THE
SILVER
WEDDING

ETHEL M. DELL

The Silver Wedding

LONDON:
HUTCHINSON & CO. (PUBLISHERS), LTD.

PRINTED IN
GREAT BRITAIN,
AT THE ANCHOR
PRESS, TIPTREE,
∶ ESSEX ∶∶

CONTENTS

PART III

PART IV

PROLOGUE

"CAN'T you sleep?" said the night-sister softly. "Would you like some tea?"

The man in the bed gave a great start and looked up at her with glassy eyes. "Did I make a noise? I'm sorry," he said; and added after a moment: "Is anybody sleeping in this infernal racket?"

"I'm afraid not," she said. "But I daresay it will soon be over now."

The whirring of engines overhead served to belie her words, and in a moment there followed an explosion that seemed to shake the very foundations of the earth. The man flinched in spite of himself; the woman remained motionless, to all outward seeming composed. The awful thunder of the answering guns made pandemonium of the night.

"Pretty near!" muttered the patient, as the roar of sound began to subside a little.

"But not near enough!" said the night-sister steadfastly.

He looked at her intently, searching her face with his feverish eyes. "Are you really like that—all through?" he said. "Or are you terrified—as I am—wanting to squeal like a rabbit?"

She moved, drew nearer to him, and, bending, laid her quiet hand on his wrist. "No, I am not terrified," she said. "But then, you see, I am lucky. I have so many things to think about."

He groaned. "And I can only lie and think about myself. There's the difference."

"All the difference," she said. "And this is your fourth night without sleep."

"I know," he said. "It plays the devil with one's nerves, doesn't it?"

"You'll get off presently," she said soothingly, "when the raid is over."

"Oh yes, I know." His tone held apology. "Afraid I'm a rotten patient. Being wounded takes more courage than I bargained for."

"Yes, the highest kind of courage," said the night-sister. "Let me see if I can make you more comfortable ! And then you shall have some tea."

She bent to her task as again the guns bellowed forth their fury. Again, through them, there came the terrific noise of a shell bursting not far away. The man straightened himself and lay tense.

A sudden call sounded at the half-open door of the little room. "Sister—sister ! Can you come ? They're beginning to panic !"

She stooped a little lower over him. "Shall you be all right if I leave you for a minute ? I'll come back."

He moved as if involuntarily. His fingers grasped her arm. "Will you really come back ?"

"I will," she said. "I promise."

His hold relaxed. "All right. Carry on !"

She was gone, her tall, straight form slipping like a shadow through the dim aperture. He was left alone in the fearful din with his sorely racked nerves and tortured body.

It went on and on, as though the gates of hell had opened suddenly close at hand. They had put him into this little room alone in the hope of giving him the rest he so urgently needed ; but now, lying solitary, he longed for the company and courage of his fellow-men. The isolation was driving him almost to frenzy.

The noise increased, became deafening. He made a piteous attempt to cover his head with the bedclothes, the pillow, anything to protect himself from it, to lessen the frightful tension, the piercing agony of hearing which made his brain feel as if it were being hammered to a pulp. But nothing made any difference. He lay alone—alone—while the fires of hell gathered and kindled all around him.

"O God !" he said. "O God ! O God ! Keep me from going mad !"

There came a sudden flare—dazzling, scarlet—beyond the window-blind, and the little room flashed from the obscurity of a night-lamp into a red inferno that burned his eyeballs unbearably. It went out in a crash through which his senses seemed to reel towards a fiery abyss from which he realized there could never be any deliverance.

In his agony he gasped strange sounds which might have been words—only they belonged to no known language ; dreadful utterances which amazed and horrified even himself, but from which he was powerless to refrain. He knew in those awful moments with the appalling insight of the doomed that his reason had gone, that he was nothing more than a gibbering maniac stripped of his humanity, being dragged like a terrified animal to the shambles. There were no decencies here, no pause for self-recovery, no companionship to keep him sane. Only Death—red Death—raging round him, while he lay helpless, waiting his turn to be thrust into the burning fiery furnace.

He flung up his arms and grasped the head of his bed, striving to drag himself up though every movement was anguish. To die like this—to die like this—maimed and powerless and alone ! O God—alone !

That was what made a raving lunatic of him—the fearful solitude, the consciousness of utter insignificance in the midst of pandemonium, the realization that whatever he did, said, or suffered, mattered not a whit to any single being in the universe. He was tottering on the edge of a cataclysm which the human brain failed to grasp, and all he knew was his own colossal unimportance and a futility through which he groped as one amazed. This, then, was Death ! On the very threshold he could hear It. Had he possessed the strength, he would have risen to meet It. Anything—anything on God's earth—would have been preferable to this unspeakable waiting in inaction. The blow deferred—the sword yet dangling—who could endure it ?

A terrific roaring of flames became audible, and with it he heard a shrieking, as of souls in torment. Had he passed the awful Gate without knowing it, he asked himself ? Was he already in the place of the doomed ? His own wild rush of utterance was over. They would not hear him shriek when they came with their instruments of torture to thrust him down. Oddly, his panic was sinking away, and he realized that it was because, contrary to his expectations, he had retained his individuality. The immensity of things had somehow lessened. The horizon of his solitude had narrowed. Those cries, awful as they were, spoke of other souls besides his own. Though his straining eyes could distinguish nothing but a fearful and lurid flickering that came and went beyond the window-blind, fitfully lighting the room, those voices piercing the din told him that he was not yet alone. Something was happening just beyond his sight which brought back to him the consciousness of mortality. Fellow-beings, and not lost souls, were waiting there.

Some of them were whimpering like frightened children

some crying aloud as he had cried. And now and then, beyond the ever-increasing roar of the flames, he heard the voice of authority mingling with the tread of feet. They were carrying the patients out of that holocaust one by one. He was not yet alone.

Not yet alone! That thought burst upon his brain like the red glare through the window-blind. Not yet alone! But how long would it be before all those others were borne out to safety and he was left forgotten? Who was likely to remember him in the confusion? Who would have time even to penetrate the secluded corner which had been secured for him only the day before by the considerate care of the night-sister, who knew the pain that racked him and the urgent need for peace?

Who indeed? Already it seemed that the fiery tide of tumult was receding from him, while drifting smoke and increasing heat told of the advancing destruction. He covered his face with his arms. There was no hope, but his reason had returned to him, and he had himself in hand. Not thus had he thought that his hour would come to him, but since come it must, he would not meet it in blind terror. He would die like a man, not like some wild, stampeding animal. His prayer for sanity had been granted. He realized it with a curious wonder. And as all hope of life went from him, he prayed again in words that were scarcely of his own choosing:

"From Thy wrath—and from everlasting damnation—Good Lord, deliver us!"

And now he was kneeling in the little stuffy village church in which he had knelt as a child, listening to the Litany that had seemed so endless, and idly speculating, as one might speculate upon the red glare of a volcano very far away, upon the meaning of the thing with the nightmare name from which deliverance was besought. The atmosphere was rapidly thickening, and he seemed to feel the hardness of the pew-front under his forehead as drowsiness overcame him. "From Thy wrath—from Thy wrath"—yes, the wrath of God must be a terrible thing. But why should He be angry with them all? Was it impossible to make Him smile? "And from everlasting damnation . . ." Ah, the volcano again! Tongues of flame shooting up through the dense smoke—the smell of burning—the taste of ashes! Stay! There was another story somewhere about a burning fiery furnace, and three condemned men walking unharmed with a Fourth in its very midst. "And the Form of the Fourth was like the Son of Man." What about that for deliverance? How did the damnation theory stand against that?

It did not stand. It crumpled like a shrivelled paper flying up the chimney. Somehow—even in his boyhood—he had always known it must. That story had always held a vivid appeal for him. It appealed to him now in his extremity, and, strangely, his fear died. He uncovered his eyes to the glare of the furnace, almost expecting to see the Form of the Divine Comrade.

And in that terrific moment he saw, indeed, a figure, though not such as he looked for. Through the lurid drift of smoke there came to him a woman, lightly and calmly, as though she moved through the sunshine of a summer day.

She reached him, bent over him, her hands touching him with a gentle reassurance, as though he had been a child.

"Did you think I'd forgotten you?" she said. "It's all right. They're just coming."

"Sister!" he gasped out, and, hardly knowing what he did, he took her hands and held them tightly against his face. "Oh, sister!"

"Ah! You poor dear!" she said. "It's all right. It's all right."

There came another crash that shook the very walls around them and brought the man abruptly to his senses. He started, and almost flung her hands away from him.

"Go!" he commanded hoarsely. "Go! Save yourself—do you hear?—before it's too late!"

She did not answer him or attempt to obey. She remained by his side.

"Go!" he cried to her again. "Go! Can't you hear? Don't you see?"

She spoke quietly, very definitely. "Nothing will make me leave you," she said.

"But why—why?" He almost raved the words. "You've got a chance—I haven't! In God's name, don't die—for my sake!"

She bent over him, spreading her hands above him, and suddenly in the shining of her eyes he saw something that struck him dumb.

"I'm not afraid to die with you," she said. "I won't leave you to die—alone."

There was no haste or impulse in the words. The gleaming courage in her eyes was like a beacon-fire. He realized in that

CHAPTER I

A GULL'S NEST

ORANGE and blue! The tawny gold of last year's bracken burning in the spring sunshine, and the blue—the deep, deep sapphire of the engirdling sea!

"There is nothing on earth like it," said Marcia Templeton. "It *is* as near to heaven as we can get."

She lay with her face to the sea, her back to a grey rock, and gazed through half-closed lids down the wonderful slope to the glittering ocean. Her pale face under its shady hat had a remote and concentrated look as though the deep enjoyment of the wonderful spectacle before her were outside her customary existence—a thing to be stored with care in the recesses of memory and kept for the grey days of ordinary life.

"I must remember it," she murmured half aloud. "I simply must. I mustn't lose it all—like a dream."

It was a day in March that might have been snatched from June. She had had to turn down her hat-brim on account of the glare. Lying there in the brilliant sunshine, there was a supple grace about her, a careless ease of relaxation, that in some subtle way expressed the charm which was never absent. She might have been twenty-three ; she actually was ten years older. But she was one of those women in whom age is of no significance. People did not pause to wonder how old she was, but there were many who marvelled at her youth. Those who had known her for years declared that she had never altered, nor ever could alter. Her quick sympathies, her warmth of personality, combined to fashion a rare spirit that outer circumstance could never change, and there were few who did not realize that she had the power to impart happiness even though they might question if she herself actually possessed it.

The capacity for keen enjoyment at least was hers, and, lying there in the bracken, she exercised it to the utmost, resolutely banishing every consideration that might detract therefrom. Perhaps that was in a measure the secret of her radiance—the power to detach herself from all burdens and gather the moment's splendour without stint or hindrance—the power to banish both past and future and revel in the glorious present with the courage that is greatness.

That wealth of English scenery now spread before her was such as perhaps only an English heart could ever fully appreciate. She had seen far richer colouring on foreign shores, but it had never held the same vivid appeal for her, had never wrapped her in this trance of delight. Only England can bestow what England as a rule most grimly withholds—the rapture and the ecstasy of spring ere spring is due—the gleaming gold in the midst of the black, unyielding seams.

Who could have expected a day like this after yesterday and the day before, and the day before that? Who could dare to anticipate such another? A child, perhaps, to whom disappointment was a thing unknown. Certainly not Marcia Templeton, who lay stretched in the sunshine, as it were receiving with her whole being the priceless and probably unrecurring gift.

But even she might not continue to revel in it to the exclusion of all besides. Though past and future might successfully be expelled, the present was not wholly unencumbered, and it was not without a certain semi-humorous air of guilt that she at length raised herself and definitely looked about her.

The result of her survey did not yield immediate satisfaction, for only the golden stretch of moor met her eyes, and after a moment or two she grasped the rock and drew herself to her knees for a more comprehensive scrutiny.

Then, still unsatisfied, she gave a clear, low call : "Goldie ! —Goldielocks ! Where are you ?"

There was no reply. Only some peewits rose near her and flew away seawards with plaintive cries.

Marcia uttered a sigh in which humour remained faintly apparent. "How naughty !" she commented. "And how exactly like her !"

Then she got up, brushing the dry bracken from her, and stood, erect and slim, searching the landscape.

There was still a smile in her brown eyes as she left her sheltered nook and prepared to walk down to the shore.

It was very rough walking, and a chill wind blew behind her as though in warning that the brilliance around was of very short duration. But the sky was yet cloudless, and the rhythmic wash of the sea held no hint of coming storm. It shone like the heart of a sapphire.

She reached a narrow beaten track that led to the edge of the cliffs, and here she quickened her pace, not from any conscious apprehension, but because slow progress was unnatural to her. As she moved swiftly down to the sea her movements had all the litheness and swing of girlhood. She sang to herself softly, still revelling in the splendour.

She came at length to the cliffs that bordered the rocky coast, and here she paused to search once more around and below her. To call again was useless, for the tide was rising and the waves breaking with a thunderous roar that washed away all other sound. Even the cries of the peewits were no longer audible here.

She turned and walked along the edge of the cliff until she came to a gap through which a steep and winding path gave access to the shore. Just as she reached it, however, a small figure with a halo of golden hair suddenly emerged, seeming to spring from the very face of the cliff, and rushed upon her.

"Oh, Mum, I was just coming to tell you! We've found a gull's nest—only fancy, a gull's! And Dennis has gone after it and can't get back. He's stuck half-way. I don't know what he'll do."

"Oh, Goldie!" ejaculated Marcia. "I might have known!"

Goldie was by no means disturbed. She was at the optimistic age of thirteen. "He's perfectly safe, Mum. I mean he can't fall or anything if he keeps still. But a big bit of rock gave way below him, and now he can't get up or down."

"Show me where he is!" said Marcia.

"Well, I don't know whether you can see him from the top. It hangs over so. And it's no good going down, as the tide's nearly up to the cliff," cheerfully stated Goldie. "I expect he'll have to stay there for a bit till somebody comes along."

"My dear child!" said Marcia. "We must anyhow find out where he is."

"Well, let's see if I can see him!" said Goldie. "If I lie on my tummy and you hold my heels, I might be able to see over."

She proceeded to carry out the idea, but without much

result, for Marcia's hold did not allow sufficient scope for her purpose.

"You hold on so tight," the child complained. "I couldn't possibly fall over if you let me go a little farther."

But Marcia would not be persuaded. "We won't risk it," she said with decision. "I'm going down the cliff-path to see if I can get a glimpse of him from there."

"Well, you won't be able to," said Goldie. "I tried, and I couldn't."

Marcia, however, determined to satisfy herself upon that point, and, returning to the gap, began the descent, which was in some places somewhat precipitous.

But Goldie was right. The path twisted in the wrong direction, and there was nothing to be gained from it but a nearer view of the approaching waves and the fluttering, wailing sea-birds all around the black rocks over which they splashed. She retraced her steps to the top.

"We must go to the village for help," she said to Goldie.

"Oh, I expect he'll get down all right when the tide goes out," said Goldie, whose experience of life so far had never included any really untoward happenings. "But there's a farm along there that's nearer than the village. P'raps there's someone there who could help."

Marcia cast an anxious glance around. "If he has to wait for the tide, it'll take hours," she said. "Oh, Goldie, why did he go?"

"I told you, Mum. It was a gull's nest," said Goldie. "I went too, only I couldn't manage to get so far. But I think I can show you where it is. It's under that big jutting-out bit of rock. Ah, here's somebody coming up from the farm! It's a man. Shall I go and tell him?"

Marcia turned in some relief. "He might be able to help, but I expect we shall have to get the coastguard. No, wait, Goldie! It's only a boy. He won't be any good."

"It isn't a boy!" declared Goldie, with keen blue eyes upon the approaching figure. "It's quite a grown-up one, anyway. I'll give him a whistle, shall I?"

Before Marcia could check her, she had made a sort of megaphone of her hands and emitted a piercing sound that carried like a miniature siren through the crisp air. It was her latest accomplishment, and one in which she took a certain pride.

"That'll fetch him," she said with satisfaction, beckoning violently to the oncoming youth, until he grasped the fact that she was signalling to him, and with an answering shout broke into a run.

Marcia looked on rather helplessly. Goldie's direct methods were always a little disconcerting but they generally gained the desired end, and she herself was for the moment completely at a loss.

She watched the stranger as he drew near, and saw in him a thick-set, powerful young Cornishman of about eighteen, who ran like a trained athlete and arrived without any sign of over-exertion. He had no hat, and his hair was wet and curly, rather like the hair of a brown retriever after a swim. His face was deeply sunburnt and wore a pleasant smile—or rather grin—as he raised a hand in salute.

"Anything I can do?" he said.

He addressed Marcia, but it was Goldie who answered him before she had time to do so.

"Of course there is! That's why I called you. My brother's stuck half-way up that cliff. He's after a gull's nest—only think, a gull's! And now he's got there he can't get back."

"I don't suppose you can help us," here put in Marcia, "but you may be able to tell us of someone who can."

"I expect I can," said the Cornishman, looking at her as if something he saw inspired respect. "I know these rocks from start to finish. Show me where he's stuck, and I'll see what I can do."

Goldie at once took command. She seemed, indeed, to consider that no small consequence attached to her position. Imperiously she led the way to the edge of the cliff.

"You see this bit of rock that juts out? Well, he's under there somewhere, about half-way down, I should say. I don't think you can get at him, but he's quite safe. He can't fall, unless he does something silly."

"I see." He looked at Marcia again and laughed, then grew sober. "Don't you worry! I expect I can get to him. There are heaps of ledges, and it's much safer than it looks. I'll try, anyway."

"Don't run any risks!" begged Marcia. "Wouldn't it be better to go straight to the coastguard?"

"Good gracious, no!" he returned cheerily. "Not till I've had a shot at it. You'd better not watch, because it looks much more dangerous than it is. I've done it heaps of times before, so you needn't be anxious. I shall be back in five minutes if I can't reach him."

He was gone with the words, striding back to the gap and disappearing from view almost before they realized that he had started upon the undertaking.

"He'll do it all right," said Goldie complacently. "Let's sit down, shall we, till he comes back?"

Marcia shook her head. "You can if you like. I do hope he won't come to any harm. We ought not to have let him go."

"Why ever not?" Goldie regarded her with a species of humorous wonder. "Fancy getting in a stew about it! Dennis won't hurt. He's not a child."

Marcia smiled faintly. "Of course not! People of fourteen can always be relied on to take care of themselves. I wonder what your father would say if he knew."

"Don't suppose he'd say much," said Goldie dispassionately. "He might punish him if he thought it worth while, but I don't suppose he would. Dad's never really interested, is he?"

"He has other things to think about," said Marcia.

Her small daughter regarded her with a sudden impish grin. "Aren't you a darling?" she said, with apparent irrelevance.

Marcia shook her head again. Goldie's appreciation was apt to be unorthodox. "You see, dear," she pointed out, feeling herself hopelessly out-of-date as she did so, "it isn't Daddy's business to be looking after children."

"'Course not," said Goldie. "So long as he never expects us to look after him, that's all that matters. Oh, I wish that man would hurry up! Wonder what his name is. Don't forget to ask him, Mum, when he comes back!"

"I hope he won't get stuck too," said Marcia.

Goldie scouted the idea. "Not likely! He knows what he's about all right. Bet you he'll be back inside five minutes and Dennis with him."

But it was fully a quarter of an hour after the utterance of this remark, and Marcia's uneasiness was steadily mounting, when the sounds of yells from the direction exactly opposite to the one they were watching directed their attention thither, and they discovered two figures swinging down towards them from the rocky headland.

"Oh, there they are!" exclaimed Marcia with relief.

Goldie whooped in answer, and ran to meet them. "Did you get any eggs?" was her cry. "You didn't? Oh, Den, you rotter!"

The person thus addressed seized her as she reached him,

deposited her on her back on the ground, and walked swiftly on, leaving her to the more polite treatment of his companion.

He was a dark-haired, eager-faced boy of fourteen, and he greeted Marcia with easy patronage. "Hullo, old dear! Hope we haven't kept you waiting. Such a scream—got down and couldn't get up again! Jolly decent chap, that! D'you know who he is?"

"I wish you wouldn't do these things," protested Marcia. You know your father——"

He checked her at once with decision. "That's all right, darling! 'Nough said! You've done your duty. Now come on and let's enjoy ourselves!"

This was the treatment invariably meted out to Marcia by her children. She was allowed to look on at their pursuits, but to take no arbitrary share therein. If she disapproved, she was hushed immediately; and she, with a smile half-comical, half-sad, was obliged to submit. They had grown beyond her control, these children of hers, during the War. It was her own fault, of course. If she had wanted to keep them her own, she should not have left them. But who that has known the fire of patriotic enthusiasm shall say that she was wrong?

Those five unforgettable years given to her country were such as she would not have been without. They had changed her as a voyage to a far land might change one who had never been outside her own. They had given her a width of out-look, a depth of understanding, such as had never otherwise been hers. They had made her live where before she had only partially existed. But it was inevitable that so much gain should also entail sacrifice, and when she resumed her home life again it was to find that her children's need of her was over. They had developed their own individualities apart from her, and she was essential to them no more.

The primary separation had not been of her contriving. It was her husband's decision to remove them to a secluded corner of Devon, out of reach of all signs of war, and she had acquiesced, not realizing until too late that such a life of inactivity would be impossible for her. She had been a popular hostess ever since her marriage, and to be suddenly cut off from the outer world just as it had been plunged into the seething turmoil of a great war was unthinkable. By her desire, then, the two children had been placed in a little home-school in complete safety on the edge of a Devon moor, and she had returned to the tumult and the strife of nations.

Perhaps no human being of Marcia's brilliance and ability could have remained outside it all. And during the two or three years that had elapsed since its cessation she had often told herself that she would not have had it otherwise. But yet the fact remained that she was still paying the price.

Her husband, Everard Templeton, a well-known K.C., had become, so far as she could judge, entirely independent of her —though she did not attempt to disguise the fact that in the days before the War his detached attitude had driven her to the children for the companionship her soul needed. She had been their adored playmate in those days, but now she was no more to them than a pleasant guest whose participation in their pursuits could never pass a certain limit. In especial was this so with Goldie—Dora, as she had been named in baptism and as her father always punctiliously addressed her. There was about the child, notwithstanding her apparent openness, all the reticence of youth ; and in her company, dearly as she loved her, Marcia always felt old and rather dilapidated. There was a barrier which she could never pass, and she was compelled to observe it. The things enjoyed by Goldie were so obviously unsuitable for her mother's delectation that she lacked the courage even to suggest that she might be allowed to partake of them.

It was not so in the same degree with Dennis. He was more willing upon occasion to treat her as a pal, but from a very superior standpoint. She always felt in her son's society that she had a great deal to learn. He did not condemn her ignorance, but he could not treat it as if it were non-existent. Marcia's five years of strenuous nursing had not tended to widen her experience of the demands of boyhood. She sometimes wondered if she had perhaps herself skipped a stage of life in the rapid growth compelled by tragic experience and so could never hope to tread again the happy playing-fields of youth towards which her soul still yearned. Her husband was ten years her senior, and she had long since ceased to aspire to stand upon level ground with him. She was too young for him, and, it seemed, regarded by her children as too old for them. She sighed her half-humorous, half-rueful sigh and accepted the inevitable.

CHAPTER II

MARCIA

"My name is Peter," said the stranger modestly. "Oh, don't mention it! Awfully glad to have been of use. Not that I did anything."

He had developed a shyness which, in the absence of ceremony which had characterized their first meeting, had not then been apparent. Marcia liked him for it. She liked his honest, straightforward countenance and manner of speech. Seeing that her gratitude merely embarrassed him, she did not press it too far.

Neither Goldie nor Dennis seemed to consider that any gratitude was owing. "Jolly good thing you turned up when you did," was the latter's airy acknowledgment, "or I might have missed my lunch. These beastly cliffs take some knowing, don't they? I'm in a filthy mess, Mum, and this is my last pair of bags."

"In that case," said Marcia, "I'm afraid you'll have to go filthy for the rest of the week."

"Make him wash 'em himself!" said Goldie, who liked to see discipline enforced upon the opposite sex occasionally. "Haven't you got another name?"—addressing their new friend with complete ease—"or do you like to be called just Peter?"

He smiled at her. Marcia noticed that his shyness melted before her direct methods. "Oh, well, yes, I have got another name," he said, "but just Peter will do."

"D'you live here?" she demanded next. "Or are you only staying?"

He nodded towards the farm nestled in a hollow of the cliffs below them. "I'm there for the present, but I've always lived about here. I was born near by. That's why I know these cliffs so well."

"You work on the farm, I suppose?" said Goldie, who liked to know the exact status of all with whom she came in contact.

"My dear," interposed Marcia, "I don't think you need ask quite so many questions."

"But I want to know," said Goldie imperiously.

Peter was smiling broadly. As he was attired in the roughest and shabbiest of tweeds, perhaps Goldie's surmises

were not wholly unreasonable, but Marcia with her deeper
intuition saw further.

Peter, however, appeared quite willing to reply to the
child's interrogations. "Well, no, I'm not a labourer exactly,"
he said, "though I've done a bit of farming. But I've just got
another job, so I'm giving it up."

"D'you go to market ?" asked Goldie.

But here Marcia asserted her authority with more decision.
"We really must get back to lunch," she said. "Thank you
very much," holding out her hand to Peter. "I am more
grateful to you than I can say, and I hope we shall meet again.
Come, children, we must go."

But Goldie also insisted upon shaking hands, and even
lingered for a few seconds after her mother's determined
departure to try to arrange the future meeting vaguely
referred to.

When she overtook Marcia, however, she had no definite
success to report. "He says he's expecting a cousin or someone to come and join him, and can't fix up anything till he
comes. Isn't that silly ? A great man of his age !"

But Marcia would give no opinion upon the subject. "I
think you talk too much, darling," she said, trying to be
judicial. "We mustn't be too free-and-easy with perfect
strangers. It isn't quite advisable."

At which gentle criticism her small daughter deliberately
caught her brother's eye and smiled aloud. "You're a pet
of a thing, Mumsie," she said tolerantly ; "but if I let you do
the talking you'd never find out anything."

Marcia did not argue the point, realizing the complete
futility of such a measure. It was only by accepting the
situation into which these children of hers thrust her that she
could hope to maintain any sort of contact with them. To
disagree with Goldie was to lose her confidence. Was she not
already completely outside their councils ? She let the
matter pass without further discussion. And Goldie, wholly
sweet-tempered and quite unaware of any lack of consideration
on her own part, hugged her arm affectionately and accepted
her forbearance.

"I like Peter," she said. "Hope we shall see some more
of him."

"I shall get him to go gulls'-nesting with me," said Dennis,
within whose breast his sister's reproach still rankled.

But at this announcement Marcia once more asserted
herself with some firmness. "If you ever do anything of the

kind again, Dennis," she said, "I shall write straight to your
father and tell him that our holiday here must come to
an end."

Dennis gave her a quick look of surprise, and met in
return a full gaze of such unswerving determination that he
deemed it best to yield the point without delay, the while
Goldie chuckled in high delight.

"Oh, if you feel qualmy about it, of course I won't," he
said. "But one's got to do something, and there isn't much
one can do here, is there?"

Marcia melted. She was blessed—or perhaps cursed—
with the gift of seeing with the eyes of others as well as of her
own, and she had an intense sympathy with the fever and
folly of youth. The two children were, moreover, recovering
under her care from measles, and it was hard to deny them
some compensation after their dreary incarceration.

She put her hand on the boy's shoulder with a movement
of gentle conciliation. "I only want you not to do anything
dangerous, dear," she said. "You see, I am responsible for
you, and I couldn't possibly have got you out of your difficulty
to-day."

He laid his cheek in swift affection upon the caressing
hand. "That's all right, darling. Don't you worry!" he
said. "I'll not do anything rash—promise!"

With which he grinned up into her face with mischievous
assurance, and the incident was closed.

Peter's share in it, however, was by no means forgotten.
The two children discussed him and wrangled about him
throughout luncheon in the semi-friendly, semi-aggressive
style peculiar to them. Dennis said he was a gentleman,
while Goldie questioned the matter and declared him
countrified.

Marcia, finally appealed to when both parties had practically exhausted their ammunition, expressed the opinion that
he might be well bred, but possibly not too well educated, a
point of view loudly acclaimed by Goldie, who considered that
it supported her own, but received by Dennis with polite
disdain. There were lots of chaps he knew in the Upper
Fifth, and Sixth, too, who hadn't half the decency upon long
acquaintance that Peter had shown at short notice. He
personally meant to see more of him, but Goldie might do as
she liked.

This started another train of discussion, Goldie not having
the smallest intention of being left out in the cold, and so the

two continued almost without cessation, while Marcia sat in the background, half-listening, half-dreaming, until the meal came to an end and they went out once more into the rare sunshine.

The beauty of the day had indeed already begun to wane. She had known that the splendour could not last, and before another hour was gone great clouds were drifting up from the north-west and an icy shower drove them indoors.   There was a good deal of grumbling on the part of the children, but these were the occasions when Marcia really could feel herself to be of some use, since they turned to her for entertainment, and she soon had them occupied with a juvenile game of cards. They always insisted upon playing for money, but the points were of too modest a nature to allow of any large sum changing hands, though they took an amazingly keen interest in their gains and losses.

Marcia alone felt the slow passage of time, since this con- sideration held small appeal for her, and if she could have left them to play peaceably together she would gladly have fared forth again over the moor, the wild weather notwithstanding. But this was out of the question.   She was considered a necessary adjunct to their indoor pastimes, and she was ashamed of her own boredom of which they were so sublimely   unconscious.   They   were   under   the   firm impression that she desired no greater treat than to join in their pursuits, and even considered it as something of a virtue when they were able to include her.   The fact that they would have been considerably at a loss without her did not enter into their consideration.   Was she not there to take care of them, and, since she belonged to them, could any more congenial occupation be desired ?

If they could have seen her a little later, when the long day was over at last and they were safe and sleepy in bed, feverishly pulling on her waterproof and running out into the chill evening to catch the last of the failing light, they would have stared at her energy, believing that a book by the fireside was all that any mother could need for her amusement and recreation at the end of the day.

Marcia herself could hardly have explained the great impa- tience that possessed her.   It was more than mere restlessness urging her to action.   It was almost revolt.   And yet she had volunteered for this quiet Cornish holiday with her children, and till to-day she had believed herself content.   But some fiery essence in the glory of the morning had upset her.   The

surface repose which she had long ago learned to cultivate
for her peace of mind was gone.   A seething longing for something which she recognized as hopelessly beyond her reach
had awakened within her.   "I want—life," she said to herself almost wildly.   "My God!   I've only lived once in the
whole of my existence."

And this was true.   Through marriage and maternity her
pulses had only stirred to fresh longing, never to fulfilment.
She remembered now the day on which Dennis had been
born, and her husband—Everard—coming to congratulate
her.   Congratulate her!   That had been his attitude.   He
had been occupied—completely absorbed—by a case which it
had taken his utmost ingenuity to defend.   His fullest
ability, which was of no mean order, had been expended, and
successfully, at length, but it had been a tremendous battle.
And the birth of his son had been an interlude—a mere
diversion—in the course of events of overwhelming importance.

She remembered his words : "Now you will be happy, my
dear !"—as if, almost hysterically she laughed at the phrase
—as if that tiny atom of humanity, precious though it was,
could fill her deep and never-satisfied soul-longing for companionship.   "You will be happy now !"   The words mocked
her.   They had mocked her for years—until the War had come,
and all that was false had become grim reality.

Happy !   Her girlhood flashed before her.   Yes, she had
been happy then—happy in anticipation.   She recalled yet
the eager pulsing of hope in her veins, the swift rapture of
surrender, when the quiet, self-contained man who had
seemed to her so perfect a knight had sought her for his wife.
Her marriage had been to her like the opening of some
golden gate leading into a realm of joy almost beyond imagination.   His courtship had been brief, but she had loved him
for all that he had left unsaid.   He had filled her world, and
she had been lost in the glad contemplation of the future.
Everyone had considered her lucky to have attracted so
brilliant a man.   The progress of her engagement had been
rather like a triumphal procession, she remembered, ending
at the altar of St. George's, Hanover Square, in a blaze of
glory.   Lucky !   She had been stupendously lucky !   Everyone had said so.   A great many people thought so even now.

But that was because she had for her pride's sake kept
up the farce ;   for farce it had become.   There, almost at
the very altar-steps, her dream had ended.   The flowers had
withered at her very feet.   Looking back now, she could

realize with pathetic clearness her own self-deception—how she had glorified the common earth into a paradise, and the inevitability of disillusion.   But at the time it had been utterly beyond her comprehension.   She had only felt stunned by the most crushing disappointment she had ever known.   And the terrible part of it was that he had never even suspected the bitterness of her broken hopes.   He had not asked for that which she had so passionately yearned to give.   He had contented himself with the little when she had desired to pour forth to him her all.   He had been reserved and repressive, deliberately calm when she throbbed with emotion, resolutely restrained when she would have flung restraint to the winds.

And so the barrier had grown up between them, day by day, hour by hour ; and though at first she had striven feverishly to tear it down, it had continued to rise in spite of her, until now she did not even know what manner of man dwelt behind it.   He had, it is true, sensed her discontent in the early days.   Hence the form of his congratulation upon the birth of their son, upon whose welcome advent he had obviously relied for its removal !   That it had continued since—that, in short, any woman with natural instincts could possibly desire anything more than a kind husband and a healthy son—was plainly a state of affairs outside his calculations.   He was very fond of her, she believed, in his spare time.   Had she been a woman of whims he would have indulged them.   Everything in a material sense for which she expressed any desire was immediately her own.   And she had wearied—how she had wearied !—of those mundane possessions.   The birth of her little daughter had for a time lifted her out of her despair.   Fondly she had hoped that this second link would indeed draw them closer.   But the hope had died.   His children at this stage were his recreation, nothing more.

And recreation meant very little to him.   Perhaps later he would take an ambitious interest in his son ; but for the present his own career was paramount.   Nothing could be allowed to interfere with that.   He was quite willing that she should have as many children as she desired, and he was fully prepared to do his worldly duty by them, to make every provision for their upbringing and education.   But he had very little spare time to spend upon them, and when Marcia unexpectedly decided that their family of two sufficed her he made neither protest nor comment.   If she did not wish to enlarge her maternal sphere, it was her affair alone.   He had given her all—more than all—that the average woman possessed, and now, as ever, he was prepared to let her take her own course.

Their intimacy did not lessen, because it had never been very close. She continued at the head of his house, and he was proud to see her lead the way in society with that brilliance for which he had originally chosen her. She was exactly the sort of wife he needed. She fulfilled all his requirements ; and now that the first fever of youth was past and she had settled down, he believed her happiness to be complete. She had taken her place as a wife to a man of fine achievements and little leisure, and she never now asked for attention which he could not bestow. She filled her life with social engagements, and was at the same time a devoted mother. He desired no more.

Then had come the world-convulsion of the War, and to his surprise she had broken away from all the ties that hitherto had bound her. She had left the children. She had abandoned the home. She had completely overlooked any possibility of his needing her that might exist. She had gone straight into a hospital and bound herself to duties which practically excluded him from her life. He had admired her for it, though deeming her somewhat headlong and recognizing in her action some survival of that old impetuosity of hers which in their earlier married days he had been at some pains to repress. He himself, though he dutifully offered his services to his country upon every possible occasion, had been regarded as too valuable to his profession to be allowed to take any share in the struggle, and he was absorbed into a Government department in which he contrived to make his unerring mark while working unceasingly to maintain his own private career at the same time.

No one ever knew how he had worked during those strenuous four years. He and Marcia met but seldom, and their meetings were brief and almost impersonal. She was wholly immersed in her work, as he was. Perhaps they were both too absorbed to have much thought for each other, and if there was any tinge of longing in her husband's attitude, Marcia was completely unaware of it. For the first time in her life she was revelling in the power to give without check or stint all the energy that was in her to the service of those who sorely needed it. Everard had scarcely counted. He had seemed like a back number. She had taken it for granted that he was as engrossed in his own affairs as he had ever

C

been, and that the fact that she too was now similarly engrossed could possibly affect him had never crossed her mind.
They met and parted almost like casual acquaintances.

But the end of the War had been Marcia's undoing. To
take up the threads again in a ruined world, to resume the
old hollow pretences of life which had become a thousand
times more hollow since Grim Reality had reigned so starkly
supreme—this was the impossible.

After two years of effort she stopped and faced it. Something in her had given way. Everything was different now.
Everard was different. Yes, even Everard was older, graver,
more restrained than before. The children were different.
They had grown up apart from her. The days of their infant
reliance upon her were over. She herself was different—
totally different. Of what use to try to pretend that anything
was the same ?

In the time of the War people had sometimes said :
"There will be nothing left," and she had refused to believe it,
refused to look forward to possible failure or to contemplate
the inevitable void ahead. But now that void had come and
there was nothing left. She seemed to have outlived both her
children's and her husband's need of her.

"If I were to die to-morrow they wouldn't care—really
care—for more than a fortnight," she told herself wistfully,
as she wandered through the damp chill of the evening. "I
am not in the least essential to any one of them."

And so far as she could see, this would be her portion for
the rest of her life. She wondered, more swiftly pacing the
sandy road in her unwonted fit of rebellion, how she was going
to endure it. The fire of youth still ran hot in her veins even
while she recognized that by now she ought to be resigning
herself to the calmer joys of maternity. And how to ex-
tinguish that fire she knew not. It leaped within her almost
like a beacon-flame kindled for the guidance of some unknown
traveller. It was terrible to have been needed—so urgently
needed—and then to be cast aside.

She was walking rapidly, almost heedless of direction,
vaguely making her way towards the moaning sea which was
now veiled in mist. It had begun to rain in earnest, but she
would not turn. She could not face the long, dreary evening
in the cheerless room with its one solitary, unshaded lamp ;
and sleep, she knew, was out of the question while this restless
mood was upon her.

It would wear itself out in time. In the morning she would

be quiescent again, ignoring the numb despair at her heart, cheerfully accepting the daily ration of stone instead of bread. She would occupy herself with the children, allowing no time for these morbid ideas which attacked her only in her unaccustomed solitude and leisure. Very soon this holiday would be over, and she would be immersing herself once more in the countless engagements and undertakings of town life. They helped at least to deaden the sense of emptiness within her—that emptiness which nothing could ever fill.

"I mustn't have any more holidays," she said to herself, "for a very long time."

And with the resolution she realized that she had left the track and was plunging in complete bewilderment over the boggy ground of the open moor.

CHAPTER III

THE MEETING

SHE felt no anxiety at first, believing that she could retrace her steps without difficulty. But within a very few seconds she realized her mistake. Night had closed in upon her almost unperceived, and rain and mist were all that she could now see of the world which a few hours before had been so fair. The wind had dropped, moreover, so that she had no guide whatever as to the course she ought to take. The dull roar of the sea seemed to come from all directions at once, and there was no other sound to be heard, though she stood for many seconds listening.

"How—foolish of me !" she murmured at last. "Almost as bad as Dennis !"

But still she felt no real alarm. She would find her way back of course eventually, though it might take some little time. She wished that she had brought either stick or umbrella to feel for the bogs, which were quite invisible in the rapidly diminishing light, but since she had neither, she was forced to move with great wariness, trying her weight with every step.

It was indeed like a maze, presenting possibilities with which she was ill-equipped to cope. Her knowledge of the

country was limited, and she was obliged to face the fact
that since leaving the track her sense of direction had completely deserted her. Very soon the darkness would be
intense. Already she could see but a few feet ahead, and the
rough ground all about her offered no reassurance.

"I can't be lost," she reflected. "If I keep on, I must
come to something."

So for a space she kept on, sometimes floundering almost
ankle-deep in bog, sometimes struggling through heaps of
dead bracken and occasional brambles that clung viciously to
her, impeding her progress.

She fought down discouragement, however, telling herself
that the whole situation was absurd. She could not be more
than half a mile from the little house near the coastguard
station in which the children were soundly sleeping. The
lighthouse itself on the point of the headland could not be
far away, but she could see no sign of it, and while she was
debating this within herself a most melancholy sound suddenly burst forth, filling the world with its long-drawn-out
wailing, and she realized that the light was failing to penetrate
the ever-thickening gloom.

Somehow that sound awakened real uneasiness within her.
It gave her an unpleasant, baffled sensation, as if there were
something hostile in the atmosphere which it was seeking
vainly to overcome. The fog smelt strongly of the sea and
made her think of some ocean-monster rising from the un-
fathomed depths and stretching great tentacles over the land
to seize and drag down its prey. It was a gruesome thought
and she tried to shake it off, but it persisted. The night held
a creeping horror which seemed to be closing in upon her.
She was a stranger in an unknown country, and beginning to
be afraid.

She made a resolute effort and summoned all her energies.
She was lost, and there was no denying it, but she could not
have wandered far, and if she kept moving she was bound to
strike a track before long. To attempt to ascertain her
whereabouts was useless, but to remain stationary was even
more so. She made another plunge into boggy ground,
extricated herself, and struck out afresh.

The siren continued to boom forth its melancholy,
piercing call, echoing round and round the wide moor with
ghostly illusiveness. She determined to pay no attention to
it since it could not help her, and to concentrate solely upon
steering a straight course.

The gloom deepened and became night; the darkness began to press upon her. The rain was streaming down her face, and her shoes were heavy with water. But still she persisted, though weariness was beginning to numb her senses to an almost overwhelming extent. She was cold too—cold to the bone—for rapid movement was impossible; and as to progress, she strongly suspected that she was making none at all. She had read that people lost in the desert invariably walked in circles, and she reflected that she was probably doing the same.

"But what am I to do?" she asked herself, suddenly pausing. "I can't spend the night here."

No answer came to her. Walls of darkness closed her in. Her feet sank as she stood. She had difficulty in dragging them free. She felt herself shivering like a frightened animal. Something like desperation came upon her. She turned, feeling for firm ground, and found her ankles entwined in thorns. It was like an enemy clutching at her. She tore them away, heedless of the pain. She struggled and fought for safety till, coming suddenly into violent contact with an unseen boulder, she pitched forward and fell headlong with a force that almost stunned her.

She stumbled up again, but she was badly shaken. One leg was torn, and she could feel the blood oozing through her stocking. And another disquieting thought came to her as she stood recovering herself. Those low boulders were mainly scattered near the edge of the cliffs. She remembered noticing it in the morning. Listening intently, she became convinced that the sound of the sea, muffled though it was in the clinging fog, was nearer than it had seemed when first she had recognized herself as lost. That meant that she had wandered in a completely wrong direction, that she might at any moment come upon the very brink of the precipice.

Again she shivered from head to foot, caught in a kind of trance-like horror from which she could not free herself. At any moment—at any moment—she might go hurtling through the darkness over and over to the rocks and the muted waves two hundred feet below.

For a space she stood quite still, picturing depth which-ever way she turned. Then gradually her natural strength returned to her and she put panic firmly away. She had encountered a danger just as deadly as this before, and had given no place to fear.

Quietly and courageously her prayer went out into the

dark: "O God, guide me safely! Keep me from falling!"
And then, without hesitation, she turned once more and
stepped out as though she trod a well-known path.

She felt the ground sloping downwards, but she did not
pause. Indecision was over, and, limping and difficult as
was her progress, she compelled herself to continue. It was
thus that she had faced unshrinking the terrors and perils of
the War. It was thus that she had once stood unblenching
in the very face of Death.

So, without pause, her hands stretched out before her, she
went blindly along a track that seemed strangely smooth
after her desperate struggle on the open moor, and in so
doing, though she knew it not, she skirted the very edge of the
cliffs on which she and Goldie had stood that morning while
their unknown friend rescued Dennis from his rocky ledge.

Finally, at the end of a long descent, she came into
collision with a rough stone wall not more than four feet high,
and, feeling her way along it, discovered a small wooden gate
half-open. Beyond it there shone a vague red glow in the
darkness that sent a thrill of thankfulness through her. Here
was light at last—light and human company and shelter from
that cold, merciless rain!

"Oh, thank God!" she said. "Thank God!"

Her tired feet stumbled up a muddy path and kicked
against a step. She recovered herself with an effort, but the
glow had increased and hope beat high. It came from a
lighted window covered with a red blind. But for that she
thought that she would have fallen prone and given up the
struggle.

As it was, she mounted the step, clinging to the last
remnant of her strength, and knocked with a trembling hard
upon the door that barred her progress.

There was no immediate reply, but as she stood there
waiting she thought she heard the sound of men's voices
talking together; and after a few moments, spent in gathering
confidence, she knocked again with more decision.

Not in vain this time! She heard a movement within.
Someone was approaching. A curious tremor that was like
an ague seized her. Just for a second she was afraid—
inexplicably and overwhelmingly afraid.

Then a bolt was drawn back and the door opened to her.
She found herself looking through another door at right
angles to the first, straight into the room from which the light
had come. It was low and oak-raftered. An unshaded

lamp stood on an oak table, and it dazzled her after the darkness from which she had come.

A man was sitting just beyond it, but she could not see his face on account of the glare. Another man stood close to her, holding the door open for her to enter. She could not see him either, with any distinctness, for her eyes were fixed upon the lamp and she seemed unable to withdraw them.

But his voice recalled her. "Why, it was you I met on the cliff to-day—with the kids! Is all well? Are they all right?"

"Oh, quite," she said, "quite!"—answering him as it were mechanically. For somehow, for a reason wholly unaccountable, her attention was attracted beyond him to the man who sat on the other side of the lamp.

The boy's voice came to her again, and it had a note of anxiety. "Come in, won't you?" he said. "You must be very wet. I wonder you found your way on such a foul night."

She entered, hardly realizing that she did so. "I didn't —find my way," she said. "I'm lost!"

And then the man beyond the lamp stood up suddenly. She saw his face clear in the shadows above the glare. He was looking at her very earnestly, with a species of incredulous recognition. And something in the sight reached down to the very heart of her, so that she halted on the threshold as if spellbound.

"I'm lost!" she said again, rather breathlessly.

And through the silence another voice answered her—a voice that was like the echo of a day long past: "Lost, are you, sister? I should say that you are—found!"

She heard herself laugh shakily in answer, and she made a movement forward to meet him, but somehow her strength failed. She was glad of Peter's arm supporting her. It gave her the sense of reality she needed.

"Sit down!" said Peter. "Sit down—and we'll get you something."

He set her in the glow of a fire that burned in a huge chimney-place, and as he withdrew she saw his companion's dark face bending over her.

"How strange to meet like this!" she tried to say, but the words would not come.

She could only smile at him—smile at him—while he gathered her two frozen hands up to his face and warmed them with his breath.

CHAPTER IV

THE RENEWAL

SHE had not realized how near to exhaustion she was, but sitting there, sunk in a chair before a blazing fire, an overwhelming inertia came upon her, and even her immediate surroundings seemed to fade and become dreamlike. She was not sure that she would not presently awake and find herself out in the mist and darkness, perhaps stuck fast in one of those terrible bogs, her tired brain wheeling inwards upon memory and visualizing that which never could be true.

The face that had bent over her was one which she had often seen in dreams but which in actual fact she had never thought to see again, and that it should fade so swiftly did not surprise her. She had always recognized it as a dream—a dream to be fondly clung to, but which must inevitably fade at length. She had schooled herself to see it fade, had as it were armoured herself against regret ; and now that it had apparently followed the usual course she was not greatly surprised. The splendour of life was not for her.

But the glow and the warmth began to take effect upon her wandering faculties. She stretched out her soaked feet to the blaze, and became aware of gentle hands that drew off the sodden shoes that weighted them and placed a cushion for their resting-place.

"How nice !" she murmured. "Oh, that *is* nice !"

And then there came a movement and a few low-spoken words, and again the face of the man who had sat beyond the lamp looked into hers. "I want you to drink this," he said, very quietly and distinctly. "It's hot. Will you try ?"

The rim of a glass was held to her lips, and she meekly submitted and drank. A scalding mixture of hot brandy and water went down her throat, and she gulped and lifted a protesting hand.

"Just a drain more !" he said. "There ! Hold it yourself ! How's that ?"

His fingers took hers and closed them upon the stem of a wineglass, but they still held and guided her own. She drank a little more at his insistence, and while she drank, her eyes were raised to his, wonderingly, incredulously.

As he took the glass from her, he answered the look. "So you haven't—quite—forgotten me !"

"Forgotten you!" she said, finding her voice again with a vast relief. "But what an absurd idea!"

She saw him faintly smile. "Three years is a long time," he said.

"It is nearer four," said Marcia.

"You are exactly the same," he said.

She shook her head slightly, though she also smiled somewhat wistfully in answer. "No, I am getting old and rusty."

"Oh, we are all back numbers," he said.

She leaned slowly forward, stretching her hands to the blaze. "Yes, I suppose we are. We had our day, didn't we?"

"A pretty hectic one while it lasted!" he commented. "What happened to you afterwards? I tried to find you, but I got on to a wrong scent and so lost sight of you altogether."

"I just carried on," said Marcia. She added half-whimsically, "I didn't want to give up at all. Though it was all so gruesome, it was life."

The blood was coursing through her veins again, and she no longer questioned the reality of her surroundings. It was no illusion, though she had a feeling that it was not without an element of magic—this dream that had suddenly come true.

"Life! I should think it was!" he said. "Life and death all mixed up! One never knew which would be handed out next—or which was preferable."

"Oh, did you feel that too?" she said with a sigh. "I often wonder . . ."

"What do you wonder?" he said.

"What it was all meant for," she said. "And—like you—which were the true gainers. You know, until this moment, I didn't even know if you were still—on this side."

"And yet you hadn't forgotten me," he said.

"No. I don't forget very easily." Her eyes went back to the fire. "And you made a special impression upon me. You were so brave."

"Heavens above!" he said. "I was the most chicken-hearted of all your charges. I've often thought since what a devilish poor show I put up."

"Oh no!" said Marcia. "You conquered yourself. You were brave in spite of it all." She began to smile again. "And now we tell ourselves life is finished—because Death is not always knocking at the door!"

"Not because of that," he said. "Only because we fee we've outlived our uses."

She nodded. "Yes, that's it. It's so blessed to be needed —to feel oneself essential." She broke off, half-laughing. "What rank egotism! As if anyone could hope to be that when their first youth was over—even if then!"

"Oh, don't tell me the War has turned you into a cynic!" he said. "Not you—of all people."

Her smile died. "No, I am not a cynic," she said. "I care too much."

"I'm glad to hear you say that, anyhow," he said. "Do you remember my name?"

"Yes. You were Major Morven." She spoke with absolute assurance. "But I never heard your Christian name. I completely lost sight of you—after that night."

"I know," he said. "I was drafted home—against my will. My name is Eric. You're feeling better now?"

"Much better, thank you." She turned round from the fire. "I ought to be going. Ah, there is—Peter!"

The lad was standing almost behind her. He came forward at her words. "I say, I'm afraid you've had a rotten time," he said. "What a mercy you found your way here! It's dense outside."

Marcia smiled at him. "We seem fated to get into trouble, don't we? And you seem fated to be our rescuer." She looked at Morven. "Did you hear what he did for my young son this morning?"

"No, he never told me anything. I only arrived myself this evening," said Morven.

"There wasn't anything to tell," protested Peter, embarrassed. "The kid got stuck on the cliff and I unstuck him, that's all. There wasn't the slightest danger. He'd tell you the same himself."

"I daresay," said Marcia. "You men are all alike. I think there was danger—considerable danger. And I am all the more grateful to you for your help. Now I think I had better get my shoes on again, don't you?" She addressed Eric Morven again. "They're very wet, I know, but——"

"My dear sister," he said, "those shoes won't go on again to-night. Why, look at your feet—your stockings!"

"I know." She pushed them out in front of her and contemplated them ruefully. "They're dreadful. But still—I've got to make the best of it. I must get back—because of the children."

"You won't get back to-night," he said.

She looked at him, startled. "Oh, but I must! It's dark, I know, but if you can lend me a torch I shall be able to keep on the road and find my way. I am quite all right now."

"You won't go back to-night," he repeated with decision. "I simply won't let you attempt it. Can't you hear that siren ?"

The long, warning boom came to them as they listened, and Marcia shivered. "I know it's very dark and horrible, but I think I ought to try. They'll be so worried about me—the children, I mean."

"Won't they be asleep ?" said Peter.

"Oh yes. They won't find out to-night, but in the morning——" She broke off in some agitation. "Really, I couldn't stay here all night."

The man on her other side uttered a low laugh. "You've done stranger things than that before now, sister," he said.

"And besides, they're not really kids, are they ?" said Peter. "I'll go round myself early and let them know you're safe. But even I mightn't get through to-night. At least, I wouldn't bank on it. I know these sea-fogs."

"You mustn't attempt it, of course," said Marcia. "But oh, I do wish I knew what to do." She looked up at Morven again half-appealingly. "I don't see how I can stay here and do nothing."

"How old are your children ?" he asked.

"The boy Dennis is fourteen, and my little girl, Goldie, thirteen. They are very independent, both of them. But still . . ." She paused.

"You have given me the surprise of my life," he said unexpectedly.

"Have I ? But why ?" Surprise on her own part supplanted perplexity for the moment.

His dark eyes looked full and direct into hers. "Well," he said, "I am obliged to believe you, but if you had told me your boy was fourteen months I should have found it easier."

"What nonsense !" she protested, flushing a little. "Didn't I tell you I was on the shelf ?"

"You must have had a considerable climb to get there," he said.

And then they both laughed, abruptly and inexplicably, while Peter stood by, looking as if the joke were beyond him.

But to Marcia that laugh in some strange fashion bridged the space of years that had opened between them, though she could not remember that they had ever laughed together before. With a gesture she surrendered to the inevitable. "Well, since you are both against me, what am I to say? Quite honestly, I don't think either of the children will have a bad night on my account. If I may really spend the night by this lovely fire, I shall be more than grateful."

"Oh, you won't do that!" declared both Morven and Peter together, and then both stopped to laugh. An odd hilarity seemed to have found its way into the atmosphere.

Peter recovered first and took up the tale. "There's a very decent spare room upstairs. I'll tell Mrs. Rider to get it ready for you. They won't have gone to bed yet. I'll get you something to eat too." He turned to the door with the words.

"Oh no, indeed!" Marcia called after him. "I don't want anything to eat. I had a very substantial meal before I came out on this foolish expedition. Do stop him!" she urged, turning to Morven. "I really couldn't eat anything more."

"Some hot milk, then," he said with a nod to Peter, who at once went out with finality.

"I don't need anything," Marcia said. "And please don't let him give up his room to me! I have a feeling that he means to. And I would much, much rather stay down here."

"Have a cigarette!" said Morven soothingly.

She began to refuse, and then changed her mind. "Just to show you I really am in my right senses," she said, as she took one from the case he proffered. "I am terribly ashamed of giving you all this trouble, only I know that that is the sort of thing you don't want me to say."

"The sort of thing that never is said between you and me," he corroborated quietly, striking a match for her. "We never were at that stage. We were long past it when we began."

He spoke with a steady insistence that commanded attention. Marcia attended, meekly leaning back in her chair. The feeling of magic was still upon her. She could not shake it off.

He also began to smoke, standing against the great open fireplace, the red glow playing over him.

She saw that he was not so tall as instinctively in the past she had pictured him, but his form was straight and active, essentially that of a man who played the part of actor rather than onlooker in the theatre of life. He had an air of authority about him. His brown smooth face, with features slightly aquiline, expressed a firmness of purpose tempered with humour that appealed to her in a fashion that she could not have explained. He seemed to her as a master among men, and she had a woman's longing to test his strength.

"I think perhaps you are right," she said after a few silent moments. "There was no time for convention in those long-ago days."

He made a slight gesture with one hand. "Not so long ago," he said; "that is, if you measure time by events. Has anything in the least like that happened to either of us since?"

"Not to me," she said, with a sigh scarcely restrained.

"Or to me," he said. "I was homeless then. I am homeless now. You were—the oasis in the desert."

She laughed protestingly. "Or does distance lend enchantment, I wonder?"

"Not in my case," he said. "In fact, there is no distance. It happened—so far as I am concerned—only yesterday."

Marcia was silent, aware of a quick sympathy warmly endorsing his declaration, aware also of an inner sense of expediency checking the first impulse to give utterance to it.

He too smoked in silence for a space, looking at her with semi-rueful amusement.

"Yes, I know," he said at last, as if she had spoken. "You are just as much married now as you were when I saw you last—perhaps a little more so, since Convention has resumed her sway. But that fact can't alter or take away. Remember that!"

"Perhaps you are right," she said. "The past is certainly beyond reach of the present."

"Why do you say that?" he asked with a certain keenness.

"I feel it to be so." she answered soberly. "We may recall it, dwell upon it in memory, but we could not relive a single hour that is gone."

"I'm not so sure of that," he said. "We can do practically anything if we have the will."

She shook her head at him slowly, smiling. "No—no! We can never make the water that has passed under the bridge turn and flow back again."

He wheeled away from her and stood leaning against the rough oak of the chimney, his face to the fire. "Perhaps we wouldn't if we could," he said.

"There's something in that, I think," said Marcia, but she spoke with an unconscious touch of wistfulness. "Should we want the moon, after all, if we had it?"

He made no reply, and a definite silence fell between them which had in it an element of understanding that made it as simple as speech.

The entrance of Peter brought it to an end. They both turned towards him.

"Everything's fixed up," he said. "Mrs. Rider's got everything ready, and she's waiting to give you some hot milk when you're in bed and take your wet things to be dried."

Marcia got up. "How very kind !"

"Don't be in a hurry !" said Morven.

"Oh yes," she said. "It's getting late. I mustn't keep her up. I suppose I mustn't ask which of you is going short of a bed to-night ?"

She looked from one to the other with that sweet smile of hers which once seen was seldom forgotten.

It was Peter who answered. "I am, and I shall love it. I can sleep on my head anywhere. I'll be up early in the morning, I promise, and will let the kids know almost before they're awake ; so don't you worry !"

"I am—more than grateful," said Marcia, holding out her hand.

He took it with a boyish embarrassment. "Well, I hope I'd do more than that for a friend," he said. "Good night ! Hope you'll sleep well."

She turned to Eric Morven. "Good night ! And thank you a thousand times !"

He held the hand in his. "For nothing whatever !" he said. "But there's one thing you've forgotten."

"Oh, what ?" she said, with simulated alarm.

His dark eyes looked straight into hers with a glint of domination. "You haven't yet told me your name," he said.

"My name ?" She returned his look in complete surprise. "You never heard it ? How extraordinary ! My name is Marcia Templeton."

"Marcia !" He repeated it softly, dwelling upon it as though it pleased him ; and then a moment later : "Templeton, K.C. ? Is that the man ?"

She bent her head. "My husband—yes."

Her hand still lay in his. She could not have removed it without a decided effort.

He spoke rather abruptly. "Do you know the name of this place that the god of chance has led you to to-night ?"

"Oh, don't say chance !" she said, and her voice had a faint tremor. "I don't believe in it. Do you ?"

"God, then !" he said almost roughly. "I arrived here this evening, and you—not five hours later. Tell her the name of the place, Peter !"

"Oh, rot !" said Peter, turning red.

Morven began to laugh, and suddenly something vital seemed to pass out of the atmosphere. "He calls it rot, you see. I call it chance. You—you will probably find a better theory. The place is called—Truelove Farm."

He paused before very deliberately he uttered the name. The smile was still on his lips. Her hand was still in his.

There was a second's silence, and then Marcia spoke, quietly freeing herself with the words, "What a sweet, old-fashioned name !"

Peter was holding open the door. She turned to pass out, and as she did so Eric Morven's voice reached her, not strained or cynical, but absolutely natural, as her own had been.

"Yes, it is old-fashioned. I like it. Don't you ?"

"Very much," she answered gently. "Good night !"

She did not hear any response. The door closed behind her.

CHAPTER V

THE MORNING

THAT she should sleep throughout the night and well on into the morning up in the little oak-raftered bedroom with its lattice-window open to the sea was a circumstance which, when at length she awoke, refreshed and calm, occasioned Marcia some considerable surprise.

She was in fact rather shocked at the lateness of the hour, and she sat up and looked about her with a sense of neglected duty. Dennis and Goldie were certainly awake by that time, and what could they be thinking ? Then she remembered Peter's undertaking, and reassured herself with the thought that the young Cornishman would certainly keep his word. She saw with relief that the fog had cleared, and the sun was shining. She could hear the laughter of the waves from the cove below, and, rising, she went to the little window and leaned forth to drink in the beauty of the morning.

The extraordinary happenings of the night before ran like a fairy-tale through her brain. She felt absurdly young, almost like a girl again standing alert and eager on the threshold of life. In her hospital days she had been sedate and womanly, but to-day all her garnered experience was gone. The strange joy welling within her was such as she had never known during the whole of her womanhood. Leaning there, drinking in the chill sea-breeze, she felt that life itself was in the draught, and her whole being thrilled to receive it.

But something besides the scent of the sea came up to her, and, recognizing it, she drew back just as a voice from below accosted her.

"Don't run away! It's only me. Have you had a good night?"

She did not resume her position at the window, but she answered him from within on a note of laughter. "Oh, a lovely night. Much better than I deserved. I'm just going to dress and come down."

"Do!" he said. "Your things are all outside, including a spare pair of shoes and stockings which Peter fetched this morning."

"Oh, how good of him!" exclaimed Marcia. "Where is he?"

"Down on the shore with the kids. Don't hurry! No one's worrying." There was amusement as well as satisfaction in this statement.

Marcia found herself laughing in reply. "And no one scolding either! I think I'm very lucky."

"I think we all are," he responded.

She retired into the room, found her clothes at the door, all dried and neatly folded by the farmer's wife, and proceeded to wash and dress while he still smoked on the bench below her window, the lazy scent of his tobacco rising like the incense of a dream.

When she was ready, she leaned forth once more. "How lucky to get another gorgeous day like this!"

"It isn't going to last," he said. "Come down and enjoy it while you can!"

Her spirit leapt at the invitation. She felt like a lonely child who unexpectedly finds a playfellow of its own age.

"I'm coming," she said, and went down forthwith to join him.

She found him seated in the sunshine in a sheltered angle of the old wall. He rose swiftly to greet her, and she saw his dark face glow with an answering eagerness to the smile upon her own.

Their hands met and clasped. "You are looking splendid," he said. "I've got your breakfast laid here. Hope you don't mind."

He pointed to a little wooden table by the bench on which a cloth had been laid and weighted at the corners with stones.

"What a lovely idea!" said Marcia, as she sat down. "But you must go on smoking to keep me company."

He laughed a little. "You were always tactful. Well, let me come to leeward of you, and you won't get it."

They sat down, and presently Mrs. Rider, the farmer's wife, came stoutly forth bearing a tray which was laden with good things.

"I feel thoroughly spoilt," said Marcia. "If Dennis or Goldie had behaved as badly as I have, I should certainly not have fed them on brown bread and honey—and ducks' eggs."

"I'll pour out the coffee," said Morven, "while you get down to the eggs. Yes, Mrs. Rider knows how to tempt the shyest appetite. Mine is doing her credit already."

"I'm sure it's a pleasure to serve anyone so kind and appreciative," said Mrs. Rider, beaming upon them. "I hope you're feeling rested, ma'am. Is there anything else you'd care for?"

"No, indeed, thank you," said Marcia. "You've brought me much more than I could possibly eat."

Mrs. Rider smiled encouragingly and withdrew.

"What a dear old woman!" said Marcia.

Eric Morven, having mixed her coffee to his satisfaction, was leaning back against the wall. "Yes, it's a good lodging, this," he agreed. "It's Peter's retreat really. He usually comes here in his holidays."

"What! Alone?" said Marcia.

"Yes. She was his old nurse, and is devoted to him. He's a good lad, Peter. We're cousins of a sort, and I've been appointed his guardian. That's why I'm back in England." He smoked in a leisurely way as he talked. His eyes were often upon her with a sort of quiet satisfaction, but they did not dwell for long.

And Marcia, eating her breakfast with relish, was conscious of supreme content. "So you have been abroad," she said.

D

He nodded. "England after the War wasn't good enough. My old father died before it was over, and there was nothing to keep me here. So I retired and went out to Canada and bought a ranch. I'm going back to it later. But I had to come home to settle Peter's affairs."

"Will they take much settling?" asked Marcia with interest.

"Don't you know who he is?" said Morven.

"No." She looked up with a smile. "Someone very special?"

"In these parts, yes. He is Sir Peter Tregassa, and owns the whole countryside." Morven laughed a little. "Poor chap! He's rather overwhelmed about it at the moment. But he'll soon get used to it; that is, if I know anything of the younger generation."

"How interesting!" said Marcia. "We met him only yesterday for the first time. There seems to be something rather fine about him."

"I agree with you: there is," said Morven. "It's a pity he hasn't trained for the Army, or, in fact, for anything except farming. He seems to have a better knowledge of that than I have."

"What a pity you can't change places!" said Marcia.

He laughed again, quietly, rather sardonically. "Odd! He said the same thing to me last night. You think I could play the country squire creditably? I don't. I'm like you— fed up—out of joint with the times. We've eaten too much of the Tree of Knowledge ever to be satisfied again with the trumpery little substitutes of ordinary existence."

"Perhaps we shall get over it in time," said Marcia thoughtfully.

He shook his head. "Do you believe that? I don't. Either we were stunted before, or we are over-developed now. We may have to cramp ourselves back into the old niches, but we shall never fit them again."

"Oh, I do understand!" exclaimed Marcia with sudden feeling. "And you went off to the New World to try for something better?"

He looked straight at her. "I didn't find it. There's nothing new left. I shall stick to it, just because I suppose I'm a sticker by nature. But it's all used up and old. Even over there we hate our neighbours and fight for the titbits when there are not enough to go round."

She met his look almost with a challenge in her own.

"I simply don't believe it—of *you*. I have never forgotten—I never shall forget—your utter conquest of self when others were clamouring to be saved."

His look fell abruptly from hers. "My dear," he said in a low voice, "you don't know me."

With the words he got up, as though goaded into action by some unseen influence, and walked away from her down the garden-path towards the sea.

She watched him with a puzzled wonder. It had seemed to her that they had been in such complete sympathy a few minutes before, and now it was as if there were something in his soul upon which he could not bear her to look.

She sat motionless, forgetting her meal, until he returned, quietly as he had gone, up the path.

It gave her an odd sense of relief to see him smile. "Sister! I mean—Marcia! Is that right? May I call you that? Why don't you finish your breakfast?"

"You may call me anything you like," she said, feeling that he had every intention of doing so—and perhaps the right also. "I have practically finished. Come and tell me some more about Peter! I am deeply interested."

"In Peter?" he said with a grimace, and passed instantly on before she could answer. "Well, the boy was the son of a younger branch of the family who never expected to inherit. The War cleared all the other heirs away, including his father. He was an only son, and his parents were wretchedly poor, too poor to give him a really decent education. His father was a gentleman-farmer when the War broke out. He joined up immediately, leaving the mother in charge. He was killed at Cambrai, and she and Peter carried on as best they could, but it broke her, poor soul. She died of pneumonia the following winter. Then Peter, who had plenty of grit, joined forces with the Riders here. I was still in France. I'd only seen him once in my life. As I say, we are only distantly related. But I knew old Sir Arthur Tregassa, and his son Percy was a friend of mine. He was dying of tuberculosis from being gassed when I went out to Canada, but they kept on hoping they'd pull him through. He lingered on for a couple of years, and then died rather suddenly, just a week before his father. I don't think Peter ever realized that he was next in succession until the old man was dead. Very little notice, if any, was ever taken of him. But then it all came out ; also that I had been appointed his trustee. That's what brought me home. I can tell you I didn't bless the chance—till yesterday."

He was still on his feet leaning against the wall. Marcia, looking up at him, caught the sombre glint of his eyes as they rested upon her.

"It is a strange story," she said.

"Yes; and perhaps you're right and there's less chance about it than I thought at first sight." She did not quite understand his tone. It had a doubtful ring, almost as if he expected some species of contradiction; but he went on without pause: "Anyway, I'm not quarrelling with it now. There's plenty to be done which will keep me over here for the next three months at least. And even after that I've got to look after the boy and keep him out of mischief till he comes of age. If I can get his affairs into decent trim, I may take him back with me to the ranch for a bit. He'd like that all right. But of course the estate has got to be looked after. It's not in too prosperous a condition at present, so I gather. I'm only just in England, and haven't had time to look into it yet."

"You'll have your hands full, I expect," said Marcia. "But I'm sure he's a very nice boy. You won't have any difficulty with him."

"Hope not," said Morven. "But we hardly know each other yet. He's very shy. Small wonder, perhaps, with the upbringing he's had."

"He's very young. He'll develop," said Marcia.

Morven began to laugh. "Yes. I fancy those children of yours have started developing him already. It'll do him good to be with them."

"Oh, have you seen them?" she asked.

"I have. They're the most self-contained couple for their age I've ever met." His tone held reserve, though his smile lingered.

"You don't like them," said Marcia.

He shrugged his shoulders. "My standards are too old-fashioned. I should have liked them better if they had taken the trouble to come and look you up before going down to the beach to play."

It was Marcia's turn to laugh. "Oh, but how absurd!" she said. "They know I'm perfectly safe!"

"So they may." His tone held a certain grimness. "And I'm not quarrelling with them for keeping out of the way. All the same, I don't admire them for it."

"What a good thing you're not married !" said Marcia.

He held out his cigarette-case to her abruptly. "And what a pity you are—since we think exactly alike on this subject ! You needn't suggest going to look for them, because I'm not going to let you. I can see you're still tired. And Peter's no fool. He'll keep them out of mischief."

Marcia accepted a cigarette. "Thank you. No, I really don't feel nervous about them if Peter's there. I like Peter immensely."

"So do I," said Morven. "The boy's a good sort, and I believe we shall be friends. You must get him to show you his ancestral castle. It's only a few miles away. He wouldn't go near it till I came. He's very shy about it. I haven't seen it myself yet. We've half arranged to go over to-day."

"I should like to see it some time," said Marcia ; "but certainly not to-day."

"Why certainly not to-day ?" he said, holding a match for her.

She smiled up at him through the smoke. "Because, Major Morven, you will get on with the job much better without us."

He threw away the match with a touch of impatience. "Can't you call me Eric ? Or are you putting me in my place ?"

She answered him quietly, her eyes still lifted. "No— Eric, I am putting myself where I consider I ought to be."

"You ought to be first—everywhere," he said quickly.

She shook her head while her smile slowly died. "I have never been that," she said. "I don't think I was ever meant to be."

Eric Morven said nothing whatever, but in his silence there was something which was more forcible than speech. A faint flush rose in her face as she turned her eyes away.

CHAPTER VI

COURAGE

PETER and the two children did not come up from the beach until the hour for the midday meal was approaching. They found Marcia seated on a camp-stool not far from the cliff-edge rapidly sketching the exquisite coast-line, while Eric Morven lay beside her in the sunshine, stretched out in sublime content.

Marcia took a swift glance at her watch as the group approached. "Good gracious! Lunch-time already! I'd no idea. What has happened to the time? Or has it ceased to exist?"

"Probably," said Morven, sitting up. "Oh, there are your young ideas at last! The call of the stomach is apparently more urgent than that of the heart."

"Oh, be quiet!" she laughed. "Children are all the same —always have been."

"What an admission—for a mother!" he said.

"Well, but what is the use of pretending?" she protested.

The group approached. They were evidently engaged in a discussion of some importance. At least, the two children were. Peter, between them, seemed to be holding the scales of justice with considerable amusement

"Oh, there's Mum!" exclaimed Goldie, as they drew near. "We'll ask her. She'll know."

"She won't," maintained Dennis. "She couldn't catch a crab to save her life, let alone cook one."

"How true!" murmured Marcia for the benefit of her companion. "Well, children! Still scrapping? What's it all about?"

"We're not scrapping," said Goldie with some assumption of dignity. "We're just discussing. Dennis has got a crab in his pocket, and he wants to cook it ; but I say he ought to dress it first. You do, don't you, Mum?"

"Rot and bunkum!" said Dennis. "She doesn't know what she's talking about. Hullo!" This to Morven, who had suddenly raised himself from his recumbent position to regard him and his sister with an attention that could hardly be described as flattering.

"Good morning!" said Morven with emphasis. "Good morning, Madam!" to Goldie.

"Oh, good morning, again!" said Goldie serenely. "I don't know who you are, but that doesn't matter."

"I am an old friend of your mother's," he explained with some ceremony.

"Major Morven," said Marcia.

Goldie smiled her approval. "Oh, that's nice for you,

Mum. Now you'll be happy. I suppose you were coming over here to see him last night when you lost your way?"

"Hardly, darling," said Marcia. "You see, I didn't know he was here."

"Well, I expect you would have if you had," said Goldie with some insight.

"Your mother had a pretty bad time last night," said Morven, still speaking emphatically. "You might have lost her altogether, and then where would you have been?"

"Oh, tut, tut, tut!" said Goldie airily. "Well, it was her own fault, wasn't it? She shouldn't have done it. You're very naughty, Mum," with an admonitory shake of the head. "No," as Marcia stretched out an arm to her, "I'm not going to kiss you. You don't deserve it."

"I'll tell you what," broke in Dennis with keen enjoyment. "If it happens again, I shall have to write to Dad and tell him that this holiday must come to an end."

"Brats!" muttered Morven, while Marcia simply laughed and resumed her sketch.

"Aren't we going to have some lunch?" suggested Goldie. "What ever are you doing?"

"Just—amusing myself," said Marcia.

Goldie came and looked over her shoulder. "You've got that cliff in the distance much too high. It isn't a bit like, is it, Peter?"

Peter had seated himself on the ground by Marcia's side. He did not attempt to see the sketch, but she showed it to him.

"No, it's exactly right," he said.

Marcia smiled at him, and Morven laughed a little.

Goldie looked round for an ally. "I'm sure Dennis wouldn't think so. Look, Den! That's the cliff you couldn't get up yesterday. 'Tisn't as high as that, is it?"

Dennis threw a perfunctory glance at the sketch. "Much higher," was his verdict.

"Ass!" said Goldie tersely. "I say, Mum, aren't we going to have any lunch?"

She stood by Marcia, and this time she allowed herself to be drawn to Marcia's side. She even after a moment passed a persuasive arm round her mother's shoulders.

"Do get up and come along!" she urged.

"Why should she?" suddenly broke in Morven. "Just because you're hungry, eh?"

Goldie surveyed him in one swift comprehensive glance

of complete disdain. "Well, that wouldn't be a bad reason, would it ?" she said. "Come along, Mum ! Do hurry up ! You can come back again afterwards if you want to."

"It's going to rain afterwards," said Morven exasperatingly.

Goldie paid no further attention to him. She laid a deterring hand upon Marcia's pencil. "Come on, darling ! Do let's go ! It's getting so late."

Marcia laughed and yielded. She looked at Morven ere she rose. "I suppose I must go," she said. "Youth must be served."

"Especially when it wants a meal !" he rejoined unsympathetically.

"I hate people who pretend they're never hungry," remarked Goldie.

"You would," said Morven dryly. "You're really going ?" He addressed Marcia. "When shall we meet again ?"

"Oh, any time," she answered lightly. "Come and look us up, you and Peter ! We are staying at the little house next to the post-office, just on the other side of the moor."

Goldie turned to Peter. "Yes, mind you come too ! We play cards when it rains, and when it's really fine we'll have some picnics."

"Good work !" said Peter heartily.

Marcia also turned to him. "And thank you so much for the loan of your room and all your care of me last night. If I can ever do anything for you in return, I will."

"Oh, but I didn't really do anything," pleaded Peter, turning very red. "I mean—not really !"

"Don't blush !" said Goldie. "It isn't done nowadays. I'm obliged to you too, for looking after her. She wants it."

With which stately declaration she stalked away past Morven, upon whom she did not deign to bestow another glance, leaving her mother to follow.

"I don't care for Major Morven," she remarked when Marcia joined her. "He thinks too much of himself."

"My child," said Marcia with unwonted dignity, "you are much too young to express an opinion which only complete inexperience and lack of judgment has led you to form."

"My golly !" ejaculated Dennis, pleased and impressed by this well-turned rebuke. "One in the eye for you, miss ! But let's hear all about him, Mum ! Come along ! I suppose he's one of your old war-pals."

Marcia turned towards him with a certain warning

brightness in her eyes. "Yes," she said. "I met him during the War. He is one of the finest men I have ever known."

"What did he do?" demanded Goldie defiantly.

Marcia paused, and over her face there came a strange look, veiling the brightness. She spoke, almost under her breath. "His courage was like a sort of splendour—like a light in a pitch-black night. I always knew it would never go out."

Goldie glanced at her in surprise. There was something here that she did not understand. "I'll bet he was frightened sometimes," she remarked.

"My dear, he was," said Marcia quietly. "He was terrified, but—he was always brave in spite of it. That—is what I mean by courage. One always knew he would be brave."

"You can't be brave and frightened at the same time," objected Goldie.

But Dennis had caught the true significance of his mother's words. "A girl couldn't," he remarked scathingly. "But"— he looked at Marcia with an odd touch of reverence—"I think p'raps you could, Mum."

Marcia's soft eyes met his with a gleam of appreciation, but she turned immediately to her little daughter as if in compunction for her late severity. "Yes, a girl could, Goldie-locks," she said. "I'm quite sure you could."

"Don't know so much," said Goldie, only partially appeased. "Anyway, he hasn't got very nice manners, and I don't like him much."

She would have liked him still less if she could have heard the remarks to which, at that very moment, Eric Morven was giving utterance as he and Peter walked together towards the farm.

"Children are an awful handicap in these days. I suppose they'll be sending their representatives to Parliament next and making the laws for us."

"Very likely," said Peter.

Morven bit through his cigarette with unconcealed irritation. "How did a gracious woman like that come to have such an impossible offspring? I don't mind the boy so much—but the girl——"

At this point it might have gratified Goldie to know that Peter took up the cudgels in her defence. "Oh, she's a sporting little beggar," he said. "Don't turn her down before you know her! She's full of grit."

Morven threw away his ruined cigarette and laughed, clapping a friendly hand on the boy's shoulder. "That's just the difference between your generation and mine," he said. "You like 'em hard, and I like 'em soft. Not that the mother hasn't plenty of strength too," he added in a different tone. "Only it isn't the bombastic kind. How do you imagine a woman like that would behave in the face of danger, Peter ?"

"Don't know," said Peter. "Expect she'd keep pretty quiet."

"Quiet !" said Morven. "She was calmness itself. She was magnificent. I've never seen such courage in a woman. It was as if she held up a lamp in the dark for us poor frightened devils to steer by."

CHAPTER VII

PETER

"Now I want to hear all about you," said Goldie, fixing blue eyes of firm determination upon Peter's reluctant countenance. "I don't even know your surname yet, or where you went to school, or anything."

"Those things aren't worth knowing," said Peter.

"Yes, they are—if you want to know them," said Goldie. "You know all there is to know about me, and you haven't told me a single thing about yourself. And that's really absurd."

They were on the beach on a rough blustering afternoon a few days after their first meeting. Dennis was with them, but he was scrambling about among the rocks some yards away, and thus Goldie, who had been awaiting her opportunity, took advantage of their temporary isolation to launch her attack.

"For," as she explained, "I do like to know everything about everybody, the same as you do. I asked Mother, and she said I'd better ask you—though I'm sure I can't think why."

"How decent of her !" said Peter ingenuously.

"Well, of course, she's that," conceded Goldie. "But I don't know why she should make a secret of things, do you ?"

"Not really," said Peter. "I suppose you've got to know sooner or later."

"Oh, there is something, then !" exclaimed Goldie with interest. "I knew there was, somehow. What is it ? Did your father make a mess of things, or what ?"

"No, he didn't !" said Peter. "My father was killed in the War. He couldn't have done anything better than that, could he ?"

"Oh, sorry !" said Goldie. "Go on ! What is it I've got to know ?"

"I'm not sure that I shall tell you now," said Peter.

"Oh, don't be silly !" She gave him a nudge with her elbow in semi-impatient cajolery. "You know you've got to. There's nothing whatever to be rattled about. What is your surname ?"

"Tregassa," said Peter.

"Tregassa !" She opened her blue eyes to their widest extent. "D'you really mean that ? You're not having me on ?"

"I'm not," said Peter. "It's my name all right."

She looked him briskly up and down. "Any relation to the man who owns Tregassa Castle ?"

"The same," said Peter.

Goldie stared a little harder. There was an element of warning in her fixed regard. "Is that the truth ?" she said.

"And nothing but the truth," said Peter. "I wish it wasn't."

"Tregassa Castle belongs to you ?" pursued Goldie, determined to get to the bottom of things.

He nodded. "There's no getting out of it—yes."

"Then you're a duke or a lord or something," said Goldie relentlessly.

"Oh no, I'm not. Only a baronet ! And I don't want to be that," said Peter, trying not to turn red under her scrutiny. "I'm not fitted for it. I've had no education."

"You are Sir Peter Tregassa ?" questioned Goldie, still pursuing her point.

"Yes." Peter's blush rose in spite of him. "Sounds absurd, doesn't it ? You see, they were all killed off in the War."

"It isn't at all absurd," pronounced Goldie, convinced at last. "I should think it's rather nice. And what's Major Morven got to do with it ?"

"He's my trustee," said Peter. "A jolly good sort! He's been very decent to me."

Goldie made no comment. She was more interested in Peter at the moment. "Well, why do you say you haven't had any education? It isn't too late, is it? You can go to college?"

"Me?" said Peter. He paused as if gathering impetus before replying; then with vehemence: "Go and be laughed at by all the public-school swells? No, I couldn't!"

"They wouldn't laugh at you," said Goldie. "I expect they'd like you."

"They wouldn't," said Peter with conviction. "We'd hate each other. Anyway, I'm not going to. I've told Eric so! He sees my point, thank goodness."

"Well, I don't," said Goldie flatly. "I think you're very silly not to do all you can to be made——" She paused.

"Into a gentleman?" suggested Peter, his face a duskier red than before.

"Well, not exactly that," said Goldie kindly. "But it's a pity not to make the best of yourself. You'd learn a lot of things at college that you don't know now."

"I daresay," growled Peter. "Spread on the varnish and make it stick in patches! That's what you'd like to do."

"No, I shouldn't," said Goldie. "It's silly to talk like that just because you've not been to a public school. You'd soon catch up."

Peter was silent, but there was more opposition in his silence than in his speech.

Goldie realized the fact, and brought all her batteries to bear. "You'll be jolly sorry some day if you don't. It's bunkum to say it doesn't matter, 'cause it does. Some day you'll come out of your shell and want to marry. And being a baronet you'll have to marry somebody decent. D'you know what'll happen then?"

"Can't imagine," said Peter, beginning to smile.

"Well, she'll look down on you," said Goldie, scoring her point with triumph. "And you'll be jolly sick about it, and it'll serve you right."

"I shan't marry her if she does that," said Peter.

"But everybody'll do it, and you've got to marry someone," insisted Goldie.

"What for?" said Peter.

"Because everybody does—everybody that counts.

You've got to have a son to leave things to," explained Goldie with some impatience.

"Oh, is that all? Then I shan't bother," said Peter. "Eric is next of kin—last of the line in fact. He can do that."

"He couldn't take the title. He's got a different name. The title would die," said Goldie severely. "And it would be your fault—all because you were too lazy to go to college."

"What an awful thought!" said Peter.

"Yes, you can laugh now," she returned, "but you won't then. You'll be simply fed up with yourself. And it'll be too late. Everything will be spoilt."

"Oh, don't!" said Peter.

"Well, but it will!" she insisted. "You can't shut your eyes to facts ; at least you're very silly if you do. And you'll never enjoy anything."

"But look here!" said Peter. "You don't look down on me, do you ? Or if you do, I never noticed it."

"That's different," said Goldie. "I'm at school myself at present. And besides, it's holidays."

"I see," said Peter. "There's no knowing what you may do afterwards. Is that it ?"

"Well, I shouldn't like to say," said Goldie with some hauteur. "One naturally gets more particular as one gets older."

"Oh, then when you're twenty or so, you won't know me ?" said Peter.

"I may not—if you don't go to college," returned Goldie with her head in the air.

"All right," said Peter, and swung suddenly upon his heel. "Then you'd better stop knowing me now. Good-bye!"

He was striding away from her over the sand before the drift of his words reached her. Goldie stood still in amazement. Hitherto she had regarded Peter in the light of a comparatively humble vassal to whom her favour was a gift of considerable value. To see him rise thus in sudden open rebellion literally took her breath away. Peter—the good-natured playfellow who had been at their beck and call since the first day of their acquaintance ! She stood and gazed after him with the wind whistling round her, too confounded for the moment for speech or action. Then, as she saw his square-built figure rapidly receding from her, a great gust of wrath went through her and she uttered a cry that was almost a shriek of anger.

Normally, Goldie was a good-tempered child. In all her

bickerings with Dennis she never betrayed any real rancour.
Dennis was a brother with whom it was necessary to hold her
own. And she did so without much difficulty, and comparatively without any bitterness. At school also she steered
an even course, taking nothing very seriously, too wholesome to be easily irritated. In all her life no adverse circumstance had very deeply affected her. She took things as they
came, seldom desiring the unattainable with sufficient keenness
to fret for it, and enjoying her pleasures without undue
excitement.

Perhaps until that moment she had never known the meaning of true mortification. Life had been a very easy thing to
Goldie. She had a certain philosophy of outlook which kept
her calm. The depths of her had so far been scarcely stirred.
But now, quite suddenly, as when a stone is flung into the heart
of a sleeping pool, her whole being was in tumult. Unconsciously she had come to regard Peter as a kindly henchman
upon whose services she could rely implicitly at any time.
He had become an essential part of their seaside holiday,
as much an established part of their entertainment as the sea
and the rocks. Her first thought on going forth in the morning
to the day's enjoyment was naturally Peter, and Peter was
always at hand and ready to join in their pursuits. She
hailed him as a comrade, but she looked on him as a slave.
And now to be abruptly flouted by him caused a revulsion of
feeling in her so violent that she was thrown off her balance.
She scarcely knew in this tremendous exigency what she was
doing.

Her scream of fury, which was half a shout of recall, and
the other half an expression of sheer passion, reached him as
he strode away from her, but he barely glanced over his
shoulder and he did not slacken his pace. With unaltered
decision he pursued his way, grimly stifling the hurt within.
If he were not to be worth knowing in the future it was
certainly better to sever the acquaintanceship at once. He
had grown fond of his little playmates, especially of Goldie,
whose normally even temper and fund of originality appealed
to him. His life had not held much in the way of pleasant
companionship hitherto. As to his position, he had barely
begun to sense its novelty. The responsibility was upon
Eric's shoulders rather than his own, and to regard himself
as a being of any importance was an idea which had not so
far penetrated Peter's humble mind.

It was natural, perhaps, that Goldie should see farther.

Goldie belonged to the far-seeing sex ; but to be weighed
in the balance on that account and to be found wanting was
not to be tolerated.   Peter pursued his dogged way along the
beach, and his progress was not without dignity.   People
could take him as they found him or do without.   If Goldie
chose to stamp and storm in rage upon the shore because he
would not bend to her will, well—there was no help for it.
His life was his own, after all, and what he chose to do with it
was no affair of hers.

At this point, however, a curious impulse made him pause.
It was true that she had no right of interference, true that she
had gone too far and had goaded him into exasperation ;
but did that justify him in treating her thus ?   Was he not
indeed in so doing betraying the very lack of culture of which
she had accused him ?   She was only a child, and no doubt
she needed a lesson, but was it for him to administer it ?
Was such a rebuff as this the act of a gentleman ?

Something like a red-hot dagger seemed to go through
Peter.   He felt scorched to his inmost soul.   Abruptly he
swung round.   This was unbearable.   It was he who had gone
too far.

And then to his amazement he saw that the wrathful
Goldie had abandoned her position and was flying to him,
heedless of rocks or pools barring her way, her hat off and her
hair standing out in a wonderful golden nimbus around her
eager face.

Swiftly he strode towards her.   The impact of their meeting knocked the breath out of them both.   As for Goldie,
she collapsed, all wet and panting, in his arms, the tears
streaming down her cheeks.

"How could you ?   How could you ?   Oh, how could
you ?" she sobbed.

Peter, firmly supporting her while she hung upon him,
wondered how on earth he could.   "I'm a brute.   I'm awfully
sorry.   Do stop crying !" he said with deep contrition.

Goldie made a strong effort to comply, and partially
succeeded.   She allowed him to lead her towards the sea.
"I never meant you—to go away—like that," she said still
tearfully.

"I never thought you'd care," said Peter.

"Well, of course I care !"   She gave his arm a hug that was
half a shake.   "I thought we were pals."

"So we are !" declared Peter stoutly.

She uttered a trembling laugh.   "You don't behave at

if we were. But never mind!" She squeezed his arm again with more warmth. "I was a pig too. I quite understand why you don't want to go to college, and I don't really mind whether you do or not. So there!"

"Thank you very much," said Peter gratefully, feeling this to be a great concession. "That's jolly nice of you."

"Well, no there isn't much in it," confessed Goldie with honesty. "There might be for some people; but you— you're all right as you are."

"Oh, thank you!" said Peter again, slightly over-whelmed. "I hope you'll always think so."

"Yes, I shall," said Goldie with confidence. "So we'll go on being friends, shall we?"

"Rather!" said Peter in a tone that left nothing to be desired.

When they returned along the shore a little later they were on the best of terms. But Dennis, who was prawning in a pool, gave his sister a suspicious glance.

"You look as if you'd been crying pretty hard. What's the matter?" he said.

Peter at once replied on her behalf. "She had a fall— a nasty bump. But she's all right now."

Dennis snorted his contempt. "Girls always cry before they're hurt."

Goldie drew in her breath to make sharp retort, but again Peter was before her. "And you'll cry afterwards if you don't watch out, my lad," he said genially. "I'm just in the mood to punch your head for you if you can't keep a civil tongue inside it."

Dennis stared for a moment in some surprise, and then turned aside. "Oh, don't make a fool of yourself!" he said. "Life's too short."

With which sensible remark Peter expressed full agreement and the matter dropped.

CHAPTER VIII

YOUTH

"I WONDER if you're really enjoying yourself," said Morven. They were walking side by side across the moorland track,

Marcia with her sketch-book in her hand. There was a certain view of the coast-line which she had seen the previous day which she was anxious to attempt to reproduce. She had been clever with her pencil in her girlhood, but of late years inclination had been wanting and she had not made any use of her gift. She glanced down at the book as she made slightly irrelevant reply.

"I am growing younger every day."

He smiled at her. "Oh, you've begun to notice it too! A pity you can't teach your children to be young in the same way."

"You're very hard on the present generation," she protested.

"My dear," said Eric Morven, "you and I belong to the present generation. They belong to the future, and a very unattractive one it is from my point of view. They'll be old before they get there. They're old already."

She smiled back, finding it impossible to do otherwise. That intimate form of address was one which he often applied to her when they were alone, and it seemed as natural as their friendship. There is a type of born friend whom one recognizes instinctively at first sight, drawn by a mutual magnetism that knows no law of convention, being in fact a law in itself which is infinitely stronger. Such a friend as this had Eric Morven been from the outset to Marcia. There had been no early stages, as he had said, no gradual linking up of bonds of union. They had known each other from the first moment as comrades ; it had been more like a renewal of a pre-existent friendship than a beginning. And so no touch of intimacy seemed out of place. The confidence between them was complete and unassailable.

"I wonder what age really is," said Marcia. "Somehow I don't think it belongs to time, do you ?"

"I don't know," he said. "There's no spiritual connection, anyhow. You and I would always be young together, even in our dotage."

She pondered the statement with a certain gravity. "Yes, I suppose we should, though I don't know quite why."

"For the same reason that you are growing younger every day," he said. "It is always springtime when we are together."

'Yes, I know," she said, not disputing the obvious. "But, why ?"

He began to laugh. "My dear Marcia you were wondering

E

what age really is. Here is another problem for you! What is youth?"

She shook her head, laughing with him. "Now that is an impossible question! I should say it is just the joy of life. The people who have never had it have never been young."

"And the people who can hold on to it will never be old," he said. "We shall have to hold on to it somehow. It would be awful to let go, wouldn't it?"

"That's, I'm afraid, what I had begun to do," said Marcia.

"So had I." He spoke with a kind of grimness. "It's easily done, you know. One gets out of touch with the things that matter, and then one loses interest, which is fatal. That ranch of mine—I tried to work up a certain keenness. But it was all make-believe—artificial. But if there were held out to me the smallest hope that you might some day see it——"

She spoke almost involuntarily into his pause. "Oh, how I should like to! It would appeal to me immensely. An enterprise of that sort really would deserve all one's energies."

He made a slight grimace. "Success for its own sake doesn't appeal to me. One has got to do something, of course, and one may as well make a decent show of it as not. But there's not much inspiration in working for oneself alone. At least, one hardly feels inclined to work overtime."

"Oh, I do understand," said Marcia impulsively. And then she paused as he had paused, conscious, as it were, of a sudden gap in the road they were travelling. After a moment she delicately skirted it, scarcely aware of its nature. "But, as you say, it's up to us to make a decent show of things. In fact, we can't do less, can we?"

"You couldn't," he said.

"I don't see you slacking at your job either," she said. "And now you have Peter to look after too. You've got to set him a good example."

"Oh, are you really old-fashioned enough to think he'd follow it if I did?" said Eric.

She laughed. "I don't know. I think you're a hopeless pessimist if the truth were told."

"And that's a contradiction in terms," he said.

"Oh, don't be highbrow!" protested Marcia. "I'm no good on stilts. Here is the place I want! Let me get my little sketch before the rain comes!"

He was carrying a camp-stool which he opened for her; and then when she was installed he wandered restlessly away, smoking his pipe with the expression of one who sees no future before him.

It was a blustering day with a sky that was generally overcast, but which afforded occasional bursts of sunshine when the wind tore a rent in the clouds. The sea was rough, and the roar of the waves had a solemn sound which in some fashion seemed to add to the man's heaviness of spirit. He moved to and fro with a dreary aimlessness, presently drifting back to Marcia where she sat braced against the gusts of wind, making her rapid sketch.

For a time he stood watching her in silence. Then: "You're a wonderful woman," he said abruptly. "Given a few coloured rags, you would turn out the loveliest ball-dress ever designed."

She shook her head, not looking up, her smile just visible at the corners of her mouth. "No, Eric, no! I'm not in the least that type of genius. I just believe in making the best of what we've got, that's all."

Again for a space he was silent, gravely watching her. "But never reaching out for a bit more?" he suggested at last in an odd tone that sounded half-serious and half-amused.

She continued her sketch deftly, unswervingly. "Reaching out—every time!" she said. "That's life, isn't it?"

He assented somewhat gloomily. "The fruit that grows out of reach is always the best," he said.

"You're very depressing to-day," said Marcia.

"Do I depress you?" he asked.

"Well, no, not really." She paused a moment to survey her work. "I know you're not quite in earnest. But if you were——"

"Well, if I were?" he questioned.

She bent again to her sketch. "Then I'm afraid you would," she said. "You see, I don't like my friends to be unhappy."

He received the statement in silence, almost as if he had not heard it, and again one of their quiet intervals succeeded, during which Morven knocked out his pipe and refilled it with a sort of automatic attention.

When he had relighted it, he spoke again in the semi-sardonic fashion habitual to him. "How long is this Cornish idyll going to last?"

Marcia's hand came to a sudden stop as if she had detected

a blunder. She sat for some seconds motionless, surveying the little picture which had sprung into being under her pencil.

"Don't let me put you out of your stride !" he said.

She recalled herself with an effort. "No. I was just wondering. One really almost forgets the passage of time here."

"One does," he assented. "But I suppose it will continue to pass as long as we allow its existence."

She looked up at him, her smile slightly tremulous. "That is the worst of letting oneself grow young again. One forgets that the good times can't last."

"Then you are really enjoying it ?" he said.

"I am loving it beyond words," said Marcia.

And then, with a definite effort, she withdrew her look rom his and returned to her sketch.

"I wonder what the children are doing," she said.

"D'you think it matters ?" said Eric. "I'll find out for you if you want to know."

She shook her head. "No, don't ! They only bore you. And Peter is there."

"Oh, Peter !" He laughed. "Peter has become an absolute rabbit—at least so far as your small daughter is concerned. You may have noticed."

"Well, yes, I have," admitted Marcia.

"Not her first conquest, I daresay," he commented.

"Oh yes, I think it is," she said, laughing also. "She is so very naïve about it. And really I don't think he is quite such a rabbit as you think. She has an immense respect for him."

"I'm glad to hear she has for someone," he commented. "Did you hear about the car he's learning to drive ?"

"Yes, he wants to take us all to see Tregassa Castle in it. At least so Goldie told me last night." Marcia spoke a little dubiously.

"And what did you say ?" he questioned.

"I said that I would consult you, and perhaps you would do the driving," she said with a smile.

"How prudent of you ! But why not let them walk—it's only three miles—while you and I go in the car ?" he suggested. "You'd like that all right, wouldn't you ?"

"Oh yes, of course I should like it. But"—again Marcia paused to survey her work—"would they mind, do you think ?"

"Would it matter if they did?" he countered. "No, look here, my dear! You're absurd. You give way over everything. That's why you get domineered over. If you'd only spanked that young Goldie of yours a littler more in her earlier youth, she'd think twice as much of you now. Well, I'm going to find Peter and tell him it's settled. I'll call round for you this afternoon and we'll take tea along. The castle is furnished, but there are no servants there. We're contemplating putting in caretakers for the present, as Peter can't take up his abode there alone."

"I shall love to see it," said Marcia.

"That's settled, then. We'll go by the coast road and enjoy ourselves. They can take the short cut across the moor." He spoke with a boyish zest. "And when that sketch is finished, I'm hoping you may be induced to give it to me in memory of the occasion."

"Do you want it?" said Marcia. "I don't think it's very good."

"I want it very badly," he said. "And I think it promises to be the best you've done."

"The work one does the quickest is always the best," she said. "Other things—that one spends hours over—sometimes never come right."

"That too is life," he said. "You've got to snatch the best. It's always so. If you miss it, it may never come your way again."

"Do we always know the best when we see it?" said Marcia in a tone that needed no reply.

"I do," he said with decision ; and, turning from her with the words, he went upon his quest.

CHAPTER IX

SPILT MILK

How seldom, looking back along the path of life, is it possible to say, "That was the place where we left the beaten track", so narrowly and so almost imperceptibly does the first divergence appear ! The mere suggestion of a trodden way through the flowers and the grass is the only indication of the spot where our feet first left the dusty high-road, to linger, perchance to rest awhile, and then to wander on. How easy that initial wandering, how blessed the relief from the glare and the noise of the crowded thoroughfare! How harmless the respite, and how inevitable the return!

In after days Marcia blamed herself bitterly for her lack of caution, but who that has known the true holiday spirit, the sense of relaxation after prolonged toil, shall blame her for failing to see that the return along that flower-decked track might prove a harder task than she anticipated?

Perhaps, at the back of her mind, she had begun dimly to suspect that the return could not be postponed much longer, but that the beaten track already lay a considerable distance behind her was a fact of which she was unaware. The time had passed so quickly, and they had all so thoroughly enjoyed it. Certainly the weather had not always been irreproachable, but it had not often upset their plans, and the children were so healthy now that there was no further need for coddling.

The expedition to Tregassa Castle, remnants of which claimed to be of Round Table antiquity, had been discussed more than once, but though it was generally agreed that it must take place some time before their departure, it had been left to Peter to make the definite suggestion.

Eric's amendment had, to Marcia's relief, been duly accepted, and, having seen the three younger members of the party start upon their ramble across the moor, she busied herself with packing the tea, which was to be transported in the car. That done, she sat down in the window to await the arrival of her cavalier, putting a few finishing touches to her pencil sketch of the morning the while.

Very soon, with the ardour habitual to her, she had become engrossed in her occupation, and it was not until the car actually stopped at the gate that she was roused from her absorption. Then she looked up smiling to greet him as he came up the path.

"We're going to have a real spring afternoon," she said.

He stopped at the window and stretched his hand inside. "May I have it, please?"

She hesitated. "It isn't good enough. I'm trying to mprove it. Mayn't I keep it a little longer?"

"No. I want it just as it is." He sounded inexorable, but she saw that he was smiling. "You can't improve it. I want the first fine inspiration untouched."

She laughed and yielded. "Well, let me put it in an envelope anyway! Come along in, won't you, and help me collect the tea-things! I'm just ready."

He pushed up the window and entered without ceremony. "I wish we'd made them take their own tea," he said. "Then we could have gone in the other direction."

"Oh, why?" said Marcia. "I've always wanted to see Tregassa Castle."

He strolled about the little room restlessly. There was a touch of lawlessness, a hint of the buccaneer, about him that afternoon; but she was glad to see that the depression of the morning had passed. "Oh, I don't know," he said. "I get tired of going about in herds, don't you?"

"You mean bored," she said. "No, I haven't been really bored for quite a long time. I think this place has done us all a lot of good."

He turned towards her with a quizzical expression. "Are you sure it's the place?"

She was putting the provisions in order, not greatly heeding the conversation. "I've learnt to love it," she said. "It must be even lovelier in summer. Will you take that basket? Mind—it's heavy!"

"I'll take everything," he said. "Have you got an extra coat? You'll probably need it."

"Yes, I have. It's in the hall. Oh, here is your sketch!" said Marcia. "I'll keep it for you till we come back, shall I? See, I'll put it in this drawer."

"Well, give me the key of the drawer, then!" he said. "I'm not taking any risks. I think you're wrong. It couldn't be lovelier in the summer. Nothing could be lovelier than this."

"Perhaps not," said Marcia. "Are you going out again by the window, because, if you don't mind, I think I prefer the door!"

He opened it for her with an obeisance. "I follow you," he said. She went out lightheartedly. The sun was shining, and the call of spring was in the air.

There was nothing smart about Peter's latest venture. It had been bought very much second-hand, by Eric's advice, for purposes of tuition, and it looked as if it had been a learner's car almost from its infancy.

"The boy's getting on," said Eric, as Marcia took her place. "He'll never come to grief, so you needn't be nervous. He's far too cautious for that."

"I'm glad of that," she said. "For Dennis and Goldie have set their hearts on going out with him."

He laughed at her. "And you, of course, haven't the heart to forbid it! But you can trust Peter all right. He's safe."

"Yes, I like Peter," said Marcia.

The road that wound about half a mile from the coast was rough and narrow, but there was no other traffic upon it, and to Marcia the scenery was the most beautiful she had ever beheld. At certain points along their route they seemed to be almost completely surrounded by sea, the sapphire blue of which was a sight to sink deep into the memory. The fiery gold of the bracken that clothed the moor and the grim grey of the outstanding rocks seemed to call into being an ancient magic to which she could give no name.

"I feel," she said presently, "as though we had gone back about two thousand years."

"The primitive woman awakening!" said Morven. "This car of Peter's is a bit of an anachronism, though. D'you think we ought to abandon it?"

"No, of course not! But go very slowly!" she begged him. "I want to enjoy every inch."

He reduced the speed to a walking-pace. "You're right. It's too good to miss any of it," he said. "I've seen quite a lot of fine things in my life, but never anything to approach this. But once again I'm not quite sure that it's just the place. Anyhow," he spoke deliberately, "I could never think of it without you after to-day."

Marcia smiled. The sheer beauty around her seemed to be reaching down into her very soul. "I'm like that too," she said. "I always connect people with places. We have been very lucky to meet again in such a heavenly spot."

"Having parted in such a hell," he said.

It was his first deliberate reference to the horrors of that earlier episode which had drawn them so closely together. She received it in silence, her eyes upon the brilliant blue that stretched to the horizon.

For a few moments he also was silent; then, very steadily and quietly, he spoke again: "It wasn't all hell—to me. I've often thought since that there was more of heaven in it than I knew."

Still she was silent, and he gradually brought the slow-moving car to a standstill. She did not seem to notice. Her look was far away

He broke in upon her thoughts with a certain imperiousness. "Marcia!"

She gave a slight start, and turned towards him. Her eyes met his questioningly, with a clear unfaltering regard. There was no embarrassment whatever about her. "Well?" she said, faintly smiling.

He spoke with a curious mixture of insistence and hesitation, as though yielding to an impulse half against his judgment. "You've never told me—I don't know if it's intentional—you may not want to—anything about your husband."

"Oh, haven't I?" she said. "I never realized that I hadn't. I don't suppose it occurred to me that you might be interested."

"I'm interested in anything that concerns you," he said rather doggedly.

"How nice of you!" said Marcia.

"No, it isn't." He disputed the point at once. "I can't help it. I want to see everything connected with you exactly as it is."

"I don't know that there is very much to tell," said Marcia thoughtfully. "My husband is a very busy man and—I should say, though he has never told me so—rather ambitious. He has already reached a very high position, and I am quite sure he will climb much higher still."

"Do you want him to?" demanded Eric abruptly.

She shook her head. "I really don't know. I want him to do whatever will make him happiest. No one can judge for anyone else, can they?"

Morven took out a cigarette. "A good many people try," he said.

"Well, I'm not one of them," said Marcia. "I think people must all choose for themselves."

"At the expense of other people?" he suggested.

"No, of course not. I didn't mean that. We ought to be able to fit in with each other so that no one is cramped or disappointed. Don't you think so?" She was still smiling a little, though her tone was serious.

"I think—in this world—that's quite impossible," he said. "But don't let my opinions upset your Utopia! It all sounds very charming, and if you are satisfied . . ." He stopped with a slight shrug.

"Ah, you are cynical," she said.

He raised his eyebrows. "Or truthful! Are you

going to tell me that you have never been cramped or disappointed?"

"It is entirely my own fault if I have been," she said. "I have had—plenty of opportunities to expand."

Morven began to laugh. "Yes, during the War, away from your home atmosphere. You expanded then, didn't you?" He became abruptly grave again. "It must have been pretty difficult going back again afterwards."

She made a quick effort to be loyal ere the occasion robbed her of the chance. "Oh, not really. I had the children, you know."

"So you had," he agreed dryly. "Also your husband. He must have been pleased to see you back."

Marcia was silent, a faint troubled frown between her brows.

"Well?" He spoke with a certain perversity. "Wasn't he?"

She turned from him with a slow, rather weary movement. "I don t know. I expect so. He had his work to do."

"And you had to make yours." There was irony in his voice. "You had to pick up the burden again just where you laid it down—with perhaps a little added thereto—and adapt yourself to the bearing of it. Nobody thought of bothering to try to adapt it to you."

"Isn't it—rather a pity—to talk like that?" said Marcia in a low voice. "You can't want to make me discontented and unhappy."

"Or to see you feeding on ashes—and satisfied," he said with almost a sting of irritation in the words. "I don't know which I want the least. You are so magnificent that I can't endure the thought of either."

"Perhaps," she said very quietly, not looking at him "you think too much of me altogether."

"And perhaps," he returned with a flash of anger, "no one else thinks half enough!"

She made a gesture with one hand as if to stay him. "No, you mustn't say that. It isn't fair—or true. The War—I think the War, though it did us good in some ways, rather upset our sense of proportion. It made some of us feel more important and useful than we really were. And—you are quite right—it was difficult to settle down afterwards. But that was one's own fault, and no one else's."

"You were always much too good to them," he said.

It was her turn to laugh, and she did so softly. "How

absurdly one-sided you are ! It wasn't being good to them to forsake them entirely as I did and give such services as had always been at their disposal to my country."

"But you were right," he asserted hotly, "quite right to do it. You would do the same again."

She was silent.

"You would do the same again," he reiterated with challenge in his voice.

"I suppose I should," she said slowly. "It's hard to say. But I am not sure that I did the right thing. It certainly seemed so at the time. But perhaps I was over-eager to hear the call. I sometimes think now that possibly, after all, my place was at home."

It was the first time that she had ever voiced that doubt of hers—the doubt that had grown and matured in her heart during two years of fruitless effort to turn her desert into a garden. Perhaps if she had realized the state of mind of the man beside her she would hardly have done so then, but the impulse that stirred her to candour would have been hard to deny, and she had no one else in whom to confide.

His tone as he made reply to that confidence of hers was gentler than before, as if he sensed her need for sympathy. "Tell me," he said, "if you don't mind—were you happier before the War than you are now ?"

Her eyes had gone back to the shining belt of ocean. They dwelt upon it wistfully. "I don't know," she said. "It's so difficult to tell, isn't it ? One forgets. But—yes, in a way I suppose I was. The children were comparative babies then. I think—even you—would have loved them in those days."

She stopped as if involuntarily, and he saw her throat work. He leaned forward and looked into her face. Then, very gently, he laid his hand upon hers, without speaking.

She uttered a faint, choked sound and put her free hand up to her eyes. "How ridiculous I am !" she said after a moment. "I am actually crying over spilt milk ! Why do you encourage me ?"

"I didn't mean to make you unhappy," he said.

She smiled at him, dashing away her tears. "What an idea ! You are far too kind, and I take advantage of it. I should think you are excessively bored. You ought to be. I really thought I had more sense."

"It isn't always sensible," he said, "to hide one's soul

from one's friends. With you, to reveal it is just an act of graciousness which I shall never forget."

"Thank you," she said, and laid her other hand for a moment upon his. "But I don't want you to think that I spend my time in idle regrets. Life means more to me than that."

"You wouldn't be you if you did," he said. "I've found out one thing about you—a thing I knew from the very outset. You may live on husks yourself, but you hand out the real thing to everyone else."

"Oh no—no!" she protested, removing her hand gently from beneath his. "Now you're talking nonsense. We had better go on."

But Morven still lingered. "I wish I might ask you something," he said.

She met his look with perfect confidence. "But of course you may ask me anything! Why not?"

"It isn't much," he said with momentary embarrassment. "Only I should awfully like to know. You give so much to other people. Are you ever sorry afterwards? Do you ever wish you hadn't?"

"Oh no, I don't think so," she said. "Besides, I really don't feel that I am as ultra-generous as you say."

"No, you wouldn't." He smiled with more assurance. "Then you don't ever regret anything that you gave—to me —in the past?"

His eyes searched hers for an instant as he uttered the question, and then before she could answer it he had turned from her and was pressing the self-starter of the car.

"Don't tell me if you do!" he said. "I'd rather not know."

She was on the verge of answering him with the warm generosity habitual to her, but something in those last words checked the words upon her lips. Only, as he set the car in motion, she spoke gently, with a touch of repression, as though instinctively she sought to spare him pain.

"Isn't it always better to look forward than to look back? That, at least, is what I try to do."

"Yes, I thought so," he said in a tone that finally closed the subject.

The next moment the car was running swiftly over the moorland road and all confidential talk was at an end.

CHAPTER X

TREGASSA CASTLE

THE wonder of Tregassa Castle was its ancient keep, which stood apart from the main building on a high eminence overlooking the sea. This, although long disused, was in a very fair state of preservation, and the winding spiral stone staircase that led up to the battlements, though crumbling in places, was still by no means difficult of ascent. The castle itself stood up rough and grey against its green surroundings as it had stood for centuries. Its western windows, like the keep, gazed out to the open sea. But its southern front was its glory. Here the efforts of many generations had achieved an effect of mellowness which the passage of time had graciously assisted. It was almost entirely covered with ivy, with the exception of a sheltered space in the centre where flourished a giant magnolia which in summer bloomed with a rich splendour once seen never to be forgotten. A formal spread of lawn and garden stretched before the gravelled terrace on this southern front, and in it, sheltered by the ancient pile from adverse winds, there grew aloes and semi-tropical palms. Here in the summer were wonderful parterres of flowers dazzling the eye with their brilliance. It was, in short, one of those ancient homes of greatness which had never been allowed to decay.

The drive, which wound round to the northern side of the Castle, was guarded at its entrance half a mile away by heavy iron gates hung on great posts of stone surmounted by enormous stone dragons of terrific aspect. A lodge, also faced with stone, stood on one side ; but the gates were open, and Morven and his companion drove straight in and up the avenue of fir trees without a pause.

"This really is a wonderful place," said Marcia. "So dignified and ancestral. Peter must indeed feel proud of it."

"He has hardly begun to look upon it as his own yet," said Eric.

"No. It feels rather like a place without a master." She looked up at the massive walls with a whimsical touch of pity. "How sad that the direct heir should have died like that !"

"Yes, it's a desolate sort of stronghold." He brought the car to a standstill before the portico. "They've kept the ancient spirit of the place, anyhow, on this side. It's less forbidding on the south. Come round to that first!"

He conducted her by a gravel path which bordered what had once been a moat to the sheltered stretch of garden below the terrace, and then up the steps, on the top of which she paused, lost in admiration of the view that lay spread below them.

"Really, Eric," she said, "this is a glorious old place!" He stood beside her, making no comment, content to observe her keen appreciation of the beauties around her.

She turned at length. "I'd no idea it was so lovely. You never told me half. I hope Peter has plenty of money to keep it up with."

"That's just the trouble," Eric said. "We may have to let it for a few years. There's nothing decided yet, but it will need pretty careful nursing, and it would be rather absurd to run a big establishment under present circumstances. Later on, when he's old enough to marry, it'll be a different thing."

"Yes, it's a pity he isn't a little older," said Marcia. "Well, do take me over the Castle! Is there really no one looking after it?"

"The people at the lodge are caretaking. The man was the head gardener, and we've kept him on. But there's no one actually in the place. It's all wrapped up. I hope you won't be disappointed." Eric turned towards a side-door at one end of the terrace and produced a key.

She followed him eagerly. "Of course I shan't be! I am intensely interested—more so, probably, than the children will be. They won't be here at present, so we can dawdle as much as we like."

"Yes, it's nice to go at our own pace, isn't it?" he said with a smile as he opened the door.

They entered a stone passage that evidently led to the domestic quarters, but out of this another door admitted them to the main part of the Castle.

"I want you to see the great hall and gallery," Morven said. "I hope you're not cold."

The atmosphere of the place smote chill like a vault, but Marcia was not to be discouraged. "Why, of course not! I am wrapped up to the eyes. How strangely the light slants through that high window, almost as though someone were pointing a torch! Oh, Eric, what a magnificent place!"

They had entered the great stone hall which occupied the major part of the original portion of the building. This had once been a vast, churchlike apartment, but like the southern front the passage of time and additions of successive owners had tempered its native starkness. It was now wonderfully panelled in oak, and surrounded by a great gallery which was approached by a shallow winding oak staircase with a massive carved balustrade.

"I have never seen anything more beautiful in my life," Marcia declared.

"Come and see the lower rooms," said Eric. "There is a rather beautiful old French drawing-room here which I think you will enjoy."

He opened one of a pair of high folding doors and ushered her into a large dim chamber with shuttered windows and ghostly draped furniture.

She entered impetuously, and then paused. "Eric! There's something I don't like about this room. What is it?"

He moved forward. "Only because it's dark. Let me undo one of the windows!"

She put out her hand sharply and stopped him. "Don't!" she said. "Don't! You'll think me fanciful. But I don't like this room. Let us go back!"

He turned immediately, his hand grasping hers. "My dear, you're not nervous of shadows!"

"I don't know what I am," she said, breathing quickly. "There's something here I don't like. Perhaps it's within myself. I can't tell. Please let us go!"

She pulled at his hand like a frightened child, and they went back into the hall.

"What is it?" he said. "What's happened to you?"

She laughed, but her laugh had an appealing sound. "Oh, it's just my silly fancy. Shut the door, if you don't mind. And shall we go out into the open again and wait for the children? Then we can all go round together."

He made no remonstrance. Perhaps he realized that she was scarcely in the frame of mind to listen to any reasoning. Silently he closed the shadowy room and accompanied her back down the stone passage by which they had come.

Out on the terrace once more, in the fitful sunshine and racing wind, she threw him an apologetic glance. "How foolish you must think me! I really can't explain myself. Please don't be vexed!"

"That is the most absurd suggestion of all," he said quietly. "Imagine anything else you like, but not that!"

She breathed more freely. "Thank you. That's comforting at any rate. Shall we walk up and down ? I'm not generally so fanciful and ridiculous. Quite absurd, as you say."

"Don't misapply my words !" he said, smiling a little. "Have a cigarette !"

She accepted one, feeling that some sort of propitiation was due to him in spite of his assurance to the contrary. They turned and paced slowly along the terrace, and her agitation began to subside. Eric walked beside her in silence —that calm, unstrained silence of his which she never found embarrassing.

She turned to him at length. "I am really sorry to have behaved so absurdly, but somehow there was something in the atmosphere of that French drawing-room that brought back to me so vividly—so intensely vividly—that *château* in France that we turned into a hospital. It was some essence —some sort of scent—that used to hang about the place. I really can't describe it. And being there with you too. In some way it brought back the ghosts of those dead days."

"And you have no use for them now," he said. "Poor ghosts !"

She flushed a little at his tone. "Oh, don't think me fickle ! Really I am not. Only—it took me rather by surprise. I felt as if I had been swept back into the past—almost like a ghost myself."

"And is the past ever dead ?" he pursued. "Do you want it to be ?"

She hesitated. "Well, perhaps not, though there are some things one would very thankfully forget."

"But not the good things," he said with quiet persistence.

"Oh no, not the good things of course." She smiled rather wistfully. "Only they are so mixed up with the bad that it's difficult to distinguish the one from the other."

"I know ; the wheat and the tares !" he said. "There's no help for it. They've got to grow together. You wouldn't like to root out everything."

"No, no ; not everything," she agreed, but she spoke with some uncertainty as though possibly her choice and his might not be identical.

"I believe you would like to wash out the War entirely," he said, half-laughing.

She replied instantly, with deep earnestness. "I would. I believe it did far more harm than good. Nominally we were victorious, but actually I believe we shall never recover from it."

"Never is a long time," he observed.

"Oh, I know. But what I mean is that the effects will go on for generations, like a stream of hatred released and spreading farther and farther every day." She spoke almost passionately. "It is so terrible to think of. One tries to see the other part—the good part ; but it is so infinitesimal compared with the bad."

"And you mean to say you let that worry you ?" he said.

She looked at him. "Don't you ?"

He shook his head. "Frankly, no ! I always knew the world was a bad place, and of course the War hasn't made it any better. No sane person ever thought it would. But as it had to be gone through——" He broke off with a shrug. "The only sensible thing to do is to save everything that's left worth having."

"One wonders sometimes if there *is* anything left," Marcia said in a low voice.

"That isn't like you," he protested. "You're not cut out or a pessimist."

"No, and I don't mean to be one." She forced a smile with the words. "I think pessimism is another word for cowardice, don't you ?"

"Well, I can't picture you being guilty of either," he said. "Your courage always stood the test."

"How little you know about it !" said Marcia.

"Do I ?" he said, and suddenly there sounded in his voice a note that almost startled her. "Do you think I've forgotten how you once—when I was in mortal terror— sheltered me in your arms ?"

She felt the blood suffuse her face ere she could repress it, but she made a quick attempt to treat the matter lightly and naturally. "Oh, but you were brave too ! Anyone else would have panicked, wounded as you were. I never felt really frightened when I was with you. I always knew I could depend on you."

She spoke a little breathlessly, but with a sincerity that could not be questioned.

"Thank you," he said gravely. "I hope you still feel the same."

She did not answer him save with a brief, friendly smile, for at that moment a distant shout of greeting reached

F

them from a group of trees below the lawns, and they saw the rest of their party approaching.

"How quick they've been!" exclaimed Marcia.

"They always are when you don't want them to be," observed Eric, only half-laughing.

She threw him an amused glance, and then turned to wave to the advancing new-comers. Goldie had broken away from them and was running to meet her.

"Hullo, Mum!" she cried. "Hope you haven't done the Castle without us! We've been simply tearing along to get here in time."

"You would!" muttered Eric venomously to his cigarette.

Marcia's clear voice called back in answer. "No, dear, no! It's all right. We waited so that we could all go round together."

For the first time Eric Morven looked at his companion as though he suspected her of some species of subterfuge.

CHAPTER XI

GOLDIE

NOTHING but an immediate inspection would satisfy Goldie, and they all accordingly obeyed her imperious behest and proceeded to explore the ancient pile from roof to cellars. Peter acted as guide, and as his visitors burst noisily into each room all ghostliness of atmosphere evaporated before them as completely as the smoke from Morven's cigarette.

Goldie went from one apartment to another like a miniature whirlwind, permitting no lingering on the part of any, admiring here and criticizing there with all the impartial inefficiency of early youth that occasionally and quite accidentally scores a bull's-eye. Eric schooled himself to endure her observations in silence, and Marcia, aware of his self-restraint, was not wholly at her ease. Fortunately Dennis remained to preserve the balance, for Peter, since the momentous occasion on which he had succeeded in administering a lesson to Goldie, had never ventured further in the matter of her education. But Dennis, having nothing to lose since he regarded his sister's favour as of small account, had no hesitation in bestowing upon her as many snubs as his brotherly ingenuity could devise, and Goldie, during her rapid progress through the grand old rooms, actually experienced some difficulty in holding her own. She returned once or twice to argue, but, to do her justice, she did not often claim Peter's support, there being a sort of unwritten law between herself and Dennis that all their contentions must be conducted without any backing on either side, their mother only being sometimes allowed to act the part of mediator.

They maintained a lively though not wholly unfriendly altercation throughout the proceedings which quite prevented the rest of the party, whatever their sentiments, from being dull. There were a great many treasures to admire in the Castle, in furniture, pictures, and tapestries, and Goldie frankly told Peter that they were all thrown away upon a person who could think of nothing but farming. He merely smiled, however, refusing to be drawn into any discussion, and she presently veered round and declared that he was exactly like one of King Arthur's knights and fitted the place to perfection.

The ancient four-poster beds in the bedrooms attracted her immensely, and she kindly promised Peter that she would come and stay with him the moment he had any servants.

"Or I'll come and picnic with you if you like," she added, still more generously. "It would be rather fun doing the work ourselves. I'll sleep in this room and you can have the one next to it. Then if there are any ghosts about, I shan't mind."

"You can't do that unless you're married," broke in Dennis. "This is 'My Ladye's Room'. It's on the door."

"I don't see why not—nowadays," contended Goldie. "People can do as they like, can't they, Mum?"

"Well, of course, dear, within certain limits," said Marcia.

At which reply Dennis uttered a rude crow of triumph.

Goldie turned round, flushed, to Peter. "I'm sure you wouldn't mind sleeping in that little room next to this with me in here without being married, would you?"

"Not in the least," said Peter with simple alacrity. "I should like it."

Morven gave vent to a brief laugh. "Well, I, as a chaperon, refuse my permission. Peter, don't be so young! Can't you see she's trying to catch you?"

It was carelessly spoken, and held no more than his usual touch of caustic satire, but for some reason Goldie's armour was pierced ; she whirled upon him in sudden inexplicable wrath.

"You sneering cad !" she ejaculated. "You—you bounder ! How dare you say such a thing ?"

This explosion of righteous indignation was as unexpected as a bombshell. Everyone stared in amazement. Even Morven looked for the moment as if some insect which till then he had regarded as irritating but harmless had dared to sting him.

As for Marcia, she was frankly horrified. To rebuke her daughter publicly was literally beyond her ability, but to pass over such an outrage as this was equally out of the question. Something had to be done, and she made a quick attempt at compromise which perhaps scarcely improved matters.

"Goldie !" she said. "Major Morven was only joking, remember."

"He wasn't !" declared Goldie passionately. "I know he wasn't ! He always means at least half he says !"

Morven made her a curt, ironic bow. "And occasionally twice as much," he said.

It was here that Peter deemed it his duty to intervene, and laboriously came to the rescue.

"Well, anyhow, on this occasion it's quite obvious nobody meant anything," he said. "So let's get on with the job ! I'm sure it's tea-time."

He laid a hand upon Goldie's shoulder with the words, and literally propelled her out of the room before any idea of resistance occurred to her. And, Dennis having already marched off with his hands in his pockets in open disgust with the whole scene, Marcia and Eric were left to bring it to any conclusion that they deemed fit.

Marcia was plainly distressed, but he took the initiative so quickly that she was not long left in suspense.

"That was my fault," he said. "I'm sorry. I shouldn't have baited the child, but I didn't know she'd take it like that."

She held out her hand to him impulsively. "Oh, Eric, how generous you are ! But it was very wrong of her. Do please forget it happened !"

He gripped her hand and released it. "I'm going to," he said. "As I say, she wasn't to blame. It was my fault."

"Shall we go downstairs ?" said Marcia. "I think we've seen practically everything."

"All but the keep," he said. "We'll leave that to the children. I'm sure you'd rather "

She thanked him with a look, and they made their way downstairs.

Perhaps it was as well that they did so, for Goldie's voice when roused was not of the quietest, and she continued to express her indignation to Peter in no measured terms when they were alone.

"I always hated him," she declared. "I can't think why Mum likes him—horrid, sneering beast!"

But Peter, much as he valued her favour, would not stand by and hear a friend disparaged. "No, you're wrong," he said. "He isn't. You don't understand each other, that's all. Your sense of humour isn't the same. He was only joking, though you didn't realize it."

"He said—he said I was trying to catch you," persisted Goldie. "As if I ever wanted to catch anybody! It was hateful of him—hateful! I'll never forgive him."

"Oh yes, you will," said Peter. "Don't be silly! You'll like him as much as I do when you know him better."

"I'm sure I don't want to know him any better," averred Goldie. "He's always laughing at one. I detest being laughed at, don't you?"

"One's got to be sporting," said Peter.

She looked at him. "Oh yes, of course, but—d'you think I'm not sporting?"

Peter's eyes met hers with absolute directness. "I shouldn't say you were—very," he said.

Goldie turned red up to her fair hair. She clenched her hands almost as if she would have pounded him for his daring. And then quite suddenly a change came upon her. She turned from him with a gulp.

"Oh, I say!" said Peter.

He put his arm round her, but she resisted him. "Don't! Go away! I don't want you."

"Oh, but I say!" begged Peter, and if the words were monotonous, it was astonishing the amount of appeal he managed to infuse into them.

She suffered his arm, but her face was still averted.

"I didn't mean to be a cad," he urged, "but I had to be honest."

"Shut up!" said Goldie. And then, as abruptly as she had turned from him, she wheeled back and threw her arms round his neck. "I like you, Peter," she said. "You're so jolly straight. I'm going to be sporting—like you are. Only it's much harder for a woman than a man,"

"Of course it is !" said Peter. And then, as she evidently desired it, he stooped and kissed the trembling lips she lifted.

She kissed him heartily in return as though thereby she sealed a peace pact with herself as well as with him ; and then, with her arm linked in his, she closed the discussion.

"Come on ! Let's go down and have it out with this tinker ! Mum's so old-fashioned, she's sure to want me to apologize—just to show how well brought up I am !"

She threw him a grimace which provoked a laugh in which she joined, and they descended to the ground floor in complete accord.

Marcia and Eric were engaged in unpacking the tea and arranging it in a sheltered angle near a stone seat on the terrace when Goldie marched up to them with a combative air with Peter and Dennis in her wake.

"I've come to apologize," she announced rather loudly. "I beg your pardon for calling you a cad and a bounder."

She stood straight in front of Morven as she uttered the words. Her eyes challenged him proudly, but her mouth was quivering.

As for Morven, having observed her defiant approach, he was completely taken by surprise. Actually for the moment he deemed that she had perpetrated some fresh impertinence, then abruptly the twitching lips undeceived him. She was on the verge of turning away, when he extended a swift conciliatory hand.

"Please don't apologize !" he said. "It's nice to be told the truth about oneself occasionally, and I'm inclined to think you were right."

Goldie looked at him with deep suspicion, but his hand remained outstretched, and after decided hesitation she laid her own within it.

"Thank you," said Eric quietly. "I hope that is the seal of your forgiveness."

She continued to survey him doubtfully, finding no words.

He released her hand. "If it isn't," he said, "I give you free permission to punch me as hard as you like."

She recovered herself with an effort. "I don't want to punch you," she said almost inaudibly. "Only—only—you needn't say horrid things—especially if you don't mean them."

"Yes, I agree with that," he said. "For the future I won't."

"Goldie dear," said Marcia, gently intervening, "come and help me make the tea '

Goldie turned with relief, and the difficult moment passed.

Throughout the meal that followed Eric conducted himself in the most exemplary fashion, and all the strain speedily passed from the atmosphere. Goldie quickly recovered her spirits, and, as Peter elected to sit beside her, they soon soared high.

Marcia, thankful to be at peace, made every effort to secure success for the picnic, and everything went smoothly. Even the kettle boiled on the spirit-stove without undue delay, and the children at least did full justice to the fare provided.

They sent the walking-party off in advance when the meal was over, as rain-clouds were beginning to drift up over the sea, Marcia and Eric remaining to pack up again.

"You smoke your pipe!" she said to him. "I really don't want your help."

He lighted his pipe, but he would not let her do the work alone, and everything was soon in order and ready for the homeward journey.

Then he paused. "Don't let's go yet! We shall get back much too soon."

"It's going to rain," observed Marcia.

"Not yet! And it won't kill us if it does." He looked at her persuasively. "Come on down to the shore! There's such a jolly little cove down there."

"Can we get down?" she said, hesitating.

"Easily," he assured her. "There's a regular path cut—and steps. Come along! You'll love it."

"You're sure it won't make us late?" said Marcia, beginning to yield.

"And if it did—say five minutes—say ten—would you mind very much?" he said, laughing. "There's the path, beyond that yew-hedge. It runs straight down. Shall we go?"

"Or shall we not go?" said Marcia, but she turned her face towards it with the words.

"That's the stuff!" said Eric lightly. "Come, I'll race you if you like!"

She smiled, refusing the contest. "I'm not so young as that—yet. We'll go straight there and straight back. We mustn't really be late."

He consulted his watch. "If we motor home twice as fast as we came, which won't be difficult, we shall easily beat the walkers. I don't suppose they will exert themselves unduly going back."

"No, I daresay not," said Marcia. Some impulse moved her to add, "Thank you for being so good to my little Goldie."

"Oh, don't, for heaven's sake!" he protested. "She put me in the cart entirely. In fact"—he gave her a humorous glance—"she has more of her mother's grit in her than I gave her credit for."

"Oh no!" Marcia said. "She is not in the least like me."

"Then let's hope she'll get so," said Eric with decision. "I shan't forbid Peter's banns if she does."

"How absurd you are!" said Marcia. "Fancy—my little Goldielocks—getting married!"

He laughed with a touch of derision. "My dear, it will happen as surely as to-morrow's dawn."

"But not quite so soon!" she remonstrated. "I shall be an old woman by the time it happens."

"If it happens in another ten years," he said, "I don't suppose you will be any older than you are at present."

"Well, I certainly ought to be," she returned. "I shall be celebrating my silver wedding by then."

A sudden silence fell upon her words. It was almost like the closing of a door. They had reached the head of the path that, flanked by bushes, wound steeply down from the cliff edge.

Deliberately Eric stepped in front of her. "I think you had better let me go first. Then if you slip, I shall catch you. You were good enough to say a little while ago that you could always depend on me."

She made no reply. There was that in the action which, if she had known the man less intimately, might have made her fancy that he did not wish her to see his face at that moment. But as it was, knowing how rarely his self-command was shaken, she accepted the suggestion with complete simplicity and followed him down the rocky way without hesitation, thinking, in truth, more of Goldie's future as he had foreshadowed it than of her own.

CHAPTER XII

THE TIDE

THE shore was grey and lonely, lying dreamlike in the evening light. Heavy clouds had drifted over the sinking sun and the cove of which Eric had spoken had a ghostly look. The waves broke outside and washed up over the rocks with almost a secret sound.

"It looks like a smugglers' haven," said Marcia.

"It probably has been," he said.

They stood together on the stones and looked out on to the white swirl of breakers. The gulls were swooping overhead with wild cries that seemed to echo among the hollows all around them.

A large flat rock fifty yards nearer to the narrow entrance to the cove caught Marcia's attention. She pointed to it. "Let's get on to that and watch the breakers!"

"And pretend we are cast up on a desert island?" suggested Eric.

She smiled at him. "Yes, just for two minutes! D'you mind?"

She did not wait for his answer, but pressed eagerly forward through the shifting shingle while he followed.

The rock was easy of access, and they were soon mounted upon it with their faces to the sea. "This is what I love," said Marcia.

Eric knocked out his pipe and put it in his pocket. He did not speak, but she found his silence as sympathetic as any words. She knew that it deeply appealed to him also.

For five full minutes they sat so with the west wind blowing in with the tide and the roar of the waves in their ears. It was to Marcia one of those rare occasions which she knew she would treasure up in her memory for all time. The splendour and the isolation of the scene were never to be forgotten. Alone she might have found them almost overpowering, but the presence of the man beside her gave her the confidence she needed for full enjoyment. She revelled in the glory, clinging as it were to each moment as it passed.

At a touch on her arm at length she turned, smiling but reluctant. "Oh, if there were only no such thing as time!" she said, and then stopped, arrested by something in his face.

He was smiling a little, but there was a certain urgency in his look. His hand had closed upon her elbow. "Or tide either," he said with a glance behind him.

"Oh!" said Marcia in dismay.

While she had sat in rapt contemplation the water had crept into the cove and surrounded them.

"It can't be deep," she said the next moment, reassuring herself rather than him.

"No more than knee-deep," he said. "I'll carry you through."

He began to pull off his shoes and stockings with the words. Marcia watched him with a semi-comic dismay. "Oh, but I can wade too," she said.

"No, you can't. At least I shan't let you." He spoke without looking at her while he continued his rapid preparations, finally stuffing the stockings into the shoes and standing up to fling first one and then the other across the strip of water that intervened between their rock and the shore.

"How could I have been so stupid?" said Marcia.

He turned to her. "You're not stupid. It was my fault. I ought to have been on the look-out. Are you ready? We'd better go before it gets any deeper. Wait while I get down!"

He lowered himself from the rock into the water which rose above his knees, and stretched up his arms.

"Oh, you will be so wet!" lamented Marcia. "Do let me get wet too!"

"Don't be ridiculous!" he said. "Come along! It's getting deeper every second."

There was no help for it. She could not refuse to trust herself to those extended arms. Also, as he said, there was no time to be lost. Every wave that broke outside the cove increased the depth between them and the shore.

With a slight gasp Marcia yielded herself to his insistence, feeling him brace himself to receive her weight, and then realizing with relief that he was fully equal to it.

"Put your arm round my neck!" he said. "And keep your feet up!"

And when she had meekly followed these instructions, he set out through the rising water, moving slowly, with extreme caution, his burden firmly borne above the invading element.

"Are the stones hurting your feet?" she asked him when midway he paused.

"No," he answered briefly. "I don't feel them."

She saw that there were drops of perspiration on his face. "Put me down if I'm too heavy!" she entreated.

"You are not heavy," he said.

They reached the shore in safety, and Marcia in her agitation almost expected to be dropped like a sack. But he lowered her very slowly, keeping his arms about her as though to steady her.

"Thank you," she said. "Oh, thank you!"

And there she stopped. For it seemed to her as though a thrill had gone through him like an electric battery suddenly directed into his taut muscles. She found herself on her feet indeed, but a prisoner in his arms.

"Marcia!" he said. "Marcia!" And his voice fell oddly broken like a jarred instrument. "I can't bear it—to hold you—and let you go again. Marcia!"

Before she knew it, his hold was a grip. He caught her close, so that her head went back upon his arm, her feet slipping from under her; and so holding her he pressed his lips passionately, fiercely, upon her own.

She was utterly powerless, completely taken by surprise. But for his supporting arms she must have fallen. One of her own was still about his neck, and instinctively she clung to him while that long kiss held her speechless, breathless, and amazed.

Perhaps he did not realize that as he held her resistance on her part was impossible, for as his lips left hers at last he spoke with a wild exultation. "You love me—you know you love me—just as I have always loved you—worshipped you—adored you! Marcia—my own—my darling!"

Again his lips held hers, and there was no evading them. She was entirely at his mercy. It was as though he forced his way thereby into her very soul, and she had no means of keeping him out.

When he released her again she was sunk upon the shingle, while he knelt on one knee beside her, supporting her, gazing closely into her face.

"Why are you so pale?" he whispered. "I haven't hurt you, have I? I'd sooner die than hurt you. You're not afraid of me? Surely you can't be afraid! Marcia!"

For her eyes had closed before the eager flame of his, and she lay as one who lacked all strength to move.

"Yes," she murmured faintly, her breath coming and going rapidly through her parted lips. "I am—afraid."

"But, darling," he said, "why—why? I wouldn't harm a hair of your head. You know that."

Tenderly he removed her crushed hat and stroked the hair about her temples.

"We've got to be honest with each other, you and I,' he said. "We can't fence ourselves round any longer with stupid conventions. We've got to face the truth—and shape our lives accordingly."

Her strength was gradually returning to her. As he stooped again to kiss her, she put up an arresting hand.

"No, Eric, please !" she said, and the entreaty in her voice stayed him more effectually than her action. "You don't know what you're doing. My dear—you mustn't."

He took the restraining hand and kissed that instead, holding it pressed against his face. "There's nothing I mustn't do," he said, "except offend you. I haven't done that yet."

The confidence of his tone did not even challenge contradiction ; perhaps she lacked the heart to attempt it. But she made a resolute effort to sit up, though every nerve was quivering.

"No, I'm not offended," she said, "only—only sorry—and rather shocked. Eric"—she lifted her eyes to his with a kind of desperate determination—"this ought never to have happened. It never must happen again."

She saw his face change. Some of the new-found ardour went out of it, and a hint of the customary semi-cynical hardness reappeared in its place.

"Are you going to tell me," he said, "that you are the sort of woman to wrench the very heart out of a man and then deliberately break it into pieces and throw it back ? If so, I don't believe you—and, by heaven, you'll have your work cut out to make me."

He covered the half-veiled ferocity of his speech with a smile, but it was a smile that hurt her almost unbearably. It was as if he bared his breast and waited for her to stab. And she could not do it. With a shiver she turned her point aside.

"We mustn't be—melodramatic," she said with a piteous attempt to introduce a lighter vein into their tragedy. "I think perhaps—we take ourselves too seriously. But anyhow—convention is the accepted rule, and can't be—quite ignored."

She drew her hand gently from his and steadied herself preparatory to rising, but he suddenly grasped her shoulder, preventing her.

"Marcia !" he said and he spoke with urgency. "Let's understand each other—at least ! You say you're not angry, only shocked. That's not possible. You must be both—or neither."

Again steadily she met his look, though her heart seemed to be slowly failing her. "I can't—quite explain myself," she said. "I've got to be—alone with myself—first." Again, but this time unconsciously, the pleading note was in her voice. "I only know that I am very, very sorry. I can't say any more than that. And now let us get back!"

"D'you expect me to say I'm sorry too?" he said.

She made a slight gesture of appeal. "I don't want you to say anything—just to take me back, that's all."

He got to his feet slowly, and quietly helped her to hers. Then he picked up her hat and gave it to her, stooping immediately to pull on his shoes and stockings with his back towards her. When he turned at length, all the fire seemed to have died out of him. His face was set and grim.

"Will you lead?" he said.

She turned, stumbling a little, towards the steps. Her knees were trembling under her. She grasped the crazy rail.

As she began to mount, a steady hand came from behind her and supported her free arm, helping her to ascend. All the way up he assisted her so, making her pause now and then to rest, but never speaking. Looking back later upon that exhausting journey, Marcia thought that she could never have accomplished it without his help. For she was shaken to the depths physically and mentally, and all her nervous strength was utterly gone.

When they reached the sloping path at the top of the steps he came and walked beside her, making her lean upon him. He seemed to understand her state without explanation. No words of any sort passed between them.

They approached the old grey walls, and Marcia uttered a deep, quivering sigh. Somehow she felt as if the magic had faded. They were face to face now with stark Reality.

He glanced at her, but he said nothing. His expression had not altered except to harden into firmer lines than before. The sky had darkened and become heavy with clouds. As they neared the car a few drops splashed down.

Eric moved forward to put up the hood, but she checked him, speaking for the first time since they had left the shore.

"Do you mind? I'd rather have it down. I don't want to be shut in. I like the rain."

He yielded in silence, but she had a quick feeling that she had wounded him.

"I only mean that I want the air," she said rather lamely.

"I know what you mean," he said, his voice dead-level, his eyes fixed straight before him.

She felt unable to cope with the matter and let it pass, her distress of mind still too great for further effort.

They set out upon the homeward journey, and Eric more

than exceeded his promise to travel at double the speed at which they had come. The rain had begun to fall in earnest, but in a sense Marcia was thankful for it. It served to revive her and restore her shaken faculties. She made no attempt to break her companion's stern silence. An impassable barrier seemed to have arisen between them. They had become almost as strangers.

Her relief when at length they came in sight of the end of the journey was intense. Not until then did she realize how near to snapping-point was her endurance. And still he did not speak to her, but drove straight on.

They reached their goal, and she glanced around, half hoping and half dreading to see the walking-party awaiting them. But there was no sign of them as she descended.

"Don't bother to get out !" she said. "I can manage."

But he had already followed her. "You go in out of the rain ! " he said. "I'll leave the baskets in the porch."

She appreciated his consideration and took advantage of it while she despised herself for so doing. But the trembling had come upon her again, and she had no choice.

With a murmur of thanks she turned and fled straight into the house, leaving him to do as he would.

Blindly she made her stumbling way up to her room and shut herself in ; then sank down by the bed, her face hidden.

"O God," she prayed incoherently, "O God, forgive us— and help us—out of Thy great mercy !"

Kneeling there in tense supplication, she heard the wheels of the car as he drove away.

CHAPTER XIII

THE DECISION

THE voices of the two children calling her aroused Marcia from what had become almost a stupor after her agony of prayer. She got up, feeling oddly numb, as if she had ceased to play any part in the human drama to which she belonged. For a second or two she stood motionless, aware of the voices, but scarcely attributing any meaning to them. Then at the

sound of a rush of feet on the stairs she collected herself
and turned, albeit somewhat automatically, to the door.

They were already clamouring at it as she opened. Goldie,
all flushed and laughing from her triumphant attempt to
arrive first, burst headlong in.

"Oh, Mum darling, hasn't it been a lark ? We're so wet.
Peter wouldn't stay. Wasn't it rotten of him ? Why, you're
wet too ! Didn't you put up the hood ?"

"We didn't stop to," said Marcia, still feeling curiously
detached and not in the faintest degree interested.

"Oh, Mums, aren't you a muggins ?" said Goldie, hugging
her to soften the reproof. "Well, you'd better change, hadn't
you ? And I'll change too. Go on, Den ! We don't want you.
I say, shut the door !"

"Shut it yourself !" said Dennis, who never allowed any
suggestion of dictation on his sister's part. "Jolly fine place
that Tregassa Castle, Mum ! Shouldn't mind being in Peter's
shoes myself. Lucky dog !"

Marcia quietly extricated herself from Goldie's boisterous
embrace. There was a faint smile on her face, but it was a
wholly impersonal one, almost like a mask held up before her
as a shield. "You needn't change, either of you," she said.
"It's so near to bedtime that you may as well undress
altogether and have your suppers upstairs."

There was a great outcry at this. To lose a full half-hour
of the day on account of arriving home wet through was
monstrous. The two children hovered on the edge of rebellion,
but Marcia merely turned from them without further words
and began to take off her own wet things exactly as if they
were not there.

It was Dennis who first discovered that her attitude was
unusual. He stood and peered at her with a sharp scrutiny.

"Why, what's happened ?" he said abruptly. "You
haven't had a spill or anything, have you ?"

Marcia continued to disrobe herself without speaking,
and a sudden silence fell. The children looked from her to
each other. Their protestations had evidently fallen upon deaf
ears. They had never seen their mother thus, as it were
completely withdrawn from them. They drew together
almost instinctively, awed by this unfamiliar experience.

Goldie spoke at length, her usually assertive voice pitched
considerably lower than usual. "What's the matter ? D'you
think she's ill ?"

"Don't know," said Dennis, thoroughly uncomfortable

and still closely observant of Marcia's every movement. "Mum"—he addressed her awkwardly, as he might have addressed a stranger—"are you all right?"

Marcia had removed her outdoor garments and laid them aside. She sat down at the end of the bed to undo her shoes, still in complete silence.

Dennis pushed forward clumsily. "I'll do that for you. Let me!" he said.

Marcia straightened herself on the instant. Her face was very pale, and her eyes had a look in them from which they shrank. She spoke with great distinctness, but otherwise without expression. "I wish you two children would be good enough to do as you are told, and leave me alone."

Dennis drew back as if he had been stung. Goldie stiffened in scared astonishment. Then, as Marcia bent again to remove her shoes, they turned with one consent and crept like culprits from the room, Dennis shutting the door with extreme caution so that it made no sound.

In the passage they consulted each other's eyes without speaking for a few moments, then Goldie pointed to her own room and made her way thither on tiptoe, closely followed by her brother. Why they took these exaggerated precautions against making any noise neither child could have said; but it was not until the second door was closed upon them that they ventured to speak again, and then only in whispers.

"What ever's the matter?" said Dennis. "Something's up. I've never seen her look like that, have you?"

"No, never," said Goldie. "I expect it's that Major Morven's done something. She was all right after tea."

"But what?" questioned Dennis anxiously. "Think they've had a row?"

Goldie shrugged her shoulders. "Goodness knows! He can be nasty enough when he tries. But he's never been nasty to her before. Shouldn't think it's that."

Dennis did not think so either, but it was difficult to know what to think. He offered no further suggestions while Goldie began to pull off her clothes despondently, but stood at the window staring out at the rain with a troubled countenance.

"You'd better go and undress," remarked his sister after a pause. "You'll get into hot water if you don't."

He turned slowly, his hands in his pockets, and walked across the room. "I don't like it," he said with decision. "It's—it's putrid."

With which expressive pronouncement he opened the door,

peered for a moment into the passage, and then stepped forth as he had entered, taking immense precautions to make no sound.

It was nearly half an hour later that Marcia came out of her room and, descending, found her two children, attired in dressing-gowns, finishing their meal in the sitting-room. They both looked up at her entrance in some anxiety, which cleared as she sat down at the table with them. For there was no longer anything unusual about her, save that she looked somewhat tired.

"Well, have you enjoyed to-day ?" she said.

"Oh, rather !" said Dennis, but he spoke with reserve, as though not quite sure of his ground.

"And you, darling ?" said Marcia, turning to Goldie who had not spoken at all.

"Yes, Mum, I've liked it all right," said Goldie, with attentive blue eyes upon her mother's face. "Why ?"

"Well, I think," said Marcia quietly, "that we have been down here long enough, and we ought to go back to Dad for a little while before the holidays are quite finished."

There was a fresh outcry at this, both children completely forgetting their newborn awe. They were loving the place and enjoying every minute of the time. Surely they needn't go before the holidays were over ! Dad couldn't possibly be wanting them back. There were heaps of things they hadn't done yet. There was Peter's car, and he had promised they should all go out in a boat as soon as it was calm enough. Besides, they had only half seen Tregassa Castle, and Peter said there was a smugglers' cove there. Altogether a great many objections were poured out, almost sufficient in fact to have justified their remaining in Pentreith for six months at least ; and Marcia sat and listened to them all in a silence which plainly revealed that her decision was made.

It was Dennis who first discovered this and abruptly ceased to maintain his part of the duet. Goldie continued for several voluble seconds before she noticed his defection.

When she did she also paused, and Marcia spoke again very gently, but with unalterable resolution.

"I'm sorry, dears, but now that you are both quite well again the time has come to make a move. It has been very pleasant, but I feel as if we've been here quite long enough. You will be going back to school in another fortnight, and we have got to get ready for it."

"That won't take more than two days," said Goldie.

G

"I think we must allow longer than that," said Marcia. 'But that is really not the point. I feel we ought to be getting back, and I am writing to tell him that we shall be home the day after to-morrow."

"Oh, but, Mum !" protested Goldie, aghast. "Oh, couldn't we have anyhow one week longer ? That would leave us a whole week at home if we *must* go back to school. One week more couldn't make much difference to Dad, could it ? He wouldn't even notice."

"No, dear, I think not." Marcia's quiet voice still held unvarying determination. "We mustn't be greedy, you know. Daddy might begin to notice if we were."

Goldie pushed back her chair with a quick movement. Her childish face was very pale. She went to her mother and wound her arms closely round her neck. "Please, darling," she begged very earnestly, "do let us have one more week here ! It couldn't make any difference to Dad. You know it couldn't. And there are so many things to do before we go."

Marcia sat passive in her embrace. "I'm afraid it's no good, dear," she said after a moment. "It's so clear to me that we have been here long enough already—if not too long. It was only meant to be a short holiday, you know, just to make you and Dennis fit again."

"And it has been—much too short !" said Goldie, laying her cheek abruptly against Marcia's forehead. "And Dennis and I don't want to go back. Do we, Dennis ?"

"Depends what Mum wants," said Dennis unexpectedly.

Both Marcia and Goldie gave him a quick look, then swiftly Goldie lifted her head and transferred her look to Marcia. "Oh, it's that !" she said rather incoherently. "You —you want to go !"

There was accusation in her voice, but Marcia met her gaze without a falter. "Would it surprise you so very much," she said steadily, "if I told you that I wanted to go home to your father ?"

The amazed silence that followed her question was more than sufficient answer. Marcia felt like a witness convicted of perjury, and a quiver of indignation went through her.

"Well ?" she said, almost on a note of defiance.

Goldie's arms had relaxed. They slipped from her. For a second or two longer the child stood staring at her, then very suddenly the tears welled into her eyes and she turned away.

"Oh, all right !" she said in a choked voice. "Then—then —I suppose we've got to go."

She slipped from the room and ran hurriedly upstairs. Dennis got up awkwardly from his chair.

"Good night, Mum," he said.

Marcia held out her hand to him. "I'm very sorry, Dennis," she said humbly.

He took her hand and patted it. "It's different for you," he said. "You don't enjoy things like we do. And of course Goldie's gone quite potty about Peter. Well, it's bedtime. I'd better go."

It was the first time in the whole of his life that he had reminded her of the fact. Marcia looked at him with a trembling smile.

"Good night, darling !" she said, lifting her lips to kiss him.

He stooped and kissed her rather perfunctorily. She made no attempt to detain him ; but as he moved away she rested her elbows on the table and her chin upon her hands in an attitude of deep dejection.

Dennis, looking back at the door, saw it and hesitated ; but the sense of injury was too strong for him. Older people had no right to be selfish. He turned and sternly went his way.

CHAPTER XIV

THE FAR COUNTRY

It was more than two hours later that Marcia sat alone at the little writing-table in the window and by the light of an ancient oil-lamp wrote her letter to her husband announcing their return.

It was not a lengthy epistle. She never wrote at any length to him now, feeling that to do so might encroach upon his time, for even when at home his briefs occupied practically the whole of it. She had no difficulty in finding words, nor any fear that he would read between the lines. He was far too busy.

When she had finished she sat for a space quite motionless, gazing at the white blind and hearing the long deep roar of the sea. The wind had died, but there was a vague patter of rain outside and a slow, irregular dripping from some drainpipe near the window. In the room behind her a small fire was sinking into a heap of ashes in the grate, and above it a clock that was always wrong ticked aggressively as if proclaiming the error of its ways in defiance of the world. She had often tried to make that clock go right without success. It struck three now with impetuous vehemence, and she looked at the watch on her wrist and saw that it was ten o'clock.

She made a weary movement as if to rise, but at that moment there came another sound, arresting her—a slow, quiet knock upon the window-pane. She gave a great start and sat motionless, her eyes upon the blind. Several seconds passed, and then the knock was repeated with the same deliberation but perhaps a little more insistence.

Marcia had not moved. She moved now with a gesture that was almost tragic and, rising, pulled up the blind. The night was very dark, but against the darkness, close to the window, she saw a face. It looked straight into hers with a half-smiling appeal, and her hand went straight to the catch.

He helped her to raise the sash, and in a moment the rush of the rain became apparent.

She stepped back. "Oh, come in out of the wet!" she said.

He climbed in over the sill and stood before her, the faint smile still on his face. "This is very unorthodox," he said. "But I couldn't sleep without seeing you again." Then, at something he read in her face : "Oh, you needn't be afraid of the flesh. I assure you the spirit has full control."

Marcia spoke, her voice curiously strained and conventional. "Won't you shut the window and come to the fire ?"

The suggestion was one which his appearance fully justified, for he had neither hat nor overcoat, and his hair and face were glistening with the rain through which he had come. He obeyed her with absolute simplicity. They confronted each other on the hearth, Marcia pale but completely steady.

"I had to come," said Eric quietly, "and explain something to you. Do you mind ?"

"No," she said.

"Are you angry—now you've had time to think it over ?" he asked.

"No," she said again.

He looked at her with curiosity, but her calm face remained quite inscrutable. He made an abrupt gesture of protest. "Look here !" he said. "I'm not really such a damned blackguard as you make me feel. I've been letting my imagination run away with me, that's all, and it went so fast at last I couldn't stop it. Can't you understand? Have you never dreamed dreams?"

"Oh yes," said Marcia in the same still voice; "very often." She added after a moment, though more to herself than to him: "But I think it's a very dangerous thing to do."

"No doubt you're right," he said, with a touch of his old cynicism. "Still, my extravaganza was after all of such a very innocent nature that I don't think even you could have taken serious exception to it. Mayn't I tell you what it was about?"

"Is it going to do any good?" questioned Marcia.

He raised his eyebrows. "I am in disgrace, then? You refuse to listen?"

Marcia moved a little, turning slightly from him. "No, it's not that. Of course I will listen. Only—talking won't undo anything, will it?"

"Certainly not," he agreed. "But it may place things in a more favourable aspect—restore our friendship to a reasonable footing. Would you object to that?"

"I am afraid," said Marcia, speaking almost under her breath, "that this is a subject that I can't very well talk about. And I think—perhaps—" she spoke with effort—"there are some things on which it is best not to be too—explicit. We have had a very jolly time—up to to-day. You have been very good to us all—you and Peter. But—it's come to an end now. To-morrow we shall be busy packing, and the next day we are all going home."

"Oh!" he said abruptly. "You're leaving, are you? Running away! Marcia, why?"

There was a certain ring of sternness in the question. She turned and faced him fully again as though compelled, but she spoke with firmness.

"I am doing the only thing possible—the only thing left to do."

"That's absurd," he said. "You're making a mountain out of a molehill. Marcia"—his voice changed suddenly, subtly—"my dear, don't!"

She made a small movement with her hands as if to ward off persuasion. "I have—decided," she said, her voice very low.

There came a short silence, during which she faced him still but with eyes downcast. She was trembling unaccountably, though she strove desperately not to let him know it. But when he spoke, she looked up at him perforce, for his voice was sharp with pain.

"All right," he said. "I understand. I'll go."

He turned with the words, and was already across the room before she could stay him. It was only his momentary pause to open the window that gave her time.

"Eric—Eric !" she said. "Stop !"

His hand was on the sash, but at the sound of her voice he checked and stood rigid, his back to her.

"Stop !" she said again, quickly, almost incoherently. "Come back ! You—can't go like this."

He turned slowly round without advancing. His eyes met hers across the intervening space, but he said nothing whatever.

It was she who spoke nervously, deprecatingly, as if in extenuation of the impulse that had moved her to detain him. "I didn't mean to drive you away, or to seem unkind. I've seen enough of men to know that—what happened this afternoon was—as you say—a mere molehill. But——"

"Marcia !" he said, interrupting.

She wrung her two hands together as if the effort to stifle her agitation were physical. "Yes ? What is it ?" she said.

"Don't—flay me !" he said.

Something in his tone—reproach of her or of himself—cut her to the heart. She drew in her breath to speak, but could not. Speech broke upon a sob. She turned from him and sat down before the fire, bending forward, her face averted.

In a moment she heard him coming back, but with the measured step of a man quite sure of himself. He reached her chair and stood behind it.

"Marcia," he said—and his voice was quiet and steady as his step had been—"forgive me ! It wasn't a molehill. I'm not —that sort of man. And if I had been, do you imagine I would insult you—you, Marcia—like that ?"

She did not answer. She could not. Tears were running down her face, and she could not check them. She could only gaze straight before her into the blurred glow of the dying embers in utter silence.

"Listen !" he said very gently. "And don't cry, dear ! Please don't ! Nothing has happened to make you. Nothing new has happened at all. I didn't even kiss you for the first time to-day. And as to loving you, I have done that from the first moment I saw you. Is there anything in that to make you want to cast me out ?"

He paused, but still she could not answer him. He did not misread her silence, but went quietly on.

"I promise you this, my dear. I will never let my love for you get out of hand again. I will never again give you any cause for distress. What happened this afternoon was simply and solely the outcome of a sort of holiday fantasy that I was fool enough to give the rein to. All the while we were up at Tregassa I was picturing myself the king of the castle, while you—beloved—were just a fisher-girl down on the shore. And I saw myself coming to you and offering all I had—all I had." A tremor crept into his voice. He stopped for a moment, then ended almost coldly : "That's all. My imagination got away with it. That's what I came to explain. It never will again. Will you accept my explanation and put the whole thing behind you ?"

He paused again. Marcia made a curious little movement like a shrug of the shoulders. Then, rather blindly, she fumbled for her handkerchief and wiped away her tears.

"It's already put behind," she said in a choked voice which he had to stoop forward to hear.

He waited for more, but nothing came. She sat huddled together, with a crushed aspect wholly unnatural to her.

"I'm forgiven, then, am I ?" he said at length. "You won't make an outcast of me for this ?"

She shook her head forlornly. "No. It makes no difference," she said.

He bent further forward, trying to see her averted face. "Marcia ! What do you mean ? You're still friends with me ? You'll keep friends ?"

She seemed to struggle with herself, and at length sat slowly upright. "But I've got to go away," she said, and, low as it was, her voice had in it something of a wail. "You mustn't—please, Eric—try to dissuade me from that. It isn't that I'm angry. You can see I'm not. But it's just my duty."

"You don't want to go," he said.

She was silent, sitting with her hands clasped in her lap, her eyes still upon the smouldering fire that was sinking lower and lower as the clock that was never right ticked off the passing seconds.

He could not see her face, but there seemed to be no need. He spoke behind her huskily. "Shall I go—and you stay ? I'll do that if you wish it."

She shook her head again with the same despondent gesture. "No. I must go. I'd much rather."

Again for a space there was silence, then quietly Eric straightened himself. He moved round her chair to the hearth and there stood looking down at her.

"Are we never going to meet again ?" he said. "Am I to be banished completely out of your life ? Is it—Marcia—is it as bad as that ?"

A hard quiver went through her. "Oh, don't let us talk of it any more !" she said, and looked up at him as she sat with eyes that openly entreated him. "Of course we can meet—sometimes—when you're in town."

She held out her hand to him with a somewhat uncertain smile. "Please let this be the end of it ! Let us be just ordinary friends again !"

He took her hand, kept it for a moment without speaking ; then suddenly went down on his knees before her and bowed his head upon it. "You shame me—utterly," he said brokenly.

"Oh, please ! Oh, please !" said Marcia. For a second she sat rigid, then the gracious womanhood of her stirred and took command. She laid her other hand upon him with a tender, pitying touch, lifted by the sight of his distress above her own. "Oh, Eric, my dear, I am so sorry," she said. "I ought to have known—ought to have realized. But somehow I thought it was all just natural comradeship after what we had been through together. I never expected this."

He bowed himself a little lower. He was clinging to her hand in a kind of gasping agony. "I don't know how to leave you," he whispered. "Oh, God—my God—I can't !"

"Hush !" she said, and drew him to her so that his bowed head rested on her lap. "God will help you—help us both." Her fingers stroked his hair, his forehead, lingeringly, caressingly. All thought of herself was gone. "Do—do be comforted !" she urged him softly. "All this will pass. You have your life to live, and I know you'll go to it bravely. This—this has only been a sort of interlude. We mustn't take it seriously. It shan't wreck our happiness. Eric—Eric, don't let it !"

"There *is* no happiness—on earth—without you—for me," he muttered, beginning to master himself, but still as it were depending upon her for support.

"Ah, you don't know," she said. "Life changes so. But even if that were true, happiness isn't everything. There is so much to be done, and happiness—real happiness—is not for everyone.   It is only like glimpses of a far country to most of us."

"Is that what it has been to you?" he said.

He raised his head with the words and looked up at her with eyes so heavy with misery that she could hardly bear to meet them.

She made a valiant effort to smile. "Well, perhaps—something like that," she said.

"Yes, I knew it," he said.   A great sigh went through him and he straightened himself while still kneeling at her feet. "Well, I'm afraid I haven't made things any easier for you. But remember this, Marcia : there's nothing to regret on your side.   If you've been too decent to me and I've taken advantage of it, that's my fault, not yours."

"Oh, never mind!" she said.   "Never mind!"

He bent towards her. "Marcia!   You kissed me once—long ago—on a night when the far country seemed pretty near to both of us.   Will you do it again, dear, just this once, as a sign of your forgiveness?"

"Oh, Eric!" she said, and drew back momentarily as if she would refuse ; then on a warm human impulse she checked herself and clasped him by the shoulders, turning her lips to his. "My dear!" she said.   "My dear!"

There was nothing passionate in action or words, only the generous offering of friendship.   Their lips met, as they had met on the night when she had stood by him, refusing to leave him to die alone. And now, as then, her kiss, pure and steadfast, calmed him, imparting the strength he needed.

"Thank you," he whispered and got to his feet with reverence as though he had received a blessing.

She remained motionless in her chair, watching him.   A great weakness was upon her, but she would not have him know it.

He turned to the writing-table by the window and took a key from his pocket.   "The sketch you gave me—may I take it?"

"Yes, it's yours," she said.

He opened the drawer and took it out.   She saw him place it inside his coat.   And then he pushed up the window and she heard again the soft sound of the falling rain.

Suddenly he looked back at her.   "Good-bye—sister ! Or may I say : *Au revoir* ?"

Her lips moved without her conscious will.   She heard her voice give answer across the dividing space : *"Au revoir !"*

And then she was alone.

PART II

CHAPTER I

IMPORTANCE

EVERARD TEMPLETON sat in his study, which might perhaps more suitably have been described as his office, very deeply engrossed in a sheaf of documents which he was perusing with great concentration, one by one. He was a man in the early forties, with a high forehead somewhat accentuated by receding fair hair which left but little impression even where it still existed. He had the quiet features and grave eyes of a philosopher, clean-shaven, very fair, perhaps inclined to severity when in repose, but not definitely stern, It was the kind of face which seemed to call for a barrister's wig, and looked rather incomplete without it.

The hour was late, but as he worked best at night he took no count of its passing. He had acquired the habit of indulging in sleep only when he needed it, and a very little sufficed him, possibly because, though he had an active brain and used it to the utmost, he never allowed it to be fussed by small or irrelevant things. He possessed the valuable power of concentration to a very marked degree, and he was able to exclude all unnecessary hindrances almost without effort. In his opinion the secret of success lay in never allowing one thing to interfere with another   All affairs that required attention were tabulated and dealt with in strict rotation according to their relative importance. If an unexpected item arose he would place it at the very bottom of the list if circumstances permitted, but if they did not, he would rearrange his programme with mathematical precision and remain unflurried and collected, free from all wear and tear, undismayed.

That to Marcia had once seemed a sign of strength, but Everard's sister, Lillith Barrowdale, herself a woman of considerable brain, described it as an utter lack of inspiration. "He follows his course like a hedgehog," she had been heard to say : "and nothing will turn him from it. It may be one way of getting there, but it is the least inspired." By which it may be concluded that Lillith either leaped her obstacles or

scrambled round them, but never pushed them from her path
or laboriously surmounted them by sheer strength of purpose.
Nevertheless, there were times when Marcia, though
she never outwardly agreed with Lillith, or indeed permitted
herself to discuss her husband's character with her at
all, wondered whether there were possibly some truth in her
assertion.   Certainly she was powerless to picture Everard in
a moment of inspiration, or even of strong emotion ; yet for
years she had not allowed herself to believe him wholly
incapable of either.

It might be that in this respect conviction was gradually
stealing upon her, but there were still occasions on which she
did her utmost to resist it.   In any case she had never given
her sister-in-law credit for understanding him.   Lillith had
never appreciated his undoubted brilliance in his profession,
and was apt to overlook the fact that he was steadily hewing
his way to the front ranks thereof.   She did not see in him a
man who must inevitably make his mark, and the fact that
Marcia did had often excited her perfectly good-humoured
derision.

"He may have 'the infinite capacity for taking pains'," she
would say jauntily, "but of genius—not a spark !"

And yet even she could not deny that his progress towards
his goal was steady and assured, and might one day become
monumental.   There was beyond all question something great
in it.   He was apparently a man whom no force of circumstance could ultimately daunt.   All that he did was the result
of well-ordered and calculated effort, and nothing that he did
was fruitless.   He had, moreover, a strict rectitude which
would not lend itself to doubtful methods, and he would never
take up a case in which he did not believe.   Perhaps it was
the reputation for straightness which had induced his sister to
refuse to credit him with genius, for, as she was wont to observe,
genius would never consider little things of that sort.   Real
genius was quite unscrupulous and above such petty details.
But in this also Marcia had been known to disagree
with her.

Her estimate of her husband had varied considerably
during the passage of the years, but never with regard to his
uprightness.   It was the one quality in which he had never
disappointed her, and which she knew could never end in
bitter disillusionment.   His sense of honour was like himself,
rock-like, impregnable.   It held her in a fashion she scarcely
realized, although in moments of sad introspection she

sometimes admitted to herself that respect might be stronger than love. She knew that whatever happened he would always command the former.

Any casual observer entering the room that night would have said that this man with his domelike forehead and eyes of unswerving concentration was one whom no one could fail to respect ; but love was a different matter, and, being a cheaper commodity, he would not probably have valued it so highly. This might or might not be the case, but certain it is that that which is the most easily obtainable is the least sought after, and thus in some lives even love may be at a premium.

At the quiet opening of the door he did not so much as raise his eyes. There was only one person who ever entered his room when he was at work without asking permission, and so it was logical to conclude that that was the person who now stood on the threshold and after a definite pause came quietly forward, leaving the door ajar.

An electric fire was alight on the hearth. She stood before it—a tall, slender woman about whose delicate figure there hung an indefinable girlish grace. There was a slight droop in her pose this evening as though of physical weariness. She stretched her hands above the stove, not mechanically, but as one who felt the need of warmth.

The man seated at the writing-table behind her made no sign whatever that he was aware of her presence for many seconds. Very methodically he continued his intent perusal of the papers he held. But at length, almost as if some knowledge were forcing itself upon him against his will, without stirring, without apparently interrupting his exhaustive study, he spoke.

"Why don't you pull up a chair and sit down ?"

His voice came through the stillness very calmly. He might have been speaking in his sleep. But the woman he addressed made a sharp movement as if startled. She turned and looked at him.

His eyes remained fixed upon the paper in his hand. He gave no sign of being aware of her scrutiny unless a slight tightening of the fingers and a slight contraction of the brows could be taken as such. Without words, she turned again to the motionless fire and resumed her former attitude.

She was dressed in some black material that clung about her like a carelessly assumed veil. Her arms and shoulders shone with a dazzling whiteness against the dark drapery.

Her face was almost unnaturally white. Her eyes looked forth gravely out of deep shadows.

There fell a long silence which there was nothing to relieve. In that *sanctum* there were no coals to fall, no clocks to tick. The stillness was as intense as the man's determined concentration.

Yet after a time there was a sound, the shuffling of papers ; and this was followed by another. Everard Templeton had turned in his chair.

"I believe I shall have to take to glasses at night," he said.

She replied without stirring : "Shall you ? That's rather sad—at your age."

His fingers drummed absently upon the chair-arm. "We're none of us as young as we were," he said.

"What a horrible truism !" said Marcia.

Something in her voice—perhaps it was its dead weariness— caught his notice. He looked at her with dawning attention.

It was impossible to see her face from where he sat. Yet after a moment he said · "You're tired, my dear. Why don't you go to bed ?"

The white shoulders made a movement. It might have been a shrug. It might have been a shiver. It certainly was a species of protest. But she spoke no word.

"You came in to say 'Good night', did you ?" he said into the silence.

She did not look round. Her voice sounded flat and life-less as she said : "It's very late—past one. Aren't you going to bed yourself ?"

"Not at present," he said. "Not till I've finished. Don't wait. The sooner you go the more quickly I shall get done."

There was no unkindness in the words ; they were a mere statement of fact. Marcia received them as such with a slight downward motion of the head.

"Forgive me for disturbing you !" she said.

His eyes were still upon her, as though he had begun to detect something not quite normal in her attitude. After a very decided pause he laid his papers down. "Well, dear," he said patiently, "what is it ?"

She made an odd gesture as though she cast something from her into the glowing imitation of living coals. Then she turned and faced him.

"I've been away a long time " she said. "Do you realize how long ?"

His brows were still slightly contracted. He looked as f

he were trying to attend to two things at once. "Well, no," he said, smiling a little. "I'm afraid I've lost count. I've had a lot of business to get through since I saw you last."

"Of course!" said Marcia. She added after a moment: "The children didn't at all want to come back before the holidays were over."

"Aren't they over?" he said. "Why didn't you stay a little longer, then?"

She answered him with that in her voice that was almost a challenge. "I didn't think it was fair to you."

"Oh, I shouldn't have minded," he said. "I have so little time for home when the courts are in session."

"I know," said Marcia.

He looked up at her shadowed eyes enquiringly. "Did you enjoy yourself, dear? I hope it did you good."

"It did the children good," she said. "That was what we went for, wasn't it?"

His survey became critical. He suffered his case to slip to the back of his mind, and gave her his undivided attention.

"No," he said with decision. "I thought you needed a change too. But you don't look as if it had been one for the better. You are probably tired to-night, though, so perhaps it is hardly fair to judge."

"Yes, I am tired," said Marcia. She stood looking down at him, meeting his scrutiny with a faint mask-like smile. "It's been a long journey. I suppose I ought to have gone to bed as soon as I had tucked up the children."

"It would have been wise," he said, still observing her. "You look as if you have been overdoing things. I hope they've not been too much for you."

"Oh no!" said Marcia. "Oh no!" There was a hint of derision in her voice. "They're too young for that. I was just thinking to myself at dinner——"

"Ah!" he said, breaking in. "I'm sorry I wasn't back in time to dine with you. It was quite unavoidable."

"But of course!" she said again. "You explained that, didn't you? I didn't mind dining alone in the least." She paused as if irresolute; then: "Well, perhaps I'd better say 'Good night'," she ended.

He got up quietly and came to her; quietly still he put his arm about her and turned her back again to the fire. "You're very cold," he said.

She stood within his hold without seeming aware of it.

H

But a sharp shiver went through her. "Yes, I am cold—I am cold!" she said.

He stooped and pulled forward a chair. "Sit down and warm yourself!" he said. "What have you been doing?"

She slipped down into the chair, and his arm was no longer about her.

"I don't know," she said, and suddenly her face had a puckered, woebegone look. "Just sitting by myself."

"Well, well!" he said, smiling down at her. "You'll soon have plenty of people around you again. You are the candle to a good many moths."

"I don't burn many of them," she said, her head bent.

"No—no," he said, and touched her shoulder lightly. "I didn't mean that. You are too popular to be left sitting alone for long, that's all. Have you read your letters? I saw quite a budget waiting for you in the hall."

"I haven't opened them yet," she said.

"Ah, well," he said, "you'll have your work cut out to-morrow."

"To-morrow!" She moved a little. "It is to-morrow already, isn't it?"

He smiled again. "Yes, if you like to put it so, I suppose it is. And I'm still at yesterday's work."

"I'm afraid I'm hindering you," she said. "I'll go."

"Never mind, dear! Get warm first!" he rejoined. "A few minutes more or less will make little difference now."

Marcia's faint smile came again over her tired face. "It was very lovely down there," she said irrelevantly.

"Then you did enjoy it," he said.

"I enjoyed parts of it immensely," said Marcia. She looked up at him suddenly. "Everard, when are you and I going to take a holiday together again?"

He leaned his shoulders against the mantelpiece, a tall man in the prime of life, whose imposing presence even in moments of ease seldom failed to make itself felt.

"My dear," he said, "that's a very difficult question. As I think you know, my activities are not solely confined to briefs."

"Oh, I know," she said, and in her voice was just a hint of impatience strangely mingled with a wistfulness that found no other outlet. "I know. But you can't go on for ever, can you? Like a machine, I mean? You must take a rest some time."

"When I feel the need for it, no doubt I shall," he said. "But I've no time to fritter away in idleness. It's no good sitting down by the wayside to rest if you mean to win a race."

Marcia sighed. "And when you've won ?" she said

He took out his cigarette-case and held it out to her open. "I'll tell you something which I think will amuse you," he said. "But keep it to yourself for the present !"

Marcia leaned back in her chair with folded hands, her attitude one of unconscious resignation. "I won't smoke, thanks," she said. "What is it, dear ? Birthday honours ?"

He lit a cigarette himself with extreme deliberation. His unimaginative, clear-cut features were almost obscured by the smoke. It seemed as if he had a moment of embarrassment. But as the smoke cleared, he was still smiling at her.

"Well ? What would you say to it ? Would you object to being 'her ladyship' ?"

Marcia made an abrupt movement, stretching her arms above her head. So for a few seconds she remained tense, gazing before her fixedly as though she would fain read the future. Her husband was looking at her questioningly, but during those few seconds she seemed unaware of him.

Then at length very suddenly she dropped her arms and rose. "I think I shall stand for Parliament," she said. "It's the only thing left to do."

He lifted his eyebrows. "Are you in earnest ?"

A queer little smile illumined her face for an instant and was gone. She put her hand on his shoulder. "No, my dear, no ! I am never in earnest. You needn't be afraid. Go on and prosper ! I ask nothing more than to be your background."

He took her hand and quietly held it as though weighing it in his own.

"It'll make a difference to you," he said. "You will be of considerably more importance in Society than you are now."

"Yes, it's nice to be important," said Marcia with a faint laugh. "Well, you've given me something to think about, anyhow. When you're a judge, Everard, I shall be more important still, I suppose ?"

He took the cigarette from his lips and blew the smoke upward. His other hand still held hers. "Yes," he said, "that is so. And I hope you will not have very long to wait."

There followed a pause that had in it something expectant on his side, something quite nameless on hers.

Then her hand slipped from his. "Well, good night, dear !"

she said. "You mustn't spring any more surprises, or I shan't sleep. I wonder how long it will be before there are lady justices in England."

CHAPTER II

AFTER THE HOLIDAYS

THE holidays were over. Dennis and Goldie had been packed off to their respective educational centres in smiling self-sufficiency, bidding their mother "cheerio !", they would meet again at the half-term. Everything was as usual, the social wheels running with their accustomed oiled smoothness. Easter was past, the season in full swing, the courts in session. Marcia alone, as one in the centre of a whirling roundabout, seemed to stand quite still.

What had happened to her she scarcely knew, but all her customary zest was gone. A great spiritual weariness was upon her, seeming to isolate her from all around. Her usual pursuits held no interest for her. All that she cared for, that had ever seemed to her attractive, had gone completely flat. She had not withdrawn herself from the general round, but it had lost all appeal for her. Its hollowness could no longer be ignored. Its utter emptiness seemed at times to hold what was almost a menace from which she could not shake free. And through it all—a memory which she dared not encourage, but was powerless to cast out—the magic of the golden Cornish moor beckoned, eluded, and compelled.

There were moments when, perhaps in the midst of some wholly irrelevant scene, it caught her as it were by the throat—a fiery thirst which nothing at hand could quench. Avoidance was impossible. She never knew when it might come upon her. Strive as she might to fill her life with other things, to satisfy herself with the husks, it was always there, waiting in the background—that vision of an oasis in the desert which she knew to be no mirage. While others danced their way through life, she was as one who toils along a dusty, crowded thoroughfare, finding neither rest nor amusement, a stranger in the throng. And yet her popularity was as great as it had ever been. She was as much sought after, as eagerly secured, as in former days.

"They haven't found out yet," she would say to herself sadly. "They think the light is still burning when it is really only a reflection of their own that they see."

That was how it was with her in those days. Though she forced herself on along the accustomed track, her very vitality seemed to be waning. The enthusiasm that she simulated was at times too much for her strength and she had an intense longing which she dared not satisfy to stop and rest.

She could not do so, however, without exciting comment, and that alone was her spur. This weariness of hers—this utter lethargy and disillusionment—must never be suspected. It had become almost a matter of loyalty with her to screen it from all eyes, but she could no longer hide it from herself, and as time went on it seemed to increase rather than to diminish.

Her sister-in-law, Lillith, meeting her unexpectedly on the lawn at Ranelagh one afternoon of early summer, regarded her with eyes of shrewd criticism. There was not much that escaped her.

"What on earth have you been doing to yourself?" she said. "Is it a new cult—or have you been crossed in love?"

Marcia met her scrutiny with a baffling smile. Lillith was her senior by five years, but she had always refused to be awed by her.

"Oh, I hope I'm not so behind the times as that," she said. "I always get thin in the season, don't you?"

"Try to," said Lillith. "But it's not too easy. You see, I'm old-fashioned enough to be happily married."

"I'm sure it's the only old-fashioned thing about you," said Marcia. "How is Cradock?"

"Still alive, I believe. He's fishing on the Spey." Lillith spoke with an easy indifference which to anyone who did not know her might have seemed to belie her previous assertion. "I stayed till the last minute, but he wouldn't budge, so I had to come South at last without him."

"He'll be following you before long," said Marcia.

"Oh yes. When the fish stop rising, he'll look round and wonder where I've got to. And how's Everard? Still coining money and briefs?"

Marcia did not answer. Her eyes had wandered to the play, though she did not seem to be watching it very intently.

"And the children?" pursued Lillith. "Someone told me they had whooping-cough or something, and you were all leading the simple life down in Cornwall."

"It was measles," said Marcia. "Goldie had it first. And then Dennis followed suit. We went down to Pentreith to recruit."

"All alone?" said Lillith.

"Yes, I gave Hobbs a holiday after the nursing. I didn't need her. The children were practically well. It's quite a long while ago now," said Marcia. "They've been back at school for three weeks or more."

"Dear me!" said Lillith. "And you've been back in the vortex ever since. I should have thought you'd have needed a rest cure after that."

"They're not babies," murmured Marcia.

"That makes it worse," declared her sister-in-law. "I'm really rather glad sometimes that I never had any when one sees what little beasts they grow up into."

She was watching Marcia narrowly, waiting for the quick protest which such a remark was almost bound to provoke ; but Marcia did not even turn her head.

"Perhaps yours wouldn't have been," she said gently.

"Good heavens!" remonstrated Lillith. "Don't make me a target for your Christian charity, for pity's sake ! Besides, mine was a bow at a venture. I haven't seen Dennis or Dora for ages. I daresay they've improved in the interval."

"They've certainly developed," said Marcia.

Lillith made a grimace. "I can picture it. And what distractions did you find down there ? Don't tell me that sea and rocks were all you needed !"

"And the children," said Marcia with a certain tenacity.

Lillith turned upon her. "My dear, don't ! It's not done nowadays. You'll tell me Everard went down for the week-ends next. A family idyll by the sea."

Marcia turned quietly and met her derisive eyes. "But I thought you were happily married," she said.

"I am," declared Lillith. "And I'll tell you the secret of it—how to do it, I mean—when I'm quite sure you want to know."

"Thank you," said Marcia.

It was generally the same with her and Lillith. People said that they were always at variance, though neither of them would have endorsed the statement. They seldom agreed upon any subject, yet they never quarrelled. But then, as

Marcia had never been known to quarrel with anyone, perhaps this could hardly be taken as evidence.

There was in Lillith Barrowdale's nature a decided vein of cruelty, but it was cruelty of a good-natured type, which she usually managed to exercise without losing her temper. She enjoyed what she termed "a good scrap", and she almost always emerged from it laughing. It ministered to her sense of humour, which was of quite a sporting variety. She liked hurting people up to a point, and it was very seldom that she got hurt in return. Being a clever fencer, she was apt to despise all who lacked a similar agility. But Marcia was not one of these. She could always hold her own with a quiet subtlety that provoked her adversary's secret admiration. She did not dislike Lillith, but she was never sure of Lillith's feeling for her.

There might be actual hostility, or it might be merely feigned. There might be a vein of bitter jealousy in her light-hearted attacks, or there might be nothing but pure mischief —"the sporting instinct", as Lillith herself called it. That she possessed no weapon wherewith to pierce her very deeply was a matter for congratulation, for that she would ever refrain from piercing deeply if she held the means Marcia did not believe. It was not so much dislike of a person as that inherent instinct of cruelty that influenced Lillith. It was even possible that she was fond of Marcia, but she would not spare her on that account. There was no silly sentiment about her.

"People must look after themselves," she would say lightly. "I'm not going to make things easy for them." And she certainly did not.

She sat beside Marcia now, and tried to discomfit her with various leading questions, but without much success. Marcia amiably but steadily refused to be drawn, and when the Dowager Lady Barrowdale, who was much fonder of her than of her daughter-in-law, came up and joined them, she displayed merely pleasure and no relief at the diversion.

"You're too thin, dear," she said to Marcia presently, with a kindly pat on her knee. "You must feed up."

Lillith laughed aggressively. "That's just the trouble, Mater. She is fed up."

The elder Lady Barrowdale looked at Marcia with kindly eyes. "Oh, I can't believe that. I have never seen any signs of it yet. You are much too young, dear, and too charming."

"That's probably the trouble," said Lillith.

Marcia laughed also without effort. "Oh, isn't that called *ennui*?" she said. "I hadn't thought of that. But it's a very prevalent disease, isn't it? I wonder who I caught it from?"

"I wonder," said Lillith.

Lady Barrowdale continued to pat Marcia's knee with an admonitory touch. "My dear, you simply couldn't," she declared. "It's a sign of spiritual anæmia, which I am sure you don't suffer from. There is far too much natural sunshine in your constitution. Now tell me—your husband—is it true, the rumour, I heard?"

"It depends," said Marcia, still smiling.

"What on, dear?" begged Lady Barrowdale, whose ardent interest in the affairs of others was her sole drawback, if such it could be called.

"On what the rumour is," explained Marcia.

"Now you're playing with me!" protested Lady Barrowdale, her own eyes twinkling. "You know very well what I mean."

Marcia turned to her sister-in-law. "Do you know, Lillith?"

"Probably as much as you know yourself," returned Lillith.

"My dear," said Lady Barrowdale, coming swiftly to the rescue, "I won't keep you in suspense. You're probably feeling a little shy about it still. He's a wonderful man, that husband of yours. A knighthood this year, and, who knows, probably a judgeship next!"

"Oh, isn't that travelling rather fast?" said Marcia.

"Not a bit of it," declared Lady Barrowdale. "He deserves it all. It isn't many men who work as he does. But then"—again she patted Marcia's knee—"it isn't many men who have such a wonderful incentive."

Lillith laughed on a derisive note, but Marcia warmly grasped and held the kindly hand that had caressed her.

"How very nice of you to put it like that," she said—"even though I'm afraid it isn't true!"

"What nonsense, my dear!" said Lady Barrowdale. "We all know he worships the very ground under your feet. And who could help it, I wonder?"

"It's to be hoped some people can," said Lillith.

"But what nonsense we're all talking!" observed Marcia. "Hadn't we better wait till some of it materializes? Oh, there is Virginia Freeman! Will you excuse me one moment while I speak to her?"

She rose swiftly to follow a dark-haired girl in yellow who had just passed, and Lady Barrowdale looked at her daughter-in-law with a quizzical uplift of the brows.

"We mustn't embarrass her," she said.

"It would take a good deal to do that," said Lillith. "Besides, she is thinking of something totally different all the time, as anyone can see. And really, Mater, I don't know how you managed to muster that fib about Everard. He doesn't care a row of pins about anything or anybody except his own professional advancement. Surely you know that!"

"I don't believe it," stoutly replied old Lady Barrowdale. "He couldn't possibly be married to that charming woman and not worship her. The man wouldn't be human who could."

"No human man remains in a perpetual state of worship for ever," remarked Lillith. "They've been married for fifteen years."

"Dear, dear! And she still looks such a girl." Lady Barrowdale spoke almost compassionately. "I hope she's happy."

"She's no reason to be anything else," said Lillith rather tartly. "A clever husband, money, position, two children, quite healthy and not more than normally objectionable. I don't know what more she can want."

"What more could anybody want?" said Lady Barrowdale. "It sounds—as you express it—quite Utopian."

"Well, it's life, anyway," said Lillith shortly. "And she's got her fair share."

"Yes, dear, it's life," agreed old Lady Barrowdale. "Whether it's fair or not is perhaps not for us to judge."

Her eyes wandered to Marcia still talking to Virginia Freeman in the distance. "She is always so sweet to everyone," she said. "She deserves to be happy."

"Oh, if we all had our deserts!" scoffed Lillith.

Her mother-in-law looked round at her with something of a twinlke. "Do you know, I sometimes think most of us do—more or less," she said.

CHAPTER III

SOMETHING NEW

A FEELING of intense languor oppressed Marcia as she went back to her home that evening. The weather was sultry, with a threatening of thunder in the atmosphere which she found almost overwhelming. She told herself that it had been a pleasant afternoon, but something within her flatly contradicted the assertion.

"Then I must be getting old," she said as she mounted the steps to the door.

She was dining at home that evening and going to a musical At Home afterwards. It was an affair to which normally she would have looked forward with zest, but somehow the prospect had lost its attraction. If she had not seen her friend Virginia Freeman who was also going, she would have felt inclined to ring up and make an excuse. But she had parted from Virginia with the assurance that they would be meeting again that evening, and she had no tangible reason for failing to fulfil her engagement. She only wished rather wearily that she had.

There were several letters on the hall-table, and she paused to collect her own. Everard would not be in yet. She never knew whether he would join her at dinner or not. By his decree they went their separate ways, since, as he said, his business must not be suffered to interfere with her pleasure.

There were also one or two visiting-cards. She looked at them idly, with half-wandering attention. Old Mrs. Leatherwaite had called. Dear old lady! She must remember to go and see her on her first leisure afternoon. The Reverend Henry Fordisty! Oh, he had come about that bazaar. What was it she had promised to do? She fancied it was the tea-stall. Or was that at the Early English Fayre for Disabled Service Men? Sir James Arleston was running that, and she had certainly promised to do something, but what she could not remember. She must look up her engagements. One more card! Who was this? A genuine friend, or only someone with something to sell? With careless curiosity she glanced at it. And then, as though some of the electricity with which the air was charged had suddenly found a means of entrance, she stiffened and stood. "Eric Morven"—so the inscription ran, and beneath it scrawled in pencil in a man's hasty writing:

I am in town for a couple of days, staying at the Regency. Will you dine with me? Come if you can, 'phone if you can't.

She stood with the card in her hand, gazing at the written

words, seeming to hear his voice at her shoulder, uttering them. "Come if you can, 'phone if you can't!" It was somehow characteristic of him. He wasted no time on words, but those he used expressed his exact meaning, neither more nor less. She imagined that most people kept their appointments with him.

Again she read the message · *In town for a couple of days* . . .

Evidently up on business! Had he brought Peter, or was he alone? Probably alone! She was sure Peter would not want to come, and being a minor his presence would not, she supposed, be essential. Yes, Eric would be alone, and he wanted a glimpse of her. She saw no reason for refusing. Had she not promised to meet him again in a friendly fashion? Everard would probably not be in to dinner, and she was under no obligation to dine alone. The only question that presented itself was, should she ring up and ask him to join her, or should she go straight to him? She knew in a moment which of the two courses appealed to her, but she stood for an appreciable time wavering between the two. If he came to her, there was the possibility of presenting him to her husband, and somehow this seemed advisable, though she did not believe the meeting would give either of them any pleasure. Everard, if he put in an appearance, would be too deeply engrossed to relish any diversion, and Eric—an odd little quiver went through her—she knew exactly the sort of impression her husband would make upon him, and she knew that she would resent it, yet be wholly powerless to alter it. Everard was not really *like that*, but Eric would think he was, and no effort of hers would induce him to change his opinion.

She abandoned the idea with a little fatalistic shake of the head. It might be advisable from some points of view, but she had no intention of carrying it out on that occasion at least. Everard would not be in the smallest degree interested, and she did not want him to be. She would cherish her "Cornish idyll", as she cherished her favourite books: treasured apart from ordinary discussion. When she knew her point of view would hold no appeal, she preferred to keep it to herself.

Her Cornish idyll! The words—his words—swept through her like a sudden whiff of the salt sea air from that enchanted coast. Ah! What a haven it had been to her! And how far off it all seemed now! And yet not one tiny detail was forgotten. It stood out in her memory with the clean purity of a photograph—the cove, the rocks, the washing waves, the calling gulls, the cliffs! A great sigh broke from her of which she was hardly conscious. She turned to the stairs and began to ascend to her room. The moor—the golden bracken —the deep, deep blue of the encircling sea!

The blinds were still drawn, shutting out the glare of the London sun. There was a heavy scent of nicotiana which had drifted in from a window-box and could not get away. It oppressed her with its exotic fragrance. Like a narcotic, it pleased the senses while it imprisoned the spirit. She felt like a bee caught in a flower-cup, trying to escape. A wild desire for the open air came upon her. She wanted the wind in her face, and perhaps the rain, with the peaty smell of the moors and the cold vitality of the ozone steeping her very being. For the moment she felt almost sick with longing. She moved blindly towards the window.

"Shall you be dining at home, madam?" asked her maid behind her.

Marcia stopped short, as though some physical check had been laid upon her.

"Oh—no, Hobbs," she said, after an instant's collection of her thoughts. "I am dining with an old friend at the Regency. But tell Wilson to have dinner ready in case Mr. Templeton comes in for it. And I should like the car at seven-thirty."

"Yes, madam. And what will you wear?" said Hobbs.

"I don't know," said Marcia, and suddenly she laughed. Eric had never even seen her dressed for dinner, nor she him. "I'll wear blue," she decided. "That lace frock of mine—anything for coolness." And, whimsically, there came into her mind the thought, "I don't suppose he will see it!"

"Your pearls, madam?" said Hobbs.

Marcia laughed. "If you like, Hobbs. But don't deck me out too much. It's not a smart occasion."

When she was dressed she caught up a thin velvet cloak of deep sapphire blue and, throwing it over her arm, turned to go.

"Won't you look at yourself, madam?" protested Hobbs deferentially behind her. "It's quite early."

Marcia paused, aware that there had been a measure of urgency in her preparations. To please Hobbs, she went back to her mirror and took an exhaustive survey of herself. There was no vanity in her scrutiny; it was completely level and impartial. She looked at herself with interest, and she turned from the sight with a funny little laugh.

"Quite satisfactory, Hobbs," she said. "I congratulate you."

Hobbs smiled at the compliment, but she looked slightly puzzled. "I've done you the same as usual, madam," she said.

"You have made me most attractive," said Marcia, turning to go.

And again on the stairs she laughed; for she knew inwardly that it was not Hobbs' hand that had waved the magician's wand.

Down in the hall she heard the front door shut ere she came within sight of it, and when she rounded the curve of the stairs she saw her husband hanging up his hat.

"Oh, Everard!" she said.

He looked up at her with his kind, rather absent smile. "You are going out, my dear? I thought so. The car is outside."

She reached the hall and stood before him. "Everard, I'm sorry. I hardly thought you would be in. I was going to dine with an old friend at the Regency."

He stooped forward and kissed her. "Quite right, dear. Why not?"

"You won't be lonely?" she said.

He looked mildly surprised at the idea. "No. I am going to be very busy. I have a lot to get through to-night."

She still stood irresolute. "I could ring him up and ask him to come round here and dine instead. Would you like that?"

He shook his head at once. It was as though he refused a suggestion proffered by a thoughtless child. "Not to-night, dear. I am much too busy. Another time perhaps. I think I will have dinner served in the study."

"I'll tell them," said Marcia.

He stopped her. "No, don't trouble! I'll give my own orders. You run along and enjoy yourself!" He smiled indulgently and took her cloak from her. "That's a very pretty get-up. Let me see you in it again!"

The cloak dropped around her. She turned, half-laughing. "Good night, Everard! I won't disturb you when I come in. You've seen me in this several times before. It isn't new."

He looked at her again. "No? Something's new, I fancy. Anyhow, it suits you. Good night, dear!" He kissed her forehead. "Have a good time!"

He went down the steps with her to the car and stood to see her go. As she turned the corner of the Square she saw him make a gesture of farewell, and she bent forward impulsively and kissed her hand to him, but he had already begun to retrace his steps.

She leaned back in the car with an odd feeling at her heart. Something new! What was it that had caught his eye? She wondered.

The Regency was in a quiet street away from the hubbub of thoroughfares. She had never been inside it before, but its shaded seclusion had always held her fancy. It had a look of peace in the midst of turmoil. It was just the sort of place that she would have expected Eric to choose.

The main entrance was on a level with the pavement. The revolving door was fixed wide open. She went into a lounge hall that was really a covered courtyard with a glass roof and a pool in the centre with a fountain tinkling over a mass of ferns.

He was waiting for her close to this, and he came to meet her with a warmth of welcome on his face that sent her back in a flash to those Cornish days of more than a month ago. His hand took hers in a vital grip.

"How splendid to see you again!" he said.

She laughed with a sense of sheer, spontaneous merriment. "Where are we? Is it past or present?"

"It's a sort of intermediate state," he told her, "somewhere between the two."

He took the cloak that slipped from her shoulders, and she saw that he regarded her attire with more than passing attention. It gave her a moment's amusement, for she had not expected it.

His next words also were unexpected. "Do you ever wear your nurse's uniform now?"

"Well, no!" she said, smiling. "Did you expect me to come in it to-night?"

He smiled faintly in reply. "I should like to see you in it again some day," he said. "It is more like—you."

She laughed. "Do clothes make such a difference?"

"I don't know," he said with simplicity. "I have never considered you in the light of *la grande dame*. But I see it really is you still."

"Very much so," said Marcia. "But not too grand, I hope."

"You would be perfect in any part," he said.

He conducted her to a dining-room with alcoves along the walls, to one of which he led her. A bunch of lilies-of-the-valley lay beside her plate

"Oh, how lovely!" said Marcia. "Did you think of these?"

"You made me," he returned.

She held them against her face. "Eric, that really was sweet of you. May I put them into water and keep them fresh?"

He despatched a waiter for water. "I'll tell you what I nearly brought you," he said—"one of those long shiny brown ribbons with frilled edges straight from the sea."

"Ah!" She drew a deep breath. "I should have loved it. How heavenly it must be down there! And how is Peter?"

"Very fit. Just the same." Eric laughed a little. "He can't get used to being a baronet. I left him down there. He seemed to think London would be the last straw."

"Poor Peter! He's such a dear. I'm sure he'd much rather be a farmer," smiled Marcia.

"He would—much. He's implored me to let the Castle for a few years. I don't know whether it's altogether advisable, but something's got to be done. We can't leave it as it is."

"And you haven't got an agent?"

"No. The old one died, and there's been nobody regular since. It's a post the boy himself would be fitted for if he were a bit older. But my property in Canada seems to attract him much more than his own."

"You ought to let him go out there," said Marcia. "It would be an experience."

"I believe I shall in the end. But the estate has got to be fixed up first. He's got to take an interest in that whether he wants to or not." A gleam of humour crossed Eric's face. "We've missed Goldie badly," he said.

"Oh, I don't believe it!" she protested.

He nodded. "Fact, I assure you. Peter was as glum as a monk in Lent after you all went. I wasn't much better myself." The gleam became a twinkle. "But Peter's lady-friend had the decency to write to him eventually, and that lightened his gloom a little. Mine didn't."

"Oh, really, Eric!" Marcia felt herself flush a little even while she laughed. "Did Goldie really write to him? I never knew."

"You wouldn't," said Eric.

"She's not in the least deceitful," Marcia declared. "It simply wouldn't occur to her to tell me, that's all."

"Quite," said Eric. "It doesn't nowadays. But I must

say I was rather grateful to her. I gathered a few crumbs of news on my own account—and your address."

"You could have got that from our old landlady," she said.

He smiled. "My dear, I don't do that sort of thing unless hard driven. It might have led to unnecessary comment."

"How absurd you are !" she said. "How could it ?" And then they laughed together. Of course it was absurd !

"Anyhow, you'll admit it was a more romantic channel," maintained Eric. "I was really grateful to Goldie for that letter. It dispelled the gloom."

"Did Peter answer it ?" she asked with interest.

He raised his brows. "You don't know Peter apparently. He is incapable of snubbing the female species, being a type of gentleman with whom one rarely meets nowadays.   I am quite sure that he answered it—though I can offer no proofs of his having done so."

"And did she write again ?" asked Marcia.

He shook his head. "Now you're asking more than I can tell you. Ask the lady herself—or Peter !"

"I will—some day," said Marcia.

But even as she said it, she knew that Goldie would conduct her own affairs without help or hindrance from her when that day came.

CHAPTER IV

THE MAGIC CARPET

"What would you like to do ?" said Eric.

They stood once more beside the tinkling fountain. They had drunk their coffee there and a pause had followed, of what duration Marcia could not have said. The soft murmur of the falling water accompanied everything they said and made music in the silences.

She had been gazing down into the dim ripples, but at his question she raised her eyes. He was looking at her with that faint smile which revealed so little of that which dwelt behind.

"What have you got in your mind?" she said.

He made a gesture as of transferring all responsibility to her. "My mind is a blank," he said, "waiting to be filled."

"How accommodating of it!" said Marcia. "But I'm afraid my ideas are not very practicable. If I had a magic carpet to-night . . ."

"Yes?" he said as she paused.

She laughed half-apologetically. "I should transport myself to the edge of water, cool and deep. But I know that is out of the question, so I won't ask for the unattainable Now it is your turn."

"My turn!" he said. "All that occurs to me is to give you what you want. I don't know why it should be unattainable. By the way, is your man coming back for you?"

She shook her head. "No. I thought you would see me home, as I wasn't sure what your plans might be."

"Good!" he said. "Then I start to make my plans from this moment. Stay here a second!"

He was gone with the words with the quick ardour of a boy, and Marcia, drawing a chair to the edge of the pool, sat down and drifted her fingers in its coolness. Curiously, his declaration that his mind was a blank seemed to apply with complete accuracy to her own. It was as if she had come to a halting-place from which she could look neither forward nor back, and now she felt that this had been the case ever since their parting in the little sitting-room at Pentreith, with the smouldering fire and the clock that was never right. They had reached a definite stage that night. And since that night nothing that counted had happened to either of them.

It was a strange reflection, but she was powerless to put it from her. Something of the magic of the moor had as it were entered her bones, and she could not cast it out. Pentreith, with its golden bracken and grey rocks and the ineffable blue beyond, was nearer to her in that hour than London with its brilliant streets and clanging traffic. It was like a secret spot within to which her soul had withdrawn itself.

Ah! She started a little. His voice spoke to her above the rippling water. "Everything is ready. Shall we go?"

She turned her face to him and met his smile. "Yes, I am ready. Where are we going? We mustn't forget the time."

"There isn't such a thing," he said.

She laughed and stood up. "No, I don't believe there is.

I

There is something about you that makes all the clocks go wrong."

He laughed with her. "Yes ; it's a useful power to have, but I'm afraid it only works in one direction. Will your cloak be warm enough ? I've got an open car."

"Anything would be warm enough to-night," she said.

Passing through the hotel-portico she might indeed have trodden the magic carpet of which she had spoken, for she was aware of nothing very clearly except the presence of her companion. Through ordinary sounds and sights which she scarcely registered she entered a small car that seemed to have been specially designed to suit her mood, and almost before she realized it they were gliding forward as if on wings through the timeless wonder of the night.

She lay back with a sense of complete security that yet was oddly vital, as though she had drunk of some elixir that soothed and quickened at the same time. Only a few hours before she had been weary, but now she was renewed and strangely happy with an exultation which she did not pause to analyse. Neither did she say to herself that the man beside her was the only person in the world with whom she could have felt thus.

They left the lighted streets behind them and ran for a space beside the river ; then they turned away from it and were swallowed once more amongst buildings. She asked no question, felt indeed no curiosity. He drove with the confidence of long experience. She had discovered that even during their brief expedition to Tregassa. She was reminded oddly of that to-night. It was all so dreamlike, and yet so real.

On they went, and on. The streets were narrow, the lights intermittent. There was a freshness in the night air, and she knew that out in the country there would be dew. The threat of thunder had passed from the atmosphere. They seemed to have entered a new world.

And now they had come to the river again and were about to cross it. It stretched dimly away on either side, soundless and remote. The flowing water gave forth a sweetness that was somehow new to her. But everything was as if renewed that night.

They crossed the bridge without hindrance, and once more they were among houses ; but only for a brief interval. Almost mysteriously they emerged among shadowy trees, and human habitation was left behind. No word was spoken. So complete was the accord between them that words would have been not only superfluous but out of place. The silence that lay upon them was as a spell binding them both.

It was like the flight of a bird, that journey through the night. It had in it something miraculous, intangible yet vivid. Some strange spring of vitality seemed to have been set free within Marcia. She tingled with a sense of glorious life which the rapid motion fed. She felt as if she wanted to go on for ever.

But when they slackened speed at length an exclamation of sheer delight escaped her. For he had brought her to that which her soul had craved, and there before her lay stretched a sheet of sleeping water, still as a glass, across the far end of which the pale beam of the rising moon shone from above the trees and made a glittering pathway almost to the very spot at which they halted.

"Oh, what a paradise!" she breathed.

Eric leaned forward and quietly opened the door. "Is this what you wanted?" he said.

"Oh yes," she answered—"yes!"

She stepped out with the words, and walked down to the water's edge as though she moved in a dream. It might have been an enchanted place, so still was it and of so unearthly a beauty. There seemed to be no sound in all the world.

Eric came behind her until they stood side by side on the very brink. "'The edge of water, cool and deep'," he said softly.

She turned towards him. "Eric, it was good of you. I shall never forget it."

"Not even in 'the garish day'?" he suggested half-whimsically.

She smiled with a touch of sadness. "It will be an oasis in the desert more especially then," she said.

Something moved him to sudden compassion. "Poor girl!" he said. "What a rotten time you have!"

She contradicted him at once, though somewhat vaguely. "Oh no, not really," she said. "I've nothing to grumble about."

He did not challenge the assertion openly; he merely said, after a moment, "I think you are the loneliest person I have ever met."

She made a movement as though she would contradict that also, and then for some reason she checked herself and held her peace.

He went on with a certain quiet intention. "There ought

to be no desert for such as you. There wasn't when we were in France, though you were often fit to drop with weariness. You just shouldered your burden and stepped out with the rest of us. It was all comradeship. You were never lonely."

"I thought we agreed that France spoilt us," she said in a low voice, her eyes upon the water.

"You said it," he returned. "But you know in your heart that it was only because we had a real life to live instead of this hollow sham of conventional existence. To my mind, it didn't spoil us ; it made us."

She answered him with a faint sigh. She looked very slim and young standing there bareheaded in the moonlight. Her cloak had fallen back a little, and her neck gleamed white against its folds.

"I sometimes wish," she said presently, "that I could take up nursing again. It would interest me enormously, but . . ."

"But what ?" he said. "You're not strong enough ?"

"Oh yes—it's not that." She spoke rather wistfully. "If I were not married, I should certainly do it. But, as things are, I'm afraid it wouldn't be possible. My husband would never agree to it."

"Couldn't he spare you ?" The old sardonic note sounded faintly in Eric's voice.

She made a slight gesture of protest. "He wouldn't consider it suitable, and in a sense I think he would be right. This social life is in a way necessary. I owe it to him to keep things going."

"Do you ?" He spoke as if not vitally interested. "You seem to owe a great deal to everybody. Does nobody owe anything to you ?"

She turned from her rapt contemplation of the lake. "Eric, you're not to try to sow seeds of discontent on such a heavenly night. Let me be happy in my own way !"

He met her face to face. "Far be it from me to preven you !" he said. "It's what we're here for. Don't ever think you owe me anything, that's all !"

His tone touched her. She held out her hand. "No," she said, "no ! There can never be any debts between us. I think that is the real meaning of friendship, don't you ?"

"Of our friendship," he said, grasping her hand very closely. "That's one of the things I've been trying to say to you—though it doesn't quite express all I mean. I just want to be your—holiday pal." There was something of boyish shamefacedness in the words. "Understand ? I want to be able to give you a strictly private little treat now and then without your saying, 'Ought I to let him ?' "

"I do understand !" Marcia said, and all the quick warmth of her generous nature was in the words. "That is the very essence of friendship—and we were always meant to be friends."

"I am glad you realize that, anyhow," he said.

She laughed a little as she withdrew her hand. "My dear friend, how could I help realizing it ? We were born to be pals."

He looked at her, and his eyes shone strangely in the moonlight with a deep and sombre glow. "You feel that too ?" he said.

"I have always felt it," she answered simply. "There is nothing else in my life in the least like it. I have never had—a holiday pal."

"How on earth have you managed to keep so young ?" he said.

She shook her head, still half-laughing. "I don't think I ever am—except when I am with you. That Cornish holiday did wonders for me."

"Do you ever wish yourself back ?" he said.

She turned back to the water sharply, as though something had pierced her.

He waited for a second or two ; then as she did not speak, with a hint of sternness he pressed the point. "Do you ? Marcia, tell me !"

She stood motionless for a space, almost as if she had not heard him. Then, as though awakening to the fact that he would have his answer, she spoke in a voice that quivered with some emotion too deep for utterance. "How often ! Oh, Eric, how—often !"

"Like that !" he said as if surprised.

She made a mute gesture of appeal. The cloak was slipping from her shoulders. He lifted it and wrapped it more closely about her.

She thanked him tremulously. "It's a pity you asked me that, for I couldn't help telling you."

"Why shouldn't I know ?" he said. "Doesn't friendship mean that too ?"

"Yes," she said, "yes," and caught back a sob. "But— you mustn't encourage me—because it's too absurd—like a ghastly sort of homesickness—only no one is ever homesick nowadays. It's out of date. Like a thirst, shall we say ? A kind of gasping in the soul !"

"I know," he said.

"Do you know?" She asked the question with a hint of piteousness. "Isn't it utterly unreasonable of me?"

He answered her very gently, almost as if he soothed a child. "No, dear, it isn't. It's quite natural and understandable. You're horribly lonely. I saw it in your eyes the moment we met. That holiday down in Cornwall was, as you say, an oasis. Some day we'll do it again, shall we, you and I— with Peter and the kids to make everything proper?"

She caught at the half-tender banter of his words. For a moment she was indeed like a child on the verge of tears. "Oh, we will, we must!" she said, and then added, almost in spite of herself, "But it'll never be the same again. Nothing ever is."

"Perhaps it'll be better," he said. "Anyhow, the sea and the rocks don't change."

"Only ourselves," said Marcia with a little quiver of the lips.

He made no answer, but there was that in his silence which contradicted her words.

CHAPTER V

FRIENDSHIP

When they returned to London the moon was high above the trees and the roads practically deserted.

Again upon the journey they spoke but little. There had been nothing to mar the peace of their companionship, and Marcia lay back in the car drinking in the soft night air with a sense of deep refreshment.

"You're not sorry you came?" he asked her as they sped once more through the narrow streets.

"Oh no, indeed!" she made emphatic answer. "I am only sorry it is over."

"Shall we do it again?" he said.

"But you are going back," said Marcia.

"I needn't go," he said.

She turned her face towards him. "Don't you think you ought?" she said.

He answered with a certain doggedness with which she was not unfamiliar. "No. There's no 'ought' so far as I am concerned, unless you want to get rid of me. Then there is."

"That certainly couldn't happen," she answered gently. "I can't tell you how refreshed I feel."

"That's all I want," he said. "When can you come again?"

She hesitated. "It's rather difficult to say for the moment. May I ring you up?"

"You may do anything," he said. "Don't you realize that all I want to do is to give you a little real pleasure?"

"You have done that to-night, Eric," she said in her warm, sincere voice. "I can't tell you how I have loved it."

"Then let us do it again!" he said.

"Shall we?" Yet for a moment longer Marcia hesitated as though some inner voice spoke, bidding her pause.

"It will give me pleasure too" he said quietly, "if you enjoy it."

There was no appeal in his voice, yet curiously she yielded as though there had been. "Then that settles it. I will ring you up. Or—if you like to come in with me now—I will look up my engagements."

"I think you had better ring me up," he said. "And meantime I will think out something more thrilling for our next spree."

She heard the smile in the words and laughed herself in answer. Then he called upon her to direct him, and the matter dropped.

When they reached the doorstep of her home in Mountgrave Square a church-clock in the distance was officiously chiming the hour of one.

"I never dreamed it was so late," said Marcia as she descended.

"Does it matter?" he said, getting out behind her.

"No, of course it doesn't." She gave him her key. "Won't you change your mind and come in? I can give you some coffee."

"No, thank you." He spoke with his customary decision as he stooped to unlock the door.

Marcia lingered for a second on the step as it opened, her face to the moonlit Square garden. "What a perfect night!" she said. "Eric, I have enjoyed it. You can't possibly invent anything more delightful."

He smiled a little. "We mustn't be monotonous," he said, "even on holiday."

She held out her hand to him. "You are never that. I don't believe you could be. Well," she caught back a brief sigh, "it's over for to-night, anyhow. And to-morrow—and the next day—but perhaps—next week . . ." She paused half wistfully.

"Whenever you like, sister," he said. "Remember, I am always at your service. I always have been." His hand held hers again with a close and friendly pressure and released it. "Good-night," he said. "Here is your key. Don't lose it !"

"Good night," she murmured back in a voice that was involuntarily hushed. "And thank you a thousand times !"

She entered the hall, leaving him outside in the moonlight, and there she turned for a final glimpse of him, but already the door was gently closed between them. She heard the spring of the latch and then the steady fall of his feet as he went back to his car. And as she stooped to draw the bolt a queer little throb went through her that was half-amusement and half-pain. Why should he shut himself out like that ? Did he imagine that anyone would be waiting for her— taking note of her absence—wanting her back ?

Slowly she ascended to her room. She would have taken some refreshment if there had been anyone with her, but in the utter solitude she forgot her own needs. Everard would be still working. She had said that she would not disturb him, and she knew with complete certainty that he would not dream of disturbing her. The servants had gone to bed, were probably all asleep. She wished with a sudden petulance that was not natural to her that she had not come in so soon. For she was wide awake, her brain vividly alert, and she felt not the faintest desire for rest. Something had aroused her from the lethargy in which for the past few weeks she seemed to have been steeped. She felt an urgent longing to turn round and go back again into the shining wonder of the night. Why had she suffered Eric to leave her ? They might have talked for an hour longer of past events, present circumstances, future plans. She was quite sure he had not wanted to go. It was only for her sake, lest she should have felt impelled to dismiss him, that he had departed so suddenly.

It was too late now to call him back, and she began to chide herself for her restlessness. She went to the window and drew aside the curtain. Again the scent of nicotiana came to her, heavy, luscious, but it was mixed with another fragrance. The night beyond was all silvered with moonlight. She looked out upon it with a curious sense of unfamiliarity.

It held something new, but what that something was she could not tell. Then again that other fragrance came to her—a compelling perfume which suddenly filled her senses like a breath of air from the Elysian fields. Lilies of the valley—Eric's lilies ! She had fastened them in her breast. She lifted them and buried her face in them, drawing their essence into her very soul. Why had he given them to her ? He could not have known that she loved them beyond every other flower for their purity and magic sweetness. Or perhaps he had known. There was a wonderful bond of sympathy between them. She had often been surprised by his intuition —his complete understanding of her moods. Surely it could not be wrong to foster such a friendship as this ! There was nothing else in life now that so met her need. And since his brief passion was mastered, it seemed that it might meet his also. And friendship—true friendship—was so precious and so rare a thing.

Looking back over her life, she could not remember anything in the least like this. She had married too young to form any close attachments, and the unfulfilled dream of becoming a real companion to her husband had for long held her back from other ties. But that was all over now. Even the bitterness of disillusionment was wellnigh past. She had grown accustomed to the idea that his need of her, never very acute, had swiftly died ; and that it could ever revive was a contingency which she had long refused to allow herself to contemplate because of the passion of longing which it was still capable of arousing within her. The only possibility that yet remained was that one day he might be ill and then he might turn to her, as men do turn in moments of need to the women who have ceased to hold any attraction for them at any other time. But this was so remote a chance that she had practically ceased to consider it. In her heart she did not believe that he could ever need her again.

But Eric was different. He wanted her friendship—her companionship—as she wanted his. It was no small thing to her, though Everard, she knew, would not take the faintest interest in it.

"You must make yourself happy in your own way, my dear." Long ago he had said it to her. "I have no time for running round in the social circle."

But he liked her to be popular, he encouraged her to entertain, and he appeared as host at such of her parties as included people who interested him. In his detached fashion he was proud of her and appreciated her success, and he took it for granted that she could desire nothing more. He never saw—as Eric saw—the emptiness and the longing behind it all. No, the man with whom that link of friendship had been forged in the past realized more of her deep soul-hunger in a few hours of companionship than Everard had realized in fifteen years of married life. A quiver of pain went through her at the thought, but she stifled it with her face pressed blindly to the flowers he had given her.

And in that still night-hour she made the resolve which was to carry her further still from that dusty thoroughfare of crowded life which she had trodden with a kind of weary perseverance for so long. She owed it to Eric to make some return for that steady devotion which he dumbly offered to her. She owed it to no one to quench the flame of this friendship which to her was sacred. And so into the heart of the lilies she breathed a promise as though she uttered a vow to her inner self.

"Yes, we will be friends. And I will be good to him always—just as he is to me. I will never let him down."

When she lifted her face the pain had passed and her eyes were steadfast. Yes, this friendship that had come to her out of the empty years was indeed a sacred thing, and she would cherish it in her heart for ever.

CHAPTER VI

PLANS

"So Everard is over the fence and well away!" commented his sister with a certain caustic pride. "I knew he'd do it if he set his heart on it. Extraordinary that he should think it worth while."

"My dear, a baronetcy!" protested Lady Barrowdale. "They're not as plentiful as they were. So fortunate he has a son! How pleased dear Marcia must be!"

"She has gone into modest retirement," observed Lillith. "I must say I don't blame her. These Press reporters really are the limit. I had one calling only this morning asking for her War record. As if anyone ever thinks of the War nowadays! He wanted a portrait of her too in Red Cross uniform, and I told him I didn't believe one existed, and the uniform was doubtless thrown on the bonfire long since."

"Oh, I don't believe dear Marcia would have the heart to do that. She loved her nursing days," declared old Lady Barrowdale. "I never saw her in her sister's cap, but I'm sure she looked a perfect darling."

"She always does," remarked Lillith without enthusiasm. "It's really wonderful how she manages to keep it up. She's been looking a little less haggard lately for some unknown reason. Perhaps the impending baronetcy has given her a fresh interest in life."

"Oh, my dear! As if it would!" Her mother-in-law laughed, but on a note of reproach. "She is much too unworldly to care about a title. In fact, I can quite imagine that she might prefer to be without one. She has such a sweet and simple nature."

"Guileless to a fault!" scoffed Lillith. "I can quite believe it too. She said she was going down to Graybourne for the boy's half-term next week-end. She really is a model mother. Much reward will she get for it!"

"I think her two children are sweet," said Lady Barrowdale, in whose estimation nothing juvenile could ever be anything else.

Lillith made no retort. She could not be always snubbing her mother-in-law; it was a sheer waste of energy when there was usually more important game to be hunted. She turned from the subject with some impatience.

"Well, Everard is off to the West for this Coulson trial to-morrow, and he tells me he shall spend the vacation when not at the Old Bailey in completing that legal tome of his, so we shan't see much of him for some little time to come."

"Dear me! I hope he will find time to take Marcia away for a holiday," said Lady Barrowdale. "She sadly needs one."

Lillith laughed. "I should think she is fully capable of looking after herself in that respect by this time, having been all through the War in France quite unattended."

For some reason this had always been a sore point with Lillith, who had no aptitude for nursing herself, and had severely blamed her brother for allowing his wife to develop hers.

Lady Barrowdale did not dispute the point. She merely wished to herself for the hundred-and-first time that dear Marcia had been persuaded to become the wife of the present Lord Barrowdale rather than that of the newly created baronet, Sir Everard Templeton.

There was no doubt in her kindly mind that Marcia was n need of some sort of succour just then. Something quite indefinable about her that had been developing for at least the past two years proclaimed it. In some subtle fashion the War had changed her, just as more blatantly it had changed everyone else. Or was it the peace that had done it ? It was hard to say. She had seen but little of her during those troublous years ; but now that they were over, now that life was dropping back to something of its old aspect, the change was becoming daily more palpable.

She did not think that Marcia was very happy, and she strongly suspected that it was her husband's fault. But to have said so to Lillith would have been to wave a red rag in front of a bull that loved stampeding for the sake of exercise and would certainly gore its victim if conditions were propitious. Lillith had an almost fanatical veneration for her own family, though in what dim virtues of the past it originated no one had ever discovered. Without being in the faintest degree in sympathy with her brother, she yet regarded him as the revered head of her house, and to suggest that any blame could possibly attach to him under any circumstances whatever was almost sacrilege. She might criticize him herself—she often did ; but no one else was qualified to do so. It was rank impertinence for the rest of mankind to express any sort of opinion concerning him.

If Marcia were not happy, no one but herself could possibly be to blame. She had everything in the world to make her so. If her children were little beasts, so were everybody else's. One could not expect anything different in these enlightened days. No reasonable mother could take a trifle of that sort to heart. In Lillith's opinion Marcia wasted more time over them than she need. To go down to each child twice a term was to her a sign of doting fondness which could only end in absurd disappointment. What child ever appreciated so much attention nowadays ? What child even wished to spend its holidays under the parental roof ?

Could she have heard Dennis eagerly laying his plans for his summer entertainment before his mother as they walked in the river-meadows of Graybourne during that leisurely week-end she would have laughed to hear her opinions so triumphantly justified.

"You see, darling, it's an opportunity I'd be sorry to miss." So ran his ardent explanation of the fact that he wanted to spend practically the whole of the holidays with a chum's family who were going to yacht in the Norwegian fjords. "It's time I began to see a bit of the world, and I can't stick town or the English coast in August. Can you ?"

Marcia did not pronounce either to be quite unstickable, but she saw his point. The chance of a fishing-holiday in the fjords was too good to miss, and it would be selfish—as he gracefully hinted—to put any obstacle in his way. She agreed to the plan therefore, and was rewarded by a warm hug of appreciation and the assurance that she was a stunner, and he was glad she had been made a lady, as he for one was quite sure she deserved it. With this gratifying declaration the matter was dismissed as settled, and Marcia spent the rest of their time together in an atmosphere of patronizing approval which ought to have given her the keenest satisfaction.

Her following week-end was devoted to Goldie, who was allowed to return home for a couple of nights for her mid-term, and who, since places of amusement were barred, insisted upon spending practically the whole of her waking hours in the Row. Riding was a pastime that never palled upon her, and she never looked prettier than when in riding-kit, but Marcia hoped, rather despondently, that she was still too young to be aware of this. She took her to church on Sunday morning, though Goldie assured her that attendance during holiday-time was quite unnecessary, but she imposed no further discipline upon her, and as a result saw very little of her until the hour for departure drew near. Then, finding that Goldie had a little time to spare, she took the opportunity to discuss the holidays and to impart Dennis's plans.

"You and I will have to think of something nice to do by ourselves, darling," she said.

But Goldie at once discouraged this idea. "Oh, I don't think that'd be much fun, Mumsie," she asserted, with clear conviction. "Don't let's be silly about it ! I'm sure you've got lots to do, and I rather think I can wangle an invitation to join a party of our girls who are going to Switzerland. Miss Robins is organizing it, and she's a great sport. If Den means to go to Norway, I don't see why I shouldn't do Switzerland, do you ? You'll be going to Scotland, of course."

It was difficult to reply. Actually Marcia was half amused

and did not know whether to be disappointed or glad to be relieved thus of all encumbrances. It was evident that Goldie expected her to be glad, and, realizing that no sacrifice on the child's part was involved, she decided to be so.

"If that is what you would like best to do, darling, of course I am quite willing to agree," she said.

"Well, I think it would be a good idea, that's all," said Goldie dispassionately. "It isn't good for families to see too much of one another, and we all had a good dose at Easter-time, didn't we? And we shall all be cooped up together again at Christmas. So I think we ought to make a real thing of the summer holidays, don't you?"

A real separation was her meaning, and Marcia was quick to grasp it; but she would not express the dismay which momentarily caught at her heart. She merely said, "You would really rather do that than pay another visit to Pentreith?"

Goldie gave her a swift look. "Peter still there?" she asked bluntly.

"I imagine so," said Marcia. "His home is there. Have you heard from him?"

She had not meant to ask the question, but it was irresistible. Yet in a moment she knew that it was unwelcome. Over Goldie's face there came a curious expression that was somehow as if she had drawn a veil over it. She smiled at her mother—a queer little taunting smile. "Darling, aren't you inquisitive?" she said. "What about Major Morven? Is he there too?"

"Goldie!" ejaculated Marcia, and felt the blood rush to her face overwhelmingly, as though she had been accused of something outrageous.

Goldie uttered a crow of laughter at the sight. There were occasions upon which Marcia was reluctantly compelled to recognize in her a very decided resemblance to her Aunt Lillith. But the next moment, unlike Lillith, she was seized by an embarrassing impulse of pity.

"Oh no, darling, not Pentreith!" she said lightly. "I should get tired of Peter if I saw too much of him. Let's have them up for Christmas—both of them!" Pity had become generosity. "I'm sure I don't care. The more, the merrier! P'raps I'll teach Peter to dance."

"Not to your piping, I hope, my dear!" It was Marcia's turn to be enigmatical; she realized that now or never must this young shoot be trained into some semblance of steady growth. "Besides, I should think he has far more interesting things to occupy him at Tregassa, and has probably forgotten your very existence by now."

"Ho!" said Goldie, with a free toss of her golden head. "I wonder!" And then, with semi-ironical repentance, she turned and embraced Marcia. "Dear ladyship!" she said. "You are the funniest, dearest thing in the world!"

There was not much satisfaction in this, but Marcia knew enough to realize that it was all she could expect.

"So we are all to spend our holidays apart, are we?" she said, as she kissed Goldie's bright face.

"That's the idea," said Goldie nonchalantly. "Awful fun, don't you think? Not that you want any holidays, darling. You never do anything, do you?"

Marcia shrank a little from the scathing question. She had asked it of herself so often. "I don't know, dear," she said after a moment. "I manage to get tired, anyhow."

"P'raps that's because you don't do enough," remarked Goldie complacently.

But to Marcia's relief she was not sufficiently like her aunt to pursue the subject further.

CHAPTER VII

THE ETERNAL LOSER

"So your family have given you the go-by!" said Eric.

She had joined him for the day in a country nook by the river, having come out by train to the nearest station, where he had met her with a car. There was no great secrecy observed in these expeditions, since there was no one but themselves to consult, but for some reason which he had not given Eric would not present himself at the house in Mountgrave Square as an ordinary visitor. Marcia, concluding that he did not wish to be drawn into the social circle in which she moved, never pressed him to do so. Their friendship was a thing apart, and she shared in his evident desire to keep it so. In it there was nothing either to hide or to reveal, but there was much of a quiet confidence to which others had no right of access. The hours that she spared to him were, as it were, filched from the usual round of engagements. Where she could escape a function without being missed she would do so, and where this was impossible she had developed a habit of leaving early which no one had time to notice. It was quite easily done, and the refreshment that it brought into her life was such as sometimes made her wonder how she had endured the ceaseless whirl without it. Their meetings were interludes of peace and contentment which were different from any other experiences. She looked forward to them, and later looked back upon them with the same deep, abiding pleasure. In his presence she was less conscious than at any other time of the great unsatisfied longing within her. In his friendship she found a solace and a fulfilment which stilled her restless longings. He understood her so completely, and he ministered to her need just as she ministered to his. It was a perfect companionship in her eyes, and what it was in his she did not question. Her faith in him was absolute— the free gift of her generous nature. She revelled in the flawless sympathy that existed between them.

At his suggestion they were reading the same books, and when they met they had long discussions on the many problems and topics therein contained. She found that his opinions, though usually more emphatically expressed, corresponded in all basic points with her own. They might disagree over details, but even this was rare, and in the main they were practically always in accord. She often declared that she knew beforehand exactly what he was going to say, and his comments, sometimes caustic, always concise, gave her the keenest enjoyment. They did not talk of the future at all, and only occasionally of the past—as though each desired to make of this ideal companionship the perfect delight of the present.

To day, however, she had been moved to tell him of the various plans which had been promulgated by Dennis and Goldie, finding herself half-laughing at the philosophies attached to their recital.

"You see, they both of them mean to avoid boredom at all costs," she said in reply to Eric's remark, and was instantly aware by his silence of his deep-seated indignation stirring on her behalf.

"It's very natural," she hastened to add. "I'm sure we were the same at their age."

"I'm sure we weren't," said Eric briefly ; and he also made addition with great emphasis : "Detestable little imps !"

"Now, Eric !" she protested.

He looked at her with that glimmering smile in his eyes, half-humorous, half-tender, which she knew so well. "My dear, I should say the same if they were my own. Only probably mere saying would not suffice me. I always told you you ought to have spanked them more when they were younger."

"I'm afraid I wasn't with them during the spanking age," admitted Marcia. "And it really wouldn't have done, you know. You're not allowed to take those sort of liberties with your children nowadays."

"I'd have done it if I'd swung for it," declared Eric grimly.

She laughed. "I'm sure you wouldn't. If you had a baby of your own, you'd adore it ; and you'd never dream of keeping it in order till it had turned the tables on you, and then it would be too late."

He shook his head whimsically over the filling of his pipe. "P'raps you have reason. If it were in the least like you, you certainly have. But if it were like Goldie——"

"Now stop !" she said. "You don't know each other, and I won't hear anything against her."

He looked at her again with one eyebrow raised. "I can't help loving you, Marcia. It's no good. You're so enchantingly silly. Why are you Goldie's mother, I wonder ?"

"Some people think she is very like me," said Marcia.

"Some people would," he rejoined compassionately. "Well, I don't. There isn't the faintest resemblance. Dennis is different. When you were a tomboy of his age, I can picture you doing the same things in the same spirit of complete inconsequence. But Goldie—no, there is no comparison."

"You're quite absurd," said Marcia. "But we won't quarrel on that account. When Goldie is a little older and more formed, you will see her in a different light."

"She will never be like you," he said with unalterable conviction. "But then, you don't occur more than once in a thousand years. It is ridiculous to talk of likenesses where you are concerned."

"Don't be extravagant !" reproved Marcia. "If your pedestal gets too high, I am sure to tumble off it, and that would spoil everything."

He returned to the filling of his pipe. "I don't think my humble adoration need make you giddy," he remarked dryly, "unless I am the only person in the world that worships you, which I can hardly believe."

K

"That is rather an exaggerated way of putting it, isn't it?" said Marcia.

"No," he rejoined bluntly. "Not from my point of view. But we won't discuss it if you'd rather not. Am I right in gathering from what you've told me that you are possibly going to be at a loose end in the holidays?"

He had not mentioned her husband; he never did so, and any reference to him that she might make he always passed in silence. It was the only subject upon which it seemed they could not speak openly, the only subject on which Marcia felt compelled by loyalty to reticence. She could not picture herself trying to explain Everard to Eric, even though she strongly suspected the latter's estimate of the former to be an erroneous one. She had not been able to hide the fact of her loneliness from this good friend of hers, but she could never have told him anything of its development. She could never have presented the situation to him as she herself saw it, tragic, inevitable, and irremediable.

He would not have allowed the fond excuses by which she had so long tried to justify Everard's preoccupation, nor indeed could she have advanced them in the face of his candid disapproval. No, the matter was better left alone between them. She knew his opinion without hearing it, and to plead extenuation on Everard's behalf was unthinkable. It was preferable to leave his prejudice unassailed. It is possible that in arriving at this decision she also realized that her cause was such a weak one that she would have found it difficult to refute his judgment with the arguments with which she tried to blind her own.

But his question contained no open reference to Everard, and she could not leave it unanswered.

"No doubt I can find someone to spend the time with," she said, "when it is quite settled that—that——" She paused involuntarily.

"That none of your family have any need of your services," he finished for her. "Marcia, there are occasions on which you infuriate me, and this is one of them."

She smiled at the declaration. "I had no idea you were so easily roused."

"Well, I am," he said. "You don't know the first letter of how to make yourself appreciated. You are a woman of practically boundless attractions, and you throw yourself away."

"Perhaps you can give me some hints," suggested Marcia.

"I could," he rejoined. "But you wouldn't take them. If I were to tell you to make yourself completely inaccessible to these hangers-on of yours, you simply wouldn't do it, so what's the good?"

"Completely inaccessible!" repeated Marcia. "Do you mean run away from them?"

"Yes; to the other end of the world." He spoke with emphasis. "They'd miss you then—probably more than you'd miss them."

"Are you in earnest?" said Marcia. "Do you really think I shouldn't miss them?"

He looked at her quizzically through the smoke of his pipe. "I think," he said, "that you would find it difficult to miss them as much as you ought."

She made a gesture of protest. "Oh, Eric, then you don't understand."

"Please forgive me!" he said, interrupting. "I do, most thoroughly. And, in some ways, you miss them more when you are with them than when you are away from them. You're such a child, Marcia." He spoke with a sort of affectionate impatience. "I'm not keen on the present age, goodness knows; but I do realize that it's got to be conformed to more or less. You don't. You still cling to the yoke and make it gall you even when it's so old and rusty that you could break it at a touch. You are still the model, rather than the modern mother. You're not nearly vain enough, frivolous enough, selfish enough, for this year of grace."

"I can't help it," said Marcia hopelessly.

"Oh yes, you can." His reply was one of gentle severity. "You've not seriously begun to try yet. The only really up-to-date thing you've done so far is to give yourself a holiday now and then in my company. You won't even contemplate the mass of jolly things you might do in this world of every man for himself. It's a pity, my dear, because at the rate you are developing you'll be a very old woman before you realize all you've missed."

She met his eyes through the drifting veil of smoke. "That sounds rather sad," she said wistfully.

"Yes, doesn't it?" said Eric. "And there's no earthly reason for it that I can see—no one to benefit by it—only one to lose. You're the eternal loser, Marcia."

"Am I?" she said. "Then I suppose it's my own fault. I must be a bad player."

He brought his fist down upon his knee with a sort of

condensed fury. "By heaven, you're not! You're just the very best—the loveliest woman on earth, and too good, a million times too good, to everyone else but yourself!"

"My dear Eric, what nonsense!" She began to laugh a little.

"It isn't nonsense." He spoke emphatically. "I'm not a fool. And I've looked on too long not to understand your trouble. It's damned unfair. You're put upon—taken advantage of—at every turn. You're expected to be there when wanted and to keep out of the way when not. And you're so incredibly sweet and patient that you put up with it all. On my soul, Marcia, I'd like to pick you up and take you away to Canada—to anywhere in the wide world, and show you what it really means to be cared for and treated with honour."

"My dear boy," she protested, flushing faintly. "Don't you think that sounds rather ridiculous?"

He got up abruptly as if he could bear no more. "No, I don't. I think it's time you thought out a decent holiday for yourself, and if you'd spend it with me I'd undertake that it was a happy one. Only I know you won't, so what's the good of talking?"

He turned away from her and walked down to the river's edge. It was the third week in June—a perfect day of summer. A light breeze rippled the water, and the woods beyond—beech-woods—were of that golden-green which only the early summer knows. A swan sailed up to the bank on which Eric stood, arching its neck, inviting *largesse*. She watched it absently, wondering within herself if she would be called upon to give any serious consideration to his last words. She did not want to do so. She never wanted to discuss the details of her daily life with Eric. She liked to regard their companionship as a thing wholly apart from it—as a kind of haven in which its trials and disappointments could find no harbourage. She had already begun to regret that she had broached the matter of the holidays to him. It had really been done from a desire to find out his plans for the future, and now she half-wished that she had been content to drift. His indignation, though quite comprehensible, rather spoilt the brightness of the day.

She heard a hiss from the swan, which, disappointed, had turned in its track and was sailing away again. The dignity of its withdrawal provoked her to a smile, and she also got up and moved down the slope, feeling that the beauty of the day was too good to waste in any sort of discontent.

He did not turn at her approach. His eyes were fixed with a certain moodiness upon the ripples at his feet. She joined him quietly.

"Eric, have you seen those beeches with the sun on them ? If not, look at them at once !"

He looked up, but he turned his eyes upon her instead of across the water. They dwelt upon her with a grave, speculative expression. He said nothing whatever.

"What's the matter ?" she questioned. "Have I done something wrong ?"

His faint smile gleamed at her for a moment under his drawn brows, and passed. "My darling girl," he said, "you are no more capable of doing wrong in my eyes than you are of walking across to that other bank without wetting your feet."

She laughed at that. "Well, I wonder if I could ! Shall I try ?"

He shook his head. "No. I should have to come too, and I at least should certainly tread too hard. Marcia, have you ever thought during these jolly times we've had together that I've danced to your piping without once changing step ?"

She turned and looked at him steadily. "My piping, Eric ?" she said.

He made a semi-quizzical gesture. "Well, it was really you who called the tune, wasn't it ? It was quite a nice tune, and I've enjoyed it. Have you ?"

She hesitated momentarily, then : "Very much," she said.

"You mean that ?" He spoke with a certain insistence.

"Of course I mean it. I don't know why you ask."

Her eyes still met his unflinchingly, but after a second or two he turned aside. "I'll tell you presently," he said. "Let's go in to lunch ! Then I'll row you up the river. And after that, or before it if you prefer, you shall walk through those enchanted beech-woods."

She turned with him. "Yes, I'm sure you're right. They are enchanted, and I shall love it. But we'll keep them till last and go through them when the sun is lower. They will be even more heavenly then."

He gave her a quick side-glance. "It will be something for you to remember—when you're alone," he said.

CHAPTER VIII

MIDAS

THEY lunched on a verandah overlooking the sparkling river, and Eric called for the first strawberries of the season and insisted upon picking out the best for Marcia, declaring that he loathed them himself. She did not believe him, but it was so obvious that he enjoyed them more in that way that she was obliged to submit. He took such a boyish delight in showering good things upon her that she found it impossible to refuse them. And when the meal was over, and they went out into the splendour of the afternoon sunshine, the old gay spirit of her girlhood had come upon her and she found herself laughing with him at the most absurd trifles. It was all a part of the day—that day of summer magic which was to have its effect upon the whole of her life.

They decided in favour of a punt after all, because, as he said, they were sure to feel lazy after such a lunch. and when he had installed her among as many cushions as he could squeeze into their craft he proceeded to propel her upstream with a slow but masterly energy that soon carried them out of sight of the little riverside hotel and drifted them into a new world of hushed ripples and willows that stooped to rest upon them, a world of sweet silences in which even the birds forgot to sing, and in which no other human being seemed to exist.

Marcia, lying among her cushions, with her fingers dipping in the running water, felt like a being strangely transformed. The busy woman with the secret unacknowledged weariness at her heart whom she had come to regard as herself had given place to someone totally different—a creature with a new-born vitality which seemed to have emerged from that former personality of hers. She could not understand the change. She only knew that out of the gold of this June day something had come to her that had never been hers before—something subtle and incalculably precious that had the dazzling quality of a fresh-cut jewel. She was half afraid to look at it too closely lest it should melt away or turn into something startling that might repel her. She only wanted to lie still and feel the warmth and brightness sink deep into her spirit like a swift ray of sunshine coursing through her after the long, dark chill of cloudless skies.

Eric scarcely spoke to her during that rapid glide through the swishing water. The murmur of it around them and through the reeds by the bank filled the world with a tinkling music that made speech seem out of place. They seemed to be floating through a charm in which sound and echo blended like a dream and the very spirit of the river found expression. He saw that Marcia's eyes were half-closed, though once they opened and she smiled at him and he knew that it was not drowsiness that held her, but rather what of late he had been striving to bring to life within her—the perfect rhythm which is happiness.

They came at last to a bend in the stream around which the rush of a distant weir floated like a mystic chanting from some far-off land. Here against a bank which was thick with moss was a nook over which the willows spread a complete screen, a fairy paradise threaded with bright spots of sunlight which fell in a shower of gold through shimmering leaves.

"How perfect!" whispered Marcia, as they slid through the shallows.

He fastened the punt to a low branch. "You like this, do you?"

"Like it!" she said. "You find something lovelier every time."

"No," he said. "It is only because you are learning how to enjoy things."

"I wonder!" said Marcia with a faint sigh. "You know, I am not at all sure that you're right. Beautiful things are somehow very often so poignant."

"That's contrast," he said. "Either looking back or looking forward, instead of basking in the present."

"Ah!" She stretched out her hands to the chequered sunlight. "I love basking, don't you?"

He looked across at her, the sombre gleam in his eyes. "Yes, I know," he said. "You were always meant to bask. It's your nature to absorb light and then to give it out again."

She laughed. "I should be a very selfish person if I did the one and not the other. But I'm not sure that I do either."

"You do when you're with me," he maintained. "You have a sort of radiance of your own that I've never met with in anyone else. That's why everyone loves you. There is something warm in your very presence."

"Oh, what an idealist you are!" she protested. "It's very absurd of you. I think the sunshine must have got into your head to-day. You make me think of Midas—of the ass's ears."

He felt for his pipe. "Why?"

"Because everything around you seems to turn to gold," she explained, half-laughing.

He pulled out his tobacco-pouch and sat filling his pipe. "There's no gold when you're not there," he said, with his eyes upon his task. "Nor ass's ears either. It's all your doing."

"Then perhaps I'd better keep away for the future," said Marcia.

He threw her a swift glance. "For your own sake or mine?"

She flushed at the curt question, for it almost held a challenge. Then, very deliberately, she answered it. "Mainly for yours, because I don't think you ought to wear ass's ears on my account."

He laughed grimly. "It's only you who see them. Tell me, Marcia : what are you going to do in the holidays?"

"What are you going to do?" she countered with sudden boldness.

He looked across at her abruptly, as though he too had heard a challenge. "I ought to be going to Canada," he said.

"And are you?" said Marcia.

She met his eyes with absolute directness, but her heart had begun to beat very fast. Were they all going to fail her, one after another?

He spoke very slowly. "Marcia—why can't you come with me?"

"Eric!" she said breathlessly.

He made a restraining gesture. "Don't! It's old-fashioned. Let's be modern for once! Why couldn't you be original enough to take a trip to Canada? Would it matter—would anybody care if I chanced to go too?"

"Oh, I don't know," she said, "I don't know."

"I think you do," he rejoined, quietly returning to the filling of his pipe. "I think you realize, as I do, that probably nobody would care a damn. And even if they did, it would be so much the better for all concerned. It's high time you made them care, just made them realize that you're not everybody's slave."

Marcia recovered her breath with an effort and produced a smile. "You are evidently in rather a fairy-tale mood to-day," she observed. "I think we had better try and find something a little less visionary to talk about."

Eric placed his pipe in his mouth and lighted it. "Are you thinking of *Midsummer Night's Dream* ?" he said. "Don't forget that the fairy queen fell in love with the chap with the ass's ears while it lasted ! Enjoyed it, too almost as much as he did !"

Marcia laughed. "I always thought that such a silly story."

He nodded. "Quite ! There are limits, as you say. Look here ! Don't stay awake on my account ! Dream if you want to ! I'm going to make a boat."

He pulled a rush from the river-bed and began to fashion it, and Marcia leaned back upon her cushions with a feeling as of tension relaxed. It amused her to watch him, for he was deft in all his actions—a born craftsman. The water rippling against the punt made soft sounds that were like fairy laughter. The roar of the weir in the distance was the background of her dream.

Idly, with lazy enjoyment, she watched him. How good the present was ! How unnecessary the future ! As for the past, it was sunk in oblivion as though it had never been.

The boat was growing between his fingers. He used his spent match for a mast and secured her ribs with coarse grass from the bank.

"Will she be seaworthy ?" murmured Marcia.

He smiled at her. "I want a hair or two, if you can spare them, for the rigging."

She took off her hat, laughing. "I'll see what I can do. I'm afraid they're not very thick." She pulled out a hair and regarded it dubiously. "Is that any good ?"

He took it from her, holding it up so that the sunlight glinted upon it. "I shall want another," he said.

"I expect the next one will be grey," said Marcia, beginning to select another.

"Your hair is golden," he said briefly.

She laughed again and pulled out the hair. "Midas once more ! My hair may have been golden once. It's sandy now."

He gave her a glance of strong disapproval as he reached for her second offering. "Your hair is beautiful, and always has been," he said in a voice that defied contradiction. "But you don't make the best of yourself. You never have."

She waved her hand at him in mock disdain. "My dear censorious friend, I wouldn't stoop. That is for other people to do. I have lived with myself too long to waste my time

over anything so depressing.   Besides, when I am with anyone as kindly as you, why should I ?"

He returned soberly to his task.   "You are always at your
best with me," he said.

"Or do you only look at the attractive side ?" she suggested.

He did not answer her, apparently finding that the business
n hand required his full attention.   She settled down upon
her cushions again and closed her eyes.

"Let me know when you're ready to launch her !" she said.
"I see you are attempting the impossible, but it may take you
a little while to discover it."

Again he made no response, and she smiled to herself as she
drifted into a happy reverie.   So perfect was the day, so perfect the companionship, that all that had no immediate part
in it grew remote and shadowy in her mind.   From a beech-
tree on the other side of the river a thrush had begun to sing,
and the clear notes thrilled her to a quiet ecstasy of delight.
It was like a golden draught held to her lips, and she drank
deeply of it, filling her soul with the magic.   Everything was
golden on that wonderful afternoon.

She had not realized that she was drowsy.   She certainly
had not intended to drift into slumber ; but it crept upon her
unawares.   Slowly, imperceptibly, as the mist-wreaths on the
Cornish moor, it enveloped and enchained her senses.   Very
gradually she forgot Eric and his fairy boat, sinking down and
ever down into a fathomless depth where only the soft rustling
of the reeds could reach her lulled senses.   The last thing she
knew was the memory that was like a murmur among their
trembling stems of the old, old couplet of her childhood :

> "List, Mother Earth, while no man hears!
> King Midas has got ass's ears."

CHAPTER IX

THE MAGIC WOOD

SHE slept, and her sleep was deep and lasting.   There was
something in the air of the river that day that made for
drowsiness.   Perhaps there was indeed magic at work.   For

she dreamed vaguely of a golden world where it was always harvest-time. She saw fields and fields of waving corn, and she told herself with conviction, though without any apparent reason, that that was Canada. She had never seen so much gold before. It stretched away on all sides of her—seas of it, all rippling like flowing water in the breeze. She had a sensation that she was floating upon it, and she laughed in her sleep because it was all so delicious. Eric was there, of course, though she could not see him. It all belonged to Eric. And he was laughing too, telling her that this was the kingdom where she was queen. But when she asked him where her subjects were he could not tell her, for there was nothing but corn stretching away, away, away, as far as the eye could reach.

Later she had a vision of Eric himself, though how she managed to recognize him she did not know; for he was amazingly transformed into Bottom the weaver, and his ass's head made strange grimaces at her which only very occasionally reminded her of Eric in a caustic mood. Still, it certainly was Eric; there was no disputing that. She knew it by the way he waggled his ears, and again through the whispering reeds she heard the tragic confidence which the whispering reeds betrayed.

After a very long time the whole thing began to appear so ridiculous that she made a definite effort to rise to the surface of life once more, and, so rising, she made the humiliating discovery that she had been soundly sleeping in the punt during the whole of that summer afternoon.

She opened her eyes with that sense of weakness which always attends the reuniting of body and spirit after deep slumber, and, gazing before her lazily, she perceived Eric, no longer smoking, but still seated in the bows and staring down into the water as though he were watching something.

At her first slight movement he transferred his look to her, and somehow she knew in that moment that, notwithstanding his apparent preoccupation, his attention had been riveted upon her for some time.

"Well," he said, "where have you been all this time?"

She stretched up her arms luxuriously. "I've been to Canada," she said.

She saw his smile, and wondered vaguely if he had had anything to do with it.

"Well?" he said. "Did you enjoy it?"

"I loved it," she said.

"I told you you would," he remarked. "What did you see there?"

Half-laughing and half-serious, she told him. "There was corn—heaps and heaps of corn, all ripe and golden. I've never seen anything like it. You didn't tell me about it, did you?"

"Was I there?" he said.

She let her arms drop. "Oh yes, you were there. At least, it must have been you if it wasn't Midas or Bottom the weaver. I think it was you." Something had caught her eye in her gesture; she raised her left hand again. "Oh, Eric! The time! Do you know it?"

"There's plenty left," he said.

She was studying the watch on her wrist with astounded eyes. "Perhaps! But this can't be right! It isn't five!"

"Ten minutes to" said Eric. "And why not, if you've enjoyed it?"

She stared at him incredulously. "I can hardly believe it. Why, it isn't five minutes since you—since you . . ." A yawn caught her unawares and she was obliged to yield to it, though the next moment she sat up with determined energy. "Eric, this is really disgraceful. You shouldn't have allowed it. I'm quite ashamed of myself."

"I don't know why," he said. "I've enjoyed it too."

"You've not been asleep, have you?" she questioned.

"No." He offered no explanation of his enjoyment, and she did not seek for one. Everything still looked a little distorted and unnatural after her deep sleep.

She abandoned the subject. "What about the boat?" she said.

"The boat?" He looked at her enquiringly.

"Your boat," she explained. "Did you finish the rigging and sail her?"

He shook his head. "No. The rigging baffled me, so I put it into my pocket-book as a memento. I sailed the boat though. She went away downstream."

"We must look out for her," said Marcia. He was being deliberately ridiculous, of course, about the rigging, and the matter was not worth discussion. "Really, I think we ought to be going, don't you? I have a train to catch."

"There's plenty of time," he said. "We'll drift back if you ike. I expect you want some tea."

She stifled another yawn. "I think I do. It will wake me

up, anyhow." She looked around her regretfully. "It has been lovely here."

"Would you like to stay the night?" he suggested.

She laughed. "I should love it. These cushions are the acme of comfort. Just a rug or two is all that I should need."

"No one would miss you," said Eric. "I'll soon get some rugs if that's all you want."

She had sunk back again into her nest, but she waved a protesting hand at him. "No. Don't be absurd! Take me back!"

He turned without further words and loosened the mooring-rope. In a few seconds he was paddling the punt out into the stream. They floated into the full warmth of the afternoon sun.

"Delicious!" murmured Marcia. "Don't bother to punt! Just keep on paddling!"

But he ignored her request and got out the pole. Very soon they were shooting down the river at a pace that left a long wake behind them in the ripples. She watched his straight, athletic figure bending rhythmically to the work with quiet satisfaction. He did everything in a satisfactory way, this holiday pal of hers.

The glow of the western sun upon the beech-woods roused her afresh to admiration as they shot by.

"I knew they would be even lovelier now," she said. "But shall we have time to go into them?"

"There's plenty of time," he said again rather doggedly.

The river was no longer deserted. They passed several skiffs, and a motor-launch going upstream sent a wave from her bows that rocked them like a miniature tempest.

"Too many people in this country," Eric remarked

"I'm rather fond of them," murmured Marcia dreamily.

He gave her one of his semi-quizzical glances. "At a distance, perhaps. Everything in its place!"

She smiled back at him. "Well, yes. I'm not keen on crowds, certainly. But they've all had tea, evidently, so we're all right."

"You don't think I'd let you have tea with that mob, do you?" he said, with a vindictive gesture towards the vanishing motor-launch.

She laughed. "I believe I'm much more sociable than you are. Well, here we are at the end of the journey! You'll get a time-table, won't you? I'm not sure we ought to stop for those woods."

He frowned suddenly. "Marcia, if you harp on that subject any more, I shall be angry."

She continued to laugh with a sort of indolent happiness. "But, my dear, there are other days. I'll come again. There'll be heaps of leisure later on."

"And if I go to Canada?" he said. "Will you come here alone?"

She gave a slight start, and her mirth passed like a flash. "Alone! Oh, of course not!" she said.

"Thank you for that!" said Eric curtly.

They reached the little landing-stage and he handed her to the bank. They walked up the stretch of shorn turf together in silence. It was as if a slight cloud had come upon them, but yet they were not ill at ease. They knew each other too well for that.

When they sat at tea under a golden laburnum a little later there was no sign of any strain between them. They talked without effort of ordinary things.

"I don't think I shall let you go back by train," Eric said at length. "I'll motor you up."

"I thought you were going down to Peter for the weekend," she said.

"Well, I'm not," he rejoined. "Peter is haymaking and can get on quite well without me. I don't know whether you think I ought to spend more time in civilizing that young man."

"Oh no!" she said. "He is much nicer as he is. I should let him go to Canada if I were you and see to the ranch."

"And stay in England myself?" he said.

She nodded. "Of course!"

"Do you want me to?" he asked her point-blank.

She handed him his tea with a faintly wistful smile. "Should I suggest it if I didn't?"

"I don't know. Yes, you probably would. You're such a mass of unselfishness." He spoke half-resentfully.

"Oh, not when I'm with you," she corrected gently. "You are rapidly turning me into the most selfish creature on earth. Don't you realize it?"

"I wish I did," he said.

"You're very blind if you don't," said Marcia.

She drank her tea with her eyes on the slow-flowing river and fell into a meditation from which for some time he did not rouse her. In fact he also ate and drank absent-mindedly, as if his thoughts were far away. The stream was deserted again,

and the beech-woods had taken an almost dazzling brightness
from the brilliant western sky. It was the hour when afternoon begins to melt imperceptibly into evening, and a very
slight coolness came up like a soft breath from the water.

"Let me give you some more!" said Marcia.

"No, thanks." He leaned his elbow on the table. "Have
you finished? Have a cigarette!"

She accepted one, lighted it, and seemed to return to her
dream.

But he broke in upon it ruthlessly. "Marcia!"

She looked at him, slightly startled, through the cigarette-
smoke. "What is it? Ought we to be going?"

"There's no 'ought' about anything," he said impatiently.
"Why do you persist in living by rule when nobody else does?"

"My dear," she protested, smiling a little, "don't be rude!
What was it you wanted to say?"

He smiled also, as it were in spite of himself. "Forgive
me! You're such an angel of forbearance that I'm always
taking advantage of it—like the rest of the world."

"Well?" said Marcia, shaking her head at the declaration.

He got up rather abruptly. "We'll go over the bridge and
walk in those woods, and you shall tell me the upshot of all
these meditations."

She rose also, faintly flushing. Her face wore a very sweet,
almost girlish look. "I don't know that I can. But I'd like
to see the woods, just for a few minutes."

They went by way of a narrow path that skirted the river's
edge, finally leading to a footbridge with white rails approached
by wooden steps.

Marcia went up them slowly, still as though she were in a
dream. The man behind her followed closely, with that
doggedness which was one of his main characteristics.

When she paused for a moment at midstream to gaze
down into the water, he quietly touched her arm. "Go on,
dear, will you? I want to ask you something."

She went on half-mechanically till she reached the further
side. Then she paused, looking at him.

"Well?" she said.

His hand touched her again with a sort of restrained urgency.
"You wanted to go into the beech-wood," he said. "Look—
there's the gate!"

She hesitated momentarily. "I wonder whether we ought.
I mean"—with a smiling, semi-apologetic glance—"I wonder
whether it's private."

"Oh, never mind!" he said. "What does it matter if you want to go?"

"Really, Eric!" she protested. "Your principles are not quite so lofty as I thought."

"No, I daresay not," he assented with a certain grimness. "I'm learning to be modern, you see. And I mean to go through that gate if they shoot me for it."

"Oh, very well," said Marcia, turning. "Then I'll come too."

They found the gate fastened only by an ordinary latch, and passed through it without hindrance.

Immediately the magic was with them again. It met them as it were on the very threshold, and they entered together an enchanted place, soundless, remote, a great carpet of dead gold under their feet, a far-reaching canopy of living gold above their heads.

Marcia moved forward a few paces, feeling as though she suddenly found herself in a cathedral of immense grandeur; then she stood still. "It's almost too lovely," she said in a hushed voice.

He slipped his hand under her arm, and they stood so for several seconds in silence. Then, as if by a mutual impulse, they began to move up one of the long golden aisles.

They left the outer world behind them. It was as though it had dropped completely away. And they went on and on through their wonderland, forgetful of time and circumstance, forgetful of all but the splendid harmony that bound them.

They came upon a fallen trunk, and again with one consent they paused. Eric pulled off his coat and spread it for her to sit on, though she tried to stay him with a soft remonstrance.

"I'm much happier without it," he said. "It's hot."

And then he sat down beside her and took her hand into his own.

She made no demur. Her vague smile seemed to acknowledge that this place was not as the world outside, that even she was not enslaved by convention during this brief hour of enchantment.

He leaned towards her and quietly spoke. "Marcia, I want to ask you something."

"Yes?" she said, still faintly smiling, her eyes upon the ground.

"I want to know," he said, "if you think I've played the game."

She nodded without looking up. "Oh yes. And you

haven't found it too hard, have you ?   I mean, you're happier now ?"

"I'm happy with you," he said.   "And you, Marcia— you are happy with me."

There was steady conviction in his voice, and she did not attempt to refute it.   "Of course I am !" she said.   "You are such a dear friend to me."

"Would you be sorry if I went away ?" he said.

It was as though a spell had been laid upon her.   She was compelled to answer him without any attempt at subterfuge— as simply as he asked.   "Very, very sorry."

He lifted her hand and laid his forehead against it.   "Marcia, are we going to see more of each other in the future, or less ?"

She made a slight movement.   "Eric, are you really going away ?"   Her voice had a faint half-piteous sound.

He did not answer her directly.   "It's got to be one thing or the other," he said.   "It seems to me we've gone too far together to make parting very easy."

Marcia was silent.   She sat as if waiting for something which was bound to happen in that quiet place.

He went on, his head still bent over her hand.   "You'd miss me a bit if I left you, wouldn't you ?"

Again she made answer as if she could not help it.   "I should miss you terribly, Eric."

"Yes, I know you would," he said.   "It isn't given to people in this world to be as you and I have been to each other and then break apart without tearing something.   You know how it is with me.   But how is it with you ?   You who are always thinking of the needs of others, do you ever think of your own ?"

"I don't know," she said in a low voice.   "I used to once. I try not to now."

"Yes," he said, "you try to ignore the fact that you have any needs.   But you won't be able to go on doing that.   It isn't right that you should.   You've got to think for yourself sooner or later.   A woman like you needs to be needed by somebody.   It's the very breath of life to you.   You'll die without it."

"I don't think so," Marcia said rather drearily.   "That isn't the sort of thing that people die of."

"No ?"   He spoke very bitterly.   "Then you'll go on living in utter misery—death in life.   Is that what you're prepared to do ?"

"I don't know," she said again, and her voice trembled a

L

little. "I'd rather not think about it. Things may change, you know."

"They won't," he said grimly, "unless you make them. Look, Marcia"—he lifted his head unexpectedly—"you're here with me now to-day, and you're happy. You've not the faintest wish to go back to your home to-night, and nobody has the faintest wish to see you there. Isn't that true?"

He was looking straight into her face, her hand still held in his. She made no attempt to avoid his look, but she winced slightly at his words.

"You needn't answer," he said. "I know it is."

"No, wait a minute!" She interrupted him gently, but with decision. "You haven't got—quite the right impression of things, Eric. It's true that under ordinary circumstances that might be a real picture; but you've left out a possibility of something different happening." She spoke rather nervously. "You've overlooked the chance—and there is still a chance—that I might be needed. And do you think I would miss that chance for anything in the world?"

"Oh, my dear!" he said. "Would you go on sacrificing yourself for the moon? Do you honestly—honestly, Marcia—believe that that chance still exists?"

She drew back a little. He saw the pain in her eyes. "Eric, please!"

He leaned suddenly to her and took her by the shoulders, not roughly, but with a determination that would not be frustrated. "No, face it—face it!" he said. "It's got to be faced. I love you, such as I am, better than my own soul. I need you as no one else in this world needs you. You don't love me yet like that. But you can, you will, when once this fetish of yours is overthrown. You know already in your heart that the man you love, or think you love, is a dream-creation of your own that can never come to life. You are never happy with him. You never have been since you found out your mistake. You are always happy with me. Why, do you think? Have you ever asked yourself why?"

She was not shrinking from him now. The intensity with which he spoke seemed in some fashion to compel her courage. She sat motionless in his hold, listening, weighing his words.

When he stopped for her answer, she gave it unfalteringly. "Because we are friends, Eric; and friendship is a very precious thing."

"Yes," he assented doggedly. "It is—very precious. Now I'm going to ask you another question—just one more—and

I charge you by all that's sacred to answer me truly. If I had met you first would you have married me ?"

His eyes looked deeply into hers with the words. There was no evading their scrutiny. She did not seek to do so, but she turned slowly very pale.

"Ah, that," she said, "is another matter. How can I tell you that ?"

"You must tell me," he said. "Ask yourself ! You have got the answer in your heart."

Her lips began to quiver, and she tried to hide it with a smile. "No, Eric, I don't think I have," she said. "I'm trying to be very honest with you—though I don't quite see what good it's going to do. I'm not trying to hide from you that I've had my illusions. You know me too well not to realize it. But you don't know the very heart of me. I'm not quite sure—quite sure—that I do myself. You may call it a dream-creation, but it's very precious to me still though it may hold more pain than pleasure. One has got to be faithful, Eric, or everything goes by the board. If I had married you, I believe we should have been happy. I don't deny that we make each other happy when we're together as it is. But—it's difficult to explain to you—I should have missed my dream, the dream that has been so dear to me in spite of everything."

"The dream that will never come true," he interrupted slowly and steadily.

She caught her breath, and then suddenly the quivering went all over her face, and she put up her hands to hide it. "Oh, you mustn't say that," she whispered brokenly. "Please don't say that ! It might, you know, it might !"

Her voice went into a sob. He drew her to him, unresisting.

"Hush, dear, hush !" he said. "I hate hurting you, only I've got to. You want so much, and you've got so little. But if you'd only take what's within reach—Marcia, if you only would !"

His cheek was against her forehead, his arms held her closely, but there was no compulsion in his clasp. He only sought to comfort.

And she leaned against him, her tears falling unchecked. "I can't—I can't," she told him. "I almost wish I could."

"You don't know what life holds," he said. "I can't bear to think you never will know. But you never will, Marcia, you never can, if you go on like this."

"No; I know," she said wearily. "It's just like that. But, you see, I can't help it."

"Why can't you?" he said.

She began to wipe away her tears, and in a moment or two she raised her head. "Oh, my dear," she said, "how miserable you look!"

"It's only because of you," he said. "I can't bear to see you like this—you of all people—neglected, alone. Marcia —look, Marcia, couldn't you possibly give it a trial?"

"Give what a trial?" she said.

"Well, me," he said bluntly. "You haven't found me wanting so far, have you? I've never overstepped the mark since you pulled me up. I think you know I never shall again, without being—quite sure—first. Look, Marcia! Where's the sense in us both being wretched—for the sake of a man who doesn't care a damn?"

He ground out the words in a fierce undertone. There was a smouldering heat in his eyes which impelled her to lay a gentle hand on his arm.

"But, Eric, what else is there to do?" she said. "No, dear, wait! Don't get angry about it! Let's try and make allowances! Men don't stay in love, you know. Even you must acknowledge that."

"I don't!" he flung out savagely. "And if you really want to know what else can be done, I'll tell you. Break away! Leave off circling round a dead planet and strike out in another direction! I may be a poor thing in comparison, but at least I'm real."

His words went into silence. She was looking at him no longer. She just sat with her hand on his arm, gazing into the golden spaces. Yet there was something about her that checked him, something spiritual, unearthly. His anger fell away from him like a quenched flame. It was as if that quiet hand of hers had been laid upon his heart.

She spoke after a few seconds, her voice low, yet resolute. "You see, dear, it wouldn't be right. I don't know quite how we ever came to discuss such a thing. Everard"—she uttered the name for the first time and almost with reverence—"is a good man in every sense of the word. And he cares for me—at least he must have cared for me once"—her words had a certain insistence as though she sought to convince herself— "or he would never have wanted me for his wife. I care for him too. I always have. And though my love may not seem to mean a great deal to him now, yet—yet"—she paused as if the uncertainty she had tried to combat were getting the better of her—"I have no right to be miserable about it. So, please, Eric, you mustn't encourage me to be discontented. Just help me, if you will, to make the best of things!"

"Discontented!" He echoed the word contemptuously, seemed to contemplate it for a moment then throw it from him. "My dear girl, if *that* were all the trouble! You don't imagine, do you, that I'd care to butt in, interfere, unsettle you, if there were the faintest chance of things ever coming even moderately right? No!" He looked down at the hand upon his arm, then suddenly he grasped it. "It's gone too far for that. You've been cheated, and you know it as well as I do. That's why I want you so desperately to take the thing within reach, even though it isn't the thing you most want. I promise you this at least: it'll be more to you from the very outset than what you've now got. It won't be your ideal, but it'll be a real solid fact, and it'll never let you down. I have the power to make you happy. You've owned it. Marcia, couldn't you trust me to keep you so?"

"I don't know," she said gently. "I ought not to let myself even think about it. I don't believe I should—anywhere but here."

"You mean you wouldn't if you could help it," he said. "Well, I've done. I don't want to persuade you against your will. I wouldn't handicap myself to that extent. I only want to say just this much: if you will give me a very small slice of your life—only a few weeks—and come with me to Canada, it can be done quite unobtrusively, and I promise you that it shall be the happiest time, apart from dreams, that you have ever known. It will bind you to nothing. You shall come back whenever you wish. That is my idea of friendship. It has no obligations."

There was no impetuosity in his speech; it was quiet and measured, yet in a way more forcible by its very restraint. As he ended, he made a movement to rise; but, strangely, she checked him. It was one of those moments when the generous impulse of her could not be denied.

"Oh, Eric," she said in a voice that trembled, "I don't know how to tell you what your goodness means to me. It is something beyond, above, everything else in my experience. You make me realize, as nothing else ever has, what love truly means. It goes straight to my heart, and it makes me ashamed. But I will tell you this: I am not the sort of woman to take all and give nothing. If—if it ever happened that I could possibly take what you offer, I would give you all I had in return."

She ended with both her hands clasped in his, and when a moment later he took her back into his arms she made no attempt to resist him.   Perhaps it was a midsummer madness that came upon her in that enchanted wood, or perhaps, like the thirsty traveller who drinks at the wayside brook when the mountain spring is out of reach, she could no longer resist the draught.   But in that hour she was vanquished.   Her spirit could battle no longer, and close against her lover's breast she found a respite all too brief from the unfulfilled longing of her heart.

CHAPTER X

THE RETURN

On the edge of the wood he paused and looked at her with a curious intentness.

"And so we go back to the world, darling!" he said.

"Is it the same world?" she asked rather tremulously.

His eyes followed hers to the winding river with its green banks vivid as emerald in the evening sunshine.   From the distance came the sound of chiming bells.   All was as it had been, a scene of utter and complete peace.

His look returned to her.   "Yes, just the same, only a little colder.   Do you really feel you've got to go back?"

She put out her hand half-appealingly.   "Yes, I really must.   Help me to go, Eric!"

"I will do anything in the world for you," he said, and pressed it against his heart.

The gate was open, but she hung back for a second.   "You really mean that?" she said.   "I know you mean it."

"Yes," he said with simplicity.   "I do.   I will do anything or nothing, exactly as you wish."

"Thank you, dear."   She gave him a fleeting smile.   "That is so like you.   Well"—she caught back a sigh—"it's been a wonderful day.   I shall never forget it."

"No," he said.   "And you won't spoil it in retrospect, will you?"

Her eyes smiled at him somewhat wistfully. "If you're sure—quite sure!"

"Darling, I am quite sure," he said. "What has happened to-day is simply the removal of a barrier between us, that's all. It binds you to nothing whatever. So don't take fright over it, will you?"

"No," she said, "no—so long as you understand."

"Sweetheart, I do," he said. "I understand completely. That's why I'm trying to guard against your saying to yourself directly you're alone, 'What have I done?' You're not to say that, Marcia, or if you do, you're to give yourself the true answer. You have done nothing." He paused a moment, and then deliberately took her two hands and held her before him. "And there's one other thing you're not to do," he said. "You're not to write to me and say we must never meet again. If you feel you want to say it, you must say it to my face."

He spoke half-whimsically, but there was a hint of sternness in the words. She stood passive in his hold.

"Is that a promise?" he said.

She smiled at him again, shaking her head. "Oh, you don't know me," she said. "I am much more selfish than that."

His sternness vanished. He drew her swiftly to him and kissed her. "My darling—my darling!" he said.

For a few seconds his hold was passionately close, then abruptly, as though putting sudden force upon himself, he let her go.

"There! I'd better take you back," he said. "You're getting more precious every instant. If you don't go soon, I shan't be able to part with you. When am I going to see you again?"

"Next Thursday," she said.

"Not till then?"

"I'm afraid not till then, but I'll let you know." She was free, and she turned once more to the gate; yet paused again with a slight shiver. "Eric, I hate leaving this lovely wood. I feel it's going to be very cold outside."

He put his arm round her and led her quietly through. "Now I'm going to help you," he said. "I'd spend the whole night here if I had my way, but it wouldn't be your way, so we won't consider it." He pushed the gate behind him and it shut with a desolate clang. "Now we go back to our dust and ashes, but we won't forget that we have a secret garden, you and I, to which both of us have a key."

Her face brightened. "Yes, that's a good thought. It's not so cold after all. Thank you, Eric!"

He laughed and released her. "Here we resume our normal decorous behaviour for the benefit of the impertinently staring world. I'm rather glad in a way that we've got to. We couldn't let anyone else into that garden of ours."

"Oh, indeed, no!" she said.

They went down to the river again side by side until they reached the bridge. Then again Marcia led the way, and again in the centre she paused.

"It's like that, isn't it?" she said, gazing down into the quiet flowing water and speaking as though she resumed some discussion.

He stopped beside her. "Yes, darling. Very like that— always flowing, yet never empty."

Her hand moved along the rail towards him. "Eric, it mustn't get any deeper," she said.

He patted her hand lightly, reassuringly. "No, dear. That's all right. That's understood. We're neither of us in our first youth. I shan't sweep you off your feet."

Her eyes left the river and wandered to the golden-green woods on the hill. "If only——" she said, and paused as if half afraid to continue.

"Only what?" he said.

She ended, almost in a whisper: "We had met before!"

His eyes shone with a sudden fire. "Oh, Marcia, if we only had!" he said. And then, sharply controlling himself again: "No matter! We'll make the best of what we've got."

"The very best," she assented, and quietly turned and walked on.

Very little passed between them during the journey up to town. The splendour of the day died slowly behind them— such a day as might not come again during the whole of the summer. But not once did Marcia turn and look back.

He did not take her straight home, but to a little restaurant in a quiet alley where they dined together almost in silence. And then when the meal was over, he put her into a taxi and they parted.

"You'll let me know?" he said, his hand holding hers at the last moment.

Her soft eyes looked straight up to his out of the darkness of the cab. "Yes, of course I will!" she said. "I'll ring you up in the morning from my room."

"As soon as you wake?" he said.

She gave him a very tender smile. "At the earliest respectable moment," she said. "Good-bye!"

He made no verbal answer. His hand gripped hers tightly for an instant and then released it. He stepped back.

As the taxi shot forward she leaned to the window and saw him standing bareheaded on the pavement—an alert, athletic figure in flannels, and something about him sent a quick pang to her heart. He had the ardent look of a man embarked upon some great adventure. She had never seen him so eager, so alive. And all for what? She did not answer the question as she waved her farewell, neither did she stifle the sigh that rose to her smiling lips. She had promised him to check all backward thoughts, but now that she was alone she could not hide from herself the knowledge that they were both striving to satisfy themselves with that which was not bread.

But perhaps that was life! Perhaps it was futile to expect or even to allow oneself to want anything more! As he had said, they were no longer in their first youth. It behoved them to have gathered some philosophy with the years. To go on longing for that which could never be was surely a childish act. It was better to take what the gods offered and be content therewith. That, she was certain, was Eric's creed, and it did not seem to her to be a bad one. At least it was better than complete starvation, perpetual disappointment. For that was all that the life she was now leading held for her. It no longer contained any aspirations, unless the continual effort to stifle her desire for the unattainable could be called one. Everything within reach had become barren and unprofitable. Letting herself into the house, she told herself that there was only one person in the whole world who really wanted her.

The place seemed vast and empty. She went up the stairs with lagging feet. She was weary beyond belief.

Her maid, Hobbs, was preparing her bedroom for the night and looked at her with a certain covert criticism. It was not late, yet her expression seemed a discreet veil to disapproval.

Marcia sat down. "I am going straight to bed," she said.

"Very good, my lady," said Hobbs.

The novelty of this form of address was obviously still a joy to her though it had a farcical ring to Marcia, as though in the maid's opinion she were not living up to her added dignity and needed to be reminded of it. She wondered what Hobbs would have said could she have known that, neglecting all the claims of Society upon her, she had spent the whole day lazing on the river.   Whatever her suspicions might be, she was sure that she could not have pictured anything half as dreadful as this !

She had brought up half a dozen letters with her, but she pushed them aside unopened. They could wait till the morning, and she did not want to think of immaterial things to-night.   She did not in fact really want to think of anything at all—unless it was of that golden glade in the enchanted wood, where the cup of love with its sparkling draught had been held once more to her parched and longing lips. She could not be sorry yet that she had drunk of it, even though she had not dared to drain it because of the bitterness that she knew to be at the dregs.

As to the evil from which she once had prayed for deliverance, though it had seemed so real to her then, it had faded now into an intangible background so dim that she barely perceived it.   To serve others had been her motto, but of what avail if none needed her service ?   She scarcely saw her husband nowadays, and in her heart was a creeping conviction that his need of her was for ever past.   He took no interest in her friends, her pursuits, her welfare. He cared only for the career which link by link he was forging for himself.   And her children needed her, if possible, even less.   Life was a gorgeous entertainment to them.   They had no time for family ties.   Already the outside world had claimed them, and the word "home" had no meaning for them whatever.   They were for gleaning every experience within reach, and, since the world was wide, there was not a moment to waste.   She could understand them, though her heart was sore.   She could even understand her husband.   It was only her own position that did not seem to be clearly defined.

And Eric—surely Eric must be somehow in the right when he told her that she was throwing herself away !   He was so emphatic about it, and her faith in her own judgment had never been of the dogmatic order.   It had dwindled terribly of late.   Moreover, he was the only friend she had, the one person in the whole world apparently who wanted her.   He understood her, too, so perfectly, all her unfulfilled, her piteously faded dreams.   And he did not flatter himself that he could remedy them.   He merely proposed to create as it were a new brain-centre and form her life afresh, to leave the ruins behind and build for her another palace more solid, if less attractive, than the first.   Surely anything was better than nothing !   Surely he could not be wholly in the wrong !

She slept at last from sheer weariness, and she dreamed that she wandered in that new castle through many lofty rooms with wonderful furnishings and tall windows that looked out upon a crystal river and golden beech-woods. It was not an unhappy wandering ; it held the spirit of adventure, and in a fashion she enjoyed it. But she came at last upon a thing that baffled her, a broken stairway, thick with dust, that led down to a heavy oaken door. There was an urgent desire within her to descend, but something held her back—something against which instinctively she fought till eventually she gained the mastery.

Then, as she took the first step, it crumbled beneath her foot and she fell to the bottom. She lay against the door half-stunned, until gradually the realization came to her that she had no means of return to her castle, and the door against which she lay could never open to her, because it was the Door into the Past.

Then she awoke and found that another day had dawned.

CHAPTER XI

THE SKIRMISH

IT was force of habit more than anything else that carried Marcia through the next few days. The London season was on the wane. Only Goodwood remained, and people were already talking of Cowes. She had received one or two invitations for the latter, but she had not accepted them. Her plans were still vague, she said, and it was generally concluded that she intended to bury herself somewhere in the country with the children. That she was deadly tired of the social round no one suspected, though old Lady Barrowdale still declared at intervals with affectionate emphasis that she was much too thin. But escape was not really a part of Marcia's programme. Her vagueness had originally been induced by uncertainty as to her husband's movements, and the lurking hope that even yet he might express a desire to have her with him during the Vacation. He was just going to the North for a final case, but after that she had not heard precisely how he meant to arrange his time. He wanted leisure for writing and study, she knew, but the house in Mountgrave Square was to be placed in the hands of workmen, and she could not imagine that he would wish to stay there.

He might still want her, or at least still count upon her for something. So long as that possibility remained she could not contemplate any other. She had confirmed her promise to Eric to meet him the following week, but she scarcely looked forward to the meeting. She was waiting with a kind of tense patience for some sign from Everard before he left her, some word with regard to the future, however lightly spoken, which should bind her to his side.

It had come to that with her, though she hardly realized it. She was like a starved creature, still hoping against hope to receive nourishment from the usual beloved hand ere turning reluctantly away to seek it elsewhere. And behind her hunger and her disappointment there was gathering a strange new feeling that had hitherto been completely alien to her—a slow-kindling fire of indignation over her wounded love. She had begun almost to despise herself for the pain she was suffering, to regard it almost as a gnawing disease from which a sharp turn of the knife might free her if only she had the courage to apply it. But still, as it were instinctively, she waited, while daily her desperation grew.

Encountering Lillith one day at a wedding, she told her briefly in answer to enquiry that she was not going down to Goodwood; and when Lillith expressed surprise, she laughed in a fashion which she knew to be insincere.

"Everard may want me," she explained. "He is going North for this Marley trial at the end of the week."

"As if he possibly could want you!" ejaculated Lillith. "You're just lazy. That's what's the matter with you. Why, I've missed you at ever so many places this year."

"How nice of you!" smiled Marcia, still feeling absolutely artificial.

"Oh, I don't mean in that way," Lillith hastened to assure her. "And I've no doubt you've been enjoying yourself much more thoroughly elsewhere. In fact, Mater and I have been looking for the counter-attraction. I've often thought you were a dark horse, Marcia."

"Thank you, my dear," said Marcia serenely. "I could scarcely hope for anything better."

"But it's absurd to suggest that Everard might want you," persisted Lillith. "A ridiculous excuse, and you know it. You'll say you're too busy darning his socks next."

"I believe he still wears them," protested Marcia ; "and they must want darning sometimes."

Lillith looked at her as if she barely refrained from begging her not to be a fool, and by mutual consent they drifted asunder.

But an uneasy sense of being under observation pursued Marcia. She knew that if she had attempted to slip away early on that occasion she would have become the subject of widespread comment. For Lillith was not a woman to keep her ideas to herself. They were usually on exhibit to anyone who cared to inspect them, and they never erred on the side of mercy. It was almost impossible to be inconspicuous anywhere when Lillith's attention was aroused. In fact, in the sporting circles in which she moved she was sometimes described as a good pointer.

For the first time Marcia definitely avoided her for the rest of the afternoon, and she was very glad when the guests began to leave and she could take her own departure at an appropriate hour.

She and Everard had a dinner engagement that night at the house of a well-known judge, Lord Bevis. It was one of the rare occasions upon which she could always count on him to accompany her. He had a great respect for Lord Bevis, with whom he was often associated in his profession. And dull as Lady Bevis's parties invariably were, they usually held a certain pleasure for Marcia because of her husband's presence. It was so seldom now that they appeared anywhere together.

She took especial care over her appearance that night, to Hobbs' open satisfaction ; for in the latter's estimation, much as she admired her mistress, she did not as a rule take sufficient interest in this all-important respect. Clothes were to Hobbs practically the only means of self-expression that existed. She revelled in arraying Marcia as the grand lady, which, to her mind, was the only *rôle* that fitted her, and it grieved her that Marcia seemed so little inclined to live up to it.

"You are looking quite your best to-night, my lady," she said approvingly as she placed the velvet wrap about her shoulders.

And Marcia smiled. "Thank you, Hobbs. I am glad you think so."

Descending the stairs, she had a curious scared feeling, almost like a premonition, as if to-night were a sort of test. If nothing happened to-night to stay her course, she believed she would drift over into the rapids to-morrow.

Eric would be waiting for her. She had promised to meet him. They were to dine together, and afterwards he would take her somewhere, she had not asked where. She had a feeling that amounted to certainty that after to-night she would know exactly what she was going to do. Either she would go forward or finally draw back. She could not possibly remain where she was. Matters had either gone too far or not far enough. To-night would decide. And it rested not with herself at all, but with Everard. If he looked at her even once with eyes that saw, the bond between them would be forged anew, never to be broken. But if he remained blind . . . A great shiver went through her, and she tried to shake the thought from her. If he remained blind, then he must go his way, and she hers. He would have his profession to comfort him—if he needed comfort. And she— ah, what comfort would she have for her lost ideals, her shattered love ?

He was in the hall waiting for her—a tall, imposing personality, very upright and self-assured. He greeted her with a bare glance. "My dear, we are late."

He hated unpunctuality, she knew, but she expressed no regret. There was only one thing that mattered that night. Either the fire was kindled afresh, or utterly and for ever quenched.

"We shall be there in time, I think," she said, and passed out to the car.

He followed in a silence expressive of a certain displeasure. She almost laughed during the short journey at the thought that she had ever troubled to make herself beautiful for his sake.

She did not utter a single word, nor did he rouse himself from his abstraction to ask how she had spent the day. From brief annoyance he passed into a groove of thought in which she had no part. There were one or two matters which he was particularly anxious to discuss with Lord Bevis that night before his departure for the North on the morrow, and, as his custom was, he tabulated them carefully in his mind beforehand. As Lillith had once said of him, he had a mind like a perfectly arranged bureau. Everything it contained was in its own neatly docketed pigeonhole.

They were the last arrivals in Lady Bevis's drawing-room, but, as Marcia had predicted, they were in time. The room contained about a dozen people in all, most of them connected with the legal world. Marcia knew them all slightly. It was exactly the type of party she had expected, and she saw at a glance that any guest who desired entertainment of any description would have to provide it for himself. Many a time under similar circumstances she had exerted herself to make some sort of ripple on the still surface, but to-night she felt tired, almost stupid. The conventional atmosphere chilled her. She felt incapable of effort.

She sat next to her host whose remarks were few and pompous and who evidently considered that no woman ought to require more than his occasional attention. Marcia wondered if she ought to appear more amused than she actually was, and finally decided that it did not matter as certainly he would never notice.

On her other side was a barrister—a man of about thirty, called Baronford, whom she had always regarded as the most cynical person of her acquaintance. He was in an obscure mood, and since she knew of old that bitterness underlay everything he said, she had but small inclination to discover the actual significance of his conversation. He was a bachelor who had done a good deal of work in the Divorce Courts, and she had a shrewd suspicion that he also held a very light opinion of her sex. It did not worry her in the least. Under ordinary circumstances she would have smilingly held her own, and even have derived a certain enjoyment from so doing. But to-night she could not rouse herself to deal with the situation. Everything seemed completely trivial, almost unreal. She saw the people around her as one views the shifting landscape through the window of an express. They were standing still while she was racing on and on—whither?

Something seemed to jerk within her and she made a definite effort to take an interest in her surroundings. She must not let herself go like this.

Across the table she saw her husband's face, calm and collected, faintly smiling as he lent his courteous attention to some slight discussion that was going on about him. His eyes chanced to meet hers for a moment, but without any change of expression. She did not think they had even seen her.

The man beside her had made some remark about the Long Vacation, and she turned towards him resolutely. "Yes, it will soon be here. How fast the time goes! It only seems yesterday since——"

She broke off. His face told her she was being banal.

"Yes," he agreed with a lazy sneer. "No holding it, as you

say. Yesterday's wheat—to-day's stale bread. Yesterday's vices—to-day's virtues. Yesterday's clean collar—to-day's soiled linen. And—as I was saying—to-morrow the Long Vacation. I was also indiscreet enough to wonder how you were going going to spend it."

"Oh, not so indiscreet!" said Marcia, with a smile. "I haven't given it very serious consideration at present. My husband——" She paused involuntarily, suddenly aware that he had something to say on the subject.

"Your husband!" he echoed, a faint inflection on the word which might have been expressive of either surprise or derision. "Haven't you heard his plans yet? He is going to be busy at the Old Bailey while everyone else is holiday-making, and I'm lending him my chambers in the Temple for the purpose. Not a lady's refuge, I fear! Didn't you know?"

Abruptly she found herself on the defensive. His tone had a jeering note which could not be ignored. In another moment he would be openly scoffing at her discomfiture.

With a swift effort she rose to the occasion. "How extremely kind of you, Mr. Baronford!" she said. "It will solve a difficulty which had been troubling me for some time. Yes, of course, I knew he would have to be in town, and our house will be in the hands of the decorators during August."

So imperative had been the necessity to shield herself immediately that she barely had time to grasp the fact that a shattering blow had fallen upon her, but as she ceased to speak she found herself breathing so rapidly that for a few seconds she felt as if she were about to faint. It took all her strength of mind to retain her faculties and to hear her companion's cynically uttered rejoinder.

"Oh, don't mention it! Delighted to be of use! It will set you free, won't it, for some pursuit more profitable than keeping house for an absent husband?"

Again the jeering note was in his voice, faint but perceptible, as though he were hinting at the existence of something which he was deliberately keeping out of sight. And again, instinctively, she guarded herself.

"Well, naturally, there wouldn't be much point in that, and I am very glad to know his comfort is secure. It will set me free to make my own arrangements, as you say."

Baronford's smile had more than a touch of irony. "I thought you would probably appreciate that, Lady Temple-ton," he murmured. "So nice to kill two birds with one stone!

Now you will be able to enjoy your holiday on the river in peace."

"My holiday on the river?" Suddenly the danger that menaced her took definite form. She gathered her woman's armour around her and regarded him in blank surprise. "My holiday on the river?" she repeated aloud so that anyone near her could have heard. "Now what should make you imagine that I was contemplating one?"

He continued to smile as though he were contemplating something she could not see that afforded him a good deal of quiet amusement. "I suppose I mustn't quote the pro-verbial little bird," he said, "or I shall be accused of perjury at once. But surely the most devoted of wives is at liberty to amuse herself on land or on water—whichever appeals to her most—when her services at home are not required!"

His eyes, dark and cold, met hers with a mocking gleam, and a sense of chill went through Marcia that was like a steel point at her heart.

He went on with barely a pause, as though filling in a gap which he knew would otherwise be left empty. "It is only a figure of speech, my dear lady. A holiday on the river is an expression almost as tangible as seeing a man about a dog."

"And what does it mean?" asked Marcia with a tense quietness.

He explained with idle nonchalance. "I should say it means enjoying oneself in the way one likes best. I personally should prefer yachting on the Broads. Have you ever tried that?"

It was as if with scornful indifference he now offered her a way of escape, but she stiffly refused to avail herself of it. "No, I think the river idea would appeal to me most," she said with a brief smile. "I shall have to consider it now that you have put it into my head. I wonder how one could get hold of a house-boat."

He gave her the wary look of the man of law who weighs his chances in a game of bluff. And then, for no apparent reason, he abandoned the contest.

"I once went up the Jumna in a house-boat," he said. "Those Indian rivers make ours seem very tame affairs. I suppose you have never hunted big game, Lady Templeton?"

The sudden turn gave her a curious sensation that had in it more of dismay than relief. She would have given much to have known what was going on behind the placid irony of that smooth countenance. It held almost an ivory tinge which

M

with the cold glinting eyes, made her think of a Chinaman. But the ease with which he now directed the conversation into far different channels, if it did not reassure her, convinced her that for the moment at least she had nothing to fear. If he had in truth wielded a weapon, he had laid it aside. Perhaps he did not regard her as worthy of his skill, or perhaps he was merely biding his time! As she recovered her composure she told herself with a curious sense of doom that it did not matter which. Her destiny was already written, and nothing now could alter it.

CHAPTER XII

THE CLOSED DOOR

It was not until they reached their home that night that Marcia brought herself to break what had begun to seem almost a spell of silence laid upon her. And when she did so, it was as if against her will, and still with the overpowering conviction that nothing now could make any difference. She was very tired and felt as if her vitality had been reduced to a very low ebb. It cost her all her strength to follow her husband into his room for those few words which somehow must be spoken.

He stopped at the open door. "My dear, you had better say 'Good night' to me. I have a little work left to do."

She passed quietly into the room. "I want a word with you, please," she said. "I shan't keep you long."

Her voice sounded hard and mechanical even to herself. She felt strangely stiff from head to foot, as if she were turning into stone.

He followed her slowly in, a faint frown between his eyes. "Well, dear, what is it?" he said. "It's getting rather late."

"I know," said Marcia. She wheeled abruptly and faced him. "But you will be busy to-morrow too, and you are leaving in the evening."

"Yes, dear, yes." He spoke with a hint of impatience. "But I shall not be away for long—a week at the outside."

"What I have to say won't keep a week," Marcia said. She was very pale, but her face was absolutely composed.

It might have been the face of a statue. Only her hand which held the velvet wrap about her was convulsively clenched.

"Well, well, what is it?" He looked at her with slowly dawning attention, as though beginning to sense something unusual in her aspect. "I hope nothing has gone wrong?"

A great tremor went through Marcia, her breast heaved as if something had suddenly sprung to life there and were striving for expression. She put her free hand to her throat, pressing it desperately.

"My dear," he said, "what is the matter?"

He made a movement towards her, but she stepped back quickly. "Nothing—nothing!" she said, and forced a ghastly smile. "I'm a little tired, that's all. But I must have some sort of understanding with you about—future arrangements. Mr.—Baronford told me to-night that you were going into his chambers in the Temple in August while the house is being renovated. Is it true?"

"Yes," he answered at once. "I thought it was a good idea. Don't you agree?" He was looking at her closely now, with surprised interrogation.

She did not meet his look; it made her feel utterly unreasonable, almost contemptible, and it was essential that for this once she should maintain her own point of view.

She answered him with a certain stubbornness, bred of that tremendous effort to hold her own. "Yes, of course, I agree it may be for you. But—you realize, I suppose, that I shan't be with you?"

"Oh yes, dear," he said. "But that really won't matter. Not that you couldn't be if you wished. But I shall be very well looked after. There is really no need for you even to think of such a thing. Don't let that trouble you for a moment!"

She caught her breath, seized by a sudden wild impulse to laugh which it took her utmost strength to subdue.

He went on soothingly. "Oh no, I'm not such a tyrant as to expect you to spend August in London, especially when I shall be much too busy to know whether you are there or not. I'm not quite so selfish as that, I hope."

"It wouldn't be selfish," she said in a choked voice.

"I think it would," he replied with decision. "Anyway, I don't propose to do it. So that's settled. Now, dear, you're very tired, I can see. You run away to bed!"

It was hopeless. She felt it was utterly hopeless. The

door was closed against her, and no battering could open it. She was only bruising herself in the attempt. Yet, though the knowledge pressed upon her, she made one more desperate effort to save herself from being finally shut outside.

"Everard," she said, and the very intensity of her effort made her calm, "before I go, may I tell you one thing ? I shall not have the children these holidays. They have both had invitations to go abroad with friends which I am allowing them to accept. I don't—of course—wish to hinder your work in any way. I realize it is all-important. But I had just wondered if perhaps there might be a spare week that we might spend together somewhere."

She stopped. It was impossible to say more. Even that much had been almost beyond her strength, which was running out now very swiftly. And she knew even before the last word left her lips that she had spent herself in vain. He had made a barely conscious gesture of exasperation that told her so.

He spoke the moment she ceased. "My dear child, you are asking the impossible. Besides, it would be far better for you to go away for a thorough change. I can see you need it. And one week—even if it were feasible—would be no good to you whatever. No"—his voice took a note of deliberate decision —"it is quite out of the question. I see no prospect of any leisure for several months to come, and I insist upon your taking a complete holiday, quite independently of me. I am glad to hear that you will not even have the care of the children for once." He smiled a little. "You really ought to have been called Martha, not Marcia ! Now, dear, that is settled, isn't it ? We won't discuss it any further."

She turned with a sudden passionate movement. For an instant she was angry, so angry that the pain was dulled. "Then what am I to do ?" she said.

Again he looked at her in surprise. Her eyes were flaming in her white face, and he saw that she was quivering. He held out a pacifying hand.

"I am sorry if I have annoyed you," he said rather stiffly. "It does not seem to me an occasion for resentment. I am only suggesting that you should enjoy yourself in whatever fashion appeals to you most."

"You really mean that ?" she said in a voice that was almost metallic in its hardness.

"Of course I do !" he said. "I am not quite unreasonable. I want you to have a good time and be happy. I thought I had made that clear long ago. Come, my dear, that's understood, isn't it?" He stepped towards her and gently took her hand into his. "How cold you are! Make Hobbs heat you up some milk! I shall have to tell Lillith to keep an eye on you. You are not taking proper care of yourself."

She shrank at his words and slipped her hand swiftly away. "You needn't suggest that to Lillith," she said, and uttered a dreary laugh. "She is doing it already. I'm not in the least cold, thank you. Good night! Or perhaps—in case I don't see you again—I had better say good-bye!"

She turned to go, but he stopped her with a hand on her shoulder. "What are you doing to-morrow?" he asked gravely.

She faced him with a sudden icy resistance. "I believe I have a luncheon and a tea engagement. I am also going out in the evening. Why?"

"I think you are going too hard," he said. "It will be a good thing when the season is over. Anyway, don't get up too early! I won't disturb you. And—as you say—in case we don't meet again—good-bye!"

He bent and lightly kissed her forehead, and his kiss held an unuttered reproof. She barely restrained herself from another recoil.

"Good-bye!" she said once more.

He accompanied her to the door and held it punctiliously while she passed out.

She did not look at him again. If he had seized and beaten her, she felt, her chastisement would have been lighter. But this quiet, almost indifferent, disapproval was an infliction against which there was no appeal. She could only gather around her such poor shreds of her pride as remained and escape.

It was over. She had made her bid—her last bid—for the unattainable, and it had eluded her as she had known it would. Something was crying aloud in her palpitating heart, and she could not still it, though she tried vainly not to listen—something fierce, possessive, insistent, that urged her to take such compensation as was within her reach and fling defiance at all the world. What did it matter after all to any but herself what balm she applied for the healing of her wounded soul? Who was to care? Not the man who had just bidden her that cold and formal farewell! Not the children, who could not spare her even a week or two of their holidays, though they seriously believed that their company was the greatest favour that could be conferred upon her—the one joy of her doting heart !

"Fools !" she whispered to herself, as she went up the stairs. "Do they think I will stay locked up in a cage for ever, looking at life through the bars ?"

Yet when she reached her room she was smiling, and Hobbs, failing to perceive the icy sparkle in her eyes, moved to help her with the remark that the evening had evidently been a happy one.

"Well, how clever of you to guess that !" said Marcia. "It has been—quite a unique evening in its way, and, curiously enough, I am not in the least tired."

"You look as if you have found a fortune, my lady," murmured the admiring Hobbs.

And Marcia laughed, raising her arms above her head so that the maid could remove the shimmering gown which she had donned with such care a few hours earlier.

"Or setting out to look for one," she said.

CHAPTER XIII

THE REFUGEE

ONCE more Eric Morven waited for the woman he loved by the side of the fountain in the old courtyard of the Regency. She had begged him to wait for her there, adding that she might possibly be late. He was not in evening dress. That also was in accordance with her desire.

"I want you to take me out in the car," she had said in her note, and he had made arrangements in strict compliance with her wishes.

It seemed an eternity since they had parted. He had tried to shorten it by a visit to Pentreith, where Peter was still pursuing his leisurely and entirely satisfactory existence on the farm ; but he had accomplished little, and it had only seemed to make the time more leadenfooted. There was in fact little to be done there at the moment. They had decided to let Tregassa Castle for a considerable term of years, and when that was at length settled he had half promised to take his young cousin to Canada. But a tenant had not yet been found, and, though Peter was keen enough for the venture, his own inclinations were very strongly against any sudden move. He had given Peter to understand that his plans were held up indefinitely until the business of the estate had been fully attended to and finally disposed of. There yet remained certain formalities regarding the will to be gone through, and he had returned to London and occupied himself with them while that interminable interval of waiting held him like a maze from which he was powerless to extricate himself.

But it was over at last. The appointed hour had come. And he waited for her with a sort of tense patience beside the tinkling fountain.

She was not late after all. Just as the clock was striking eight she came quickly through the vestibule looking for him.

He moved swiftly to meet her ; their hands clasped, and she smiled at him with a murmured, "Eric !"

She was dressed in a thick coat for motoring, with a high collar that partly shielded her face from observation, but he saw that she was very pale.

He kept her hand in his, feeling it throb in his hold. "What is the programme ?" he said.

She glanced around her. "Can we dine somewhere quietly ?" she said. "Not here, I think."

"Certainly we can," he said. "I've got a private room."

"Oh, have you ?" she said, and he caught the relief in her voice. "Let's go there, then !"

He turned, her hand still in his, and led her through a curtained doorway close by which concealed a short flight of stairs. "Up here," he said.

She breathed a deep sigh of thankfulness. "Oh, Eric, how you always understand !" she said.

They reached the top of the stairs and he turned along a passage and opened a door. "In here," he said.

They entered a small sitting-room with a dinner-table in the centre, softly lighted by rose-shaded electric candles. He closed the door behind them and drew her to him.

"My darling," he said under his breath, "you've come !"

She was in his arms, a passive prisoner, but she was trembling as if in an ague.

"My darling !" he said again, and, turning her face to his own, kissed her quivering lips closely, closely, holding her faster and ever faster to his heart.

She submitted, but rather as if all her strength were gone and she had no choice than with a willing surrender. In that supreme moment it was more as master than lover that Eric Morven claimed her for his own.

It came upon him with a curious force even while he drank his fill of the cup he had so ardently desired, and he paused at last, his face still close to hers.

"Am I going too fast for you?" he said. "Forgive me if I am! I didn't mean to be a brute. Marcia! Speak to me!"

He uttered the last words with sudden alarm, for her eyes were closed and her face deathly in its pallor.

At his tone she opened her eyes and faintly smiled at him. "No," she said with an effort, "no, it's all right. But I'm deadly tired, Eric. I had a ghastly night, and such a tearing day. I want rest—oh, so terribly."

"My own love!" he said, and led her to the table. "Sit down! Let me take your coat! I can see you've had—a damnable time. Well, just leave everything to me! I'm going to take care of you now."

He lifted the coat from her and she sank into a chair, leaning her head on her hand. He poured out a glass of wine.

"Drink this, dear! You need it. You're dead beat."

She took it and drank it in silence.

He stood watching her, rigidly restraining himself, realizing that her need was great.

She moved at last, stretched out a trembling hand and laid it on his arm. "Thank you, Eric," she said. "You're always the same—ready to help. Aren't you going to drink something too?"

She spoke with a half-smile. The colour was coming gradually back into her face.

He laid his hand over hers. "I can wait," he said. "You're feeling better now?"

"Yes, much better, thank you. I've had—rather a nightmare day. You know—when one makes a sudden decision—what a lot of things there are to arrange."

"So you have decided!" he said, his voice low and very deep.

She sat motionless, her hand still on his arm, her eyes downcast.

"You have decided, Marcia," he said, reiterating the words slowly and with insistence.

Her look came up to his as if compelled. Her smile was infinitely sad. "I've decided," she said, "to offer you what nobody else wants, because I feel you have—the right of refusal."

He bent towards her. "Did you think I should refuse ?" he said.

Her hand grew tense on his arm, almost as if she held him from her. "No, Eric, no ! But—I want you, please, dear —to be very kind to me. I've done it—but it has taken all my strength to do. All I have is yours, but—please, dear—don't take it all at once !"

"My dear," he said, "I will take nothing except what you offer in your own time and of your own free will. You know I love you, don't you ?"

"Yes, I know," she said, and caught back a sigh. "And by and by—when I've got over all this—you'll know I love you too. But—but——"

"Don't !" he said, as she paused in distress. "I understand. It's been a horrible wrench to break with everything—to give up all your—dreams." He smiled at her tenderly. "Of course I understand, dear. I love you too well not to understand."

"Thank you," she said. "You're always so generous. I only wish"—her voice quivered a little—"I were worthier of you. But I shall try to be."

"Oh, don't talk like that to me !" he said.

"Mustn't I ?" A faint gleam of humour shone in her eyes. "Very well, I won't. But I think I ought just to tell you this : you're not bound to take me because I have come to you. I haven't told anyone of what I have done. I didn't think it was fair to you."

"Marcia !" he said. "Don't you know me better than that ?"

She did not answer him in words, but there was that in his look that moved her inexplicably. With a small sound like a sob she lifted her lips to his, and he took her face between his hands and kissed her.

"Don't ever say anything like that to me again !" he said. "Promise !"

"I promise," she said. "It had to be said—just once but never any more."

He released her. "Let's have some dinner ! And then we'll discuss what we're going to do. We must get out of here to-night, anyhow."

"Oh yes, let's get away !" she said. "I've left a suit-case in the cloak-room at Victoria. I thought we could go round in the car and pick it up. And then—I want you to take me to your ranch in Canada. Eric, will you ?"

"Will I ?" he said.

She laughed like a girl. "There's a boat sailing from Southampton to-morrow at noon. Couldn't we go down to-night and catch it ? Or is that quite impossible ?"

"Nothing's impossible," he said. "We ought to book some berths, that's all."

"Not this time of the year," she said. "Everybody's coming East. I'm sure it'll be all right."

He laughed with her. "It's to be a last-minute affair in every respect, is it ? Well, we'll be down there as soon as the office opens. If they turn us away, I shall have to row you across."

She laughed again. Her eyes were alight. "That would be an adventure ! More exciting than the river, anyhow."

"That's right," he said, watching her. "You're beginning to get young again."

"I always do when I'm with you," she said. "Now do ring the bell for dinner ! I want to get under way."

He complied, for there was an urgency about her that would not be denied. She had mastered her weariness, but in its place was a tension that told of nerves sorely overtaxed. It had not cost her nothing to come to him thus, though at the long hours of irresolution and ever-deepening despair he could only dimly guess. Knowing her as he did, he realized that nothing but despair had goaded her to take this step. She was like a person driven mad by thirst, and the wonder crossed his mind in spite of him as to what might happen when her sanity returned. For was she indeed wholly responsible for this act ? Would she never regret what she had done ? Deep in his soul, below every other conscious thought, lay a knowledge which he would fain have cast out but could not, a deadly certainty that what she had done had been wholly foreign to her whole nature and inclination. She had been forced thereto by bitter circumstance, unable any longer to endure the persistent neglect of the man she loved. That was the whole crux of the situation, and he was too shrewd not to know it. He was only the substitute for that which her soul so urgently needed.

She loved him as a friend indeed, but she would never have come to him as a lover unless driven by a revulsion of feeling which compelled her to seek a refuge from the daily torture which was no longer endurable. Even now—even in her extremity—she shrank from a full surrender, and that in itself was evidence which could not be ignored. It confirmed what he had always dumbly known. He had come into her life too late to save her. He could only give her the second best, and in the giving, the unfulfilled longing, the secret regret, would always be there to taunt him. It was possible that she herself did not wholly realize this yet. But when realization came to her, what then—what then?

He thrust the thought away from him, but he could not cast it out. There was only one thing now to be done, and that was to go blindly forward, shielding her as far as in him lay from all further suffering. At least she should have the very best that it was in him to give, and it might be that in time she would come to see that the substance which now she grasped was of more value than the shadow she had relinquished. But he knew that was a man's reasoning, and with a woman it might not serve. Life was like that ; human nature had no logic. But this was no moment for meditating upon it. If he had not the wherewithal to satisfy her finally, at least he would not offer her the bare husk of the fallen grain. For he loved her—as he had always loved her—with a love that would not count the cost. And though it was not given to him to see the drawn sword barring the way, yet, had he seen it, he would not have turned aside.

CHAPTER XIV

THE DRAWN SWORD

"Yes, you are right," Marcia said. "I am getting younger every minute."

It was a perfect summer night, and they sped along a moonlit road that seemed as if it had been made for them alone.

"We'll stop at the lake—where I brought you that first night," he said. "The water cool and deep that you wanted ! Do you remember ?"

"Of course I remember !" she said. "That was the night you became my holiday pal." She smiled over the words, but rather sadly. "And I made a little plan that night that I never told you of."

"I guessed it all the same," he said.

She made a small gesture of surprise. "Eric, you guess everything!"

"I can't help reading your mind," he said. "Besides, we talked about it, didn't we? Cornwall and the sea. I knew well enough that you were planning to bring the children down again for the summer holidays."

She stifled a sigh. "Ah, well, they planned otherwise. Perhaps it's as well. A thing is so seldom a success twice over."

"Practically never," he said, "where there are more than two people concerned. No, the only way to be happy is to cut out the rest of the world. I found that out long ago."

"It sounds rather selfish," she objected.

"It's the only way," he reiterated doggedly.

On they went through the quiet night. The country around them was all silvered by the moon. The very air seemed to sparkle, and the road before them shone like a strip of metal winding on and on into the misty distance, caught here and there by a tree-shadow so dense that it appeared to cleave it.

"How wonderfully you drive!" Marcia murmured presently.

"Do I? She isn't much of a car," he said. "It's difficult to get any speed out of her."

"But we needn't hurry. We have the whole night before us." She smiled over the words. "After all, it's only seventy miles."

"I don't propose to take the whole night over it," he told her with a certain grimness. "You've got to get in a rest somehow. I am wondering if we had better make a halt at that hotel near the water."

"Oh, don't let us risk missing the boat!" she said.

He laughed. "No, we won't do that. But if we leave it too long, they may not take us in anywhere."

"I am sure we can find some small inn by the wayside further on that will," she protested. "If not—well, it's a lovely night—we can have a sleep under a haystack in the early morning."

"Marcia, you're magnificent!" he said.

They went on through the sleeping world till they came to the lake all a-shimmer in the moonlight, and here once more they descended and walked along the edge. An owl was calling among the trees with a weird and strangely human cry.

"I used to think they were hobgoblins when I was a child," whispered Marcia. "I've often lain and shivered while I listened to them."

There was a wistful note in her voice which made him take

her hand and draw it close. "You're not shivering now," he said.

"Oh no, I'm not afraid of anything to-night," she said. "I've got you to protect me, haven't I ?"

"I will always protect you, Marcia," he said.

Her fingers moved in his. "Thank you," she murmured gently. "That is a great comfort to me."

They walked on together for a space without talking, in a comradeship that seemed to draw them closer at every step. The vast peace of the night seemed by some mystic process to give them to each other more fully than ever before, welding more firmly still the links of that sympathy which had sprung into being in the raging furnace of war a few years earlier. There was to Marcia something sacred in that hour of quiet companionship which she was to remember all her life.

When they returned to the car at length she thanked him again under her breath.

"But what for ?" he said, pausing to look at her with a whimsical lift of the eyebrows.

"For your great goodness to me," she answered earnestly, "which is so very wonderful."

He bent to kiss her hand, which rested on the door. "My dear," he said, "I haven't even begun to be good to you yet."

And then he got into the car, and they sped on again over the shining road into the deep heart of the country.

They spoke so little thereafter that presently a drowsiness began to steal over Marcia and she found herself drifting into a state of semi-consciousness. Once or twice she tried to rouse herself, but it closed in around her like soundless, moonlit billows, and she was obliged to yield to it. Even the rush of the wheels and the rhythm of the engine faded finally into her dream, and it was as if the shabby little car of which Eric had spoken with such disparagement had been endowed with wings and now soared into the shining unknown, bearing them to a new world above the furthest heights of fancy.

It seemed more than a dream, amounting almost to a vision, and while it lasted she was conscious of a strange ecstasy, as if after the long strife and bitter uncertainty a peace which as yet she could hardly grasp were spreading like a dawn above her soul. Though it was still beyond her reach, that winged flight through space gave her the sense of hope growing into the joy of certainty—a joy of which nothing but a crashing fall could deprive her.

The thought was actually in her mind, she was as it were already stretching out to grasp the wondrous gift, when, like the flash of a sword severing her very life asunder, she saw the pathway barred. In that moment, with terrific violence, she came to herself and knew that she was falling. Over and over, down and down, clutching at empty space she went, the moonlight blinding her—repudiating her—the darkness at length receiving her. And in that darkness, like a lost soul, she wandered as it seemed for countless ages. . . .

She was still wandering when the light dawned once more upon her, aimlessly struggling to climb a bare hillside that seemed, like the moonlight, to repudiate her at every turn. She realized dimly at length that she was trying to find her way back to the shining road that led to the stars, and that it was somewhere very far above her.

A little later, pausing from exhaustion, it came to her that something terrible had happened, that that fall from the height had been no dream but a ghastly reality, that some frightful force had somehow broken loose and hurled her into this pit. She looked around her, her dazed faculties slowly recovering, and saw that she was half-way up a steep, grass-covered hollow. Her feet were sliding on the slope, and she sat down to steady herself and take further stock of her surroundings. Her brain was still swimming dizzily, and her heart beat with a strange uncertainty, but gradually some measure of steadiness returned to her and she became capable of coherent thought.

Yes, something terrible had happened. She could not remember what, beyond a vague sense of shock. She had been asleep, and her mind had failed to register more than that. But now she was awake, wide awake, and she knew that it was no dream-abyss into which she had been plunged.

Sitting there on the hillside, she sent her trembling thoughts backwards, recalling as it were inch by inch the circumstances that had led to this. She saw again the gleaming road, cut here and there by deep tree-shadows, heard afresh the whir of the speeding car which in her fancy had taken wings. But now she faced the fact that it was only fancy. The car had been on the road the whole time, until—something—had happened. Suddenly a great shudder caught her. That awful feeling of falling through space, of turning over and over, had not been a dream. That had been actual experience. She clutched instinctively at the earth, on which she sat huddled. It was all wet with dew, but it gave her a species of comfort because of its solidity. She clung to it in desperation, giddy with the effort to think.

It was then that a voice seemed to speak to her—out of the night—out of her quivering soul, she knew not which. "Eric!" it said. "Eric—where is Eric?"

It was a question which, whatever its origin, could not be ignored. She raised herself from the almost prone position to which she had sunk, pressing her hands very tightly to her head.

"Yes—where is Eric?" she said aloud, and looked slowly around her.

Only the dazzling moonlight and dew-drenched grass met her eyes, but her normal powers were returning to her and she compelled herself to face this fearful ordeal unflinching. It was obvious that the road ran along the top of the slope on which she crouched, and the car must have shot over the edge while travelling at high speed. Unless Eric had managed to fling himself out, or had been pitched out as it was evident that she had been, he must have gone to the bottom of the hollow with the car, and must be lying there in the wreckage. Her heart began to thump again in panic-stricken distress, but she summoned all her mental strength to control it. She must be brave in this emergency. Whatever happened later, she must have courage now. There was no one to help her. She must act for herself. It might be that Eric's very life hung at this moment upon her wavering strength.

Desperately she braced herself. The whole world felt empty. The silence was in a way colossal—like eternity. It seemed almost to mock her. And the sky above her was like the dome of a bell—soundless and remote—a boundless prison. Whichever way she looked—above, below, around—she saw no chance of help.

With quivering effort she dragged herself up and gazed down into the deep shadow beneath. She could see nothing with any distinctness. Only, several yards below her, as it were at the bottom of the cup, there seemed to be a few clumps of bushes grouped together.

In any of these might lie that which she sought but dreaded to find: the twisted wreckage of that which had once been a car—the mangled and disfigured remnant of that which had once been a man.

She was on her feet now, but a horrible sense of sickness was upon her, a nausea which for a few moments she was unable to control. She battled with it in a kind of frenzy, and it passed. Then, cold to the very heart, she set herself to the task of descending the slope.

It was not easy, for the grass was wet and slippery, and more than once she nearly lost her footing altogether, but at length after prolonged effort she reached the shadow and trod more even ground. Here for a space she had to pause to rest and accustom her eyes to the dimness. It was like a terrible dream from which the sleeper strives in vain to shake free. Only she knew with a deadly certainty that this was actual experience making its indelible mark upon her life.

Gradually at last the vague objects below her began to take more definite shape. Here was a molehill and there a clump of gorse. And there, a little further on, a dark mass of something which was certainly neither of these.

The feeling of sickness came upon her again. Her heart was throbbing with a violence that seemed as if it must choke her. More by instinct than by sight she knew that she was on the verge of discovering that which she sought. And even as she stood there, halting, irresolute, tortured by doubts and agonizing fears, there came to her faintly out of the shadows the sound of a voice she knew.

CHAPTER XV

THE OPEN WAY

"Marcia! Marcia!" There was gasping entreaty in the voice; it pierced her every nerve. "Where are you? Marcia —for God's sake—speak to me—speak to me!"

She went forward, all her dread faded into the one tremendous thought that he still lived. There was no longer any desitation in her movements or any shrinking in her soul.

"I am here," she said. "I am coming. Where are you?"

She heard no answer, but a sure instinct guided her. In ten seconds she had reached the shapeless bulk beyond the gorse-bushes and was kneeling by his side.

"Eric—Eric!" she said, seeking to lift him.

He was lying in a position which she could but dimly

grasp owing to the wreckage of the car, with which he seemed to be inextricably mingled, but she very quickly realized that it was beyond her strength to help him. He was pinned by a weight from which she was powerless to free him.

"Don't," he whispered, "don't!" as she tried to raise his head and shoulders. "You can't. You'll only hurt yourself. Marcia—tell me—you're all right?"

She caught the desperate anxiety of his voice, weak as it was. "I am quite all right," she said.

And he murmured, "Thank God!" and lay motionless for a space.

She thought he was slipping into unconsciousness, when, with less effort, he spoke again. "I'm all right too, in a sense. That is, I'm not in any pain, though I'm afraid I'm damaged somewhere. You—I suppose you were flung out?"

"I must have been," she said. "I can't remember. I was asleep."

"Yes—yes, you were asleep. I remember now." He spoke with increasing coherence. "I saw you were, just before things went wrong."

"What happened?" she whispered.

"I can't say. It must have been the steering-gear. I couldn't brake in time. The curve was too sharp. You're sure you're not hurt?"

She heard the anxiety rising again in his voice, and hastened to allay it. "Yes, yes. I am quite all right. But—oh, Eric—you!"

"Never mind me!" he said, and she heard the old character-istic grimness in his voice. "I don't matter. I've had hard knocks before."

"You do matter!" she said, and suddenly, inexplicably, found her voice choked by tears. She fought them back with all her strength so that he should not know, and in a few moments was able to continue. "I'm going to get help. Will you be all right—if I leave you—just for a little while?"

His hand came groping out to her. "Oh, Marcia!" he said, and as she grasped and held it she had the feeling of one who seeks to comfort a panic-stricken child. But in a second or two he had himself under control. "Yes—of course—perfectly all right. Only—so awfully sorry you should have the trouble."

She hung over him in the darkness. "My dear!" she said. "Oh, my dear!"

Her voice trembled in spite of her, and instantly his own

N

broke in, rallying her. "That's all right, darling. Don't you worry! We'll win out yet. Now don't hurry! Take it easy! I shall be perfectly content to lie here for the next two hours. If you can climb back to the road, I think there's a lodge at the bottom of the hill. There used to be—that is, if we're where I think we are. But it may be further than that. Don't hurry! Just say to yourself all the way how damned lucky we are to be alive!"

She caught the smile in his tone and wondered how much it cost him. Impulsively she stooped, his hand pressed to her breast, and kissed him on the forehead. It felt cold and damp to her quivering lips.

"Good-bye, Eric darling!" she whispered. "I won't be long. You shan't lie here a single second longer than I can help. I won't fail you. Don't be afraid!"

"My own love!" he answered. "That's the last thing on earth I could ever be afraid of."

She stood up and pulled off her coat. "See, I shan't want this. I shall get on better without it. No, really, Eric"—as he began to protest—"that's the truth. I shall be much happier if you have it for a pillow." She rolled it up and slipped it under his head. "There, dear; now I'm going. And I shall be back very soon—very soon."

"God bless you!" he said faintly.

She turned from him resolutely, feeling as if something were dragging at her heart, and struggling as she went to stifle the wonder if she had left him to die alone.

Back once more into the moonlight and up the slippery slope she forced herself. Her limbs felt leaden, but there was no time to think of that while Eric lay there a prisoner. To obtain help to release him was the only thought in her mind, and she put forth her utmost strength. There were places where the ground rose so steeply and her foothold was so precarious that she had to use her hands as well in that difficult upward progress; but nothing stopped her, nor did she slacken her efforts for a single second. And at last, reaching a more gradual ascent, she straightened herself to see the road just above her, winding away like a metal ribbon into the distance.

It seemed completely deserted. She had certainly not expected to find help near at hand. Scarcely indeed did she look for it. But as she came out upon that shining surface she heard a far-off thrumming that was as yet hardly more than a vibration on the still air, and with a great throb of thankfulness she stood still. There was no mistaking that sound, and it was steadily and swiftly growing. Help was coming. She waited for it, panting.

In a few seconds more she saw the advancing car. It topped a distant rise and appeared on the highway like a spider running down its web. It was moving very fast, and she saw in a flash that she must make a determined effort to check its progress or it would shoot past her. She took a few paces forward into the middle of the road and stood with arms extended.

She was none too soon, though there had seemed to be plenty of time. The driver of the car swerved at the sight of her, checked sharply, and came on at reduced speed.

"Hullo!" he shouted. "Hullo! Anything wrong?"

Marcia's arms fell to her sides. The car stopped close to her. She went up to it.

"There's been an accident," she said. "Can you help me?"

"I can try," came back the gruff response. "What's happened?"

She found herself confronting a man with a red face and the keenest grey eyes she had ever seen. They looked at her searchingly, not without suspicion. An urgent need for support came suddenly upon her. She rested her hands on the door of the car and began to tell him.

"We were in a car and the steering went wrong and we went over the edge. He's down there now, pinned under the car. We shall want men—several men—to free him."

The man in the car continued to gaze at her with an unswerving scrutiny, almost as if he did not believe her. Then, just as she was beginning to lose hope, he broke into speech again.

"Where is he? Down there? Have you tried a jack?"

"I don't even know if we've got one," she said.

"Let me get out!" he said.

She stood back and he opened the door and alighted—a man of enormous bulk and height who towered gigantic in the moonlight to her overwrought imagination.

"You sit down somewhere!" he said, and turned and rummaged in the back of the car.

She sank down on the step, thankful for the moment's respite. She could hear him turning over the tools, and then abruptly he threw something out on to the road.

"That's the thing! Now where is it? Down there? Mean

to say you plunged right down into that hollow and weren't killed?" She heard incredulity in his voice.

"I was flung out," she said.

"And not even hurt?" he questioned.

She stood up. "No, I don't think so. I'll show you the way down. Can I carry anything?"

"No, you look after yourself!" He spoke with a sort of rough sympathy. "But don't go straight down! There's a path a few yards up. I know this part of the world."

His gruff kindliness gave her confidence. She breathed a great sigh of relief. The terrible weight of responsibility pressing upon her had begun to lift. She followed his guidance in silence.

When they reached the bottom of the hollow at length the moon's rays were beginning to penetrate further downwards and the shadows lay less deep. But there was a deathly stillness all around which sent an icy shiver through Marcia.

She saw the shapeless mass of the wrecked car and stood still, literally afraid to go forward. But her companion had no such qualms. He strode on past her. And that gave her courage to follow.

She came again to the spot where she had left Eric. He was lying just as before, with his head on her coat, but no voice greeted her as she stooped over him. He made no movement of any kind.

"Fainted, has he?" said the big man above her.

"I don't know," she said with a sinking heart.

"Well, we'll soon have him out, anyhow. Jolly lucky the thing didn't catch fire." He bent to examine the situation. "Yes, I think I can get a hold for the jack under there. My word! It's a pretty thorough smash-up. Still, we'll manage somehow."

He went to work without further delay, and Marcia, kneeling by Eric's side, watched trembling as he raised the twisted mass inch by inch, dreading every moment to see it slip and crash down again upon the helpless man.

But the rescuer was no fool. He secured his progress with stones wedged scientifically under the lifted bulk, and presently he turned round to Marcia.

"I think I can pull him out now. Let's try!"

She gave place to him dumbly. Eric was unconscious, but his heart was still beating. So much she had ascertained. She clasped her hands tightly over her own while the big man bent to his task.

It was no easy one. Eric was a dead weight in any case, but she saw with quivering thankfulness that the lifting operation had freed him from that crushing weight. Very slowly, with infinite care, the big man dragged him from beneath it. His legs trailed helplessly over the grass as his rescuer laid him down.

"That's all we can do for the moment," he said. "Now I'll go and get help. Will you stay with him ?"

"Of course !" Marcia said. "But—can you get help at this hour ?"

"Yes, I can." He spoke with reassuring confidence. "I'm the landlord of the Castle Hotel at Martinworth. It's not five miles away. I'll go to the cottage-hospital and get the ambulance if possible. But it may take a little while. Shall you be all right ?"

"Oh, quite," she said, "quite. Don't stop to think of me ! Do whatever will bring help the quickest—and—thank you !"

"Better wait till I've done it," said the big man.

He departed. She heard the regular tread of his feet as he made his way up the winding path that ascended to the road, and in a very few minutes she heard the whir of his engine as he started it and then the rush of the car as it sped away.

The sounds faded into the distance. The night was still again. But the moonlight had found them. It was shining upon Eric's face, and as she bent over him she saw that his eyes were open, watching her.

He spoke, and his words had a strange distinctness as if he were making an immense effort to be intelligible.

"Marcia !" he said, and as she bent closer, "Marcia ! I want you—to go."

"To go ?" She repeated the words in some bewilderment. His eyes were fixed upon her, wide and startlingly dark, seeming to beseech her.

"Yes." His voice was husky, but his meaning was unmistakable. "You mustn't stay with me. You must go back. Promise me—promise me you will go back !"

"Eric !" she said in distress. "My dear, I couldn't leave you."

"You must," he said. His speech was gathering clearness. She heard the old dogged quality beginning to assert itself. "Listen, Marcia ! I won't have you throw yourself away on me now. I'm badly damaged. I may die. You've got to go—for my sake. I couldn't endure to—ruin your life—and then go out. No, listen!"—as she began to protest. "It's no good talking—arguing. I know you'd stand by me till the end if I'd let you, but I won't. Understand, Marcia? I won't. You must go."

"My dear!" she said. "I couldn't—possibly—bear to leave you. You mustn't think of it."

"I do," he said. "And I must. It's just everything to me, Marcia. Don't you understand? We can't go on. We must go back. At least you must. You can send for Peter. He'll come to me. But you must go. It's the only way, and—thank God—it's still open." He paused, panting a little. There were great drops on his forehead. She wiped them tenderly away. "You'll do it?" he said, and suddenly she saw an agony in his eyes that was not physical. "You'll do it for me, Marcia?"

"You know I would do anything for you, darling," she said.

"Would you?" he said. "Would you?" His gaze was still upon her, as if it would penetrate to her very soul. "Bless you, I believe you would." He spoke slowly, as if aware of failing strength. "Then you will go back—and never—let anyone—know. Only Peter; but he's loyal—he'll stand by. You'll do that, Marcia? You promise?"

She hesitated momentarily, but there was no resisting the imploring of his eyes. Was it death that looked at her behind their pleading? Was it eternity into which they gazed?

"I'll do my best, dear," she said. 'I promise you that."

"Ah!" It was half-sigh, half-groan that broke from him. His eyes drooped suddenly but jerked open again, gazing widely, seeming to search the sky for her. "You'll keep—your promise," he said. "I—shall know."

And then—it was like the drawing of a veil between them—she realized that he saw her no longer. He continued to stare sightlessly for a space, murmuring incoherently, stubbornly, fighting the slow creeping of unconsciousness, until like a rising flood it spread and overwhelmed him.

To Marcia it was relief unspeakable when at last his eyelids closed.

CHAPTER XVI

THE MESSAGE

LONG afterwards, looking back, it was to Marcia as if a woman quite alien to herself went through the subsequent happenings of that terrific ordeal. Though they were indelibly stamped upon her memory—though she was to carry the marks for the whole of her life—she came to regard the events of that night as in some fashion totally apart from herself. Just as in pleasure there comes at last satiety, so in suffering there is a point of exhaustion beyond which there is no further reaction. What she endured in those final hours seemed to her as unreal as it was inevitable. She went through all like an automaton.

Eric did not move or speak again, and she sat beside him, half-dazed in the moonlight, until help arrived. Then she saw him lifted on to a stretcher and carried to an ambulance on the road, following herself as one follows in a procession, with no sense of direction and scarcely any of movement. It all passed through her consciousness like pictures on a screen, and she saw herself taking part in it while scarcely recognizing that it was indeed herself.

Then came the arrival at the cottage-hospital at Martinworth. They had put her into the ambulance with Eric and one of the stretcher-bearers, and as she descended she saw the first flush of the summer dawning behind the hills that sheltered the old grey town.

Then had succeeded a period of waiting, and she had been alone save for the uneasy coming and going of Dan Bellamy— she supposed he must have told her that was his name, though she had no recollection of his having done so—the big landlord of the Castle Hotel. He was very good to her in a gruff, unobtrusive way, and it was he who eventually came and told her that everything that was possible had been done for the patient, who was still unconscious, and that for the moment they could do no more. Undoubtedly there was some spinal injury, but they could not as yet say how serious. He asked for Eric's name, and she gave it, and then remembered her promise regarding Peter. He undertook to transmit a message to Peter, regarding her thoughtfully the while. She found comfort in the look of his large red face, even though the eyes still held a certain suspicion.

"What are you going to do?" he asked her bluntly at length. "Can I put you up at the Castle Hotel?"

She hesitated, then almost before she knew it she was telling him the truth. "He says I'm not to stay. I've promised to go back to town."

Normally she could never have uttered those words. It seemed exactly as if another woman had spoken them. But it was the understanding in the man's face that had called them forth.

And he had responded instantly, as if he were too sorry for her to enquire too closely. "All right. I'm going up myself. I'll take you."

And he had taken her. In retrospection that was always to her the extraordinary part, that he had offered and she had accepted almost as a matter of course.

Through the exquisite crystal and gold of the early morning they had travelled back along the road which she had travelled by moonlight, leaving the tragedy of the night further and further behind. She had but a dim impression of the dew-steeped country through which they passed. Her brain had almost ceased to register ordinary things. She was as one walking a tight-rope over a deep abyss who might at any moment fall over into nothingness.

They had reached London at length, crossing the river all shimmering in the early rays of the sun. The market-vans were lumbering in, and her companion threaded his way among them with a dexterity that seemed to her rather surprising in a man of his bulk.

He spoke at last, breaking a silence that had lasted practically throughout the journey, to ask for directions.

She gave them almost mechanically, and he proceeded to follow them, but checked again a little later to say, "I'd better not take you right up to the door, had I? You'll have to explain that the car you were out in broke down."

She looked at him then with vague astonishment filtering through the numbness of her brain. "You seem to think of everything," she said. "I don't know why."

He explained briefly. "I couldn't place you at first—or Major Morven either; but I was sure I knew you. I was one of the R.A.M.C. orderlies at Fontenelle when they fired the hospital. I helped carry you both out. You were the night-sister, weren't you?"

She was staring at him with a growing wonder. "Yes, I was the night-sister," she said. "I don't remember you."

"Well, of course—you wouldn't," he said with simplicity. "It's a long while ago, isn't it ? Look here ! I'll give you my address. Then you can ring me up for news." He drew up pulled a note-case from his pocket, and extracted a card. "Just ask for Bellamy !" he said, giving it to her. "I'll tell you everything. And I'll send that message as soon as I get back. That's Mountgrave Square down there, isn't it ? Had I better leave you here ? Can you walk as far ?"

She saw the trees of the Square at the end of the road. "Yes," she said, "yes, I can manage." And then, collecting herself with a great effort : "But what do I owe you for all this ? You've done—so much."

"I don't want anything," said Dan Bellamy almost aggressively. "I'll always stand by any of the old crowd. It's one of my mottoes. Those were good days, those were. Good-bye—sister !"

She gave him her hand, and found it enveloped in his enormous clasp while she tried to utter a few confused words of thanks.

"Don't !" he said. "It spoils things. We never bothered about that in the old days. I'll help you any time I can. Good-bye !"

And then she was on the pavement and walking up the quiet road towards those trees that waved in the morning sunlight.

.   .   .   .   .

She was home again. That was the next thing she knew. She found the door unbolted, and she opened it with her latchkey and walked in. There was no stealth whatever in her movements. It did not seem to matter whether she met anyone or not. Straight in, closing the door behind her, and straight up the stairs she went.

No one met her. No one seemed to be stirring. But as she reached her bedroom door she heard a sound. The door was ajar, and Hobbs started up from a chair as she entered, as near to dishevelment as it was possible for a person of her prim niceness to be.

"Oh," she gasped, "your ladyship is back at last ! Thank God for that !"

Marcia paused, faintly disconcerted by this fervent reception ; then, Dan Bellamy's words recurring to her, she made quiet use of them. It was no effort to her. It seemed to be the other woman who spoke, quite calmly and collectedly.

"Have you been sitting up for me?" she said. "I'm sorry. I have been out motoring and the car broke down. It was some little time before we could get help."

She stopped, looking at Hobbs questioningly, for to her surprise she saw that the woman was in tears.

"Oh, madam—oh, my lady, I don't know how to tell you," she sobbed. "I've been sitting up all night—and that anxious. The message came—after Sir Everard left. We didn't know—what to do."

"Why, what is the matter?" said Marcia, and as she spoke the words her own self stepped forward, as it were, and took possession. "What has happened? What message?"

Hobbs, unnerved by prolonged strain, was weeping unrestrainedly. "I don't know how to tell you," she reiterated between her sobs. "I said we'd ring up—the moment you came in—but it may be—may be—too late by now."

A sudden light broke upon Marcia. She took a step forward and grasped the maid's quivering shoulder.

"Hobbs—for heaven's sake"—she spoke through white lips—"tell me—what is it? One of the children?"

Hobbs made an agonized gesture and choked forth an answer. "Yes, madam, yes! It's Master Dennis. An urgent operation; they wanted—your consent. Appendicitis—very bad—very critical, they said. And—Sir Everard was gone—and Lady Barrowdale's at Goodwood—and there wasn't anybody. And you—I thought you'd been killed too! It's been dreadful waiting here!" She broke into a further paroxysm of sobbing.

Marcia stood for a moment perfectly stiff and motionless, conscious of no feeling but a terrible coldness. It was as though she had been turned into a block of ice.

Then, with a curious movement that was almost like the violent flinging off of some shackling force, she turned to the telephone beside her bed, mechanically throwing aside her hat as she did so.

"Please be quiet, Hobbs, or go outside!" she said. "I want to hear clearly."

Hobbs checked her tears with a gasp as though a shower of water had been thrown over her.

And with absolute steadiness Marcia sat down and picked up the telephone.

CHAPTER XVII

THE VISION

IT was raining at Graybourne. The slow drip, drip of the eaves had a ceaseless monotony that made a dull background to the cawing of the rooks in the ancient elm-trees that bordered the playing-fields. Beyond the trees flowed the misty grey river along the banks of which Marcia and Dennis had walked together a few weeks before, when he with his young ardour had poured out all his eager plans for the holidays, and she with an ache at her heart had listened and acquiesced. How long ago it seemed! How strange the space between!

And now, all alone in the matron's room, she waited to hear whether her boy was to live or die. Somehow, looking out upon those age-old trees, it was hard to realize that human life was any more than the merest incident, so transient, so unimportant, so vain. The world went on perpetually, but life—human life—was no more than a flickering flame upon its surface, coming and going, waxing and waning—a fleeting spark, bound to be quenched at last. Her own life, viewed in perspective, seemed a mass of futility. There had once been a time when the fact that she had brought two splendid children into the world had been a matter of pride to her. Where was her pride now? Life—human life—was so small a thing, pathetic in its aspirations, almost contemptible in its achievements. And always Death standing by to cut off those who overcame all other obstacles! There could be no lasting victory anywhere, she reflected drearily, with Death so close at hand. There was no bargaining with Death.

Back over the past hours went her thoughts. Till now there had been no time to think. She had been like a driven animal, afraid to stop, afraid to go forward, compelled by the goad of relentless circumstance. But now the power to think had returned to her. Now while she waited for the verdict upon her son, her mind went back with a heavy fatefulness to the lover who had also been stricken as it were by an unseen Hand. It came upon her like a sudden blinding flash of illumination that but for that shattering blow she would by now have been out of reach, and Dennis might have died with neither father nor mother within call. She shivered as the knowledge went through her. It was like a sword piercing her. Even now the delay might cost him his life.

And what of that other life ? What of Eric—the man who loved her—lying helpless and alone in that far-off cottage-hospital ? Was his life also to be forfeit, and all because of her ? She clasped her hands together with a gesture of entreaty, but no word of supplication passed her lips. She was as one cast out into the desert where there was none to hear, as one against whom sentence had been pronounced. And was that to be her doom—to remain unscathed while all around her were stricken down ?

Heavily the time rolled on, punctuated by that forlorn dripping which was like the fitful ticking of a phantom clock, like the gradual but inevitable approach of Fate. There was no escape. The curse had been laid upon her. She was as one branded and turned adrift in the wilderness, condemned to walk for ever in waste places. Her life was in ruins, and it seemed to her in that hour that nothing could ever build it up again. Dennis was dying—Eric was dying. Of her husband she did not dare to think.

A sudden sound came to her, drifting through the mist and the rain, and she gave a start of horror. The tolling of a bell ? No, surely it was only the school clock striking the hour of noon ! Her clasped hands parted and went up to her face as, quivering, she counted the slow notes. Twelve o'clock ! And somewhere in the direction of the quadrangle a door opened and there came a rush of feet and boyish voices through the stillness. Instinctively she turned inwards. She could not endure the thought of curious young eyes upon her in her misery.

Very soon now the door would open and the kind-faced matron would enter. She had promised to come and tell her the moment it was over, and till she came there was nothing to be done but wait. She began to walk up and down, aimlessly but persistently, like an animal prowling its cage—or, perhaps more accurately, like a condemned prisoner awaiting execution and chafing at the delay.

Anything to get it over, was the scarcely conscious thought in her mind. Dennis first—and then Eric ! From death-bed to death-bed ! And when it was all finished—the empty desert and the outer darkness for herself !

Vaguely the stir and life of the school reached her physical senses, but they did not pierce within to the place where her soul crouched waiting for the voice of doom. Pacing to and fro, to and fro in torment, with all her buoyancy gone and hope in ashes, she faced only the stark reality of her punishment. She had sinned, and she must pay the penalty. She only asked that the payment might be swift.

The drip, drip of the eaves was lessening, and a pale light had begun to show above the elms. It was very pale, remote as the shining of a far-off star, but it had potentiality. It spread, very slowly, wedge-shaped, across the grey sky. The cawing of the rooks had almost sunk into silence, but now it was renewed to a positive babel that seemed to vie for the supremacy with the gay shoutings of the youngsters scampering in the wet grass below.

Nor sight nor sound reached Marcia in her agony, but something—some inner unseen power—touched her. It was as if an angel had entered her prison and bidden her turn and look. She turned trembling, hardly knowing what she did.

And there before her, spread to her gaze—wide, all-encompassing, amazing—she saw that which she was to carry with her as a precious memory through the whole of her life—a great arch, many coloured, vivid with the splendour of a Divine promise, overhanging the earth as though it had been the gateway to heaven. . . .

The door opened and someone came in, came quietly to her and paused. For Marcia's face was as the face of one who sees a vision and who cannot turn away.

After a few moments the matron spoke. She was a small thin woman with the steadfast eyes that only a loyal soul ever looks out of. They also rested upon the glory while she uttered her message.

"He has come through the operation, Lady Templeton. Would you care to come and see him for a few minutes?"

Marcia turned at last very slowly, with a strange long sigh. It was as if she called her spirit back from heights undreamed of and saw once more the prison walls around her. But there was no tremor about her now, no sign of fear—only a great peace beyond understanding.

She did not attempt to ask the question which so short a time before would have quivered on her pale lips.

"Yes, let me see him!" she said quietly; and so passed, unfaltering, from the room.

The first face that Dennis saw when he recovered consciousness was his mother's, and the first words he succeeded in uttering were addressed to her. "Oh, Mum!" he whispered. "Mummy darling, how I've wanted you! Don't—don't go away!" And tearfully he laid his cheek upon her hand.

PART III

CHAPTER I

THE KEY

IT was not till Marcia returned from her ten weeks' sojourn on the East Coast with Dennis that her husband marked the change in her. He had paid them two flying visits to assure himself that all was well, and to his unobservant eyes there had been nothing unusual, nothing whatever to cause him any uneasiness, in what they saw. The boy was well on the road to recovery, and it was natural that his mother should have been completely absorbed in the care of him. She had always—except during those hectic years of the War, when no one had regarded life from a completely normal standpoint—taken her maternal duties seriously, and he was content that she should be so absorbed.

But when the holidays were over, the children back at school, and all anxiety at an end, he saw the change.

It came upon him rather suddenly one evening in October when unexpectedly he wanted to speak to her and found a locked door between his room and hers. Surprised, he went out into the passage and applied for admittance there. Her voice at once gave him permission to enter, and he did so, to find her lying quite idle on a sofa near the window. The daylight had almost gone, but there was no illumination in the room. Only a lamp-post on the road outside gleamed with a shifting glow through rustling leaves.

He paused on the threshold, sensing something within with which he was unfamiliar. "What, Marcia! All alone in the dark?"

"Yes." Rather wearily her voice answered him. "All alone in the dark! But switch on the light if you like!"

He did so, and advanced, looking at her questioningly. "Is anything the matter, my dear? Aren't you well?"

Her eyes, shadowy and inscrutable in her pale face, smiled at him. "Yes, I am quite well. Just resting, that's all."

Her quiet words did not hold dismissal, yet he paused again

as if arrested by something. "Am I disturbing you?" he said.

The warm denial which once she would have uttered did not come in answer. "You have got in early," was all she said.

He came to a chair near her and sat down. "Yes. I thought you might be interested to know that Lord Bevis has finally decided to retire at the end of the year."

"Oh, I see." Marcia still spoke with a certain weariness. "And the vacant judgeship——"

He stroked his chin, faintly smiling. "Well, my dear, if it s offered to me, I shall be the youngest judge."

Marcia lay silent. A wind was stirring the trees of the Square outside with an indescribably desolate sound, but no draught seemed to reach the room. The stillness within was almost like that of a death-chamber by contrast.

Sir Everard sat for several moments absorbed in contemplation of the news which he had just imparted, then at length slowly his first impression began to reassert itself. He looked at his wife with renewed attention.

"You're not looking very well, my dear," he said. "I am afraid you didn't get much of a holiday after all this summer."

"I am taking one now," she said quietly.

"You are going away again?" he questioned.

"Perhaps I may," she said; adding after a short pause: "It wouldn't matter if I did, would it?"

"I think it would be a very good idea," he said. "But it is getting rather late in the year, isn't it? Where would you go?"

She did not reply, and a shade of uneasiness crossed his face as he watched her.

"I am afraid I couldn't possibly come with you now," he said. "I am leaving for Cardiff to-morrow—this Bonsor case."

Marcia smiled again faintly, enigmatically. "Oh no! I shouldn't ask you to come, Everard. I would rather go away quite by myself. It would be—more of a rest."

The uneasiness still lingered on Sir Everard's face. "I would come if I could," he said.

"Thank you," said Marcia.

Again she dropped into silence, her own eyes downcast as though unaware of his upon her. There was something rather statuesque about her stillness; it expressed apathy.

He leaned forward at last to survey her more closely. "I wonder," he said, "if you had better see a doctor."

Her eyes came up to his on the instant, and he had a curious, disconcerted feeling that was almost like an electric shock. For, dark and remote as they were, they held a gleam that was strangely vital.

It seemed to vibrate in her voice also as she answered him. "No, I don't think that is necessary. There is nothing the matter with me. But I think a rest-cure might possibly do me good. Thank you for suggesting it."

"Where will you go ?" he said.

She hesitated a moment, then once more very quietly : "I don't think I will tell you—or anybody—that," she said. "I have often thought a week—or even a fortnight—out of every year spent in complete retirement and obscurity would be a very excellent thing for all Society women. If you don't mind—that is the sort of holiday I propose to take."

It was a suggestion which a few years before would have astounded him, but the War had instituted a change of outlook which it was impossible to ignore. She had gone her own way during those four years, and he had permitted it. There had been occasions then when he had not known with any certainty where she was. He had even become accustomed to uncertainty. That she should propose thus to efface herself from his life again for a set period did not surprise him as once it would have done. It did not meet with his genuine approval, but he recognized that he had no actual grounds for displeasure.

It took him a full minute to arrive at this decision, but when he had done so it was final.

"I am willing," he said, "to agree to anything that is for your good. But I should certainly prefer not to be left more than a week without news of you."

"Very well," she said in the same quiet voice. "A week. One week in every year. You will agree to that ?"

He stiffened a little. It was almost as if she were driving a bargain with him. "I think provision for one year at a time is enough," he said, and passed on deliberately with the air of putting an end to the subject. "And now for another matter ! Did you know that that door was locked ?"

He indicated the door that communicated with his own room.

It was behind Marcia's couch, but she did not turn her head. "Yes, I knew," she said. "Why ?"

"That is what I want to ask you," he said somewhat ponderously. "Why?"

Dead silence followed his words, and again the rustling of the trees outside became very audible, like the warning of an approaching storm. Sir Everard got up. There was something in the room he could not grasp, something hostile that quickened his blood as if in answer to a definite challenge.

"Tell me why!" he said with authority.

She remained absolutely passive, save for her eyes. They were alight, burning, somehow dreadful. She broke her silence, and again he heard that strange vibrant quality in her voice.

"I didn't think—that you ever used it," she said.

Again he stiffened like a man in expectation of a blow. "That is no reason," he said. "Please unlock it again!"

"I am afraid," she said slowly, "I have lost the key."

His hands clenched. He was suddenly angry, over-whelmingly angry, perhaps more so than he had ever been in the whole of his well-ordered life. His anger astounded himself, but there was no resisting it. It swept him like a flame.

Standing over her, he spoke in tones half-strangled. "Then you will find it," he said. "Do you hear me? You will find it—to-night!"

"Everard!" she said in utter astonishment. It was almost like a cry. He had never been angry with her before.

He stood looking down at her, and he saw that she was deathly pale. With an enormous effort he controlled himself, but he spoke with indomitable determination. "I mean what I have said," he told her grimly. "I always do. That door will be unlocked to-night. You understand?"

"Very well," she said faintly.

He stood a moment longer, looking upon her with a deep intensity, then without another word he turned squarely, compelling himself, and left her. The only sound that remained in the room was the unhappy rustling of the trees with their burden of doomed and shrivelling leaves in a wind that seemed the harbinger of storm.

CHAPTER II

THE VISITOR

"HE is onging to see you," said Peter.

He took the suit-case from her hand and surveyed the slim tall figure he had come to meet with a species of wonder mingling with the old boyish respect.

"Is he, Peter?" she said.

He nodded, turning beside her towards the station-barrier. "He's had a ghastly time—a rotten time. There's the hotel bus waiting. Do you mind?"

"Oh, let them take my suit-case and we can walk," she said. "It isn't far, is it?"

"No, not far," said Peter. "We'll cut through the churchyard and across the fields."

"Tell me everything!" she said, as they walked away together.

But Peter, never very ready of tongue, seemed to have some difficulty in complying. He tramped beside her with a worried look.

They left the station-yard and walked along a stretch of road that ran by a sawmill. The clatter and shrieking of the machinery filled the silence. Then they came to a narrow passage between stone walls, and up this Peter turned. The October sunshine gleamed golden upon beech-trees at the end, and under their feet was a litter of leaves.

The noises of the timber-yard dropped behind them, and they came to a white gate that led into the old churchyard. They passed through it, and then, as if by mutual consent, under the shadow of the thinning beech-trees they paused.

"Now—tell me!" said Marcia.

He looked at her with his straight boyish regard. "Well," he said, "you've got to know it—even if he hasn't told you. It's hopeless."

Her eyes were on the drifting beech-leaves. "You mean he is—dying?" she said.

He made a rather desperate gesture. "One man gave him a few months. The last said it might run into years. But anyhow—it's hopeless."

"He is—quite crippled?" she questioned.

He ground his heel into the path. "From the waist

downwards. It's—it's damnable. You wouldn't—ask a dog—to endure it."

The sudden passion of speech and action moved Marcia. She put a light hand on his arm. "We must try to make it bearable between us, Peter," she said.

He grasped the hand unexpectedly. "I'm so fond of the old chap," he blurted forth, and turned his face aside.

She saw his chin quivering. "Let's walk on!" she said.

They moved forward between the grave-stones, and Peter found his voice again. "It was awfully good of you to come down. I hope Dennis is all right again?"

"Oh yes, he is back at school now," she said. "He was terribly ill for a week, but it's all over now."

"And you?" he said. "You're awfully thin, aren't you?"

"I am quite all right," she said, smiling a little in anticipation of his next question.

It came rather self-consciously. "And Goldie? She's all right too, I suppose?"

"Yes, quite," said Marcia.

They were passing the old grey church now, and Peter seemed to be deep in thought. He spoke at length very abruptly.

"I'm rather keen on Goldie. I hope you don't mind."

"My dear boy, why should I?" said Marcia.

His face was a hot crimson. "I daresay it'll never come to anything, but I thought I'd like you to know. I'm going to Canada directly—as soon as Eric is fixed up with someone decent to look after him. That landlord chap—Dan Bellamy— is a good sort. He'll keep an eye on him too. And you—you will?"

"Of course I will!" Marcia said warmly.

"Thanks! You see"—the boy spoke with more confidence —"I may be away for some time. There's a lot to see to out there. Tregassa Castle is let for ten years, so that's off our hands. All things considered, I'm glad."

"And you're going to take charge of the ranch?" said Marcia.

"Well, it's the least I can do for him, isn't it?" said Peter. "If he hadn't come over here after my beastly affairs, this would never have happened."

"Oh, Peter!" she said gently and very sadly. "Don't let us talk of—that sort of responsibility!"

"No; all right," said Peter quickly. "I'm sorry."

She wondered how much he knew, but it was impossible

to ask him. There was about him a delicacy, a quiet chivalry, that held her back. She turned instead to that which she more earnestly desired to know. "Tell me how he bears it !" she said.

"He is wonderful," said Peter simply. "I've never seen him give way—never once. He says he won't waste any more money over specialists, for it's evidently beyond them. The local doctor—just an ordinary country practitioner—has a theory of his own and sticks to it, that if he lives, as the other fellows declare he won't, it may eventually, quite suddenly, right itself. Some shock to the nervous system or even some violent wrench—if it were the right sort of wrench and didn't sever the spinal cord—might do it. But they're all in the dark. Even the X-ray doesn't seem to help. It's damnably hard"—he glanced at her half-apologetically—"when one would give one's right hand to help."

"One would," said Marcia. "But—Peter—I sometimes think—that that sort of case belongs to God alone. He makes His prisoners—and He releases them—as He sees fit."

"You always find something decent to say," said Peter.

They had reached a gate at the other end of the churchyard which led into fields. Below them lay the town, nestled in its hollow with the river winding through and the towers of its ruined castle rising beyond.

"What a sweet, peaceful place !" said Marcia, as she passed through.

"Yes, he likes it," said Peter. "It's off the beaten track and away from the week-end racket. I believe he'll stay here —anyhow, for the present."

"I hope he will," she said.

They went on down the slope, talking little, both occupied with thoughts of the man who was awaiting them at the Castle Hotel.

"He's got a decent room on the ground floor," said Peter presently. "He sits up for a bit in a chair already. We're hoping he may manage to wheel himself about in the garden by and bye—in the spring, perhaps."

"But he's got to get through the winter first," said Marcia.

They descended into the valley, crossed the narrow, winding river, followed it for a little way along the bank until they came to a mill ; and then, turning away from the running water, they reached a wooden door which led into a garden which Peter opened.

"This is the shortest way to the hotel," he said.

Marcia passed in. The place was full of autumn flowers and warmly enclosed with walls of mellow brick. They went through a kitchen-garden to a wide stretch of lawn shadowed by an ancient yew-tree.

"He'll be sitting in his window," said Peter. "It looks out this way."

Marcia stopped suddenly in the shelter of the yew-tree. "Peter !" she said.

Peter stopped also, looking at her questioningly, for there was something in the sound of his name that seemed to plead.

She made an effort to smile at him, but her voice was low and agitated as she answered his look. "I wonder if you would go on and tell him I'm here. I will follow—in a few minutes."

"Yes—of course," said Peter, but lingered for a moment as if in doubt. "He's expecting you, you know. And—he isn't changed."

"No—no !" She spoke almost feverishly. "Still—if you don't mind—I would rather."

"Just as you like," said Peter.

He turned away with the words, and Marcia wheeled blindly, as if she would flee from the place, and stumbled back through the sunlit walled garden till she stood once more upon the path that skirted the mill-stream.

Here for a space she stopped, striving for self-control. He was the same—he had not changed. But she—it was as if æons had passed over her. The whole aspect of the world had become different since that terrible night when last she had seen him. The madness had passed long since, burnt out as it were by the searing flame of suffering, and she felt an unutterable reluctance to renew a relationship which Fate and time had so completely severed. It could not be renewed, and yet—neither could she forsake him. Something was due from her who had brought him to this plight. He had not changed —he had not changed ; and deep in her secret heart she knew that the words were true in every sense. He would not change, simply because he did not possess a changing nature. And because of that, she stood here. Because of that, she could not throw back all that she had accepted from this man. The obligation was too heavy to be ignored. She was bound— almost morally bound—to give what in her lay. To count the cost now—when he had given so much—was contemptible. And yet her shrinking from the task before her was for the moment wellnigh uncontrollable. Fiercely despising herself she yet felt like a scared child seeking wildly for some means of escape from a terrifying ordeal. It was as if the rushing waters into which she gazed were pouring over her soul.

But in a few minutes, gradually, some measure of composure returned to her. The agony of indecision passed, and a deep sense of shame succeeded it. What was she doing here when the man whose life she had ruined was waiting for her so short a distance away, longing for the first glimpse of her ? What right had she, who had emerged scathless, to keep him waiting ? Had she not come to make—if possible—some sort of restitution ? What was she doing here ?

Resolutely she turned from the racing water. The garden-door had swung to, and she did not reopen it. She would go by the public path which ran beyond some white posts by the side of the stone wall.

She did not hesitate again, but pressed steadily forward, until, passing between some more white posts, she emerged upon the open space in front of the hotel. Then, past a row of green tubs filled with ivy-leafed geraniums, she entered at the main door.

The first person she encountered was Dan Bellamy. He came forward to meet her, and, with an instinctive movement, she gave him her hand.

He took it into his big square clasp, and she saw a smile of welcome in his direct eyes which helped her wonderfully.

"So you've come at last !" he said. "I'm very glad to see you again, sister."

His mode of address and the friendly grasp of his hand helped her still further. "How nice of you !" she said.

He turned and led her along a passage at the end of which she saw the autumn sunshine gleaming through a conservatory. He stopped at a closed door half-way down.

"He's in here. You've heard everything ?" His grey eyes interrogated her.

"Oh yes," she said. "His cousin met me. He went on—to tell him I was coming."

Dan still paused, facing her. "Look here, sister !" he said abruptly. "This isn't a hopeless job. They can say what they like. It isn't. But—I'm bound to say it—there's a lot depends on you."

She knew his meaning, and something within her shrank, though she gave no outward sign. She waited in silence.

"I'm doing my bit," he said, "and I know you'll do yours. We were all comrades together a few years ago. It's up to us to stand by each other now. At least, that's my way of thinking."

He spoke with a curious mixture of pride and appeal. It touched her in a fashion she could not have explained. "It's my way too," she said gently.

He stared at her for a second, then with a deferential gesture he turned, knocked upon the door and opened it. "She's come, sir," he said. "Go in, sister!"

She went into a flood of sunlight, and the door closed behind her. She had a momentary impression of Peter at the open window, but he vanished instantly into the garden. And then—though still half-dazzled—her eyes came to Eric.

CHAPTER III

THE PRISONER

His face was turned towards her, and it was his face that she first saw—dark, not greatly altered, save for the eyes ; and they were alight, fevered—the eyes of a famished man. Among all the many forms of suffering which she had seen, she had never looked upon starvation. But she looked upon it then.

He was lying in a great chair, propped by pillows, the lower part of him covered by a rug. An invalid-table stood beside him, and on it were books and papers and cigarettes. The room was a large one, evidently a converted sitting-room, with French windows that opened directly upon the lawn and its spreading yew-tree. A more cheerful apartment could scarcely have been found, yet there was that in the atmosphere which smote upon Marcia with a strange chill.

His voice, bridging the space between them, put it into words. "So you've come," he said, "to see me in prison !"

She went forward swiftly, for the bleak desolation of that sentence sent such a flood of pity through her that she could not have held back.

She reached him, bent over him. "Oh, my dear !" she said.

His hand came up to her and held hers. He did not speak again ; she saw that his lips were trembling.

"My dear !" she said again. "Oh, my dear !" And, stooping lower, she kissed him.

His other hand clasped her—clung to her ; and something in her that was deeply maternal moved her to take his head upon her breast.

"How terrible for you !" she whispered. "Eric—darling !"

He leaned against her in silence for a few seconds, during which she felt that he was nerving himself to fight down his emotions. Then at length very gently he withdrew himself from her close embrace.

"It's an absolute joy to see you again," he said in a voice that shook but very slightly. "I can't tell you what it means to me. And you are just the same, Marcia ! Not a whit the worse ?"

"I am—perfectly all right," she assured him tremulously. "You didn't mind my coming—at last ? I—couldn't have kept away."

"Thank you, dear," he said simply, and pointed to a chair close to him. "Come and sit by me and we'll talk." Then, as she complied : "I don't think you are quite the same, are you ? You look tired and very thin."

"I told you about—Dennis," she said.

"Yes, of course—yes ! You've had a rotten time." He spoke gently and rather slowly, as if to gain time.

She looked at him, piteously smiling. "And what of you ? Eric, I've never had—one easy moment—since that night."

He smiled also, but with a hint of restraint. "My dear, I'm used to hard knocks. You shouldn't have worried."

She was recovering herself, but rather in response to his evident desire than of her own volition. "I've thought of you," she said, "continually—sleeping and waking. To have left you like that—I don't know how I did it !"

"It was my wish," he said quietly. "It was—inevitable. How is Dennis ?"

He was pushing the cigarette-box towards her along the table. To please him she took one, though her hands were trembling almost too much to light it.

"He is much better," she said, "practically well, in fact. He is back at school now."

"And you are free ?" he said.

She did not wholly understand his tone, but again she seemed to feel a chill in the room. She held the cigarette-box towards him, but she could not meet his eyes.

"I would have come sooner if I could," she said.

"My dear," he made quiet answer, "I think only an angel from heaven would have come at all."

"Oh, don't, Eric !" she protested. "It—hurts !"

"It shouldn't," he said. "I have never—voluntarily—hurt you in my life. I never will."

He took a cigarette and struck a match for them both. She bent forward and kindled hers at it, but her eyes remained downcast. Her agitation was passing, but the coldness remained. It was as if a great gulf had opened between them, widening slowly but surely, which she was powerless to bridge.

He went on deliberately speaking, as though unaware of it. Or was he merely marking time till she should see and understand ?

"It was very sweet of you to come—the sort of thing you would do. I needn't begin to tell you what it means to me. But—I'd like to be sure of one thing : is it quite safe ? You are running no risks ?"

"None," she said. "None whatever."

"Because you never must do that," he continued. "If it meant that"—he paused, then ended very decidedly : "well, I simply wouldn't consent to it, that's all."

"It doesn't mean that," she said. "I arranged to take a quiet week on my own, and nobody knows where I am."

"Nobody ?" He echoed the word sharply, as if he desired to enquire more closely but could not bring himself to do so.

"Nobody, Eric," she repeated firmly. "I go my own way, you know, to a very great extent. And, after all, it is not so very unusual to take a rest-cure in these days."

He nodded, looking across at her, the famished gleam still in his eyes. "And so—you've come to me—for a whole week ?" he said.

Again she tried to smile. "Will it be too long for you ?"

He drew a hard breath and choked over his cigarette ; then, with an effort, "So long as it is—perfectly safe for you," he said. "There must be—no possibility of being found out. I don't know—if I ought to let you."

He coughed again with his hand over his face, and she knew instinctively that he was trying to hide something from her, trying to hide the depth of longing in his soul.

It moved her almost more than anything that had gone before. She leaned to him and laid her hand upon his arm. "You make me feel so worthless," she said, "so contemptible. Eric, I couldn't have borne to stay away. Don't you understand ? I simply had to come."

He took her hand and held it without looking at her.

"That's—so like you," he said.   "But—everything is different now.   You've heard about me—a log for the rest of my life !   I've nothing left to offer you."

A curious tremor of passion went through Marcia.   It quivered in her voice as she made reply.   "Eric, don't ever say that to me again !   Don't you realize that it was just because you needed me that I came to you ?   Is your need of me any less than it was ?"

He uttered a groan.   "God knows it isn't !" he said.   "But —you !   I'm thinking of you."

"Then stop !" she commanded.   "Let us think of you instead !   It's my turn to offer now and yours to accept. Listen, Eric !   Everything may be different, as you say ; but not—dear, not our friendship.   That at least is not going under like everything else.   I refuse to contemplate such a thing.   Sooner than that, I will give our secret away and come to you openly."

"Marcia !"   He was gazing at her now in utter amazement, and she met his gaze fierily, with a dominance he had never seen in her before.

"I mean it," she said.   "In some ways it would be a relief—a luxury—to tell the truth.   But that's not why I say it.   I say it because I too value our friendship, and—the only reason that would induce me to give it up would be because you thought—as you very well might—that it had cost you too much—had brought you—bad luck."

A sudden rush of tears came upon her with the words— tears of shame, tears of remorse—and she bowed her face upon his hand and wept.   Only a few minutes before she had dreaded the meeting beyond all words, had actually longed to avoid it.   And now—the bare sight of him lying there, broken but full of courage, moved her thus to the depths. She could remember only that he had given her all he had, had wrecked his whole life in the giving, and that now he scrupled to take the very little she had to offer in return.

His voice, very low, but deeply urgent, came to her through her weeping :   "Marcia — darling — don't — don't !   You couldn't bring anything but blessing to any man.   Please, dear, you've got to believe that.   Whatever there is left— it's all yours.   I'm not giving you anything.   It belonged to you before—for all the years I've known you.   It's only— only—I can't take a sacrifice from you.   Don't you see ? Don't you understand ?"

His hand was gently drawing her.   She went to him in her

distress, but as to a trusted friend and not as to a lover.
She slipped down upon her knees beside him, her face
hidden against his shoulder, while he tenderly soothed and
comforted her.

"You're worn out," he said. "I saw it the moment you
came in. Don't cry, darling! It doesn't help. We can't
alter things. Perhaps—for your sake—it's as well we can't.
No?"—whimsically, at a sound of dissent from her. "Well,
I'm not so sure. But I do know one thing. If you are as
adamant—so am I. If we are to meet at all, it must be in
secret. I will not take a sacrifice from you when I have
nothing to give in exchange. Marcia, nothing on earth will
move me on that point. I'd shoot myself first."

"That wouldn't help," she murmured drearily through
her tears.

"But it may hinder," he rejoined, with some of his old
sardonic humour. "There, dear, you see there's nothing to
cry for, and your cigarette is burning a hole in Dan's carpet—
which really is a matter for regret."

She retrieved it with a difficult smile and a sob. "I
didn't mean to be so foolish," she said.

"You're not—and you never could be," he answered.
"You are just the divinely unselfish woman you always have
been. But you've got to realize, darling, that so far as I'm
concerned you're free—free as air. I told you long ago that
there was no obligation between us, and it's more than ever
so now. So long as you recognize that—and so long as it does
you no harm to come and see me sometimes"—he paused again
as he had paused before, then very steadily · "that's my only
condition," he said.

"You want me to come and see you?" said Marcia.

He hesitated an instant, and—because she knew him so well
—she saw him strive against the truth and fail. "Do you think
I want food and drink, Marcia?" he said in a husky undertone.

She gave him her hand again. "Thank you," she said.
"Then I'll accept the condition—and come."

He lifted the hand to his lips. "God bless you," he said,
"and forgive me!"

"Forgive us both!" she whispered.

He did not ask her what she meant.

They sat for a space in silence; then without apparent
effort he began to talk of other things, of Dan Bellamy, of the
wrecked car, and, in casual terms, of himself, repeating what
she had already heard from Peter but suppressing all personal

details.   It was in what he suppressed rather than in what he uttered that Marcia sensed the desolation of his ruined life. For no complaint escaped him.   He took his punishment unflinching, and in so doing he awoke in her an admiration— even a reverence—which she had never felt for him before.

"Can—nothing—be done ?" she asked him once.

And he answered grimly : "Yes, a miracle—nothing else. I've had the best opinion available—Peter saw to that.   I've also had two operations at the hospital.   There's nothing left but a miracle, which may happen—according to the local surgical engineer—this week, next week, some time, never. I incline towards the last."

"One never knows," murmured Marcia.

"No, one never knows," he agreed.   "To-day, the prison, to-morrow—perhaps—the open road.   Would you still take the open road with me, Marcia ?"   He smiled at her with the words and passed on, not waiting for her reply.   "Well, perhaps prison is the safest place, after all.   It keeps us out of mischief, doesn't it ?   These open roads—some of 'em— are beastly dangerous.   And, anyhow, I can't complain of my quarters, can I ?   What do you think of them ?"

It was a relief to turn to a less tragic subject, and she followed his lead thankfully.   It was clear that he had no intention of bemoaning his fate, still less of allowing her to do so, and gradually, as she grew accustomed to the situation, there crept back into their intercourse something of the old careless friendliness which had made of their comradeship so easy and so unique a possession.   When presently Peter appeared at the window with a blunt request to join them, it seemed to Marcia that it only needed the presence of the two children in the background to restore completely the happy springtide atmosphere of Pentreith.   And in her heart she realized that this was exactly what Eric himself desired—to go back a little way along the path already trodden since to go forward was forbidden.

CHAPTER IV

CONCLUSIONS

"So Lady Templeton is taking a holiday from family cares !" said Maurice Baronford with the suggestion of a smile on his smooth face.

He leaned back in his chair in Sir Everard's dining-room, his fingers idly toying with the stem of his glass of port, his eyes half-closed, quite inscrutable.

Sir Everard, at the head of the table, was peeling a walnut with considerable precision and frowning slightly over the process. "I think I told you," he said, "that our boy had a very serious illness some ten weeks ago. One of those unsuspected cases of appendicitis and an almost eleventh-hour operation. I was travelling North at the time and heard nothing of it until the worst was over, so that the entire burden fell upon her. She took charge of him during the holidays, and was rather worn out after it."

"The ideal mother!" murmured Baronford, still watching the wine in his glass.

"Yes, she has always been that." Sir Everard's voice had a slightly defensive note. "At Easter-time it was measles. They were both down with it then. She took them down to Cornwall—a place called Pentreith."

Baronford nodded. "I've heard of it. Virginia was telling me—Virginia Freeman, you know. An uncle of hers has taken a mediæval estate in the neighbourhood. She was quite excited about it. I don't know quite why. But—well, you know Virginia."

Sir Everard vouchsafed a somewhat preoccupied smile. "She is the sort of girl who is always excited about something."

"A trifle unbalanced," commented Baronford. "She will have to improve considerably in that respect before——" He paused, and finally decided to say no more.

Sir Everard finished peeling his walnut and glanced at him. "Quite so," he said.

Baronford laughed a little with a complacent sort of amusement. "She has her points," he said in the tone of one making a concession. "By the time she's thirty they may be worth considering."

"You're in no hurry, then," observed Sir Everard.

Baronford's smile became slightly more cynical. "It never pays, does it?" he said. "One thing at a time is my motto, and I imagine—if I may be permitted to judge from appearances—that it has a certain attraction, my dear sir, for you also."

"Well, up to a point—perhaps," said Sir Everard.

"There is no other way of getting there," resumed Baronford. "At least, none that I know of. And I am no believer in women marrying too soon. Let them sow their wild oats first!"

"I admire your philosophy," said Sir Everard.

The younger man looked at him with raised brows. "Well, as you know, I am fairly well acquainted with that side of human nature. And if I ever marry, it's going to be for good. I'm not for this quick-change business personally, even if I do make my living by it."

"There," said Sir Everard, "I'm inclined to agree with you. Have a peach!"

Baronford shook his head, smiling. "Too luscious, thanks. They don't keep well, do they? Peaches, Sir Everard, are only intended for occasional enjoyment, and must be finished at once."

"Ah! The ordinary apple appeals to you more for every day," suggested his host. "There again—speaking in a general sense—I agree with you. But it doesn't apply in every case."

"You mean," said Baronford deliberately, "that some peaches can only be reached by means of the matrimonial ladder."

"Don't you agree?" said Sir Everard.

"Not entirely." Baronford closed his eyes meditatively. "At any rate, I don't think Virginia Freeman is one of them."

"Possibly you're not in love with her," observed Sir Everard.

Baronford opened his eyes and closed them again. "I hope I have sufficient self-control to avoid that," he said. "My one theory, as a matter of fact, is that only the female ever falls in love—or, shall we say, ever needs to fall in love? The male, unless he is completely brainless, can get all he wants without."

Sir Everard ate his walnut and drank his wine without comment.

"You don't agree with me," remarked Baronford after the passage of several seconds.

Sir Everard smiled a little. "I may have done so—once," he said.

Baronford shook his head again. "No, you don't. You never did. But that doesn't disprove my theory. You may be the exception that proves the rule—though I doubt it."

"A very tactful way of putting it!" said Sir Everard.

"No, I don't mean that. But I'm sure you agree that there are very few women nowadays who can be relied upon to amuse themselves harmlessly while their husbands are busy in the market-place. Looking after a wife when she's young is a whole-time job. You must admit it." Baronford's dark eyes held a half-sneering challenge as they met the other man's steady gaze.

"I never found it so," said Sir Everard. "My wife was only eighteen when I married her."

"And she is still young—and attractive," said Baronford.

"And a most devoted mother," added Sir Everard.

Baronford raised the wine to his lips with a sweeping gesture. "And what happens when she is unable to exercise the maternal virtues ? Does she lead a completely dormant existence except during the holidays ?"

A certain steeliness shone in Sir Everard's eyes. He recognized that for the sake of the argument his guest had given the discussion a personal turn, and he was too broad-minded to resent it openly, but he could not wholly conceal his distaste.

"I think she fills in her time pretty completely with entertaining and so on," he said. "She has a great many friends."

"Do you know them all ?" demanded Baronford keenly.

Sir Everard laughed a little. "My dear fellow, I really can't tell you that. Have another glass of port !"

Baronford refused with a wave of the hand. "There you are, sir ! You don't know ! That's how things begin. Ignorance on the one side—monotony and boredom on the other. Of course you can blind yourself to it. Anyone can do that. But for real peace and security—well, they're simply not to be had until a woman has had her fling. If she doesn't drag your name through the mire, you're lucky."

"Am I, indeed ?" said Sir Everard.

He spoke quietly, but his tone had a warning note which sent a quick gleam of comprehension across Baronford's face. He covered his point immediately.

"I can see you prefer to take things for granted," he said, "so it isn't for me to raise doubts. In nine cases out of ten I should call it rash, but this may be the tenth. There are some women who manage to do their sowing—and their reaping— in secret."

"I think," said Sir Everard, "that you are rather apt to forget that there is such a thing as virtue as well as vice even in these days."

Baronford began to laugh. "The weak and sickly growth

of old age, nothing more ! Equality of the sexes has uprooted all that nonsense. It's called fair play now, but I've yet to meet the woman who knows the meaning of the words."

"In that case," said Sir Everard, with an effort at humour which was not conspicuously successful, "I think you are wise not to contemplate the idea of marriage until you do."

"I may have to wait a long while," said Baronford.

"It would be wiser to wait the whole of your life than to marry a woman you couldn't trust," said Sir Everard, rising to ring for coffee.

"You speak as one who knows," said Baronford carelessly.

"I ought to—after fifteen years," his host rejoined with the determined composure of the man who refuses to be ruffled.

Baronford turned in his chair to regard him. "How on earth do you do it ?" he said.

"Do what, my dear fellow ?" Sir Everard remained on the hearthrug looking down at him. There was a touch of conscious superiority in his pose.

"Bring yourself to consider any woman as above suspicion," explained Baronford, still half laughing. "It seems to me extraordinarily rash. No, please don't think I'm making unpleasant insinuations !"—catching a glint in the grey eyes above him that seemed to express a certain remote antagonism. "I'm only interested to know how you can arrive at such a conclusion regarding any being of the female species. You may call it my life-study if you like. I'm collecting evidence, as it were."

"Well ?" said Sir Everard rather curtly.

"Well," Baronford turned round more fully to face him, "you have been married for fifteen years. You have a wife who is an ideal mother—in the holidays. You admit that for the rest of the time she has to find her own amusements. She has friends whom you have never met. She comes and goes exactly according to fancy. At the present moment, for instance, you probably haven't the faintest idea where she is." He paused. "Isn't that so ?" he demanded unexpectedly.

Sir Everard made a faint gesture as if taken momentarily unawares, but immediately he was his own master again. "I'm afraid I'm not a very good subject for cross-examination," he remarked, smiling coldly. "I know too much of the tricks of the trade."

"You don't like that question," retorted Baronford, icily triumphant. "I draw the customary conclusion. You have not the vaguest notion where she is at the present moment. Now, how long is it since you saw her last ?"

Sir Everard stiffened ; his smile seemed to crystallize. "Really, Baronford," he said, "I begin to think the joke has gone far enough."

Baronford leaned his arm on the back of his chair in an argumentative attitude. "Is it a joke ?" he said. "If it were—allow me to say I think you would treat it as one ! If you refuse to answer that question also, I am compelled once more to draw the obvious conclusion. You have not seen her for a considerable period. Now—again I ask you— on what do you base your confidence ? Mutual love and respect ? Mutual fiddlesticks !"

"Well," remarked Sir Everard dryly, "it seems to give you great satisfaction, anyhow."

"It does not," declared Baronford. "To my mind the whole structure is so damned shaky that it would collapse at a touch. I should like to hear the lady's evidence."

"I am sure you would." Deliberate irony sounded in Sir Everard's voice. "You would like to pick to pieces and dissect every action and every motive—probable or otherwise —that could be ascribed to it. I know the process quite well, and I must say that I should be sorry to have it applied to anyone I cared for."

Baronford began to laugh. "You prefer not to enquire too closely ! Your motto is peace at all costs ! Well, perhaps you're wise. We will leave it at that."

He turned his head as the door opened to admit the butler with the coffee-tray, and Sir Everard relaxed his attitude as though he felt the interruption to be something of a relief.

Wilson approached, wearing a look of sedate importance. Having served the guest, he turned ceremoniously to his master.

"Her ladyship has returned," he announced in a confidential aside. "She is having dinner sent up to her room."

"Oh, thanks !" said Sir Everard quietly.

"She said she wouldn't disturb you, sir, as you had company," Wilson added.

"That's all right," said Sir Everard.

As the door closed Baronford looked up again with an enigmatical smile playing about his smooth lips. "Won't you go and welcome her ?" he said. "Don't let—the company —stand in the way !"

Sir Everard's eyes came down to him and regarded him

steadily for several seconds. They held a very definite expression of disapproval, but when at length he spoke his voice had its usual calm and friendly tone.

"Oh no, Baronford! You're not in the way. Don't you worry yourself! You couldn't be if you tried. Have a cigar!"

CHAPTER V

THE DOOR INTO THE PAST

IT was late that night when Sir Everard softly opened the door that led from his own room into that of his wife and looked in.

She was not in bed, but seated before the fire with a shaded lamp on a table beside her and a blotter on her knee which she closed and laid aside with the pen she held at his approach.

"Oh, Everard, come in!" she said. "Wilson gave you my message, did he? It was really too late to dress and join you. And I was sure you and Mr. Baronford wouldn't be wanting any frivolous interruptions."

She did not look frivolous as she sat there, only tired and rather anxious, in spite of the smile she raised to greet him.

He stooped and kissed her. "I think it was very wise of you," he said. "You would only have been bored."

"What an idea!" she said. Her hand slid down his arm and hesitatingly found his. She turned her face to the fire. "How is everything?" she asked. "I see you won your case at Cardiff. Is the matter of the judgeship settled yet?"

He did not answer her immediately, and in a moment her hand slipped free. But he bent and took it gently back into his own. "Yes, practically settled," he said. "But I mustn't bore you with my affairs. Have you had a restful week?"

She glanced up at him quickly, nervously. "Everard! Of course I am not bored! Do tell me everything! I am longing to hear."

"My dear," he said "there is very little to tell. I am not sure that you will find that being the wife of a judge is very much more entertaining than being that of a K.C., but I hope at least it will not be less so."

She leaned back again with a faint sigh. "I suppose I may be glad for your sake," she said.

"Thank you, my dear," he answered quietly. "It is certainly pleasant to gain what one has worked for—that is, if it does not cost too much."

She made a slight restless movement. "If it is the thing one wants the most of all, I suppose it couldn't," she said.

"I wonder," said Sir Everard.

He laid her hand down with a kindly pat and straightened himself.

Marcia spoke almost in the same moment. "I agree with you that there are very few things that come up to one's expectations, but I think we have ourselves to blame. We expect too much."

Sir Everard leaned against the mantelpiece and looked down at her thoughtfully. "It is certainly very easy to do so," he said. "On the other hand, it may be that some of us possess far more than we realize."

"Do you think so?" said Marcia.

Her eyes had gone back to the fire, and her voice had a weary intonation as though she would fain close an unprofitable subject.

Sir Everard remained motionless also, but his look dwelt upon her, scrutinized her. "Yes," he said at length, as one giving utterance to a conclusion arrived at after considerable thought. "I do think, Marcia, that some of us are far luckier than we know. We all of us strive and long for something more. I suppose that is human nature. But I think we should be wise if—just sometimes—we were to stop and count up all the things—the precious things—already within our grasp."

He paused. She had made again that small uneasy gesture, but she said nothing, nor did she raise her eyes to his.

"Don't you agree with me?" he said. "I am sure you do."

She spoke with an effort. "Well, of course. It is the obvious."

"Yes," he said gravely. "You are right. It is. But we are very apt to ignore it, unless something unusual brings us to our senses. But"—he spoke impressively—"when that something happens, it is like a direct warning which it would be madness to ignore."

Again he paused. Her eyes had suddenly flashed up to his, but they were lowered again immediately. Her face was very pale in the glow of the firelight. Her hands clasped each other very tightly.

He went on. "I am not a man to take warning very readily, I am afraid. I have always held that to get the best out of life one must work one's hardest. Slackness has never been a part of my creed. I believe that all who really love work for work's sake can find it. But even work can be a tyrant and demand too much. Perhaps you have realized that, too?"

"I don't know quite what you mean," she said in a low voice.

"No?" he said. "And yet there was a time when you worked so hard that I scarcely saw you."

"You mean the War?" she questioned.

"Yes, I mean the War." He spoke sombrely. "I let you go because I saw that I couldn't hold you back. It was a time for sacrifice. But that time is past. Perhaps you think it cost me nothing. Do you?"

"Why do you ask?" said Marcia.

"Because"—he spoke with a sort of tense suppression—"I have been asking myself lately if the woman who went—the woman who was my wife—ever really came back to me."

"Everard!" she said. Her eyes were raised now. She was gazing at him with a wide look that was almost of horror. Her hands were gripped upon the arms of her chair. She spoke again through lips so stiff and cold that they would scarcely move. "Why—are you saying this—to me?"

He stood up quietly to his full height. Her agitation seemed in some fashion to restore his own composure. After a second or two he came to her as she sat and laid a steady hand upon her.

"Marcia," he said, "do you remember a week ago—only a week ago—how you locked me out of this room?"

She turned as it were mechanically under his hand. She had begun to tremble. "Is—that it?" she said, almost in a whisper.

"I wouldn't have it," he went on, in the same level tone. "In fact, I believe I was rather brutal. Anyhow, you made me feel I must have been. I'm sorry if I was. You see, my dear, in spite of my work, in spite of everything, I am still a man, and I am still your husband. Perhaps you thought I had forgotten that?"

He paused, but she did not reply. She only sat, still gripping the arms of her chair to still her trembling.

"I still won't have it, Marcia," he went on. "I have been thinking about it all the week. It's been the longest week I have ever lived through, but every hour of it has made me more determined. I may have deserved it. I am not saying I didn't. But—it has brought me to my senses quite effectually. I can't live under the same roof with you and feel you are inaccessible to me. If"—his voice suddenly sank—"your love for me is dead, well, it has got to come to life again—or—we must separate. There can be no half-measures—no wife-only-in-name business for me." He paused again as if to steady himself, then continued more evenly : "You may think my need of you is small. That is where I have gone wrong. I take the blame. I have come to my senses. I have been reckoning up my possessions. And you—I can still count you as the first and foremost of them, Marcia ?"

His voice had an urgent note. He was bending as if he would take her into his arms. But she still sat rigidly fighting the tremors that assailed her. Her head was bent, her face averted.

She spoke almost inaudibly, as he waited for her answer. "If you like to regard me—as such."

"Ah!" he said. "You haven't forgiven me yet. Perhaps that is a good sign. I couldn't wound your love—if it were dead."

"My love is not dead !" she said, and somehow, though the words were low, they sounded like a cry.

"Thank God !" said Sir Everard. And still he waited for her to turn to him. And still she did not turn.

He uttered a deep sigh at last and slowly straightened himself again. "I would like you to know," he said, "that I blame myself for what has happened. I have not been watchful enough, careful enough. I didn't realize what I was in danger of losing. It came upon me—like a bombshell. I ought to have seen it before. I blame myself."

He reiterated the words with a kind of dreary insistence, as though he had repeated them to himself a good many times before. Marcia stirred a little, but she made no answer to them, save that she very slightly shook her head.

He moved back to his place by the mantelpiece and took up his stand there again as though determined not to press for that which she was not prepared voluntarily to offer.

For a space he was silent, contemplating her. She had relaxed her rigidity and had sunk back in her chair as if exhausted. Her eyes were almost closed, and, watching her, a touch of pity came into his own, softening the melancholy severity of his look.

"Have I made you—very unhappy?" he asked.

She answered him almost automatically. "I am used to it now."

He made an uneasy movement. "If I could only see into your mind, Marcia!" he said. "Surely you can't wish—to be a stranger to me?"

"I am not sure," she said, "that I can help it."

He turned from her with a gesture of despair and leaned upon the shelf, his head upon his hands. When he spoke again his voice was low and strained. He seemed to be fighting back some impulse that leapt and tore for freedom.

"Listen!" he said. "I can't stand much more of this. There must be a way back—for both of us. You say your love is not dead. Marcia, neither is mine! For the sake of our love, then—for yours and for mine—let us open this door that seems to have shut behind us—the door into the past— and get back—get back—somehow—to where we were before!"

His voice jerked into silence. His hands were clenched, as though the utterance of that appeal had been almost too much for him. It had moved him to the depths.

And into Marcia also in her chair behind him some electric force seemed suddenly to have entered. Swiftly and silently she rose, but she did not go to him. If any inner urging were upon her, impelling her to do so, she resisted it. She stood, tall and quiet, facing him, and she spoke with a strange fatality, a power with which she was wholly unfamiliar.

"There's no getting back into the past," she said. "That door was shut—for ever—years ago. You didn't know. You were too busy to notice. We can only go forward now."

He made a blind, almost an agonized, movement. "Don't tell me—I've lost you!" he said hoarsely.

"No." Again with that strange, half-prophetic calmness she answered him. "I still—belong. But it isn't as it was in the past, though God alone knows how hard I tried to keep it so. It slipped away from me in spite of all that I could do. We're getting old, you know, Everard." A tinge of her former weariness crept back into her voice. "We've grown into different ways—different habits. It's a very long time now since we ploughed a furrow side by side— if indeed we ever did."

"But it isn't too late," he said.

"I don't know if it is possible any longer," she answered. "I am not even sure if we have ever been anything but strangers to each other—have ever come anywhere near to knowing each other. I don't suppose any two people have ever lived together and yet been so completely apart as you and I have."

"Marcia!" he said; and turned to look at her, his face drawn and haggard as she had never seen it. "Do you actually mean that?" he asked.

"Isn't it true?" she made answer. "Didn't you arrange long ago that I must go my way and you yours? No, don't think I'm reproaching you! It was probably quite inevitable —just as this is inevitable too. It seemed to me a terrible pity once, but—I am used to it now. I don't suppose I could give up going my own way even if I tried to. It has become such a habit." Her voice shook unexpectedly. "Surely," she said, "our only hope now lies in pressing forward—and making the best of what is left!"

"My dear!" he said. "Marcia!" and stretched out is hands to her with the words. "That's what I'm asking—what I want. Don't you understand? Just to know you are still my own! This past week has been like a nightmare—like hell— to me."

Marcia smiled—a very sad smile. "It needn't have been," she said.

She did not move in answer to his gesture, and the open misery in his eyes hardened slowly into stern endurance. He dropped his hands to his sides. "I suppose it will take time," he said. "Well, I can wait. And I have no wish to curtail your liberty in any way. You shall even have that week—every year—you asked for. Perhaps I deserve that. Anyhow, it will keep me from forgetting again that I have forfeited the right to enquire into your actions. That—was what you meant to convey, wasn't it?"

"Perhaps it was," Marcia said. "I think—that if you don't insist too much upon your rights—it will be easier for us both." She paused; her eyes were suddenly full of tears. For a few seconds she stood irresolute, then with an impulsive movement that yet had in it an element of reserve, she went to him and laid her face against his shoulder. "We must make—a fresh beginning," she said almost inarticulately.

His arm slipped around her. He held her in silence for a space, then bent mutely and kissed her forehead.

It was a tacit reconciliation, a tacit resolve to set out anew side by side along the great thoroughfare in travelling which they had become so widely separated. But it did not open again the door into the past. For they had lost the key.

PART IV

CHAPTER I

"OH, drat the man!" said Goldie, snatching the cigarette from her lips with a gesture of exasperation. "For sheer damned impertinence I've never met his equal. I wonder why I don't refuse him for good and all—tell him to git!"

"I wonder sometimes too," said Marcia.

She looked at her daughter with a faint smile of wisdom hovering about her lips ; but she offered her no advice. During the five years of Goldie's decidedly syncopated career in Society she had learned the mother's lesson, and she looked on in silence save on the very rare occasions when she was invited to do otherwise.

Goldie reverted with an impatient toss to the letter in her hand, resuming her cigarette at the same moment with the air of one who has little time to lose.

She read the letter straight through and slapped it down upon the table. "Really, I think I shall retire from public life!" she said. "Oh, darling, how nice and serene you look! I wish we could change places."

"Would you like to be twenty years older?" said Marcia.

Goldie screwed up her face for a moment, then laughed. "Well, it's something to know the worst, isn't it ? I have an awful presentiment that I'm going to get married this year. But who to is a point I can't discuss even with myself."

"I had been married for five years when I was your age," remarked Marcia.

Goldie gurgled a little. "I know, darling. It was hardly decent of you. How you must have wished you hadn't!"

"No. I never did that."

Marcia spoke with a gentle decision which caused Goldie to open round eyes at her.

"Oh, darling, never ? How desperately dull! And Dad —was he always a good boy too ? But no"—with an airy wave ; "you needn't answer that question. I should convict him of the most blameless virtue and perfect integrity without calling a single witness. As the dear rector would say, 'What a lamentable lack of initiative!'" She pushed back her chair and rose. "And so you married in your first season! Most dearly beloved, how precious!" She moved round to her mother's side and stood looking down at her with dancing eyes. "What a lamb you must have been!" she said, and, bending swiftly, kissed her forehead.

The smile still lingered about Marcia's lips. "I fell in love, Goldie," she said.

"Poor darling!" said Goldie. "It was your only excuse. I wish I'd been there. I'd have put a stop to it."

Marcia broke into a laugh. "Goldie! Why?"

Goldie sat down on the edge of the table and surveyed her critically. "You're very beautiful," she said.

"I don't think I am," said Marcia simply. "I never have thought so."

Goldie nodded. "In the eyes of men, you are," she said. "That's my trouble too. It keeps one so busy fending them off that it doesn't leave much time for anything else."

"Darling!" protested Marcia. "Are you as beset as all that?"

Goldie nodded again darkly. "I think men are the devil, don't you? So plausible and beastly. I'd hate to fall in love. I'd feel I was gagged and bound."

"I know what you mean," said Marcia slowly.

"Do you? I didn't think you would." A certain wistfulness shone for a moment in the girl's eyes. She made an unexpected snuggling movement downwards towards her mother's breast. "Don't let me marry Maurice Baronford, darling!" she said. "I don't want to in the least."

Marcia's quiet arms enfolded her. "I don't want you to, *chérie*," she said.

"Well, don't let me!" reiterated Goldie. "You know I should hate it, don't you?"

Marcia hesitated momentarily. "If you don't love him," she said.

Goldie gave a wriggle that might have been a shudder vehemently suppressed. "But I do!" she said in a choked voice. "I do! I do! I—lie awake at night because of him. I—count the hours when I'm away from him. I feel—quite sick whenever I see him. Isn't that that disgusting thing called love?"

"Dearest!" Marcia said. 'What am I to say to you?"

"I don't know. You needn't say anything." The girl's

arms were tight around her ; they had almost a desperate clutch. "Don't let me marry him, that's all ! Don't let me !"

"He has asked you ?" Marcia said.

"He keeps on asking—or, rather, taking for granted. I hated him at first. I do still—in sane moments. But I'm not so sane as I was. That's the beastly part of it. I'm losing my balance. I'm getting undermined. I'm——" She broke off suddenly and drew a deep hard breath. "What frightful rot I'm talking !" she said, and stood up with a jerk. "And how sweet of you to listen ! How on earth did we get on to it ? Oh yes, it was you—marrying the man you loved at eighteen !" She uttered a hard little laugh and inhaled her cigarette-smoke with exaggerated deliberation. "You know, darling, you don't look much older than I do now—though I'll bet he's the only man in the world who doesn't notice it."

Marcia looked up at the pale defiant young face above her, but she veiled the anxiety in her eyes. "That also is nonsense, dear," she said, "sheer rubbish, and you know it."

"It isn't," asserted Goldie. "I often think that in my five years afloat I must have weathered ever so many more storms than you have in all your married life. Why, you must have forgotten the very taste of a love-affair by now."

"Oh, not quite !" said Marcia. "But I am pretty sure of one thing, my child, which you may or may not relish my telling you. And that is that you have never yet tasted the very first beginnings of what I call love."

Goldie laughed again. "You mean the dear old-fashioned laid-up-in-lavender style of thing ! Well, darling, you'll laugh at me when I tell you that I did sample it once long ago —years and years ago—when I was a kid at school. And I liked it frightfully then of course, but I doubt if it would appeal to me now."

"When you were at school ?" Marcia said. "You never told me."

"Of course I didn't. Darling, don't be so antediluvian —though I doubt if the little Noahs told their mamma such things even then !" Goldie threw herself down in a sprawling attitude in an easy-chair ; her pale face with its crown of gleaming hair was in shadow. "I'll satisfy your romantic curiosity by telling you now if you like," she said. "It was Peter."

"Peter !" repeated Marcia. She also turned from the table, but not to obtain any closer view of Goldie, who drew in her feet to let her pass. She moved across the room to a bureau at the farther side and sat down before it with her back turned. "You mean Peter Tregassa, of course!" she said.

"The only Peter in the world!" declaimed Goldie dramatically. "Yes, I was very gone on' Peter at one time, and he was rather gone on me. But then he went to Canada and turned into a farmer. And he wrote to me that he had dropped his title out there—which I thought rather plebeian of him and told him so; and after that I'm afraid the correspondence ceased. There was nothing left to feed the flame, and I had other things to think about."

"But you were so young," said Marcia.

"I know, dear. But I belong to a precocious generation. And at least I wasn't headlong enough to get married at eighteen," rejoined Goldie. "You can give me points there. You must have been a very keen angler. I only dallied with my fish—whereas you hooked and landed yours." She blew a cloud of smoke upwards with pursed lips. "Yet I believe I should have married Peter if he'd had the sense to stay in England and get civilized," she said. "He was a ripping boy."

"Perhaps he is the reason that you haven't married," suggested Marcia, idly taking up a pen.

"Perhaps he is." Goldie yawned. "I'm sure I don't know. But, anyhow, I don't propose to remain single for his sake all my life. Do you remember that Major Morven?" She shot the question rather suddenly.

"Who?" said Marcia. She had begun to make dots with her pen on the open blotter, still idly, yet with a hint of purpose.

"Major Morven, darling," her daughter explained with a chuckle: "the man you had that innocuous flirtation with at Pentreith all those years ago—to the deep indignation of my crude and undeveloped mind. Don't say you've forgotten him—while I still remember Peter! That would indeed make me feel an anachronism!"

"Oh no!" said Marcia quietly. Her voice was perfectly steady; it had a faint ring as of amusement. "I remember him quite well. I very nearly smacked you once for being rude to him. But—luckily for you—you apologized before I had the opportunity."

Goldie laughed aloud. "That would have been a very dreadful affair—but something to remember, anyhow. In all the precious memories of childhood I can't trace a single one even remotely suggestive of a smacking from you—though I'm sure I often deserved one," she added generously. "Maurice says I do still. Beast !"

"I wonder you allow yourself even to think of him," said Marcia to the blotting-pad.

Goldie made a terrific grimace. "I don't. I'm compelled. I loathe thinking of him—but I want to all the same. To-night I'm going with him to the *Carte Blanche* Club. I don't know why. I've refused twice, and I wouldn't even discuss it with him on the 'phone yesterday. Yet—here is his letter announcing the fact !"

Marcia turned sharply. "But, Goldie——"

Goldie interrupted. "Don't say it ! It won't make the faintest difference. I'm going. Because why ? Because if I don't go, he'll take Virginia—and I shall be awake all night wondering."

"Goldie !" Marcia spoke with more insistence. "You're not to talk like that. It's absurd—it's——"

"I know it is, dear." Again, humorously, Goldie inter-rupted. "It's positively indecent. But what am I to do ? After all, she's had about ten years' start. He never even looked at me till the day I snubbed him for saying something beastly about people going into annual retreat—meaning you. I really was furious with him that day." She uttered a brief laugh at the memory. "That anyone should dare to cast a stone—however carefully wrapped up—at a dear innocent lamb like you !"

Marcia's eyes shone with an unusual light. "What did he say ?" she said.

Goldie clicked her fingers in the air. "I truly don't remember. It was just one of his cynical little digs. He doesn't like you, dear heart. You're too honest for him. He can't picture anyone taking a week of complete oblivion and rest in the country just once in a year for sheer refreshment and nothing else. His whole being is composed of the most complex intrigue—like a jig-saw puzzle. He just can't help trying to fit bits into other people's gaps, and they are always highly coloured. He really can't help it. It's just his foul nature."

"And do you actually mean to tell me that you're attracted by this man ?" said Marcia.

"Not attracted, darling,—fascinated, mesmerized, enthralled !" Goldie threw her hands wide. "I say 'No' to him. He says 'Yes' to me. I say 'No' again. But it's no

Q

earthly use. There simply isn't another man that counts. And he knows it."

"Really, Goldie!" Exasperation sounded in Marcia's voice.

Goldie sprang laughing to her feet. "Yes, really and truly, darling. It's a funny life, isn't it? Full of reverses, as the old man said when his wife contradicted him. When I've been married as long as you have—how long have you been married, by the way?"

Marcia was looking at her very steadily. "Goldie," she said, when the girl ceased to speak, "I want you, please, darling, to write at once to Mr. Baronford and tell him definitely that you are engaged to-night."

Goldie snapped her fingers again, blowing an airy kiss in the same gesture. "Oddsbodikins, sweetheart! That won't cut any ice. The man has second sight. He always knows where to find me."

"Goldie, don't!" There was definite appeal in Marcia's voice. "If you've told me even half the truth——"

"Ye gods and little fishes! What must the whole be?" chanted Goldie. "No, dear innocent, you can't keep me at your side. You must think of some other means of deliverance. I know!"—with a dramatic flourish: "produce—Peter!"

She was at the door with the words. Looking back, she threw her mother a lovely, impudent smile, and the next instant would have been gone but for the fact that she encountered her father on the threshold, and, being the quicker of the two, had to draw back to avoid a collision.

"Hullo, Dad!" she ejaculated. "Why, you're just the very person we wanted. How long have you been married? Mum and I can't remember."

CHAPTER II

THE PERFECT WIFE

SIR EVERARD, tall and spare and looking older than his years, entered the room with his habitual dignity. He regarded his daughter with a kindliness that was yet not unmixed with severity.   During the years that he had been a judge his attitude towards young modernity had not developed very favourably.   He was fond of Goldie, and in his way proud of her, but he had a shrewd suspicion that if ever he came to know her better he would approve of her less.   That Marcia had steered her successfully through the shoals and rapids of five London seasons was certainly a matter for congratulation ; but he was beginning to think that it was time that Goldie married.   She had had her fling, and she ought to be thinking of settling down.

He stooped and gravely kissed her bright face.   "Good morning, Dora !   What is that you say ?   How long have we been married ?   Why, I am almost afraid to think."

With his hand upon her shoulder, he turned her back into the room.   Marcia still sat at her bureau.   Her eyes were troubled, but she smiled at his approach.

"Oh, Everard !   I thought you'd gone."

"It's early, dear," he said.   "I had less correspondence than usual, and have left Grant to deal with it."

"Well ?   How long *have* you been married ?" said Goldie, beginning to chafe a little.   "It seems ages ago to me."

He smiled a little at her flippancy.   The hair had receded from his forehead, and he had a very legal look.   His eyes rested upon his wife, who had the appearance of being many years his junior.

"It isn't a very difficult sum, is it ?" he said.   "How old are you, Marcia ?"

"She's just a year younger than me," said Goldie, with an arm round her mother's neck.

He shook his head, still smiling.   "Let me see !   You are five years younger than Lillith.   That makes you——"

"It doesn't !" cut in Goldie.   "Aunt Lillith is as old as the witch of Endor."

He allowed the interruption, somewhat to Marcia's surprise.   "Well, then, shall we say, how old is Dennis ?   Our marriage is just a year older."

"Good gracious !" exclaimed Goldie, in the tone of one making a startling discovery.

They both looked at her.   "Well ?" said Marcia.

Goldie stooped and impulsively kissed her forehead. "Why, darling, Den's twenty-four.   You're going to have a silver wedding-day this year !"

"What a discovery !" said Marcia.

"Ah !   You knew it !" declared Goldie.   "You can't

pretend to me ! You were just waiting like a modest matron for Dad to remember ! And he never would have done but for me. Well, well, we must do something about it, mustn't we ? What's the date ? In October some time, isn't it ?"

"The eighteenth," said Sir Everard with precision.

"St. Luke's Day," said Goldie, "when one always expects a little summer and doesn't get it ! Well, we must have a wedding reception, that's certain. I know what I'll do. I'll arrange to get married myself on that day, and then one ceremony will do for the two of us. We'll have a double wedding, darling, and I'll share my bridesmaids with you. And they'll all be dressed in silver with bouquets of rosemary and white heather. Now, how does that appeal to you ?"

"Are you thinking of getting married, Dora ? It's the first I've heard of it," said Sir Everard with a hint of pomposity.

"My dear Dad, I've been thinking of it for years," she returned nonchalantly. "Just waiting for a superman, that's all. But I've taken to reading the stars lately, and I fancy he'll turn up soon——if he hasn't already. Well, so long, ye lovers !" She turned once more to the door. "Gather ye roses while it's May ! I must go and get a frock tried on."

Neither of her parents attempted to delay her departure, and the door closed lightly behind her. They heard her fresh young voice go singing up the stairs.

"What does she mean ?" said Sir Everard.

Marcia had turned back to her desk and was once more, rather forlornly, pricking out a design in dots on the blotting-pad. She spoke, slowly and reluctantly: "I'm very much afraid—that she means to marry Maurice Baronford."

"Oh !" said Sir Everard in some surprise. "Have you any good reason for thinking so ?"

Marcia hesitated. "He is certainly—seeking her out," she said.

"Indeed !" said Sir Everard. "Well"—he began to smile —"he's a brilliant barrister, and a rising man. It would be an excellent match for her—as far as I can see."

"I don't think so," Marcia said, her voice low and distressed. "He may be a successful man, but he is too old—too sophisticated—too cynical. He would never, never make her happy."

"My dear," he protested, "I don't know why you should say that. He's only forty ; and as regards sophistication—

and cynicism too—I should imagine Dora to be quite a match for him."

"Oh, you don't know her," said Marcia in the same wrung voice. "She is a child at heart. He would give her none of the things she needs. It would be—torture for her sooner or later."

"My dear Marcia!" he said. "It's rather absurd of you to talk like that."

"I can't help it," she rejoined, with her head bent. "Maurice Baronford is a man intent only upon making his mark. He has no scruples of any kind. Women are mere playthings to him—just to occupy his leisure moments. He has been playing with Virginia Freeman for the last ten years, and he will neither take her nor let her go. Is that the sort of man to give a girl happiness?"

"I must say," remarked Sir Everard, "that so far as Virginia is concerned I imagine that she is the one who won't let go."

"And it may be she has good reason," said Marcia, suddenly pausing with her pen uplifted. "Do you really think he is the sort of man to content himself for all these years with mere trifling? Why hasn't he married her? Tell me that!"

"For reasons best known to himself, I should think," said Sir Everard.

She dropped the pen abruptly and turned to him. "Yes, no doubt!" she said, and her voice was passionate. "Because he can get all he wants from her without! Because she has made herself his adoring slave for years. And now he is ready to kick her from his path. Or—it may be—not even that! It may be just—quite kindly—to set her on one side for a little while—until he needs her again!"

"Marcia! My dear girl!" he said. "Really—you're going rather far. You've no evidence to support such an accusation."

She got up as if goaded, and went to him. "Everard, I can't help it. No, I've no evidence, as you say. Only the misery in that poor woman's eyes! Virginia and I used to be friends long ago. We are not now. She gave me up because I saw too much." She clasped her hands suddenly and very urgently upon his arm. "Everard! Goldie must not marry this man. Help me to save her from him!"

He laid his hand at once and very kindly upon hers, but his eyes told her that he thought her unreasonable. "You're a little overwrought this morning, dear," he said. "You shouldn't allow yourself to get these exaggerated ideas!

am sure they are quite unjustifiable. I can't possibly interfere in the matter in any case. Dora is of an age to choose for
herself, and I must admit it would be a considerable relief to
me to know that she had done as well for herself as to marry
Baronford. She might do very much worse."

Marcia's hands fell. She turned from him. "I might
have known," she said.

"No," said Sir Everard quietly, "that is not fair to me. I
don't think you are being very fair to anyone over this.
And you have always been prejudiced against Baronford."

"I think that might be regarded as mutual," she said.
"He detests me, as you know."

"My dear Marcia!" he said again.

She wheeled and faced him. "You do know it, don't
you?" she said. "Even Goldie knows it."

"Well," he reasoned, "he has probably discovered your
suspicious attitude regarding Virginia. It would certainly
cause antagonism if he understood it."

"Yes, it would. Perhaps he has," said Marcia. "Well,
we needn't discuss it further. We can't agree."

"I don't like to hear you say that, dear," he said. "You
know I always try to understand your point of view."

She made a conciliatory gesture. "Oh yes, dear, I know.
And of course, a woman's intuition is bound to seem worthless
to you who are always weighing concrete evidence."

"Well, no, not worthless," he said with a smile. "But I
daren't attach too much value to it. You see, I have to take
into consideration the fact that the particular woman whose
instincts are in question is so rigidly loyal herself that she
may be apt to regard the laxer principles of others with too
severe a judgment. What, my dear? Surely that can't
offend you!"

She had turned from him with a deep sigh and seated
herself once more at her desk, her head upon her hand. "Oh
no! Not offend!" she said.

He came behind her and bent over her. "Don't think I
would have you any different, Marcia!" he said. "If you saw
the sort of things I see so often—the lying and corruption,
especially among women—you would realize how precious that
unbending integrity, that stainless honour, is to me. I
sometimes feel"—his hand gently pressed her shoulder—
"that you are the only woman in the world that I could ever
dare to trust—the perfect wife!"

She shrank sharply, involuntarily, as if from the prick of a weapon. "Oh, Everard!" she said, and hid her face in her hands.

"Marcia!" he said, startled.

She recovered herself instantly, and looked up at him with a desperately quivering smile. "Oh, I'm sorry. Forgive me! I am stupid and upset this morning. I think mothers have rather a bad time of it nowadays."

"You mustn't worry so, dear," he said, lightly stroking her hair. "After all, each must live his own life, you know. We can't live other people's."

"No, I know," she agreed wearily. "And yet—we have our responsibilities too. We can never be free from them."

"You're tired," he said. "I shall have to prescribe you an extra week's rest in the middle of the season if this goes on."

Again she made a slight movement of shrinking, and after a moment reached up and stayed his hand. "No, I couldn't do that," she said. "You forget—Dennis is coming home. Besides, I am perfectly all right, thank you, dear. Now I must really get down to my letters. It's late."

He stooped and kissed her forehead. "Well, well, I must go too. Don't fret about Dora, my dear! I am sure the matter will right itself. And try to remember, as I said before, that Baronford is certainly a coming man, and she might do much worse."

"Oh yes, I shall remember," said Marcia.

She was alone. The May sunlight streamed in upon her. Yet she shivered.

After a long pause she opened a little secret drawer in her bureau and took from it a letter. She spread it out before her with fingers that trembled.

It began:

"Beloved Queen of my Heart,

"Truelove Farm is ours at last for our week of heaven! How am I going to wait for the first week in October? I'm dreaming already of the sea and the bracken—and you."

CHAPTER III

THE SUITOR

"WELL?" said Baronford, with his complacent smile. "Still sitting on the fence?"

"No," said Goldie. "Preparing to jump off it !"

A month had gone by since that talk with her mother, and during that month it was as if Marcia had spread protecting wings about the girl, shielding her unobtrusively from the threatening danger, for the two had scarcely met. Circumstances had helped her considerably in the return of Dennis from Eastern Europe, where he had an appointment in connection with a British Embassy. And Baronford himself had been absent for a week or two upon business. But he was free now for a few days before the opening of the Law Courts, and he did not even pretend to Goldie that his meeting with her was an accident.

On her side it was different. She had not expected to see him. It was a dance for unmarried people under her Aunt Lillith's auspices, and she had come to it with her brother. That she must meet Maurice Baronford again in the near future she had known, and she had lived in a fever of anticipation in consequence. But now that they had met, she felt oddly cold, as if the palpitating restlessness of the past few weeks had left her too exhausted for further emotion. She had wanted, at times she had yearned, to see him, and now that the desire was gratified she wondered with some impatience at the absence of rapture within herself.

He received her statement still smiling.

"On my side or the other ?" he asked.

"The other," she returned promptly.

Baronford was a faultless dancer, but on that particular night Goldie was inclined to find him exasperating. It seemed he was in an exasperating mood, and he compelled her to follow it in all its tantalizing phases and to obey his slightest whim in spite of the faint frown between her brows.

"It's good practice for you," he remarked presently. "When you're completely plastic, perhaps I will give you something more exciting."

"I hate you !" said Goldie under her breath.

He continued to smile. "What for chiefly ? Going away ? Or coming back ?"

She did not answer, and he laughed with an enigmatical kind of triumph, as though he had scored some hidden point.

"I'm sure you've missed me," he said.

She remained silent, her face turned from him.

"Are you tired of dancing ?" he asked her suddenly.

"No," she answered, almost in spite of herself.

"Then I'll show you something," said Maurice Baronford.

Two seconds later the almost forgotten fascination of the man was thrilling her once again, and she was dancing with an abandonment that was pure passion. How he managed thus to dominate her, to inspire her, she could not have told. Something in his personality—a hint of the lion-tamer—and the physical magnetism of perfect rhythm, enslaved her; and ere she knew it he had bound her anew with fetters too subtle and too powerful for her to evade or break. Until the music ceased she was his captive, to do with as he would. She danced as though she were in a dream, and even when it was over she remained for some seconds still under the spell.

"That was wonderful," she breathed.

He drew her out of the crowd. It was as if he bore her, for she was not conscious of personal effort; but as they went up the stairs she came to herself, and, reaching the top, she made a definite stand.

"I think this is far enough."

"How prudent!" was his comment, and as he uttered it he drew her behind a thick curtain and took her in his arms. She had a moment's repulsion, a moment's hot resistance; then she yielded. His lips were on her own with a deep, increasing insistence, and an unknown electric force within herself leaped up in swift response. All that was practical, all that was individual in her, were completely overwhelmed. She clung to her captor, half-laughing, half in tears.

"Don't—stifle me!" she gasped, as his lips left hers at last.

"You deserve to be," he said. "How dare you trifle with me, you little devil? You knew you were marked down."

"I haven't—trifled," she protested, still gasping. "No—Maurice—please—give me a chance!"

"I won't give you anything of the sort," he said. "Here! Come in here!"

He pushed her into a dark room near at hand, still closely holding her, for she made a brief effort to hold back.

"It's Aunt Lillith's boudoir. She wouldn't like anyone in here."

"I don't care what it is," he said, "or who likes or doesn't like." He locked the door as he spoke. "I'm going to hold you in my arms. I'm going to——"

She switched on the light.

"Why did you do that?"

She retorted rather desperately, "Why did you lock the door?"

He laughed a little drawing her closer. "Because I don't

make love for all the world to see. Now, darling, look at
me—look at me! Let me see 'Yes' in your eyes!"

But Goldie still hung back. The dream had passed,
though some of the glamour yet remained. "I'll tell you
to-morrow," she said.

"To-morrow!" he scoffed. "D'you think I can wait till
then? Why, you've had a month already!"

"It'll be a month to-morrow," she returned. The practical
in her was gaining the upper hand, and she realized with a
tinge of self-contempt that she had allowed herself to be carried
away. "It won't hurt either of us to wait till then. Let's
go back and dance!"

She spoke with a hint of coaxing, for deep within her she
knew that this man was not, as he himself suggested, to be
lightly trifled with. The close hold in which she stood told
her as much, but she avoided his eyes, warned by an instinct
she could not question.

"Are you still playing with me?" he asked, his voice
dropped very low.

She shook her head with vehemence. "No, I'm not.
I'm in earnest. I want to go. I want time to think."

"Someone has warned you against me," he said, in the
same quiet tone which had in it a deadly directness impossible
to evade.

She made a small gesture of protest. "Don't be absurd!
Why shouldn't I have a little more time to make up
my mind?"

"Because you're trying to make yourself say 'No'," he
returned, "when you don't want to. I know. I can read
you like a book. You want to say 'Yes', but you're afraid.
Who are you afraid of? Your mother?"

He shot the question as though he were cross-examining
a witness, and she shrank involuntarily before she had time
to answer.

"I thought so," he said. "These blameless people who
contrive to place themselves beyond suspicion are always
the ones to throw stones. What has she said about me?
I may as well hear it."

"Nothing," said Goldie in swift indignation. "And you're
not to say one word against her, for I simply won't hear it.
It's enough to make me say 'No' here and now!"

He drew her quickly to him. "You won't! You can't!
You're mine already. You gave yourself to me downstairs."

His lips were close to her own, but she resisted him with

sudden ferocity. "No! It wasn't really giving. You made me."

"Then I'll make you again," he said, deliberately mastering her. "Look at me—look at me!"

But she would not. Powerless as she was, she yet clung to that which he had so nearly wrested from her, in blind obedience to an instinct of self-preservation which she only vaguely recognized.

"Let go of me!" she panted. "If—you kiss me again it'll be against my will!"

"Don't be so young!" he said.

But Goldie withstood the taunt. She was openly fighting for her freedom.

"I don't care what you call me. Let me go! I'm not enjoying it any more!"

He held her still.

"Are you going to deny that you love me?" he said.

"I don't know," she flung back. "I'll tell you to-morrow—not to-night. Oh, it isn't fair—it isn't fair!" For his lips were on her neck in spite of her, and his kisses had the scorching quality of a flame. She put up her hands suddenly over her face and burst into tears.

"My darling!" he said.

But she dragged away from him like a wilful child. "I can't bear it! I can't! Go away! I'll see you to-morrow. I can't—I won't—say anything to-night!"

There was finality in words and action, and Baronford relinquished his hold.

"Don't get hysterical, I beg!" he said. "There is no occasion for that, I assure you."

"Me—hysterical!" gasped Goldie, suppressing her emotion with a violent effort. "We'll go back now, shall we? I've got a partner for the next dance. And—and"—she could not resist it, for he had stung her—"I expect—Virginia—is waiting for you, isn't she?"

He stretched a hand to the door. "Ah!" he said. "So that's the mischief, is it?"

She saw her mistake in a flash, but it was irretrievable; the spoken word was her master. She stood in silent mortification.

He unlocked the door very quietly, but he did not immediately open it. "It may interest you to know," he said, "that you are quite two years behind the times. The lady you mention has given up waiting for me."

Goldie's face was crimson. She murmured something inarticulate that might have been an apology.

He held out his hand to her with an enigmatical smile. "All right, Goldie!" he said. "We won't quarrel over that. What about to-morrow? Will you lunch with me at Frangipani's? Or must I come to you?"

She hesitated, reluctantly conscious of that thrill of awareness which he seemed able to produce in her at the first unguarded moment. She gave him her hand at last, very slowly.

"I think perhaps," she said, "you had better come to me. Four o'clock—if you don't mind."

He kept her hand. "Tea with you alone?" he said.

She nodded. Her face was still burning. "Yes. But I don't promise anything. You understand that, of course?"

"I'm going to ask you for one promise," he said.

"What?" She was trying secretly to release her hand, and, as secretly, he prevented her.

"Don't panic!" he said. "It's only this: that you won't mention to anyone whatever that I am the visitor you are expecting. That's a fair condition, Goldie. It ought to appeal to your sporting mind."

She nodded again, understanding him, and by no means anxious for an explanation. "All right; I promise. I won't tell a soul."

He released her and opened the door. "That's settled, then," he said in a tone of calm satisfaction. "By this time to-morrow I hope all our troubles will be over."

"Oh, so do I," said Goldie fervently.

She passed him swiftly and went away without looking back, fearing only lest he should see into her soul and realize how nearly he had stormed the fort.

CHAPTER IV

THE LOVER

"You're a fraud," said Dennis rudely. "I don't believe you've got a headache any more than I have."

"I don't care in the least what you believe," returned

Goldie with extreme politeness. "I'm afraid it doesn't interest me. Please go away—and don't leave the door open!"

Dennis did not. He shut it with such decision that his sister frowned and said, "Damn!" as if the headache she had pleaded as an excuse for remaining in her room had more reality in it than she had managed to convey.

There was no pretence as to her being tired. She was weary to the soul, having lain wide-eyed for six leaden hours, and the breakfast-tray at her side was a welcome diversion though she was quite unable to eat. It would have been relief unspeakable to have been able to cry her heart out on the pillow; but tears were the luxury of a bygone age, and she burned with shame whenever she remembered her brief weakness in that respect on the previous evening.

Why she was so completely miserable it would have been hard to say. Perhaps disappointment was at the root of it—disappointment in Maurice whose tactics had somehow disillusioned her—disappointment with herself for being disillusioned. For, after all, what had she expected? What could any girl expect as a sequel to the first wild thrill of anticipation? Men were but mortal. They had only one way of expressing themselves. And she supposed that Maurice was as much in love as could be expected of any man of his age and experience.

"They're all beasts, anyway," she said to herself desolately as she drank her coffee. "I shall have to marry him, I suppose. The sooner the better, and get it over!"

Then she lay down again and resumed her wide-eyed musing.

Presently there came quiet steps outside her door and a gentle tapping.

Goldie did not so much as turn her head. "Just want to be left alone, please, darling," she called rather woefully. "Rather bad atmospherics this morning!"

"Can I get you anything, dear?" asked her mother's voice.

"No, nothing, thanks, Mum. Just let me rest!" pleaded Goldie.

And she heard the quiet steps going away.

A curious little convulsion went through her at the sound, and she buried her face for a few seconds in the pillow. Why was she such a fool as to send her away when what she wanted most on earth was loving arms around her?

Slowly the hours of that interminable day wore on, and instead of growing calmer her nerves became more and more tumultuous. At times she got up and paced about her room to try and ease the tension, at others she lay stretched stiffly on her bed, listening with strained intentness to every sound. He would come at four. At four she would go down to him and make the dread surrender. It was no use hanging back any longer. Already she seemed to have fought her destiny beyond her strength. Last night—she knew it now—she had felt the iron of his will encompassing her, and though she had secured a brief respite she knew that she was no match for him. He attracted her, he dominated her, and it was useless to pretend that any other man in her world counted beside him. He had made her his prisoner, by what means she scarcely knew, and she was too weary and too bewildered to resist him any further. He deprived her even of the active desire to resist. There was only this intangible sense of repulsion—which might after all be only stupid old Nature's idiotic instinct always urging the female species to run away. She laughed at the thought, but it was a very dreary laugh, and her luncheon-tray also went down almost untouched.

Marcia did not come to her again. She was probably lunching out somewhere with the indignant Dennis. Goldie herself had had a social engagement, but she could not keep it, and was too bemused even to find out what it was. She would have to make her excuses afterwards. It would scarcely be necessary, indeed, for the announcement of her engagement to Maurice Baronford would be its own excuse. Girls did not get engaged every day, and she had heard Maurice described as the most incorrigible bachelor of his time.

Well, it was no good lying there squirming like a schoolgirl. To do so was really verging on the hysterical. She could picture Baronford's smile of cynical amusement could he have seen her, and, having successfully worked herself up to a still higher pitch of nervous irritation thereby, she sprang up and went to the bathroom and douched herself severely with cold water in preparation for the coming ordeal.

Returning to her room, she found Hobbs awaiting her— Hobbs a little more ceremonious and prim with advancing years.

"There is a gentleman downstairs waiting to see you, Miss Dora," she announced. "He gave no name."

"Good heavens!" ejaculated Goldie, glancing at her watch. "It's only three! What is the man thinking of?"

"I'm sure I don't know, Miss Dora," replied Hobbs with pursed lips. "Would you wish me to go and ask?"

"No. Don't be an idiot, Hobbs!" rejoined Goldie with a tremulous laugh. "Go and put him in the morning-room, and tell him I shall be down in two shakes! Oh, and we shall want tea presently. I'll ring for it."

"Very good, Miss Dora," said Hobbs, and departed.

Goldie proceeded to leap into her clothes with fevered haste. It really was absurd of him to come so early. Absurd of Hobbs too to pretend she did not know his name! She must have seen Maurice scores of times. Part of her overwhelming sense of propriety, no doubt!

She combed her hair rapidly, dabbed some rouge on her cheeks, and then furiously rubbed it off again. What did it matter if she was pale? She would probably be much too red very soon. He had a knack of making her feel hot all over.

Ready at length, she went to the window for a moment and drew two or three hard breaths. Below her, very far below, was an empty passage between blank walls. She stared down into it. How strange if she overbalanced and fell down there! Would she be sorry? Would she be glad? She could not tell. She only knew with a certainty that admitted of no evasion that she would have given all she had to have escaped the interview before her.

With a dash of self-ridicule, she drew back and went downstairs.

At the door of the morning-room for a moment she paused, feeling ridiculously like a schoolgirl about to be punished for some escapade; then with a defiant swing she threw open the door and entered.

A large square figure was standing at the window. It turned to meet her.

"I say, I hope you don't mind," said a voice—the last voice in the world that she had expected to hear.

And, "You!" cried Goldie.

The door banged behind her—she sprang forward. They met in the middle of the room.

"You!" she cried again, and, sobbing and laughing, she threw her arms around his neck. "Peter—you darling!"

Their lips met just as inevitably as long ago on the shore at Pentreith. He clasped her in a great bear-hug that was infinitely satisfying to her torn spirit.

"Oh, Peter, you do me good!" she said, and the tears were running down her face.

"I'm awfully glad," he said in his frank, honest way. "I say—you're crying!"

"Don't stop me! I'm enjoying it!" sobbed Goldie. "Kiss me again, darling! Hold me tight! Oh, why did you stay away so long?"

Peter kissed her again several times over, a little astonished by the warmth of his reception, but by no means unbalanced. "Fancy your remembering me!" he said, squeezing her closer in his large, comforting embrace.

"Remember you!" gasped Goldie. "Why, you haven't changed a bit!"

"Nor have you," he said. "You don't look a day older. There! That's better, isn't it?" He pulled out a handkerchief and dried her tears with clumsy gentleness. "It's awfully jolly to be together again, isn't it?"

"I don't believe it's true yet," said Goldie, still clinging to him. "I shall wake up in a minute and find you've gone back to your vile ranch in Canada."

He laughed softly—the laugh of a big happy boy. "I'll take you with me if I do—that is, if you'll come."

"Like a shot, I will," said Goldie—which was all of proposal or acceptance that ever passed between them. She added somewhat resentfully: "I'd have done it long ago if you'd given me the chance."

"Would you?" said Peter in surprise. "I say, I wish I'd known! But I thought you'd chucked me many years ago. I never dreamt——"

"Idiot!" said Goldie tersely. "Of course I chucked you! You weren't worth keeping. You don't suppose I *wanted* to carry you about in my heart all this time, do you?"

"And yet . . ." said Peter, slightly puzzled, but hoping for the best.

She laid her head down on his shoulder. "I just couldn't help myself, that's all. You simply spoilt the rest of creation for me. I've often hated you for it."

"Hating me now?" suggested Peter, bracing himself to hear the worst.

She turned her face up to his again. "No, loving you—loving you—loving you! Why—darling—why—didn't you come back before?"

He kissed her quivering lips once more and was silent for a space, battling with a certain emotion of his own. "Let's sit down and I'll tell you all about it," he said at length. "You see, Goldie, I never thought you'd look at me again, and it was no good coming over and making myself miserable, was it ?"

"Would you have been miserable ?" said Goldie, pressing closer within his encircling arm.

"I was damnably miserable when I went," said Peter.

"But you got over it ?" she suggested.

"I made myself get over it," he said, squaring his jaw. "I never left off loving you. I couldn't do that. But when you chucked me——"

"I never really chucked you !" protested Goldie.

"Well, darling, I thought you meant to," he said. "I can show you your letter if you like. It certainly sounded quite definite. You said——"

"Stop !" commanded Goldie. "Where is that letter ? Give it to me !"

"I'm not parting with it," said Peter.

"Yes, you are ! Give it to me at once ! Dash it all, Peter ! You've got *me*. What more do you want ?" She lifted her head from his breast to survey him with sparkling eyes.

Peter meekly yielded. "It's in my pocket, darling. You can take it if you want it."

She laid her head down again. "Presently will do. Well, go on ! When I chucked you, as you put it, what happened then ?"

"You just became a dream to me," he said, speaking with reverence. "I put you into a secret corner of my soul that no one else ever came near, and I worshipped you in private."

"You didn't forget me, then ?" said Goldie, mollified.

"I never forgot you," he answered simply. "I couldn't. And I didn't want to. But I had to make good somehow— though I was only a farmer." Goldie stirred restlessly. "So I just carried on and pulled the ranch together and made a decent thing of it. Then—this year—the lease of Tregassa Castle expires, so I always knew I should have to come home to see to it. And I used to say to myself that p'raps I'd see you again. But I never thought you'd look at me."

Goldie stirred again. "Because you were only a farmer, I suppose ?" she said.

"That was how you put it," said Peter.

"Pig !" said Goldie. "I don't mean you this time. I'm a horried beast, Peter, and I loathe myself. And oh, d'you know, an awful thing is happening this afternoon ! There's a man coming to ask me to marry him."

"Well, you can't," said Peter.

R

"No, I know. And I shall have to tell him so." She rubbed her cheek against his shoulder. "Peter, the awful part is, I was going to say—'Yes',"she whispered.

"Poor devil!" said Peter gently.

"You needn't pity him. He's had a jolly lucky escape. Besides, he doesn't really know what love means—not—our sort of love," murmured Goldie in the hushed tones of one making confession. "It was only—a sort of makeshift with me too. I thought it was the most I'd ever get. You came—only just in time, Peter."

"You'd better let me see him," said Peter, pressing the golden head against his breast. "Maybe I can explain better."

"I think we'll see him together," said Goldie with a shiver. "I shall be very glad when it's over."

The thought of Baronford indeed threw a very definite shadow over that first happy hour of their reunion. Goldie was inclined to start at every sound, and when at length the long decided ring at the door-bell announced his arrival, she turned so white that Peter thought she would faint.

"Don't you come, darling! You're not up to it. Leave it to me!" he urged.

But Goldie would not be persuaded. "You wouldn't think much of me if I did," she said. "And I should despise myself—even worse than I do already. But you can come too," she added. "I don't think I could make him believe me alone."

"All right," said Peter quietly.

Goldie got up and straightened her hair.

The butler opened the door. "Mr. Baronford, miss. Would you wish me to show him up?"

"In the drawing-room is he?" said Goldie. "No, Wilson, I'll come down." She turned to her companion. "Come on, Peter! Let's get it over!"

Wilson's eyes opened very wide as he ceremoniously ushered them out. Peering over the stair-rail, he had a glimpse of them descending hand in hand, and murmured, "What-O!" to himself with much emphasis.

They were still hand in hand as they entered the drawing-room where Baronford was waiting.

He turned sharply at their coming, and then he stood still and watched them with a slow malice dawning in his eyes till they reached him.

Goldie spoke, her voice very clear and resolute. "Maurice, this is a very old friend of mine—Peter Tregassa—who has just come back from Canada—to marry me."

"Indeed !" said Baronford. He gave Peter a single comprehensive glance from head to foot, and then addressed himself to the girl as if they were alone. "This is a very good act," he said. "How did you manage it ?"

The colour flamed into her face. "Ask him !" she said.

Baronford's lips drew back. He did not give Peter a second look. "I fancy that has been done already," he said, "by—Lady Templeton. Please congratulate her for me on the success of her manœuvre !"

"She had nothing to do with it," declared Goldie hotly. "He came entirely on his own—didn't you, Peter ?"

Peter turned to her. "I came on my own, certainly," he said.

"By Lady Templeton's invitation, I think," put in Baronford smoothly.

Peter was silent.

Goldie gave him a quick look and plunged for safety. "Well, it doesn't matter, anyhow. We've cared for each other for the last ten years, and now we're together again we're going to get married."

She lifted her chin defiantly. Maurice Baronford was laughing. "Ten years ! My dear Goldie, you must have been in your cradle when it began ! Well, I congratulate you—and your mother too. Don't forget to ask about her share in the transaction ! You'll invite me to the wedding, I hope ? And, by the way, if it doesn't interfere with your plans, I shall hope to see you at mine. Virginia and I—on the thirtieth ! I came in this afternoon to tell you all about it. But, as you are otherwise engaged, I won't stay. Good-bye—both of you ! Allow me to wish you—all that you deserve !"

He was on his way down the long room as he spoke the last words. He effected his exit with dignity, and Peter checked Goldie as she made a nervous dash at the bell.

"Don't, darling ! Let him show himself to the door ! It's—kinder !"

Goldie yielded to his arm. She was pale and trembling. "Aren't I a fool, Peter ? I feel as if—the powers of evil have been let loose !"

"They shan't touch you, anyhow," declared Peter stoutly.

"And—what did he mean about—Mother ?" questioned Goldie. "It wasn't her doing, was it, Peter ?"

Peter hesitated a second, then spoke with simple directness. "Your mother has been very good to me, Goldie. I told her all those years ago that I cared for you. And she did send me a message to say it was now—or never !"

"The artful dodger!" ejaculated Goldie.

"Or the fairy godmother!" amended Peter.

Goldie broke into a laugh—the merriest she had uttered for months. "The same thing, my dear boy, but belonging to different periods! No, darling, you mustn't dishevel me again at present. Remember, I've got to face Wilson! Let's go back and have some tea. I'm dying for a drink."

"Come on, then!" said Peter, catching the infection of her gaiety. "I'll race you up the stairs!"

CHAPTER V

THE HOLIDAY PAL

"She'll soon be here now, sir," said Dan Bellamy in the tone of one who seeks to soothe a petulant child. "It's gone five o'clock, sir, so she can't be much longer."

"Perhaps she isn't coming!" said Eric with a twisted smile.

"Oh, you bet she is, sir!" responded Dan.

Yet he looked with some anxiety at his charge's face, which was grey and strained under the fast-greying hair. Every year it was the same—the anxiety of waiting, the rapture of fulfilment, and afterwards the long, long silence of desolation. Not once yet had she failed him, this faithful friend of his, though the trysting-place had always hitherto been the Castle Hotel under Dan's benign patronage. This year, against Dan's own judgment, they were realizing a long talked-of dream and keeping their high festival on the rocky coast that had seen their first reunion. It had long been Eric's most earnest desire, and with Peter's return to take possession of his inheritance the proposition had become feasible. But Peter was not now on the scene, and Dan rather uneasily wished he were.

He had been present a week before to assist in transporting his cousin to this far-off spot on the Cornish coast; but Tregassa Castle was not to be vacated finally by its tenant until the end of the month, and so he had stayed only long enough to establish the cripple at Truelove Farm in the care of his old friends the Riders before hastening away to rejoin his *fiancée*. Goldie, adhering to her prophetic decision, had fixed upon her parents' wedding-day for the ceremony of her own, and it was Peter's plan to take formal possession of Tregassa Castle immediately afterwards. He wanted Eric to remain for this, but Eric's decision in the matter was not yet made. He could not, or would not, see beyond the present—the one week in the whole year in which it could be truly said that he lived. How he had counted upon that week, dwelt upon it, made every provision for it, only Dan Bellamy knew—Dan who had become his self-devoted slave through the long period of his imprisonment and who had come to regard that week as almost a sacred observance.

He shared in his charge's anxiety, laboriously as he sought to conceal the fact, just as he shared in his rejoicing when it was over, just as in silence he sympathized when the long grey desolation came down upon them again. The tie that bound him to the helpless invalid was too spiritual for definition, but it held him as with bands of steel As he himself sometimes remarked in expansive moments, Major Morven was a man after his own heart—the sort of chap you'd go to hell for—and there you were. Eric himself never attempted to define it. He only occasionally with a twinkle referred to him as Brother Dan, and thus expressed a link unbreakable in the great chain forged between so many in the furnace of the Great War.

He had never openly taken Dan into his confidence, yet Dan knew the truth as no other man knew it, and that vigil for the yearly visitor meant almost as much to him as it did to Eric. In his opinion Eric drew practically the whole of his vitality from that one week of bliss. Certainly his sole desire to live hung upon it.

The fact that a fresh rendezvous had been chosen made him vaguely uneasy. The widespread golden moor with its upstanding and wholly incomprehensible grey rocks held small appeal for him. The persistent calling of the plover was a melancholy sound in his ears ; the great expanse of the ocean with the long incessant roar of its breakers troubled him inexplicably. He told himself uneasily that this was a wild sort of place where anything might happen, and indulged a depressed wish that his own more wholesome suggestion of a week at Brighton—"the very place for you, sir, cheery and all that"—had received more favourable treatment. Rocks and curlews were not in Dan Bellamy's line. Morbid he called them.

But still stoutly in Eric's presence he adhered to his declaration that the expected visitor would not now be long in arriving, interrupting the third repetition thereof to give utterance to an exclamation of complete astonishment at the sight of a car rounding a bend in the moorland road.

"Well, I'm dashed !" he ejaculated. "Why, there she is !"

Eric gave a sound that was half laugh and half an inarticulate expression of thankfulness. A gleam of sunshine shone on the advancing car, and he watched it with the eyes of a captive who sees a deliverer at hand. She had come to him again, and their one week of paradise had begun.

Helpless there in his invalid-chair, with Dan by his side, he awaited her, seeing the quick wave of her hand out of the car-window before he could distinguish herself. And something rose in his throat that was never there at any other time—something which it took his utmost strength of will to master.

"What did I tell you, sir ?" said Dan joyously, forgetful of all gloomy doubts now that ocular evidence had dismissed them. "Here she is again and looking just the same as ever !"

The car stopped close to them. Her slender figure, clad in grey nurse's uniform, descended. She came to Eric, smiling, radiant.

"How sweet of you to be waiting for me !" she said. "And how good to see you again !"

His hand held hers fast. He looked up at her with a sort of painful relief. "I've been waiting—a long time," he said.

"Oh, not so long, sir !" protested Dan officiously. "Good afternoon, sister ! It's a pleasure to see you again."

She gently freed her hand and gave it to him. "How do you do, Mr. Bellamy ? So you've found your way down to this lovely place ?" She turned her face to the ocean and drew in a deep breath. "I'd almost forgotten *how* exquisite it is."

Dan did not agree with her, but he liked her too much to say so. Also, it was quite obvious that his opinion was of no importance at the moment. He turned his attention to Eric. "I'll wheel you inside, sir, shall I ? Sister and you will be glad of a cup of tea."

They did not pay much attention to him, but it was he who managed everything, put a judicious end to any embarrassing moments, and with solid common-sense conducted them both into as practical a situation as his extremely practical brain could devise.

The farm parlour was to his mind a very poor substitute for the spacious bed-sitting-room which Eric was wont to occupy at the Castle Hotel, but he had done his best to create comfort there, and when he had finally established them near the window where the fitful rays of the sinking sun streamed in and had pulled the table with the tea-tray on it close to Marcia's side, he gave a last look round and effaced himself.

"Good chap!" said Eric. "I believe he's almost jealous of you coming to take care of me. He treats Webb like a worm—and a poor one at that."

"He loves you very dearly," said Marcia. "But I expect you miss Webb, don't you?"

"There's only one person in the world I ever miss," he made answer. "Without her, I live in a sort of torpor and never notice who comes or goes."

"Eric!" she protested. "But you have my letters!"

He smiled at her. "Yes, dear, every one of them—placed in a sacred box which is labelled, 'To be burnt at my death'. Dan will see to that."

She shook her head. "You shouldn't keep them. They're not worth it—so sketchy I am often ashamed of them; but life is so full——"

"They fill my emptiness," he said. "They give me a vision of you which keeps me alive and sane. I can't tell you what they are to me—but perhaps I needn't try."

"Don't!" she said gently. "Tell me about the journey down! Peter wasn't sure if it was too much for you."

"Nothing is too much when you are on the way to achieve your heart's desire," he said. "Besides, Peter's a big noise now, and getting quite good at managing other people's concerns."

It was her turn to smile. "Yes, I love Peter," she said. "He has turned out exactly as I hoped he would. You haven't seen him and Goldie together yet?"

"I have not." Eric spoke with a hint of firmness. "I thought it kinder—to Peter I mean—to postpone a meeting with her until the irrevocable step had been taken. You may remember—we were not the closest of pals ten years ago."

Her eyes met his meditatively. "Was that the reason, I wonder?" she said.

"Perhaps not the only one," he admitted. "It's a complication—this engagement—isn't it?"

"But you're not sorry?" she said swiftly.

"Sorry!" He echoed the word with a faint laugh. "Could I be sorry for anything that brought you the most infinitesimal fraction of an inch nearer to me? No, dear, I'm not sorry. And Peter's a good chap. He'll never give us away."

Marcia's face, slightly flushed, was turned to the window. She was gazing out over the richly coloured moorland with an odd concentration, as though seeking to distinguish something not as yet in sight.

He broke in after a few moments almost imperiously: "It's not going to make the faintest difference really. Peter and I are great pals, but we've never lived together. I don't expect to see a great deal of him, especially when he's married."

"You will go back—with Dan—to Martinworth?" she said.

"That I don't know. I haven't decided." He spoke with a touch of exasperation. "I never can look beyond our holiday week together. Perhaps—if I can endure it when you're gone—I may stay on for a bit when Webb comes back, to please Peter. He wants me here when he takes possession of Tregassa Castle. The people there don't clear out before the twenty-ninth. They got a month's extension for a house-party. They're a hunting crowd."

"It would do you good to stay here," said Marcia gently. "It's a very long journey for only a week."

"I'm not sure that I shall stand it without you," he said stubbornly.

She turned her look upon him. "Now you're exaggerating, aren't you? But it's wonderful to be here again—quite wonderful. Do you remember that night I got lost and came struggling here through the fog?"

"I remember—everything," he said.

Her eyes went back to the window and the sunset glow on the moor. "I can't believe it is ten years ago," she said. "Look at those sea-birds, Eric! Surely they are the same!"

"Are we the same?" he said, with a smile that was slightly twisted.

She shook her head slowly. "Not in all ways, perhaps, but in some—I think in many. Tell me more about yourself! Are things—just as they were with you?"

"I don't know," he answered sombrely. "I imagine so.

But I gave up consulting doctors long ago. They can't do me any good."

She turned back to the tea-tray with a look of sadness on her face. "I wish you hadn't given up hope," she said as she filled his cup.

"Have you any ?" he asked her point-blank.

"Of course I have !" she said. "You are still so young. I can't picture you with your life finished. I never have in all these years."

"You think a magician will come along," he suggested with bitter humour, "and wave a wand over me, and up I shall leap like a jack-in-the-box, shedding my grey hairs in all directions, and dance the giddy jazz of youth ?"

"Well, not quite like that perhaps !" She was smiling as she put his tea-cup within reach. "But all the same, I don't believe the curtain has rung down for you yet. I never have."

"No," he said, "I know you haven't. And—in a way— that optimism of yours has kept me going all this time. You're a very convincing person, Marcia."

"Am I ?" she said. "Well, it's because I am convinced myself."

"Even after ten years ?" His tone held irony, but it held something besides that sent a very tender look into her eyes.

She nodded quietly. "Yes, Eric. Even after ten years. I wish you would consult a surgeon again."

"Just to be told that by all the rules of the game I ought to die in the next six months ?" he suggested.

"No. No one would tell you that now." With steady conviction she answered him. "You've outlived that at least. And you've not lost ground. There must be a cure—I am sure there must be a cure—for a case like yours."

"Why should there be ?" he countered. "There are heaps of fellows crippled in the same way—fellows younger than I am—for whom these wonderful specialists can do nothing. Why should I be an exception ?"

He spoke almost fiercely, but still that something which had brought tenderness into her eyes was in his voice—as if he were appealing against himself, desiring to hear his argument refuted.

But Marcia did not attempt to refute it. She merely reiterated her own unalterable conviction. "I can't tell you why you should be an exception," she said. "I just feel you are, that's all. And I want you—very much—to give yourself another chance."

"To please you ?" he said.

Her eyes looked straight into his. "Certainly to please me—though not for my sake alone."

He pushed aside his plate and felt for his cigarette-case. "You have confidence enough to save an army from rout," he said. "Do you really want me to do it, Marcia ?"

"Haven't I told you so ?" she said with her faint smile.

"You haven't told me why," he said, watching her.

"I thought I had," said Marcia.

He made a slight negative gesture. "Why do you want me to be sound again ? Would it mean a great deal to you ?"

"It would mean a very great deal," she made warm reply. "Much more than I could possibly tell you."

His eyes lighted. "As much as that ?" he said.

She smiled at him, but her lips were trembling. "I think I want it—almost more than anything else on earth," she said in a low voice. "Eric, don't you ever say to yourself that but for me—but for my miserable moral weakness——"

"Stop !" he said sharply. "We're not going to discuss that. And at least we were partners in that show. Is that your only reason for wanting me to get well ?"

"My dear !" she said, and all the gracious sweetness of her was in the words. She stretched her hand to him across the table in mute protest.

He took and held it. "You're so wonderful, Marcia," he said. "I only see you for one week in the year, and each time it comes round I torture myself with the thought that you will have changed. And then you come to me just the same— just as beautiful—as generous—as splendid in your giving——" He broke off. "I don't know how you do it. Your ways are beyond me. There is no other woman in the world who could do the same."

"But what nonsense !" she said. "I call that sheer morbid-ity—if there is such a word." Her eyes smiled at him, rallying him. "Now light your cigarette and let's enjoy ourselves ! I'm going to have another cup of tea."

Her hand was free. She busied herself with the tea-pot while he sat gazing at her. Then, when she was ready, he held the cigarette-case out to her.

She took one and lighted a match for them both. The sunshine on the moor was deeply golden and beginning to take a ruddy tinge. The atmosphere had a crystal transparency as though rain were not far distant. Here and there against the grey rocks tufts of brilliant bracken stood out with a fiery vividness. Overhead the peewits and sea-gulls were calling, and from the distance came the long deep roar of the sea—the eternal accompaniment to life's fitful dream.

There fell a long silence between them, and a strange peacefulness settled slowly upon the face of the man as though his spirit were aware of some healing touch beneath which the weary fret of circumstances seemed to be smoothed away.

The face of the woman in that quiet hour—with all its serenity and its strength of purpose—was the sadder of the two.

The sun dipped lower and lower to the heaving grey waters. The glorious colours of the moorland began to fade. And there in the western sky, hanging as it were between earth and heaven, there shone a gleaming curve like the fragment of a severed golden ring.

Marcia was the first to see it, and, rising quietly, opened the window wide. "Look !" she said.

"Ah ! The new moon !" said Eric. He looked up at her, took her hand again for a moment and held it against his face.

She patted his shoulder. "I saw it through glass, but you didn't, so all is well."

"Why should my welfare come before yours ?" he said.

"Perhaps because you need it more," she answered.

He smiled and released her. "Don't be subtle ! Sit down and have another cigarette ! Do you know I can't quite get over Peter being received into the bosom of your family ? Does everybody approve ?"

"Of course," she said lightly. "I made the match, didn't I ? No one would dare to disagree with me."

He laughed. "Sorry ! I forgot you were so formidable. Then why didn't you arrange for the wedding to take place earlier in the year ?"

"Oh, that !" said Marcia, and hesitated for a second. "That was Goldie's doing."

"Thought she'd keep him dangling for a bit, eh ?" suggested Eric with some of his old sardonic humour.

"No, no !" protested Marcia. "Don't be so uncharitable ! The child had a particular reason for wanting to be married on the eighteenth of this month. It was just a fancy—and a very pretty one."

"Well, what was it ?" he said.

Again she hesitated, but only for a moment. "Do you

really want to know ? Well, I'll tell you—though I expect you'll laugh. She is going to be a silver bride—and a very lovely one. It is to be—a silver wedding altogether, so she says. It sounds romantic in these prosaic days, doesn't it ? But it was entirely her own idea. She insists that I am to wear silver too."

"Afraid I don't see the point," said Eric.

She laughed rather tremulously. "No ; I hadn't come to it. It is to be a sort of double silver wedding, you see ; hers—and mine."

"Yours !" said Eric, as if startled.

She bent her head. In the falling dusk her face was in shadow. "Yes. My silver wedding," she said.

He made a sudden movement of the hands that was almost like a gesture of despair, then sat in absolute immobility during the passage of many seconds.

When he spoke at last, his voice was cold, curiously edged and concise, as though the irony of it were lifted as a shield, protecting his soul. "Have you actually been married twenty-five years ? I should have thought you had hardly been alive as long as that."

Her faint laugh had a deprecating sound. "Ah !" she said. "It's time I left off pretending to be young—even with you."

He did not answer her, and she turned and softly closed the window, for a chill air was blowing in from the sea.

As she turned back, he spoke suddenly, jerkily : "Marcia ! Will you—kiss me ?"

She bent immediately, with a movement that was largely maternal, and—as once long ago—her lips touched first his forehead and then met his own. He clasped her with a desperate closeness, finally pressing his face against her breast.

"Forgive me," he whispered almost inarticulately, "if I ever ask—too much !"

She laid her hand upon his head, holding it to her heart as though she comforted a child. "I shall never have to forgive you for that, my own dear holiday pal," she whispered back very tenderly.

And in the silence that came upon them all sorrow and all bitterness were put away.

CHAPTER VI

THE DINNER OF HERBS

THE return to Pentreith and the passing of those early October days had a dreamlike quality for Marcia which she would have found it difficult to define. Almost insensibly she had come to regard this one week in the year not so much as an oasis, but as a stretch of quiet water between the roaring rapids of her life. Often as she approached it, it was with an unacknowledged dread—the fear of a possible undercurrent more dangerous than the open vortex ; but always when she reached it she found calm, complete understanding, unruffled peace.

After that first evening no faintest ripple agitated the still surface of their intercourse, no difficulties of any sort rose between them, no urgencies disturbed their quiet idyll. To all outward appearances they were patient and nurse, and there was but little in their more private moments to indicate any closer tie.

During the years of his helplessness a deeper reserve had grown upon Eric Morven—such a reserve as only strong feeling could penetrate, and that but partially and for very brief periods. With the loss of his physical independence he had as it were developed an inner and more solid self-reliance that kept all casual compassion and even sympathy at bay. He lived his own life and bore his own burden, neither giving nor accepting confidence ; and the darkness he went through, the suffering he endured, were not spoken of even to Marcia. That was the splendour of him in her eyes, and a tie that bound her to him more closely than any other. She did not realize that it was here—rather than in any similarity of tastes—that they trod common ground together and faced the world as comrades. They were one in a glorious standard of courage which each sensed in the other, but to which neither gave utterance.

Quietly the golden days slipped by, each one perfect in its own fashion, untroubled by regrets or premonitions, filled only with the sunshine of complete content. Though the progress of their friendship had been wellnigh imperceptible, it had reached a stage of development in which it seemed that passion no longer played an important part. In their most

intimate moments they were lovers of the spirit rather than
of the flesh, and it was seldom that any endearments passed
between them. Only at rare intervals a word or touch would
rekindle the spark, but it was never apparent for long. It
died down again as swiftly as it arose, and the steady comradeship would take its place. Though it may be given to no two
people to know each other wholly, yet between these two
there was a knowledge which bred an almost flawless sympathy
in the ordinary ways of life, and that week on the Cornish
coast was to them a period of peace and deep enjoyment
which diffused a healing influence in varying measure on
the souls of both.

They spent practically the whole of their time on the moor
or on the grassy track that ran up to the headland where
once Dennis had gone in quest of gulls' eggs. They seldom
spoke of those past days, yet to Marcia they often seemed
very near, so unchanged was the place and so vivid was the
memory. Save for a few showers which were soon blown away
by the brisk west wind, the weather remained favourable,
and during one or two days an actual summer warmth
prevailed. They had brought books to read together, and
sometimes Marcia brought out her sketching-block, though
this was only at Eric's urgent insistence.

"I must have some memento of this to take back with
me," he said, "or I shall never persuade myself hereafter
that it hasn't all been a dream."

She yielded to him as always, half-laughing, half in earnest,
for he was impossible to resist, and any reference, however
indirect, to his hours of loneliness went straight to her heart.
And so, sitting beside him on a campstool, on the verge of the
cliff, with the sound of the sea in their ears and the sea-birds
calling all around, she sketched for him the downward sweep
of the coast, with Truelove Farm standing among its stacks
in the middle distance.

He watched her while the picture grew under her hand—
the slim, grey-clad figure with its pale and strangely vital
face, still retaining its look of youth and the charm which
belongs neither to youth nor age—the transcendent gift
bestowed only upon the few. What was the secret of it, he
wondered, as many others have wondered through the ages?
How was it that this woman alone possessed the power
to awake those inner harmonies which without her were for
ever silent? Though she donned that simple nurse's uniform
for him, she wore it like a queen, and had it been cloth of

gold it would have given her no greater splendour in his eyes. Was it because in all she said or thought or did there was nothing trivial or ungenerous ?

Sometimes he criticized her work, but never severely, for she was always so humble about it that he was half afraid of discouraging her. More often it gave him deeper satisfaction to sit in silence and watch. It seemed to give him a closer hold upon the precious hours which were slipping so fast away.

"When we come here again," he said on the afternoon of their fifth day, "I want you to do the cove down there with the tide coming in, just as it is now."

Marcia turned her head to look. "I wish Dan wouldn't put your chair so near the edge," she said. "I told him so yesterday."

"And I'm afraid I countermanded the order," he rejoined. "I can't see the cove properly unless he does."

She looked at him with an attempt at sternness. "Eric, you are not to countermand my orders. If you were alone up here, it wouldn't be safe. Suppose a gust of wind came up——"

"My dear, it would have to be a very powerful one to send me over the edge at this distance," he pointed out. "And may I remind you that the wind invariably blows from the opposite direction ? Also that there are stones wedged under the wheels ? Also, that the odds are all in my favour ? Nobody ever goes over the edge twice !"

She shuddered a little. "Well, I don't like to think of it, so please be sensible ! What was it you were saying about the next time we come ? Oh, the cove ? I don't believe I could ever do that. Besides, by then——"

"By then ?" he repeated as she paused.

She began to smile. "I was going to say something that may sound cruel, though you know I don't mean it so. By then, I think—very possibly—you will be getting about on your own feet."

"Ah, do you ?" he said, and stopped, as if for the moment something prevented him from saying more.

She had turned back to her sketch, and she waited for his next words with a trepidation that made her hand almost too unsteady to continue its work. When his pause became a definite silence, she ceased to attempt anything further, and sat waiting.

He spoke at last very slowly, filling his pipe the while

with no hint of agitation. "Do you really think that possible, Marcia ?"

"I wouldn't say it, dear, if I didn't," she answered gently.

"No," he said, "I know—you wouldn't. But I wonder why you think it."

She turned and looked at him. His face was as calm as his words, yet she was conscious of strain behind his composure. He did not meet her look, but continued firmly intent upon his task, and in a moment, with that intuition which never failed her in her dealings with him, she had averted her own look again.

"Simply because you are certainly stronger," she said. "If I had been with you all the time like Dan, I might not have noticed it. But seeing you as I have, after a year's interval, well, there is no getting away from it. There is a difference."

"You're quite sure of that ?" he said.

"In my own mind, quite sure," she answered. "I have noticed it during this week, over and over again. You move with far greater ease than you did. You are not so quickly tired. And I have sometimes thought, when Dan was lifting you, that in certain positions you were able to help a little."

He finished the filling of his pipe with quiet concentration and put it into his mouth, and she, though no longer looking at him, was aware of everything that he did, heard the rasp of his match and the calm puffing with which he kindled the tobacco, and wondered rather desperately if she had been wise in speaking with such freedom upon a subject which meant so much to him.

Then, very deliberately, his voice came to her, faintly humorous, and she was conscious of a deep relief.

"What an observant sister !" he said. "And suppose all these wonderful surmises are true—suppose the miracle were to happen—what then ?"

She turned towards him again, as if his words had given her tacit permission. Her eyes were lovely with a light that seldom shone there. "Oh, Eric," she said, "if it did happen, how I should thank God !"

He looked at her with a species of semi-whimsical adoration. "Darling, I wonder if I should," he said.

"Oh ,surely !" she said. "Surely !"

His look went beyond her to the distant sea, to the sky-line. "Or whether I should find that my 'dinner of herbs—with love' had been more satisfying," he said.

For once she did not understand him, but something restrained her from asking his meaning. She laid her hand upon his arm in a mute gesture of friendship. . . .

A dull thudding on the moor behind them interrupted their silence.

Marcia gave a swift glance over her shoulder and turned back to her sketch.

Eric laughed a little, softly, and resumed the enjoyment of his pipe.

In another moment two riders passed them—a man and a woman—accompanied by a half-grown Alsatian and an Irish wolfhound. The two dogs were jesting together. The riders were silent. As they came close they checked their horses to a walk, but Marcia, glancing at them, saw only their profiles as they went by along the cliff track. Neither turned to look their way.

Yet when they were past, a burning colour was on her face, and the hand that sought to continue her sketch was powerless.

"That's some of the crowd at Tregassa Castle," murmured Eric, as the two quickened their pace and passed out of earshot.

He did not notice anything peculiar in Marcia's silence for some moments ; then he was concerned by it. He turned and looked at her closely.

"My dear, what's the matter ?" he said.

She mustered a smile with difficulty, not meeting his eyes. "Nothing, dear, nothing," she said, and stooped to erase a few aimless marks upon the block before her. "I know them both, that's all. I wonder whether they knew me."

"Who are they ?" he asked briefly.

She answered as it were mechanically. "The man is a certain Maurice Baronford who at one time was very keen on marrying Goldie. The woman is now his wife. They were married last summer. Her name was Virginia Freeman. She used to be a friend of mine."

"Used to be !" He echoed the words half-laughing. "That's very expressive. Well, she certainly didn't look at you as she went by, if that counts for anything. Do you imagine she saw you ?"

"I don't know," said Marcia gravely ; her eyes were following the figures dwindling in the distance. "Well, nothing can alter it now if she did."

"And if she did ?" he said.

Marcia turned back to her sketch and put in a few deft

S

touches. "As a matter of fact, he is the one most to be feared," she said.

"And why?" questioned Eric.

She hesitated a little. "Because I—circumvented him," she said finally. "Men in his position—K.C.s—don't like being circumvented."

Eric laughed suddenly and unexpectedly. "Was he in love with Goldie, then?"

Again she hesitated, but only for a second. "No," she said then very quietly. "He was not in love with her. He desired her, that's all."

"Ah! And the mother hen flapped her wings in furious indignation and drove him away. Was that it?" teased Eric.

"It may have looked like that to him," she admitted.

"Ah well, never mind!" he said lightly. "He didn't look at you either. And even if he did, no one could see you with the same eyes in that nurse's garb of yours."

"I hope not," said Marcia still gravely.

It was he this time who made the reassuring gesture. He touched her shoulder gently. "My dear," he said, "there is always a way out for you. Never forget that!"

She did not turn her head. Her attention was apparently focussed upon her sketch. As his hand fell, she uttered a faint sigh. "But is there ever a way back for those who have wandered too far?" she murmured under her breath.

CHAPTER VII

THE MIRACLE

IT was over. The world was empty, incredibly empty, save for the crying, wheeling sea-birds who seemed merely to emphasize the desolation. The sky was a heavy uniform grey, the moor a dull drab, the sea a tragic, changeless waste, veiled in a leaden mist through which its waves sent a perpetual muffled moaning.

The only definite thought in Eric's mind was that it was somehow more endurable than laughing waters and radiant sunshine. He had sent Dan away. Somehow the fellow's sympathy, silent though it was, was more than he could bear.

To be an object of pity was a situation that revolted him. He was in a state of mind to loathe the entire human race, with the exception of the one being who had passed beyond his reach, had gone back to the ties that bound her, the love that called.

How was he going to face it? How present an unchanging front to the world at large while this amazing pain racked his heart? It was true that he scarcely believed in that other love, yet it held her—beyond belief it held her. Somehow there was a fascination, the existence of which he could not deny, of the strength of which he had no gauge. She loved, possibly she was beloved, and it was all beyond his scope, outside his experience. And his love for her—that great, abiding force which nothing could quench—was only a secondary consideration in her life. She had other claims which were paramount. It was not that his love was nothing to her, but it could not hold her.

She gave him all she had to spare, and there was even joy in the giving; but the thing unknown, beyond, possessed her as he could never hope to possess. He was the comrade, the intimate friend, in some ways the most intimate friend she would ever know, but it was not friendship that drew her from him, leaving him thus forlorn and stranded on the desert shore of life. It was an infinitely stronger, and at the same time a weaker thing, a thing of the earth, all the more potent because of its mortality, a thing that gripped and held the faster because it could not last, was made subject unto death. And for this she sacrificed the greater, the eternal. For this she laid aside his devotion, gently loosened the almost frenzied clinging of his spirit, and went her way, leaving him lacerated and alone. O Life, that holds so little! O Death, that gives so much! . . .

He had made Dan, though sorely against his will—"for it's going to rain, sir; you can see it coming up, one of them nasty sea-mists"—wheel him up the grass track to the point where they had been wont to sit together.

Peter had wished him to stay on for a time, and he wanted to find out if human endurance could be induced to stand the strain. But he had soon sent Dan away with curt insistence, because the honest grey eyes held such a wealth of compassion that he was perverse enough to feel sick and surfeited. Of what use was pity when there was no remedy? Better far to suffer alone. Let pity be given to those who ask for it! Its only effect upon him was to send him into a state of fierce revolt. He could have cursed Dan for not being cheery on that particular morning, and he reflected with thankfulness that his own man, Webb, who was blessed with a peculiarly wooden temperament and could scarcely be described as an individual at all, was returning to him on the following day. Dan was a good fellow, one of the best, but he belonged to the intermediate type in which sentiment and the tactful expression thereof conspicuously fail to collaborate. Dan was honest and obvious in all his ways. And the most humiliating thing about him was that he would have laid down his life for this man whom he loved, and done it decently too.

So much for Dan! He flicked him from his mind as he might have flicked an intrusive fly from his person. And again the desolation came upon him, a vast wave of it, towering, threatening, finally overwhelming. . . .

"My God!" he said a little later, as he tasted a drop of salt water that was not of the sea on his lips. "Keep me sane if You can! What would she say to this?"

What would she say? Ah, nothing, save perhaps "My dear!" as she wound warm, protecting arms about him. And suddenly he remembered how once, that first time, she had said to him: "There is nothing to be afraid of. God is here."

Later he asked himself, drearily, incredulously, if it could possibly have been only the call of duty that had taken her from him.

The slow hours crept away. It was cold up there on the cliff, but it was infinitely preferable to the simple homeliness of Truelove Farm, the warm firelight, the shadows on the wall. He had told Dan not to come back for him until four, but he had a shrewd suspicion that his faithful attendant was not far away, that a brief whistle would call him to his side.

But he hesitated to give it. The tide was beginning to run into the cove below him, and it was a sight that always held his fancy. He loved the roar of the breakers just outside and the swirl of the great waves rushing in and then drawing out again, leaving only the spread whiteness of their foam. It was like life, so full one moment, so empty the next; only, unlike life, it was bound to be filled to the utmost at last.

The scene took on a greyer shade. The afternoon had begun to wane. He pictured her seated at a window in the tearing eastward-bound express, seeing what he saw, pitying him in his loneliness—only her pity was divine and had no sting. And he remembered quite suddenly that at the last she had made him promise to go in early that day. In his misery he had forgotten it. Well, he would summon Dan at once.

The impulse, even as it moved him, was checked. There came behind him a thudding sound, and abruptly a man's voice called a sharp order.

In the same instant he heard the taunting bark of a dog at play. Two animals rushed panting up behind his chair. He did not see them, but, swift as the stab of a knife, came realization of that which was upon him. There came a shock, a startled yelp, and the chair was in motion, gliding down the grassy slope, and gathering speed as it went, towards that grim grey edge of rock which had aroused Marcia's misgivings two days before.

It was like an avalanche, paralysing, inevitable, transforming in a moment complete security into vivid and appalling danger. And in that moment there flashed into being in Eric's soul that which he had believed to be long dead—the urgent and most primitive instinct of all, the desire of life. It went through him like a flame, consuming all beside. Frantically he sought to grip the wheels that were racing him to his doom.

It was a wild effort, conceived and executed in an access of terror so stark and so compelling that even as he made it he felt himself like a stone flung at random over that unguarded precipice. And he was conscious of the startled sea-gulls screaming all around him, and the awful rush of the wind, and the immense roar of the sea that was like the triumphant shouting of a wide-throated monster claiming yet another victim for its prey.

Then came darkness, a strange darkness fretted with tiny points of light, and little inconsequent sounds that came out of a heaving silence, quite inarticulate and meaningless.

He was down on the rocks now, and the wheeling sea-birds were far, far above him. Curiously he found himself repeating his own words: "Nobody ever goes over the edge twice." And somehow, though of course he was dying, he wanted to laugh. It had been such an extraordinary catastrophe.

Then he remembered the tide, the tide that was coming in. "Damn it all!" he said. "I don't want to be drowned as well!"

So with a movement that was oddly unfamiliar, he wrenched himself upwards. It was like the forcing of rusty joints, and he likened himself whimsically to a suit of armour that had stood in one position for the passage of centuries.

Then came pain, colossal and piercing, and a cry of agony escaped him. He rolled over on his face.

"Oh, God!" he gasped. "Oh, God!"

And—was it in answer to that agonized appeal?—suddenly he found strength. His knees were doubled under him. He raised himself up on them, and they bore his weight. The darkness passed like a film from his sight. He saw the green grass around him, and two men—Dan and the stranger who had passed him on horseback two days ago—were rushing to help him.

So he had not gone over the edge again after all! The odds had been justified. But what was this new thing that had come upon him? He had fallen, fallen headlong. That he grasped. The wreck of his chair, upturned, with wheels in air, was within three yards of him. But he himself—he himself—what new thing was this?

They had almost reached him when he made a sudden, stupendous effort. He forced himself back upon his feet. He straightened his bent knees. He stood up, swaying, and raised his arms to the grey sky, half-involuntarily, half as it were in homage to a Power above him.

"My God!" he cried aloud. "The miracle!"—and dropped prone to the earth.

CHAPTER VIII

THE WEDDING-DAY

"And now you're ready, Miss Dora," said Hobbs with solemnity. "And may you always look as beautiful and be as happy as you are now!"

"Gosh!" said Goldie irreverently. "It's no good hoping for the moon, Hobbs, my dear. You ought to be old enough to know that."

Nevertheless, she regarded her shining reflection with some pardonable satisfaction and even a little awe. For Goldie as a bride was a very lovely thing indeed, robed in silvery white with silvery blossoms in her hair which shone deeply golden in contrast. Even in Court dress she had not looked so exquisite as now.

She turned from the glass impulsively and, bending, embraced the prim maid beside her. "Bless you, Hobby!

You've been a good friend to me," she said ; a remark which from Goldie meant a great deal and actually brought tears into Hobbs's eyes.

"It's—I'm sure it's always been a pleasure to oblige you, Miss Goldie," she murmured rather incoherently.

Someone knocked smartly on the door. "Oh, damn !" muttered Goldie. "That's Aunt Lillith."

Aunt Lillith it was, resplendently attired in ruby velvet. Being Goldie's godmother, she considered herself entitled to the freedom of her bedroom.

"Well, my dear, and how are you feeling by this time ?" was her greeting. "Keeping quite calm, I hope ?"

"Bored to tears," Goldie assured her, bestowing a very perfunctory salute upon the well-preserved cheek presented to her. "Have you seen my darling mother yet ? She is the real heroine of the occasion. Peter and I will consider ourselves lucky if we can squeeze into a couple of back seats."

"Don't be affected, my child !" said Aunt Lillith with a smile that tried to be indulgent ; for there was something about Goldie at times which made her wonder uneasily if what she termed affectation were not in some way a terrible and inverted form of sincerity.

"I quite see what you mean," said Goldie. "But I'm not. Let's go in and look for the real bride shall we ?"

Aunt Lillith shrugged slightly. After all, the younger generation—what could one expect ?

They passed out into the passage, the bride with her train slung over her arm and her filmy veil with its gleaming sequins thrown back and billowing out behind her.

"Now," said Goldie, approaching her mother's door, "prepare for a great surprise !"

But before they reached it, it opened, and Marcia herself came out.

She was dressed in silver tissue that gleamed at every turn, and she carried a splendid bouquet of deep red roses. She wore a large hat in which silvery threads also glimmered, which cast a kind of ethereal shadow over her sweet face.

"Darling !" her daughter exclaimed. "You look like a Peri emerging from a cloud ! But I can't understand how anybody had the moral strength to shut the gate against you."

"I was just coming to you," Marcia said. "Ah, Lillith, I thought I heard your voice. I hope you approve of us both."

Lillith looked at her with a sort of grudging appreciation, but before she could give it expression Goldie cut in effusively.

"The meeting of the brides ! Do let's go and find a Press man with a large camera ! Quite ready, are you, darling ? I must say you look a dream. Has Dad seen you yet ? Well, he must, at once ; and if he doesn't fall down and worship your silver feet, I disown him for ever. Look, Aunt Lillith ! We're wearing exactly the same shoes, except that Mum's are a shade darker than mine. A cute idea, isn't it ? Quite my own."

"My dear child, don't be so frothy !" said Lillith with austerity. "I remember when I was married——"

"Oh, my dear *tante*, not really !" protested the bride with incorrigible hilarity. "I'm sure I shan't when I've been married as long as you have, though as a matter of fact I've been married for the last ten years, though I've never mentioned it."

Lillith turned to her mother for explanation, but Marcia shook her head half in amusement and half in deprecation.

"Your aunt will think you are quite mad, Goldie," she said. "Come down now to your father ! I think he is waiting for us in the study."

"In that case I shall not be wanted," said Lillith in the tone of one who desires to be affronted. "I will go and make myself useful in the drawing-room."

"That would be very sweet of you," said Marcia, while Goldie sniggered her delight.

They were alone for a moment on the stairs, and with one consent they paused.

"Happy, sweetheart ?" whispered the mother.

"Crazy !" whispered back the daughter, kissing her ardently. "I hope I shan't dance a fox-trot all up the aisle, but Dad'll have to put the brake on pretty hard."

"I'll give him a hint," laughed Marcia.

Then they went to Sir Everard, who, immaculately dressed, awaited them in his study. Curiously enough, he had the look of a man about to face an ordeal, and though he smiled at them it was not without a certain restraint.

He kissed Goldie and drew her to his side. "I couldn't ask to see a happier bride," he said. "I need not put all that I wish for you into words, my dear. We can't expect the sun to shine always, but I hope, and I believe, that your happiness is of the sort that does not depend upon perpetual sunshine for its existence."

"Hear, hear !" said Goldie, and then went suddenly close to him and gave him a warm kiss. "I always knew you were a bit of a darling," she told him. "Now what do you think of your own bride ? Isn't she a rose ?"

He laughed a little and pressed a packet into her hand. "One at a time, Dora ! This is for you, to spend exactly as you like and not on this occasion to save. I would like you while on your honeymoon to buy something as a reminder that even in absence your father has always loved you."

"Oh, but you are a brick !" protested Goldie, genuinely moved. "I shall remember that without any reminding."

He kissed her again. "Well, run down now, dear ! You will find Dennis downstairs. He wanted to see you before starting for the church."

"Right-ho !" said Goldie. "I'll vanish. But don't be too long, for Mum's got to get there ahead of you this time, remember !"

She was gone, singing as if she could not help it, and even the shutting of the door did not immediately drown her song.

"God bless her !" murmured Marcia, and the tears came into her eyes also.

"You are happy about her ?" he asked, with a hint of stress upon the last word.

"Yes, completely happy," she answered. "She and Peter were made for each other."

"Ah !" he said. "I know the Baronford idea never appealed to you. Well, things are probably better as they are."

"I am sure of it," she said warmly. "It was only a passing fancy on his part. Besides, he owed it to Virginia."

He waved her assurance aside. "I wonder to whom he owed the frustration of the passing fancy," he said.

She flushed suddenly and deeply. "Well, naturally I used such influence as I had," she said rather haltingly.

"Naturally," agreed Sir Everard gravely. "I think he appreciated that."

"What do you mean ?" she said.

He made another quiet gesture as of putting away an un-desirable subject. "That is of no importance at the moment. Time is getting short. I am glad that you are happy, Marcia." He took her two hands very gently into his own. "And I would like you to know this, on our own wedding-day : if it is ever in my power to make you happier, I shall not shrink from doing so."

He stooped with the words and kissed her, and there was that in his kiss which held her back from attempting to pene-trate their significance. She could only kiss him in return, feeling as if he had ordained it, and conscious, strangely conscious, of a force encompassing her for good or evil, she knew not which.

CHAPTER IX

THE WEDDING

"My dear, how lovely you look!" whispered old Lady Barrowdale, as the bride's mother, graceful and radiant in her robe of shimmering silver, paused to greet her. "You are a picture out of a fairy-tale, or a Grecian goddess! I am not sure which."

The sunshine, mistily golden, falling through countless fragments of stained glass, gave a fairylike atmosphere to the whole church. It was crowded already, and Dennis and his fellow-groomsmen were busy.

"Wait till you see the bride!" murmured Marcia.

Lady Barrowdale, snowy-haired, attired in the peculiar shade of violet considered most appropriate by old ladies, patted her arm caressingly. "My dear, you couldn't show me anything lovelier than yourself. What a proud day for Everard! You are no more than a girl even yet."

Marcia laughed a little. "I have had some beautiful gifts. Isn't it ridiculous? And yours is in the place of honour. I want you to see them all."

"And where are you going for your silver honeymoon, dear?" said Lady Barrowdale.

Marcia shook her head. "Ask Everard! I think we are more likely to play at being the old folks at home."

"That is ridiculous, if you like," said Lady Barrowdale. "Ah, here is Dennis! What does he want?"

Dennis, extremely well-dressed and looking like a slim and youthful edition of his father, was at Marcia's elbow.

"I say," he said hurriedly, "could you have a word with Peter? I don't know if he's got cold feet or anything. But he wants you."

"Of course!" said Marcia. "Where is he?"

"Over there near the vestry-door. I must go," said Dennis, and was gone with the words.

Marcia looked across the church, encountering as she did so the vaguely supercilious stare of Maurice Baronford's wife, Virginia, who was seated with her husband a few pews away.

Marcia met the stare with a conventional smile. She and Virginia hardly knew each other in these days. They had barely exchanged greetings since Virginia's wedding in the summer. Maurice Baronford's smooth, expressionless face gave her a faintly cold sensation. She could imagine that as an enemy this man might be formidable, quite implacable, even ferocious in a grim, well-calculated, Chinese sort of fashion. The bare memory that he had once nearly ensnared her precious Goldie into marriage with him made her shrink. She wondered if Virginia had ever encountered the merciless steel of which that snare had been composed. But Virginia was different. Virginia was hard and calculating herself. She had none of Goldie's warm quick impulses. It was strange to feel that in womanhood Goldie had drawn so much closer to herself than in her childhood she had ever been.

But Peter—poor Peter was waiting, and she passed the Baronfords by and went to him.

Peter as a bridegroom, though bravely facing the situation, was not at his best. His square British figure was not of the type to grace a Society function, and when Marcia reached him she thought she saw signs of strain. Fortunately the organ was playing with an emphasis that made it possible to converse without any fear of being overheard.

"Well, Peter," she said giving him her hand, "everything's all right. Goldie will be here directly, and she isn't in the least nervous."

"Of course not! She wouldn't be," said Peter. He grasped her hand. "Look here! I've got something to tell you—a bit of a surprise. You won't let it upset you?"

She knew in a moment with whom his communication had to do. It was as if something stirred very deep down below the beating of her heart, and she knew that she would have to be brave too.

"What is it, Peter?" she said.

He hesitated for a moment, then he told her. "It's Eric. He's coming to the reception. Don't be startled when you see him, that's all! He told me to prepare you. There was no time to let you know any other way, except by ringing up, and he didn't like to do that."

"Eric!" She repeated the name with a kind of dazed

incredulity. "I thought he was still at Pentreith. Surely
. . . Why, I had a letter from him only——"

"I know," Peter cut in bluntly, almost brusquely for
him. "He ought to have told you. I don't know why he
didn't. I never thought he meant to turn up at this show, but
he says he has his reasons. So he's asked me to let you know.
I think he's mad to risk it. Still, it's no business of mine."

The curt grim sentences told of an agitation which she
would scarcely have expected him to betray even on his own
account. Looking at him, she saw that he was almost too
deeply stirred to remember that he was one of the principal
actors in the wedding drama about to be enacted. Actually
he seemed for the moment to have forgotten the very existence
of Goldie, his bride, who was already probably on her way to
the church.

"What are you trying to tell me?" said Marcia.

The swelling notes of the organ covered his reply. He
drew her slightly behind a pillar, and, bending, spoke into
her ear.

"He had an accident ten days ago—the day you left. I
wasn't there. It was a fall. And—well, it's done what they
said it might do years ago. He's able to walk."

"Able to walk!" She echoed the words unconsciously
almost uncomprehendingly. "Peter!"

"Yes, but look out!" Peter's words held a deep urgency.
"He's not up to much at present. He ought not to exert
himself, but he will do it. He's worried about something, or
somebody, who knows too much. And he said he wouldn't
leave you to face anything beastly alone."

He jerked out the information with an effort so palpable
that she realized that its utterance was one of the hardest
tasks that he had ever undertaken. His hand was still
gripping hers with a spasmodic violence.

"You know what I mean," he said—"what he's afraid of?"

His insistence would have told her, had not full understanding already burst upon her. It had come, then, at last,
this stroke of Fate which she had feared, and dared, for ten
unruffled years. The ground on which she stood had suddenly
opened, and she looked down into an abyss that appalled her.
For a space of several seconds, while the organ thundered
triumphant chords that seemed to shake the very walls around
them, she thought that her heart would never beat again. . . .

It was the desperate concern in Peter's face that brought
her back. She saw it first as through a mist, then more

definitely, till it dawned upon her that but for his upholding grip and the unyielding solidity of the pillar behind her, she must have fallen. The urgency with which he regarded her came suddenly upon her, imparted itself to her, and, with an effort that tried her strength to its utmost limit, she smiled at him, and even, after a moment, uttered a gasping laugh.

"Oh, that's all right," she said, and hardly knew that it was herself who spoke. "Don't let us make mountains out of molehills! Yes, I quite understand, Peter. Thank you for telling me. Now we must go back to our various stations, mustn't we? The bride will be here directly."

She scarcely knew how she extricated herself. The only thing of which she was acutely conscious was the pressing necessity to meet that sea of watching faces with smiling composure. Her heart was beating again jerkily, uncertainly, like a stopped clock suddenly shaken. She did not know if her limbs would support her, but she kept her smile as she went back past the pew whence Maurice Baronford's glance—cold, incurious, yet alert as a coiled snake—marked her coming and her going, and they did not fail her. She spoke a few words of greeting to a friend or two, and then a slight hubbub at the west door told her of the coming of the bride. Quite calmly she went back to her own place, and she saw that Peter had been pushed into his. Across the intervening space she sent him an affectionate and reassuring smile.

A hymn was announced, and the congregation rose. She was on her feet still, her flowers held closely to her. They had been her husband's only gift to her on that wedding-day of theirs. The scent of them was like ascending incense, and she remembered with a strange inconsequence that she had carried pure white roses to the altar on that far-off day.

The voices of the choir filled the church, and something swelled within her heart, something that made her bend her face to those deep red roses in a quiver of emotion that was beyond all control.

The procession came slowly up the aisle, slowly began to pass her. She lifted her head to see the uplifted cross borne upwards into the flower-decked chancel. Then for a space she seemed to know nothing. It was as if all agitation, all anxiety, all earthly turmoil, were blotted out. She saw only that gleaming cross shining as a beacon-fire above the world, the light unfailing by which all weary travellers might set their course.

Then, as if a hand had touched her, she became suddenly

and keenly aware of another power close to her. She turned, wholly involuntarily, and met her husband's eyes ; and in that look, which endured but for a moment, she sensed a depth of tenderness and understanding such as she had never even dimly experienced before. It was as if a veil hanging perpetually between them had been drawn away, and the revelation was almost more than she could bear.

He passed, and she saw Goldie's slim white form beside him, sparkling with a silvery brightness wherever the misty sunshine fell upon it. Then came the train of silver brides-maids carrying bouquets of palest pink that filled the air with fragrance. Goldie's plea for white heather had been ruled out by Marcia herself, who had counter-pleaded for a little colour.

The bridal procession stopped at the chancel-steps, the hymn died away, and a deep silence fell. Through it there came unexpectedly the chirp of a bird, and she looked up to see the flash of wings high up in the arched roof above her. She could not have said wherefore, but it comforted her over-laden spirit like a message of hope.

Then the service began, and she saw Peter, sturdy and unflinching, standing by Goldie's side.

A few minutes more, and she heard his voice, very steady and reverent, uttering his marriage vows. There was nothing superficial or perfunctory about Peter. He ceased to speak, and Goldie's tones, unusually earnest and almost defiantly audible, followed. A great passion of mother-love welled up in Marcia's heart as she listened. She wished with a pang of self-reproach that she had somehow managed to be a closer friend to Goldie in the past.

Then the bridal couple were kneeling, to be pronounced man and wife, and a flood of memory came over her that almost made her forget even Goldie.

It had been just such a day as this, a golden day, on which she had knelt where Goldie was kneeling now, with Everard by her side, and had heard those holy words spoken over their clasped uplifted hands : "Those whom God hath joined together, let no man put asunder."

It was like a sword through her heart, and suddenly the tears welled up within her so that she did not know how to stay them. She felt them falling upon her flowers, and bent lower and lower, striving to hide them. How nearly, ah, how nearly, had that sacred tie been put asunder by her ! The bitter repentance of ten long years was in those scalding tears.

There came a movement, a faint rustle from the fashionable crowd, and then the chanting voices of the choir. Peter and Goldie were passing up to the altar.

She became conscious of someone beside her, but she could not lift her face. It was only when a quiet hand took one of hers and held it that she realized with an odd mixture of relief and apprehension that her husband was by her side. She moved a little to make room for him, and he bent towards her, whispering : "It will soon be over now."

His words, his presence, helped her. Gradually her composure returned, until at last she lifted again the smiling face which she must keep for the watching world. She slipped her hand free with a gentle pressure, realizing with a throb of wonder as she did so that he had no desire to let it go.

She did not look at him again ; she could not. But she had a sudden odd suspicion that he had deliberately placed himself there as a shield between her and the watching eyes about her. And again she felt as if her heart were bleeding from a mortal wound. Very soon, terribly soon now, his heart would be bleeding too.

CHAPTER X

THE WEDDING GUEST

IT was over, the marriage ceremony, the signing of the register, the procession down the church, and the somewhat undignified hustling of the newly wedded pair into the waiting car, while half a dozen cameras focussed and snapped upon them like a string of racing hounds. The applause of the bells was deafening as they drove away.

"Such a fuss about nothing !" commented Goldie. "I feel as if we'd been married for years, don't you ?"

"No," said honest Peter. "I feel, somehow, delirious."

"Silly ass !" said Goldie consolingly. "It's only reaction. You'll soon get over that. I was like it this morning, till I saw you. Look here, Peter. When we've been married twenty-five years, we won't cry about it. See ?"

"Who wants to cry ?" demanded Peter.

"Nobody at the moment. But Mum was absolutely sloppy

in church, whether on my account or Dad's I don't know. People shouldn't," said Goldie dispassionately, "unless they have very special cause. And I'm sure she hasn't, has she ?"

"Hope not," said Peter.

"Of course she hasn't," said Goldie with confidence. "It's just sentiment, you know—lack of grip. After all, she engineered it all, so she ought to be pleased. Did you see the Baronford couple ? I thought they were looking pretty poisonous, though one wouldn't imagine she would have much cause either, anyhow, at present."

"Sweetheart," said Peter, "I don't care a damn !"

She turned upon him. "Really, Peter ! Within five minutes of starting our wedded life together ! This is worse than delirium !"

"I don't care," he repeated with growing emphasis. "Not a damn ! Not a tuppeny damn !"

"Oh, that's extravagant," protested Goldie. "No, darling ! Not here ! Not in the streets of London ! Wait—oh, wait ! Peter—you beast !"

"You darling !" said Peter, holding her hard against his heart. "There, it's done ! Be as angry as you like ! I couldn't have lived another second without kissing you."

Goldie recovered her equilibrium with a gasp. "You ought to be ashamed of yourself," she said with a radiant smile, "if you weren't incapable of shame. Now no more deliriums, Peter ! Pull yourself together and be strong and silent, as every decent cave-man ought to be ! If you so much as look at me again in the next two hours, I'll disown you."

"Oh, I must look at you," pleaded Peter ; "because if you are ever a bride again, I shan't be there to see."

"How dare you ! How dare you !" said Goldie.

Certainly, as old Lady Barrowdale was heard to remark a little later, they made no secret of their happiness. It was their gala day, and they enjoyed it like children. But Goldie still insisted that it was a double wedding. She seemed indeed to regard it as an even more important occasion for her parents than for Peter and herself ; for, as she said, twenty-five years of marriage was really an achievement to be proud of in these days, if only for its originality, and it was an example that she and Peter had every intention of following.

She delivered a little speech about it, since when the moment for a speech arrived Peter was tongue-tied, and, as shyness had never been a failing of hers, she made a success of it, diverting the general attention quite cleverly from herself to her mother, who stood, a tall, graceful figure, by her father's side.

Everyone applauded at the end of it, except the silver wedding pair and Peter, who was staring at someone near the door with a hint of anxiety on his brown face.

The great room was crowded with people, and it was not particularly easy to pick anyone out in so dense a throng. But Peter, his happiness notwithstanding, had been on the watch for some time, and now apparently his vigilance was rewarded.

Goldie did not notice his absorption ; she had turned amid the laughter and cheers around her to cut the cake that towered on the table before her. But Marcia was watching also, and though she could not see who was standing at the door, she had caught the look on the boy's face, and she knew.

A great tremor went through her, but she subdued it, and moved at Goldie's call to give her help with the cake. She suffered herself to be swept into the seething vortex of merriment around her, but she was cold from head to foot. Oh, it had been better, surely it had been better, if he had not come ! Yet she knew the reason. Peter had made that terribly clear.

Across the room she heard Wilson's official voice proclaiming like a herald : "Major Morven !"

And Goldie at her side gave a start. "Good gracious !" she said. "Peter ! You never told me he was coming. I thought he was far away, down at Tregassa Castle !"

"So he was," said Maurice Baronford's smooth voice behind her. "But doubtless, like myself, he thought this was too important an occasion to miss."

Goldie shot him a swift glance that was not of a strictly complimentary description, a glance which told him clearly that she had not realized his closeness and did not appreciate it. It provoked no more than a quiet smile from him, but open laughter from Virginia, who stood beside him.

"We certainly ought to know," she said. "We were down there ourselves a fortnight ago. He was in a bathchair then, with a nurse in attendance."

Goldie's look swept her informant. She was angry, yet it was the tone and not the information that angered her. But at a touch from Peter she turned away.

"How people gossip !" she muttered. "Where is he ? Why can't they make room for him ?"

"He's not in a bathchair now," said Baronford at her

T

shoulder. "He's made a miraculous recovery. Didn't you know?"

"Of course I knew!" snapped Goldie without looking at him. "I know everything."

"Even the name of the nurse?" gibed Baronford in an undertone.

Goldie did not answer, for suddenly something about her mother caught and held her. Marcia was standing rigid as a statue, gazing straight before her. As Goldie's quick glance took her in, she made a sudden, convulsive movement; and then very clearly, with a distinctness that rose above the low buzz of talk around her, she addressed her husband.

"Everard, I think you have never yet met Peter's cousin, Major Morven. I have known him for a great many years. How do you do, Eric?"

It was done with superb dignity. The throng of guests parted to let the late arrival pass, and they saw her move to meet him with outstretched hand. A thin man of medium height and slightly stooping, came slowly, with a somewhat halting gait, to receive her greeting. His hair was silver-grey, but his dark face with its sunken eyes held a gleaming vitality that made him remarkable. He was such a man as could not have passed through that crowd unnoticed. There was about him a sort of ironical endurance that gave him a strangely combative look, and yet he seemed entirely unaware of the people all about him.

His hand held Marcia's for a moment, and at once released it. The deep lines about his mouth had relaxed into a smile. "I couldn't resist such an opportunity as this," he said. "I am only just out of prison. Did you know?"

She laughed, and her laughter had a brave note. "Well, yes, I had heard," she said. "But only a short time ago. This is my husband. We are very pleased to see you here."

Sir Everard, standing stiffly close to her, offered his hand to the wedding guest. "A friend of my wife's and a cousin of Peter's is doubly welcome," he said rather conventionally.

Eric's eyes gave him a straight hard look. "Thank you, sir," he said. "That's exceptionally kind of you." His look travelled further to the bridal pair. "And the deed is done, I take it? May I congratulate?"

Goldie stepped forward, flushed, momentarily embarrassed. "And you're really well again?" she said. "Why haven't we met before?"

"We were probably too busy," said Eric enigmatically.
"But I always intended to renew acquaintance with you when
you and Peter were safely married. May I be allowed to wish
you every happiness?"

She waved his felicitations aside. "And is it true that
you're only just able to walk again?" she said. "What
happened? Was it a miracle?"

They were the centre of attention, for there was about this
meeting an element of unexpectedness, and perhaps something
more than that excited the curiosity of all within hearing.

Maurice Baronford's cynical laugh cut smoothly through
their conversation. "A miracle, indeed," he said—"for
which I hold myself partially responsible! Lady Templeton,
will you not share the honours with me? I'm sure it was
your unselfish and ever-faithful devotion that paved
the way."

"Indeed, I wish it had been," said Marcia.

She stood facing him fully, breathing very rapidly, but
with no sign of flinching. Very curiously in that moment,
with her whole world toppling around her, she felt no fear.
In a way, she was even conscious of relief.

He laughed again at her words. "Oh, but surely you can't
deny you were in attendance upon the sufferer for a whole week
before the miracle!" he said. "It was my privilege, and also
that of my wife, to see you, suitably attired—or dare I say dis-
guised?—in a nurse's uniform in close attendance upon the
invalid. Major Morven himself could scarcely deny that!"

Very suave and merciless, with the practised skill of a
counsel baiting a trembling victim in the witness-box, his quiet
words fell through the grim, unnatural silence. He was
master of the situation, serenely and confidently master, and
the fact that he did not point the finger of scorn at the woman
who stood so courageously facing him was merely a tribute to
his unswerving presence of mind. Figuratively that finger was
upraised, and the whole thronging crowd saw it.

But in that moment of his triumphant attainment of an
end which he had long had in view, there was one force with
which he had not reckoned. It was not the sudden invective
of the man who stood as a stranger in the midst of them, for
that by some unforeseen influence was restrained. Nor could
it have availed to do other than further establish his advantage.
Neither was it the steady front of his quarry now standing at
bay, though that never varied.

It was a power so different and so overwhelming that in a

second the whole carefully laid train of damning facts and incontrovertible sequence was destroyed.

Very quietly, faintly smiling, Sir Everard, who had tried many a vital case without the smallest change of countenance, passed his hand through his wife's arm and established himself by her side.

"My dear," he said, "I am afraid you will have to make full confession of your charitable deeds, or I must for you. I think, Baronford, you are referring to what has come to be known as my wife's yearly rest-cure, which has lasted for exactly a week out of each of the last ten years. Well, ladies and gentlemen, it is perhaps fitting that on our silver wedding day you should hear that that week every year has been spent, with my full consent—I may even add, to my deep admiration—in the service of an old friend of hers, who during that period has been a hopeless cripple, and has now, I am delighted to see, recovered the use of his limbs. As to her use of a nurse's uniform, some of you may remember that she earned her right to wear that during the War, in which she risked her life—also to my unspeakable admiration—not once, but many times. For a man in my profession"—he was smiling openly now—"there is not much time for acts of charity, so I have been compelled to perform mine by proxy, and I am fortunate in possessing so able a proxy as the woman who has been my beloved wife for twenty-five years."

He ended, and there was a brief silence, followed by a cheery "Hear, hear! Good old Dad!" from Dennis, who suddenly thrust his head between them and bestowed a swift and unsentimental kiss upon his mother's cheek.

"But really! Is it true?" said Lillith in the background. "I always knew there was something; but really, this! I must say, it's rather unheard of."

Virginia's slightly hysterical laugh provided a fitting accompaniment to this expression of incredulous surprise.

"That's just it," said Dennis, with a hand on Morven's shoulder. "People never hear of the decent things, do they? —or believe 'em when they do! Such a jolly world, isn't it, Aunt Lillith? Well, sir, you're a dark horse, I must say. You've kept us all guessing. Almost time you made a speech, isn't it?"

"It might be," said Eric with his faint inscrutable smile, "if I were ever guilty of such an indiscretion. As it is, I only regret having taken up so much more of the general attention than I deserve. Sir Everard having so kindly and accurately expressed the whole situation, may I be allowed to continue where I left off, and salute the lady who is now my cousin by marriage—the bride?"

The dramatic moment was past. Everyone realized it, though some with a feeling that they had been in some fashion cheated of what ought to have been a first-rate scandal. It was as if Sir Everard, whose reputation for fairness was beyond reproach, had deliberately ruled out all incriminating evidence and calmly pronounced that there was no case to be tried.

Certainly Maurice Baronford, K.C., was completely deprived of his brief. Cold, sardonic laughter was the only weapon left to him, and even this could not with dignity be wielded for long.

Goldie, receiving her salute with a mingling of astonishment and relief, remarked: "Of course you and Mum were old war pals! I ought to have thought of that. But I don't know why you didn't tell anybody."

"Do you always tell?" said Eric with gentle irony. "Even when there's *nothing* in it?"

And Goldie flushed a little and said no more, coming to the hasty conclusion that this man was not one whit more attractive than he had been in the past. There was obviously nothing strange in the fact that her mother had chosen to withhold the matter from her, since they had never been in sympathy over him. And as Dad had known—well, of course, equally obviously, there could have been nothing in it.

She dismissed the whole matter from her mind very sensibly while Eric and Peter were grasping hands.

"Get him some champagne!" she said to the latter. "And I think it's about time I went and changed."

So, like a dissolving view, the scene faded, and the audience were left vaguely wondering, but not dissatisfied. At least, Goldie's "double event" had been one of considerable interest.

CHAPTER XI

THE DARK NIGHT

THREE hours had passed since the last car had swerved round the corner of the Square and shot away. Dusk had fallen, and a bevy of starlings were discussing the events of the day in the trees of the garden before retiring to roost. Somewhere in a neighbouring street a woman's voice, inexpressibly dreary, yet not devoid of a certain musical quality, was singing an old, old song. It came like a long wail from the past through the falling darkness, rising and falling, but the words were strangely distinct, unmistakable against the far roar of London's traffic, like a dark archway etched upon a grey intangible background.

> "After years of life together,
> After fair and stormy weather,
> After travel in far lands,
> After touch of wedded hands;
> Strangers yet—strangers yet."

In an unlighted room, with windows that looked upon the Square garden, a man sat alone at his writing-table and listened to the pitiful old song while the chill of evening crept all about him. He was in an upright position in the straight-backed chair he had occupied in his own home during all the years of his married life, but his head was bowed, and he sat completely idle, the papers in front of him in their neat piles all undisturbed. The silence in the house was as the silence of death, and without, save for that dim distant roar, were only the twittering of the birds and the slow, mournful voice approaching through the mist of autumn, almost as if the spirit of autumn itself had somehow found a means of expression.

> "Will it evermore be thus?
> Spirits still impervious—
> Shall we never fairly stand,
> Soul to soul as hand to hand?
> Are the bonds eternal set
> To retain us—strangers yet?"

The wailing verse came to an end in the Square itself. The man in the chair made a slight movement such as a patient under chloroform might make at the first keen piercing of the knife. Otherwise he made no sign. He seemed to be so rapt away from ordinary things that he might have been in a trance.

The singer was nearing the house now, walking slowly with a weary gait—a woman dimly discernible in the failing light, who seemed to have come from nowhere, to belong nowhere, merely to drift aimlessly through a world which itself had become nebulous.

Under the lamp-post in front of the house she came to a pause. She uttered a painful racking cough. Then again in that husky voice, with its illusive, lingering sweetness she sang to a tune older than most churches would recognize .

> " Lead, kindly Light, amid the encircling gloom,
>   Lead Thou me on !
> The night is dark, and I am far from home,
>   Lead Thou me on !
> Keep Thou my feet ; I do not ask to see
> The distant scene : one step enough for me."

It had its effect. The man before the table made a sudden. desperate movement, as of one literally wrenched into activity. He started up and almost flung himself at the window, pushing it up with one hand, while with the other he fumbled feverishly in his pocket. He found a half-crown and tossed it out into the misty circle of light. It fell at the singer's feet.

"Go away !" he said hoarsely, and in his voice was more of entreaty than command. "For heaven's sake—go right away !"

The woman stooped and picked up the coin, then stood up again to thank the giver, but he had disappeared. The banging of the window told her that he had retreated ; and with a sigh, remembering the urgency of his words, she turned and drifted away down the path in silence, a wandering shadow among the shadows.

She reached the street whence she had come and turned down it, meeting as she did so a taxicab that spun round the corner and ran straight to the lamp-post beneath which she had sung that piteous appeal of a soul in darkness. As the occupant of the cab descended, her voice came drifting back down the empty street, receding into the mist.

> "Lead, kindly Light, amid the encircling gloom,
>   Lead Thou me on !
> The night is dark . . ."

A shiver went through the man on the pavement. He spoke brusquely to the driver.

"Look here ! I want you to wait. I may be some time, and again I may not. Probably not ! But I'm going back to the Regency sooner or later."

"Right-o ! I'll wait, sir," said the driver.

He stopped his engine and pulled a crumpled paper from

his pocket as his fare went up the steps which a few hours before had been red-carpeted and sheltered with awning for the passing of a bride.

Twenty seconds later Wilson knocked ceremoniously upon the study door.

"Come in !" said Sir Everard's voice.

The butler opened, to find the room in complete darkness save for the glimmering lamplight outside.

"I beg your pardon, Sir Everard," he said formally. "There is a gentleman—Major Morven—who has called to see you."

"To see me ?" said Sir Everard ; then briefly : "Switch on the light, Wilson, and draw the curtains before you do anything else !"

Wilson switched on the light and discovered his master seated quite upright before the writing-table, looking at him with a sort of level intensity which somehow did not seem to be concerned with him at all. He obeyed his instructions with soft-footed dexterity, then stooped to turn on the electric fire.

"Would you wish me to show the gentleman in, Sir Everard ?" he enquired deferentially when this was done.

Sir Everard had not stirred from his original position. His eyes were still fixed in the same direction as before, but they obviously did not take Wilson into their consideration.

He was silent for a moment before he made deliberate reply : "Certainly show him in if he has asked for me !"

Wilson retired with that species of dignified servility which is only attained by years of practice. There followed a few seconds during which nothing whatever happened in the room. The grey-faced judge sat in his wooden-armed chair gazing at the door with a perfectly unchanging regard.

He was still seated thus when Wilson's voice became once more audible as he threw it open. "Major Morven, Sir Everard !"

And the thin, slightly bent, prematurely aged man with the dark alert eyes, who had so strangely made his way through the throng of wedding guests that afternoon, entered with his slow, halting gait, and stood still. The door closed behind him. They were alone.

Sir Everard spoke very quietly, as he might have spoken to an official in court. "Sit down, if you have really come to see me !"

Eric moved to the fireplace and rested an arm upon the

shelf. The newly kindled fire cast a red glow upwards, throwing the deep lines of his virile, faintly cynical countenance into strong relief.

"Yes, I have come to see you," he said ; "and I am obliged to you for admitting me."

Sir Everard made a slight gesture, as if to indicate that preliminaries were unnecessary. "I presume you have something to say to me," he said.

"Yes, I have." With a steadiness as unwavering as his own, Eric answered him. "I have been thinking—hard—since I left. And I have come to the conclusion that there is nothing else to be done."

"Well ?" said Sir Everard, as he paused.

Eric still paused—as though he were making some sort of inward calculation. Then he spoke. "You did a thing this afternoon which no one else could possibly have done—and which it was certainly not up to you to do. It's because of that that I've come."

"Yes ?" said Sir Everard.

He was looking narrowly at his visitor now, yet without any emotion. Exactly so had he looked many a time at prisoners who had been brought before him for trial.

And with equal resolution Eric's eyes met his—the eyes of a man with a definite purpose from which he would not be turned aside.

"If I had known," he continued in the same level tone, "that you were going to take that attitude, I should not have intruded myself—at least not then. But I did not know even that you were aware of my friendship with your wife."

"I gathered that," said Sir Everard.

Eric went on quietly still, but with a slowly gathering force. "You expressed the situation exactly as, if I had been called upon to do so, I should have expressed it myself. But what I want to know is, how did you come to know and to understand the exact position so perfectly ?"

"Is that of any consequence ?" said Sir Everard.

"It is to me." With absolute decision Eric made answer. "Your wife's goodness to me has been beyond words. I think you realize that. Yet I don't think it was from her that you obtained your information. Was it ?"

Sir Everard did not immediately reply. He sat surveying his questioner with eyes as cold as steel. At length, "I don't quite see the drift of this," he said. "But neither do I see any practical reason for withholding the truth from you.

What you want to know is whether or not my wife told me of what you describe as the friendship existing between you. Well, I am prepared to answer that quite plainly. She did not. She has never so much as mentioned your existence to me—as far as I can remember."

"I see," said Eric. He straightened himself with an effort. "Then it was Baronford who told you the whole thing. But he certainly did not present it to you as you presented it to the world at large this afternoon. He was out for blood. I saw that. But—may I take it that you didn't believe him?"

"No," said Sir Everard. He had not stirred in his chair, nor had his gaze wavered, yet there was something about him quite indefinable that seemed to indicate a force under strong restraint. "Baronford did not tell me the whole thing. Had I given him the chance he would doubtless have been far more illuminating. But his revelations—such as they were—were of merely a confirmatory character, and I did not need to go very deeply into them, even had I desired to do so. In fact, my knowledge of the matter went very much further than his."

"I see," Eric said again. "And may I know what your knowledge amounts to?"

He spoke with a curious simplicity, as though he had suddenly decided that there was no other means of dealing with the business in hand.

But Sir Everard's attitude remained unaltered. "Is that necessary?" he said.

"Yes, it is necessary. Can't you see how necessary?" A certain vehemence sounded in his voice. His arms were stretched out on each side of him, gripping the shelf against which he leaned for support, but he stood up straight. "You thought it your duty to defend your wife from calumny this afternoon, apparently against your own convictions. If so, it is my duty to defend her now. But was it against your convictions? I've got to know that."

"Why?" said Sir Everard.

Eric made a jerky movement with one foot as though he would have stamped on the ground had he had the strength. "Because"—he spoke with a touch of savagery—"her happiness counts with me, if you want to know, and it's essential that you should know the truth."

"Essential to what?" Sir Everard's voice was cold as ice it held very little interest, and no suggestion of sympathy.

But its effect upon the man facing him was almost like a

goad. He left his support very abruptly and came forward to the writing-table. Leaning his hands upon it, he looked full into the stern still eyes that watched him.

"Look here!" he said, almost in an undertone, "I should like to know what you imagine I stand to gain by lying to you. You must know a good deal of human nature by this time. Do I strike you as a liar?"

"No," said Sir Everard in the same calm, aloof voice. "Certainly not a habitual one—any more than I am myself."

"Ah!" A gleam of triumph shone in Eric's eyes for a second. "Then you did speak against your own convictions! I felt you did. You came forward and defended her because you wouldn't see her pulled down in front of you by a dirty pack of slanderers. I was there for the same reason—only I should have defended her with what I knew to be the truth. And that's what I'm here for now—just to let you know that you spoke the truth. I've nothing to gain by telling you; in fact, I've a good deal to lose—because at least"—a note of bitter irony sounded in his voice—"I might once have been counted a good second. But that's over—has been over for years. I tempted her. I persuaded her. I did my damnedest to take her from you. I succeeded almost—but never quite. God only knows why she loved you so persistently, but she never left off. You were always ahead of me—miles ahead of me—though you never cared—as I did!"

He broke off with a deep breath drawn between his teeth. There was a look of torture in his eyes.

And the man facing him stirred at last. He leaned forward very slowly in his chair, but his face remained fixed like a judicial mask. "Perhaps even you," he said, "are not in possession of the whole truth. But that is not the point now. You have come—I gather—to tell me something which so far has been kept from me. I have no wish to hurry you, but might it not be as well to get on with it?"

His voice was clear and concise, as though he were putting some point before a jury. And Eric Morven responded as it were in spite of himself, yet with an odd relief.

"Yes, I'll tell you everything," he said, "as—but for me— she would have told you years ago. It's fairer in a way that you should hear it from me, for she has never done herself justice."

"I am listening," Sir Everard said gravely. "Hadn't you better sit down?"

"No, I'll say it standing." With a grim effort Eric steadied himself. "And mind—what I'm telling you is the truth—before God, the truth."

"That's understood," Sir Everard told him in the same emotionless voice.

'Well, listen, then !" With another hard breath he took the plunge, like a swimmer diving into depths unknown. "I met her first in France—in hospital. She stood by me one night when the place was bombed, and we went through hell together. We were rescued at the last moment. She was magnificent, and—I adored her for it. No man could have helped it."

Sir Everard nodded silently. There was no need for speech.

With scarcely a pause, Eric went on : "I didn't see her again for years—never even heard her name. I went out to Canada, but I never forgot her. I've never seen any other woman like her. Then I came back on business, and met her almost immediately—at Pentreith. You may call it chance. It didn't seem like chance to me." His voice sank momentarily, but almost at once he continued : "She was with the children. I was with Peter. We all got friendly together—and I still worshipped her. There was always a wonderful sympathy between us. I saw she wasn't happy, that she was lonely and disappointed with life—though she was far too fine to admit it. In the end, I couldn't keep it back any longer. I told her that I loved her."

He stopped deliberately and waited for some comment ; but none came. The judicial mask facing him never varied.

He went on. "It upset her, but she took it in her own generous way, and when I begged her to go on treating me as a friend, she was too kind to refuse. And so afterwards—in London—we met again, and I got the impression, though she never said it, that you had left off caring. I think she had that impression too. No doubt we were both wrong, but you never knew how lonely she was. Anyhow, the thing went on. She was trying to hold back, but there was nothing to help her. None of you ever wanted her. Even the children always had something better to do. In the end she suddenly gave in and came to me. But not because she loved me. Only because I wanted her—desperately—and no one else took any notice. She had been keeping herself free for the holidays—she was always at someone's beck and call—but you had all arranged to do various things on your own, and she was left out. So she came to me."

Again he paused, then very slowly stood up and turned

away as if there were something in that stony face upon which he would not look.

Back again to the red silent fire he paced, and bent a little over it, staring downwards.

"I took her at her word," he said. "We left town that night. I drove her in a car I'd hired several times before. We set off for Southampton to catch a boat for Canada. We hadn't gone more than half-way when the steering-gear went, and we took a pretty steep drop at about fifty miles an hour. We were both knocked out, but she came to and got help. I was paralysed from some spinal injury. I thought I was dying, and I made her promise to leave me and go home. That went against the grain with her, but—I simply wouldn't let her refuse. She went back. That was when Dennis had appendicitis. She got back just in time. I was taken to a hospital to die."

He stooped a little lower, spreading his hands before the red glow so that his face was in shadow.

When he spoke again, it was almost as if he had forgotten the very presence of the man behind him.

"I didn't die—unfortunately. I lived on—a helpless cripple. And she—out of the goodness of her soul—came, as soon as she was free, to see me. She stayed a week with me, and made life bearable. And after that—she promised me a week out of every year, simply to help me to live. I consented on the sole condition that it was kept secret. I'd realized and faced the fact by then that she didn't love me—except as an old comrade. Women can love like that—at least some can—like men." An odd note came into his voice—a note of humour that yet was inexpressibly dreary. "In a way, I could hardly have borne it if it had been otherwise. I had so little to give. But at least she never felt unwanted when she was with me."

He choked suddenly, and then, as if some inner force had escaped him unawares, made a violent effort to restrain himself.

"That's the whole story," he said finally. "We spent our week this year at Pentreith at my special request, and on the evening of the day she left I had the accident which somehow put me on my feet. Baronford can tell you all about it—only he will probably throw some doubt on the fact of my ever having been a cripple. That, of course, could be proved if necessary ; but I don't think it is." He stood up again, then deliberately turned. "I have told you the whole truth," he said, "so that you may never—even in thought—do her a wrong. She has belonged to you—and to you only—as long as I have known her."

So he finished, and a silence fell in the room that was pregnant with many emotions. Perhaps he had fulfilled the hardest task of his life in thus giving expression to the secret which he had so closely cherished ; but a harder yet remained for the man to whom it had been revealed.

As he stood once more facing his listener, Sir Everard rose. His face was very pale, but it held no sign of shrinking. It was only its remoteness that made it somehow tragic. It was as if he stepped upon a scaffold, looking far beyond.

Very quietly he came to Eric, and as he reached him his hand was outstretched—as though he would shake hands with his executioner.

"You have told me the truth," he said, and their hands met on the words. "I will do the same to you. If I have misunderstood her—so have you. It is not I that she loves— perhaps it never has been. It was only that once—many years ago—she thought I was the type of man to give her happiness. And she was wrong. She knows that now. She has known it ever since she met you. And so—I give you leave—to take her—and make her happy. Do you understand ?"

"You—what ?" Eric said, as if wondering if he heard aright.

And then suddenly their hands fell apart at the opening of the door. Marcia came in upon them—Marcia robed as a queen, yet pale as the palest flower that grows.

"Everard !" she said, and stopped short.

"Eric !" she said in the voice of despair.

Both men turned to her, but one—her husband—drew back ; the other moved forward and spoke.

"Marcia," he said, "I came here to-night because I couldn't stand out any longer. I have told your husband the whole truth. I had to. And he believes me—except in one particular."

"And what is that ?" she said, her voice cold with the most utter helplessness.

Eric was close to her. He looked full into her eyes. "I can't convince him," he said, "that he is the only man on earth that you have ever loved. Perhaps you can."

"Oh—Eric !" she cried out in distress.

He smiled at her almost as if she had been a child. "Tell him not to be such a dam' fool !" he said. "Go on ! Tell him !"

She moved forward as if bewildered, yet compelled by his urgency.

"Tell him!" he said. "Tell him we're only old war pals, and if I've been devil enough to tempt you to be anything else—at least I never succeeded! Tell him, Marcia! Can't you see it's for his happiness as well as yours? Make him understand!"

There was more than compulsion in his voice; it held a wild high note of passion.

"For God's sake," he said, "let us—all three of us—be honest—if for the only time in our lives! You are man and wife. You love each other—and always have. I am nothing—less than nothing—to come between you! Damn it! I'll make an end of myself if there's no other way!"

"Eric—stop!" she said, and through the room her voice fell clear and steadfast with a ringing quality that held its own as if against a surging tumult. "It's absurd to talk like that. Everard—Everard!" She came to her husband and stood before him. "You know it's absurd as well as I do. You know that whatever madness I may have been through in the past, I couldn't—possibly—be other than true to you now."

Sir Everard spoke through stiff lips. "My dear," he said, "we are not concerned with the past now. I have just said to this friend of yours—and I say it again to you—I wish you, for your own happiness, to go to the man you love. I intended to tell you so to-night in any case."

"The man I love!" she said, and in her voice, wrung though it was, there sounded a curious note of victory.

She stood for a few seconds looking full at the grey-faced man before her; then very quietly she turned to the man who waited, grimly expectant, in the background. She went to him, laid her hands on his shoulders.

"Good-bye, Eric!" she said, and kissed him.

He said nothing whatever. He only paused a moment as though in that kiss there were something sacred from which he could not immediately turn away. Then without any gesture of farewell, yet with a finality there was no mistaking, he went straight from the room. . . .

Beyond the closed door they heard his retreating feet. They heard the hall-door open and close.

Outside on the steps they heard him whistle, and an engine started running in answer. There came the swirling clamour of a taxicab. It seemed to rush all round the Square like an intrusive insect in a quiet room. Then it was gone, and silence came instead.

Marcia was still facing the door. She turned round at last, and as she did so a faint, faint thread of sound wafted in from the outside world.

> "The night is dark, and I am far from home,
> Lead Thou me on !"

She saw her husband sunk in a chair as she had never seen him before. His head was in his hands. She saw his shoulders heave.

And a power that was deeper and stronger than passion welled up within her, driving out all lesser things. She went to him, knelt before him, took his head upon her breast.

"The man I love !" she said softly. "The man I love !" And then—with tears : "The man I—have always loved !"

And so the door into the past opened to them once more.

THE END

HUTCHINSON & CO.

have pleasure in giving the following brief notices of many important new books and novels of interest for the Autumn, 1931.

The following, either as subjects of biography or as writers and novelists, are amongst the many here represented.

HIS MAJESTY
  KING EDWARD VII
KING ALFONSO
GRAHAM SETON
DAVID DEVANT
GILBERT FRANKAU
RAFAEL SABATINI
LADY CYNTHIA ASQUITH
CAPTAIN SIR MALCOLM
  CAMPBELL
ANTHONY GIBBS
GEORG KOPP
JANE DOE
BRUCE GRAEME
J. H. WHILE
ETHEL BOILEAU
JOSEPH STAMPER
JOSEPH DELMONT
LEO GREX
WINIFRED GRAHAM
ISABEL C. CLARKE
TICKNER EDWARDES
ANNE HEPPLE
FRIEDA HAUSWIRTH
"RITA"
MARGARET PETERSON
ANDREW SOUTAR
MARGARET
      BAILLIE-SAUNDERS

GENERAL SIR CHARLES
  CARMICHAEL MONRO
GENERAL SIR GEORGE
  BARROW
GLADYS COOPER
SYLVIA PANKHURST
SIR PHILIP GIBBS
CECIL ROBERTS
ETHEL M. DELL
HERBERT ASQUITH
HOUDINI
GEOFFREY MOSS
JOSEPH CROZIER
URSULA BLOOM
NORMA LORIMER
CECIL FREEMAN GREGG
PHILIP SERGEANT
OWEN RUTTER
JOSCELYN FOXCROFT
HUGH CLEVELY
E. W. SAVI
SIMON DARE
ALLAN FEA
C. T. STONEHAM
TALBOT MUNDY
DOROTHEA CONYERS
ANTHONY WYNNE
HELEN M. FAIRLEY
EDWARD MOUSLEY

HUTCHINSON & CO. (PUBLISHERS), LTD.
34-36, PATERNOSTER ROW, LONDON

Biography & Memoirs

Personal Letters of King Edward VII

Together with extracts from the correspondence
of Queen Alexandra, the Duke of Albany, and
General Sir Arthur and Lady Paget.

Edited by
Lieut.-Colonel **J. P. C. SEWELL**, C.M.G., D.S.O.

THE life of Queen Victoria's eldest son, during the period in which these letters were written (1878-1910), may be divided, roughly, into two parts. The first when, as Edward, Prince of Wales, and the centre of what was described as the "Marlborough House Set", he lived for the most part under the searchlight of an inquisitive and generally unjust publicity; and the second when, as King Edward, the light beat upon him even more brightly, but no longer to reveal him to the critical glare of the later Victorian eye.

These letters, published for the first time, reveal King Edward's real genius for friendship, combined with a very human passion for getting his own way. We see him in hours of joy and sorrow, as he appealed to those who knew him as a man and not as a public institution. This volume, satisfying as it does a long-felt need, is of the first importance. Without intrusion upon the privacy of King Edward, they supply an intimate picture of a widely loved and popular monarch which will appeal to every type of reader.

Illustrated. Approximately, 10s. 6d.

The Life of General Sir Charles Carmichael Monro, G.C.B., G.C.S.I., G.C.M.G.

GENERAL SIR GEORGE BARROW, G.C.B., K.C.M.G.

With a Foreword by Field-Marshal Lord Plumer, G.C.B., G.C.M.G., G.C.V.O.

Although Sir Charles Monro was the man responsible more than anyone else for the wonderful skill in rifle-shooting of the British Army in 1914, it was not until the Great War that his name came prominently before the public. It was in August of 1914 that he took the 2nd Division to France, commanded the 1st Corps in succession to Sir Douglas Haig, and, upon the formation of the Third Army, was appointed its Commander.

In 1916 he was sent by Lord Kitchener to report on the Gallipoli situation. He advised the immediate evacuation of the Peninsula and adhered with unflinching firmness to his recommendation. After carrying out this evacuation, Sir Charles returned to France to command the First Army. Towards the end of 1916 he was requested by the Government to go to India as Commander-in-Chief in order to put life into the measures for the development of India's military resources, and it was here that he performed what was perhaps his greatest work. Himself a distinguished soldier, Sir George Barrow is particularly qualified to write this notable biography.

Illustrated, 21s. net.

Twenty-Nine Years—
The Reign of Alfonso XIII of Spain
From Authentic Sources
MRS. STEUART ERSKINE

The dramatic escape of King Alfonso from his native country was an event that stirred the imagination of the world. It proved that the age-old romance of kingship was not dead, and that the kings of to-day may be called upon to face hazards fundamentally similar to those which confronted their sires generations ago. Thus this series of impressions of the life and reign of one of the most vital characters of our times cannot fail to be of wide interest. The author has an inside knowledge of Spain and the advantage of knowing people on both sides of the chasm which has just divided Spaniards into two distinct groups.

Illustrated, 12s. 6d.

Footslogger

An Autobiography

GRAHAM SETON

(Lieutenant-Colonel G. S. Hutchison, D.S.O., M.C.)

Author of "The 'W' Plan", etc.

HERE is a thriller from real life. Although Graham Seton insists that he proceeds at "footslogger" pace, he hurries us from one adventure to another. We meet, in these fascinating pages, kings, smugglers, soldiers, priests, strikers, diplomatists, mayors, farmers, chefs, artists, film stars, drunkards, desert-chiefs, authors, scouts, politicians, buffoons, go-getters, gardeners, company-promoters. We travel in Egypt, the Sudan, India, Ceylon, Australia, South Africa, Rhodesia. We fight on the Western front, conduct a plebiscite, arrest a Polish Putsch. We are immersed in diplomatic intrigue; lead a victorious bayonet charge; stage an international Fashion Fair; adventure in Fleet Street and in America.

The author has figured prominently in events which have made history, and his comments are arresting and often provocative. This, then, is the story of a man whose life has been filled with varied activities, who has played an active part in many affairs, and who believes in his race and has confidence in himself.

Profusely illustrated from the author's drawings and sketches and from unique photographs
18s. net.

A special edition of 100 copies, printed on special paper and signed by the author, of which eighty are for sale. *2 guineas.*

My Magic Life

DAVID DEVANT

HERE, for the first time, David Devant, acknowledged Master of Magic, tells the story of a lifetime devoted to the Art of Mystery. Past President of the Magic Circle, that exclusive Association of the Wizards of the World, and the Magicians' Club, David Devant has an international reputation as a past-master of the Arts of Magic and scientific illusion.

He has probably "deceived" more people more often than any other man alive to-day, and in this book he makes retribution with some fascinating glimpses behind the curtain of some of his most famous illusions. *Illustrated, 12s. 6d. net.*

My Life

GLADYS COOPER

MISS COOPER, in private life Lady Pearson, is a shrewd and extraordinarily able woman. By sheer ability and hard work she has climbed from the Gaiety chorus to her present position as the foremost dramatic actress on the London stage.

Her reminiscences are anything but gushing, tiresome, and trivial. She writes with complete frankness about every side of her life, and does not hesitate to tell many good stories against herself.

In Miss Cooper's dressing-room hangs a parchment scroll bearing the signatures of hundreds of her friends—they include those of a reigning monarch, a Royal Princess, a Prime Minister, a Bishop, and scores of celebrities. Her encounters with the great and distinguished people of the world provide entertainment of outstanding human interest, and in addition to the events of her crowded life Miss Cooper discusses secrets of beauty and fashion which will fascinate every woman.

Illustrated, 12s. 6d.

A Marriage to India

FRIEDA HAUSWIRTH (MRS. SARANGADHAR DAS)

WHEN the young artist, Frieda Hauswirth, married Sarangadhar Das and went to live with him at Brahmakunda, she little realized the tremendous gulf she would have to bridge, not merely in linking herself with a husband of a dark and alien race, but also fitting her life to customs and to a culture totally different from her own. Tried by the ordeal of experience, many of her easy assumptions and much of her blind idealization vanished, but in their place came a new and even more sympathetic understanding of Mother India and of the problems faced alike by India's Hindu and Moslem sons. Her encounters with these personages are fully described in this volume. The account of Mrs. Das' experiences is unique, in that here, for the first time, a white girl, who became a wife of a Hindu, discusses frankly the intimate problems she faced. *Illustrated*, 16s.

The Life of Captain Sir Malcolm Campbell

J. WENTWORTH DAY
Joint author of "The Life of Sir Henry Segrave"

THOSE who lament that the golden age of adventure and romance has passed have only to read one chapter of this book to realize that the Sir Galahad of to-day dares dangers and takes risks of which no knight of old ever dreamed.

No racing motorist in history has won more trophies and honours than Sir Malcolm Campbell, holder of the world's speed record, who has packed his life with such adventure—flying, hunting for pirate treasure, motor-racing and yachting—and has even been lost in the Sahara and captured by Riffs. He has explored most of the civilized and uncivilized world, and has escaped death on land and sea probably more often than any man alive.

This book will stand as one of the most amazing records of a man's heroism, courage and flirtations with death.

Illustrated, 12s. 6d.

The Secrets of Houdini

J. C. CANNELL

IN this remarkable and original book there are disclosed for the first time secrets which, for many years, have been closely and jealously guarded. But Houdini's secrets did not, as many people suppose, die with him.

The task of the revelation of Houdini's secrets has been undertaken by Mr. Cannell, a well-known Fleet Street journalist and a Vice-President of the Magicians' Club, who here describes in the fullest detail Houdini's mysterious escapes from a huge bank-safe in London ; from a boiler into which he was riveted ; from a sealed paper bag ; from a packing case dropped into the river ; from a coffin in which he had been buried alive for an hour under six feet of earth ; from a heavy, bolted iron box ; from handcuffs, leg-irons, cells, and prison vans ; from knots, rope ties, strait jackets. The illusion of walking through a brick wall, the vanished horseman, and making an elephant disappear are also fully explained. *Illustrated, 12s. 6d.*

Less than the Dust
THE MEMOIRS OF A TRAMP
JOSEPH STAMPER

YOU have seen them on your rambles. **Tramps.** Repulsive, frowsy, dirty. But a tramp has ears, has eyes. What does he hear? What does he see? This book tells you, for the writer was a tramp. Without a thought of writing then he wandered about the country, and some automatic part of his subconscious registered impressions of all he saw and felt to be written down later. From this book you will see life from an unfamiliar viewpoint; you will glimpse a world you may never have known. Tragedy, humour, drama, all come within the experience of a tramp. *With a Frontispiece,* **7s. 6d.**

A Yellow Sleuth
Being the Autobiography of
NOR NALLA
(Detective-Sergeant, Federated Malay States Police).

HERE is a quite astonishingly unusual autobiography. Nor Nalla's early life gives us a glimpse into a typical Malay *ménage,* and his subsequent career carries us the breadth of the Peninsular. We are with him watching bewildering magic performed by a medicine-man in the jungles of the Far North; we escape with him from a Chinese junk lying south of Singapore. We visit the gold-mines at Raub and the crowded streets of Malacca. During the war Nor Nalla was employed in North France and England doing detective and Secret Service work, and had escapes equally hair-raising with those he had experienced in his native jungles. *Illustrated,* **10s. 6d.**

Fifty Years of Fire Fighting in London
JACK WHILE

IN this original book Mr. While, the official reporter to the London Fire Brigade, reviews the history of that Brigade from its creation, after the great Tooley Street fire in 1861, by the late Captain Sir Eyre Massey Shaw to the present day. A good deal of space is devoted to descriptions of famous fires, and the result is a book full of drama, excitement, and resource. *Illustrated,* **12s. 6d.**

History

Two Lone Ships

"Goeben" & *"Breslau"*

GEORG KOPP

Translated by Arthur Chambers

THE author of this book was on board the *Goeben*—the fastest ship in the Mediterranean—when in August, 1914, she and the *Breslau* made their thrilling escape from the Allied fleets and successfully dashed to Constantinople through the Dardanelles. This exploit is famous, but less widely known is the subsequent war-career of these two ships.

After being joined to the Turkish fleet, though keeping their German crews, they wrought such havoc against the Russian Black Sea Fleet and bases, and displayed such daring, that they became a legend among their enemies, who named the *Goeben* the "Devil's Ship". Battered and maimed as a result of many unequal contests, the *Goeben* survived the war and is still the pride of the Turkish navy.   *Illustrated*, 10s. 6d.

In the Enemy's Country

JOSEPH CROZIER

(Lieutenant Pierre Desgranges, of the 2nd Bureau de l'État-Major)

THIS quite amazing book tells in the first person of the war adventures of Joseph Crozier, a secret agent known to the inscrutable Second Bureau of the French General Staff as "Lieutenant Pierre Desgranges". During the most dangerous years of the War, M. Crozier directed the French espionage in Germany from Holland. The story of his ingenuity, of the perils he ran, of the secret organization he built up behind the enemy's lines, of the hidden and often fatal warfare it conducted against the German counter-espionage, and of the several fates of its members, forms a grim epic of the great struggle.

With a Frontispiece, 7s. 6d. net.

The Home Front
SYLVIA PANKHURST

THIS notable and important book is a graphic presentment of life at home during the Great War ; its labours, humours, and sorrows, privations and bereavements. The author, who threw herself unreservedly into the work of relief and assuagement, writes from a store of unrivalled experience of the calling up of the men, the panic closing of the factories, the food prices rising to famine height, of food queues and profiteering, the munition girls and their hard toil, and of all the weariness of those dreadful years followed by the inevitable and difficult reactions of peace. There are, also, piquant and poignant reminiscences of many of the leading people of the time.

Illustrated, 21s.

Gamblers All
PHILIP W. SERGEANT
Author of "Dominant Women", etc.

THE present day seems an appropriate time at which to bring out a book bearing such a title—with the Irish Sweep craze at such a pitch and a genuine movement in favour of relaxed legislation against lotteries in this country.

Mr. Sergeant, in his usual brilliant and entertaining manner, has gathered together many most famous gamblers, both of to-day and of the past. The story of their extraordinary luck and their subsequent behaviour makes most interesting reading.

Illustrated, 18s.

Rooms of Mystery and Romance
ALLAN FEA
Author of "Secret Chambers and Hiding Places", etc.

THIS is a subject which Allan Fea has made entirely his own ; and a very engrossing, exciting subject he has made it.

In *Rooms of Mystery and Romance*, we are shown in graphic style the actual thing, without any fantasy of the imagination. The range covered is wide, for besides the hiding-places of priests and cavaliers of long ago we are taken to the secret repositories of modern crooks and smugglers, and are also told stories of little-known haunted rooms thrilling in the extreme. *Illustrated,* 12s. 6d.

Travel

To the South Seas

GIFFORD PINCHOT

THERE is no region on earth so many people would like to visit as the South Seas. There is no region so filled with glamour and romance. This book takes you there and makes you feel as if you had made the cruise yourself. It tells how a dream of a lifetime—a cruise in his own schooner to the South Seas—was carried out by Mr. Pinchot after forty years.

The party had many adventures. They caught fish so big that surf broke on their backs as if they were reefs. They barely escaped being wrecked on a desert, waterless island. They visited the most beautiful islands and walked among wonders, recording them in photographs. The story is told simply, just as it happened, and with a quiet humour that makes it easy reading.

Illustrated, 18s.

General

Trade and Technical Writing for Profit

BERNARD BROWN, B.Sc.

THE prime object of this quite invaluable little book is to provide practical and straightforward advice for earning a definite income by trade and technical writing. The book tells how this may be achieved, how first acceptances may be obtained and then amplified into a continuous output, and how this output may be enlarged. All who aspire to the writing of commercial articles will find the advice contained in this book of the utmost help.

4s. 6d.

General Fiction

Christopher Strong: A Love Story
GILBERT FRANKAU
Author of "Martin Make-Believe" (35th thous.), "Peter Jackson, Cigar Merchant" (224th thous.), etc.

A NEW novel by Mr. Frankau is always an event of the liveliest interest, and the success of his last long story, *Martin Make-Believe*, will not readily be forgotten.

"In the face of such competence as Mr. Frankau's," said the *News-Chronicle*, "let us salute it. For Mr. Frankau has all the airs of a novelist and most of the graces. He is a model of easy manners and a master of difficult situations." 7s. 6d.

A New Novel
HERBERT ASQUITH
Author of "Roon" (5th impression), "Young Orland" (15th impression), etc.

SOME two years ago Mr. Asquith published the successor to his triumphantly successful novel, *Young Orland*, upon the publication of which the *Morning Post* wrote, "Mr. Asquith has surely arrived as one of the first English novelists—perhaps as the great novelist."

This announcement of a new novel will arouse the liveliest interest and speculation. Mr. Asquith has taken for his central figure a young and penniless girl who tramps the roads of England with her sailor father. It is a story of love and adventure, containing a wide and various gallery of characters in different planes of modern life. 7s. 6d.

Eve the Enemy
TICKNER EDWARDES
Author of "The Honey-Star", "Sunset Bride" (3rd impression), etc.

MR. EDWARDES, who has lived for many years in the quiet villages of Sussex, is a shrewd yet kindly observer, and in *Eve the Enemy*, he recounts, with deft touches of humour and pathos, the story of South-Down village life—its joys, disappointments and sorrows, its aspirations and loves. 7s. 6d.

A New Novel
CECIL ROBERTS
Author of "Scissors", "Sails of Sunset", "Half Way", etc.

THE publication of Mr. Roberts' autobiography, *Half Way*, was one of the events of the publishing season, and certainly one of the most astonishing volumes which has been issued for many years. This announcement of a new novel will be widely discussed, for Mr. Roberts is nothing if not provocative. The story, we are told, is very different to anything he has yet written, and is set, very largely, amongst the mountains of the Tyrol. There is little doubt that its publication will prove something of an event. *7s. 6d.*

Good Time
GEOFFREY MOSS
Author of "Sweet Pepper", "Wet Afternoon", etc.

SINCE the publication of that triumphantly successful novel, *Sweet Pepper* (now, by the way, issued for the first time at 2s.), the work of Geoffrey Moss has been followed by a vast company of readers with tremendous interest and anticipation. His last novel, *Little Green Apples*, was described by many as unquestionably the best book he has given us since *Sweet Pepper*. That honour, we feel, it will not hold for long. Indeed, it is not impossible that this new novel will supersede *Sweet Pepper* as his best work. It is unexpected, original, and very clever. *7s. 6d.*

Alone
NORMA LORIMER
Author of "Moslem Jane" (6th thous.), "The Shadow of Egypt" (14th thous.), etc.

THE novels of Miss Lorimer are notable for the excellence of their characterization and the originality of their setting. It was these two qualities which brought such high praise from the critics upon the publication of her last story ; and the success it consequently achieved will, we feel confident, be shared and enhanced by this, her latest novel. *7s. 6d.*

The Silver Wedding

ETHEL M. DELL

Author of "The Bars of Iron" (721st thous.), "The Hundredth Chance" (641st thous.), etc.

THIS is the story of a woman—Marcia Templeton—who, after marrying the knight of her girlhood's dreams and becoming the mother of his two children, finds herself very far from attaining her early ideals. The tremendous crisis of the war, whilst separating her temporarily from her husband and family, brings her into contact with another man with a spirit so akin to her own, that in a moment of fearful danger they cling together, awaiting death. But death does not come, and they are separated, but each after the ordeal bears the indelible memory of that strange communion. When they meet again, years later, they are immediately drawn by it, and the gigantic contest begins which leads at length to the triumph of the greater love. **7s. 6d.**

Turnip Tops

ETHEL BOILEAU

Author of "The Arches of the Years" (4th thous.), "Hippy Buchan" (8th thous.), etc.

"ONE of the most exciting stories I have read since *Under Two Flags*", said Gilbert Frankau of Mrs. Boileau's fine novel, *The Arches of the Years*.

"A really worthwhile novel," was W. B. Maxwell's opinion; "finely conceived, firmly executed. Its author shows noble thought and high purpose."

It was, indeed, a novel of exceptional quality, and achieved immense popularity. This, her latest work, will be eagerly read by her countless admirers. **7s. 6d.**

A New Novel

HELEN M. FAIRLEY

A new and exciting story by the author of "The Greater Freedom", "Kali's Jewels", "The Justice of the White Sahib", etc.

Page Fourteen

The Golden Years

PHILIP GIBBS

Author of "The Winding Lane", "The Middle of the Road'
(145th thous.), etc.

A NEW novel by Philip Gibbs is an event looked forward to and welcomed by many hundreds of thousands of people. For, as a reviewer wrote in the *Sunday Times* : "Sir Philip Gibbs is a writer of sympathy and experience, novelist and philosopher— one of the rare examples of successful journalist turned successful author. He is therefore a gleaner both of facts and emotions, and by training adapted for converting his intellectual harvest into a loaf of quality that may be digested of the multitude."

7s. 6d.

The New Poor

"RITA"

(Mrs. Desmond Humphreys)

Author of "The Grandmothers", "Calvary" (43rd thous.), etc.

IN this, her latest novel, Mrs. Desmond Humphreys illustrates the era of a new class of poverty : that of the well-born and at one time wealthy aristocrats of England, who, within the last ten years, have found incomes lessening and estates a mere ruinous outlay, and the general effect of life one of endeavour.

In the character of Lady Vivienne St. George the author has drawn a charming and somewhat unusual personality, and the story of the changes in her life brought about, if not by poverty, at least by loss of wealth, is not only amusing and entertaining, but is enhanced by an underlying and more serious application.

7s. 6d.

Just Luck

E. W. SAVI

Autnor of "A Man's a Man" (40th thous.), "Idol Worship" (6th thous.), etc.

TWO girls, closely related, who start life under widely different conditions, and how their natures react to circumstances make this story. Fate, in whimsical mood, turns the tables so that the reader is well entertained in following the fortunes of characters, who, under Mrs. Savi's art, come to life and make a book of great charm and merit. *7s. 6d.*

The New Crusade
ANTHONY GIBBS
Author of "Heyday" (5th thous.), "Young Apollo" (8th impression), etc.

HERE is Mr. Anthony Gibbs in merry mood. *The New Crusade* concerns a millionaire, Lord Surbiton, who plans to turn England naked. He buys a newspaper to plug the idea of nakedness; he parades the Dawk (a most entertaining gentleman) naked through Surrey carrying a banner proclaiming the New Crusade. By skilful work in the Press, by the most elaborate and far-reaching campaign, the idea begins to spread. After a number of quite fantastic adventures the Crusaders begin to get the idea across. There is a heat wave, and wild scenes on the Serpentine "Lido" and amongst Surrey "hikers". This story makes a most joyous piece of fun, and those who read into it a little deeper than others, will find it a searching skit on modern conditions and the power of the Press. *7s. 6d.*

Managing Ariadne
DOROTHEA CONYERS
Author of "The Strayings of Sandy" (84th thous.), etc.

THIS is another of those cheerful, gay stories of the Irish hunting-field for which Miss Conyers is so famous. In it one finds adventure, romance, and a touch of mystery. The adventures of Hugh Armstrong from the day that he attended the Doncaster September Sales; the romance of Anne, whom he met there, and of one or two other delightful people as well; the mystery of the stolen jewellery.

And through it all there runs that humour, and that inimitable light-heartedness of style which has caused the sales of Miss Conyers' novels to swell into hundreds of thousands. *7s. 6d.*

Winter Wheat
EDWARD WOODWARD
Author of "The House of Terror", etc.

AGAINST a background of the countryside, the hunting-field, and Aintree on Grand National day, Mr. Woodward has fashioned this human story. The love of two men for the same girl—none the less poignant through its frequency—brings here disaster and a mystery of unusual ingenuity. *7s. 6d.*

Blow Bugles Blow

AN ENGLISH ODYSSEY

EDWARD MOUSLEY

THIS long, dramatic novel portrays character in intense action on a big canvas. The story opens on the hero's last night at Cambridge, "on the threshold". He meets a young German girl living in a London attic. Life had begun to weave a standard pattern when the Great War bursts into being and he crosses to France. His romance with the German girl feels the full impact of war. With increasing passion the story reaches a turning point in No Man's Land, where religion is thrown dramatically in silhouette against the horror of battle.

Then the scene changes from the dug-out to the desert, and the vast opening out which has proceeded from the first page is surpassed. The struggle for Kut is dramatized from the outside, the problem of God in the war is flung into still sharper relief, and increasingly the spectacle becomes less that of war than of destiny, fate, and life itself. A closely knit theme of love and death that works itself out to the end, revealing war not as making for the degradation of the spirit of man, but as calling forth everything that is sublime and splendid. The story, which ends on Armistice morning, is conceived on the high plane of Rupert Brooke's immortal words which are illuminated with grim irony.   7*s*. 6*d*.

Those Others

SIMON DARE

Author of "Where No Wind Comes", "If the Tree Fall", etc.

HERE are the love-stories of a little group of people by an author whose popularity is growing with each succeeding publication, and whose novels are selling in their thousands. *Those Others* is a charming story which shows that love, even though it may be the beautiful flower, has many thorns upon its symbolic stem which pierce and wound until the sap dies down and the blossoms fade. . . . Thus are life and love only plants in the garden of the world. They breathe a little, grow to beauty, and slip away into the limbo of forgotten yesterdays.   7*s*. 6*d*.

The Power Behind The Throne

WINIFRED GRAHAM

Author of "The Last Laugh"(4th thous.), "A Wolf of the Evenings" (4th thous.), etc.

Mrs. Graham, having received permission from His Majesty the King to film Hampton Court Palace, decided to write a novel around this beautiful and historical setting. Thus, this story came into being. Barbara Greville, a beautiful Lady-in-Waiting to Queen Catherine of Arragon, is the heroine, and Henry VIII and Anne Boleyn play conspicuous parts. Thrilling incident succeeds thrilling incident, and Mrs. Graham, with her customary brilliance and skill, recreates with unusual vividness and clarity the atmosphere of those past days.   *7s. 6d.*

Green Sanctuary

MARGARET BAILLIE-SAUNDERS

Author of "Scarlet Sails" (9th thous.), "Mary Simnel's Marrying" (7th thous.), "Upstarts" (3rd impression), etc.

Green Sanctuary is a novel of absorbing interest—an alluring study of a loveable rake who stands midway between the influence of two women—an angel and a robot—and the tragi-comedy which results. As one reads to the surprising end of this fine story, one is conscious of a challenge and a question. Which of the two men who figure most prominently in it possess in greater degree the spirit of saintliness?   *7s. 6d.*

Folly's Coombe

JOSCELYN FOXCROFT

Author of "The Virgin Widow"

"There is some charming descriptive writing in this competently constructed and satisfying novel," wrote the *Graphic* of Mr. Foxcroft's successful first novel, *The Virgin Widow*. There can, we think, be little doubt that *Folly's Coombe* is a definite advance and an exceedingly readable story.

Disappointed in love, and fresh from the war, its hero, unconsoled by riches, removes into his chosen wilderness. Amidst the glories of South Devon, so vividly portrayed by Mr. Foxcroft, he loses grief and finds solace in work and altruism, visualizing existence anew.   *7s. 6d.*

Strange Bedfellows
ANDREW SOUTAR
Author of "The Devil's Triangle" (4th thousand), "Not
Mentioned——" (5th thous.), etc.

SIR THOMAS SHADROW was a little inflated Baronet in a country
town; he knew nothing of life outside the own little world
which was himself Then came impoverishment and he was
reduced to financial beggary. His second son returned from
the States with an American girl; they had no money either,
but they had brains and resource, so they took the whole family
on the road in a caravan, which they named "The House with the
Golden Windows". This charming story is totally different, not
only from Mr. Soutar's usual style, but also from the commonly
accepted idea of a novel. *7s. 6d.*

The Altar of Sacrifice
ISABEL C. CLARKE
Author of "As the Gentle Rain" (4th impression), "Italian
Adventure" (1th thous.), etc.

LESLEY MARVELL, a struggling and impecunious young
artist, found herself suddenly the heiress to a large fortune.
But in Italy, by the Greek Temples of Pæstum, there came
to her the first call to sacrifice, and she is awakened to the fact
that, owing to a clause in her grandfather's will, it would be
impossible for her to retain her "great possessions".

This is a powerful and challenging story, written with that
sincerity, charm and sympathy that a succession of consistently
fine novels have led us to expect from Miss Clarke. *7s. 6d.*

Gay Go Up
ANNE HEPPLE
Author of "Jemima Rides", "The Untempered Wind", etc.

HER real name was Eliza Heron, but her sisters called her
Gay Go Up. They christened her in the duckpond. She
was one of those people born with the itch to set the world to
rights; to quote her sister: "Gay would help lame dogs over
stiles, even if they wanted to go the other way, and even if they
bit her." This characteristic led her into many disasters,
comical and otherwise, from which she was nearly always rescued
by her adoring lover Angus. Gay could not understand why
Angus loved her, and so she nearly broke his heart . . . *7s. 6d.*

Slander

JOSEPH DELMONT

Author of "In Chains" (9th thous.), "Circus-Show", etc.

JOSEPH DELMONT, through his novels and his adventurous book on the catching of wild beasts alive, has shown us many sides of life, and here, in this novel, he shows us yet another. Berthold Turner was a shy young man, saddled by an old wag of a coachman with a reputation for amorous intrigue, which spread and grew like a conflagration and, through its effects, started an imbroglio in which broad farce and deep pathos intermingle.

It is a novel containing all those distinguished qualities which have earned for its author so great a reputation ; and the whole story sweeps forward with the impetuous force of a torrent.

7s. 6d.

The Enchanted Duchess

JANE DOE

THE Enchanted Duchess, London's Brightest Young Thing, Atalanta, Duchess of Killarney, was widowed, young and beautiful. In one of her Brightest moments she had the misfortune to offend, outrageously, John Stoneroof, a brilliant young newspaperman. He played on her—the queen of practical jokers—the world's best practical joke. Furthermore, he made her not only his prisoner, but his servant. So this elegant young lady was suddenly precipitated from Society butterflydom to the position of domestic drudge without the rest of the world knowing anything about it for three months.

Could such a thing be ? It sounds preposterous, but there were reasons. Glamorous and quite enchanting reasons. . . .

Jane Doe is known, through her brilliant journalism, to countless thousands of readers. This is her first full-length novel —and a very brilliant affair it is !

7s. 6d.

Historical Adventure

Scaramouche the Kingmaker

RAFAEL SABATINI

Author of "Captain Blood" (178th thous,), "The Sea Hawk"
(192nd thous.), etc.

"THOSE who search the Sabatini pages in search of adventure",
wrote a *Daily Telegraph* critic, "will not fail to enjoy a bold
story told with all the vigour we are accustomed to expect in
one of our most romantic novelists." There is, indeed, a thrill
and an undeniable glamour to be obtained from the novels of
Sabatini which can be got from few living authors. For he
creates so vividly and so intensely the colour and life of past days,
whilst his characters are bold, strong and alive.

Scaramouche is one of his most notable and lovable creations ;
and in this story we meet him again moving, working, planning
behind the turmoil of the French Revolution. His adventures
are breathless, but he survives them all, and from the first page
to the last of this fine romance the reader is carried along, held
enthralled by the fine magic of Rafael Sabatini. 7s. 6d.

White Rajah

OWEN RUTTER

Author of "Sepia", "Lucky Star", "Cain's Birthday", etc.

MR. OWEN RUTTER has here returned to the setting of his
earlier novels : Borneo and the Eastern Seas, which he
knows so well. The central character is James Brooke, who
became the first White Rajah of Sarawak in circumstances as
exciting as they were extraordinary. Mr. Rutter presents a
dramatic reconstruction of Rajah Brooke's life and a sensitive
realization of his character, and by revealing certain intimate
facts which have never before been published, is able to give full
significance to the passion for adventure which drew this strange
man to the East. It is a glowing and romantic story, through
which strides the White Rajah, dogged, frank and fearless, intent
on sweeping pirates from his realm, and swift to avenge his
friends. 7s. 6d.

Adventure
Jungle Jest
TALBOT MUNDY
Author of "Jimgrim" (2nd impression), "Om" (21st thous.), etc.

Mr. Mundy is already world-renowned for his realistic tales of life in India. Now, in this book he gives us another enthralling story in which tigers, the great forests, red-rebellion and a fearless man play the leading parts; it is a story full of drama, mystery, and adventure. *7s. 6d.*

The Lion's Way
C. T. STONEHAM
Author of "The Whistling Thorn", etc.

This is the intensely exciting story of a child reared by a lioness in Africa to become leader of a wild lion pack, imbued with all the characteristics of his terrible friends. "It is the best thing of its kind I have read," writes Sir Philip Gibbs, "and I believe it will attract an unusual notice as something quite off the beaten track." How Kaspa became a man and learnt the meaning of love and friendship, and how he strove to abandon these things to return to the wild life he craved for, is told in this magnificent story by an author who has spent most of his life in the study of African lions in their native jungle. *7s. 6d.*

Ghostly!
When Churchyards Yawn
Compiled by LADY CYNTHIA ASQUITH
Who also compiled "Shudders".

Here is another volume of Ghost Stories written by Lady Cynthia Asquith's unbeatable and almost unplayable team of story-tellers. Hugh Walpole, G. K. Chesterton, Walter de La Mare, Somerset Maugham, Elizabeth Bowen, Algernon Blackwood, Oliver Onions, Mrs. Belloc Lowndes, L. P. Hartley, Enid Bagnold, and Lady Cynthia herself—all are represented in this volume of unsurpassable entertainment. Of *Shudders* the *Spectator* said: "A better collection could hardly have been brought together." And so we all thought until this new collection came along! *7s. 6d.*

Detective & Mystery

Unsolved

BRUCE GRAEME

Author of "A Murder of Some Importance" (4th impression),
The "Blackshirt" novels, etc.

THE Clavering family were happy and united. They were gathered together to welcome David's bride; a time of jollity and blissful happiness for everyone concerned. Then, unexpectedly, tragically, Mr. Clavering died, a victim of poison, which only somebody amongst that happy company could have administered. And so suspicion grew in their minds as to whom it might be. . . . Bruce Graeme is a brilliant mystery-maker and a brilliant novelist into the bargain.   *7s. 6d.*

The Nightborn

LEO GREX

Author of "The Tragedy at Draythorpe" (2nd impression), etc.

ON a dark, squally night in early autumn a mysterious submarine emerged from the North Sea close to the English coast and surrendered to a waiting motor-boat two prisoners, a young girl and an old man. On the same night the Honourable Ronald Blassington—better known to his friends as Ronnie—lost his way on the East Anglian moors, accompanied by the urbane Hannibal Skeats, valet, philosopher, and pugilist. The two eventually stumbled across an inn, the Moonrakers, and there they fell foul of "Madame" . . .   *7s. 6d.*

The Preston Mystery

CECIL FREEMAN GREGG

Author of "The Rutland Mystery" (2nd impression), "The Murder
on the Bus" (4th thous.), etc.

ON the face of it April Fools' Day would appear to have little connection with a terrible murder and its consequences. And even when the victim is a constable posted within Scotland Yard itself, the position would scarcely seem to lend itself to tragedy. That it can, and does, however, the reader will discover in this new and thrilling story by an author whose popularity is rapidly assuming mammoth proportions. You will again meet here Inspector Higgins, who, with his customary good nature, conducts us through the thickest tangles.   *7s. 6d.*

Gang Law

HUGH CLEVELY

Author of "Hell to Pay", "The Gangsmasher", etc.

"HUGH CLEVELY," wrote a wise gentleman in *The Field*, "has a brave knack of direct description that allures and holds you." And so will this vigorous, crisp adventure story hold you. It contains no fashion plate detectives drawing their red-herrings laboriously across the trail to mystify the reader, but there are half a dozen first-rate characters, and as many gorgeous free fights.

James Stretton was a quiet, simple man, fond of beefsteak, beer, and good Virginian cigarettes, and the two things he hated most were underdone potatoes and a peaceful life. Moroni was a super-crook: huge, pig-headed, courageous, and brutal. Then the alluring, the provocative Tania Ramenoff . . . an unusually fascinating heroine.

This book is gay, humorous, and entertaining. What more can anybody want? *7s. 6d.*

Fatal Shadows

MARGARET PETERSON

Author of "The Eye of Isis" (5th thous.), "Moonflowers" (44th thous.), etc.

THERE was a fatal shadow at Rose Cottage. It stalked behind all the beauty of the roses; it leered behind the laughter of lovely Yvonne. Jealousy is the most fatal shadow that can darken love's day. Mrs. Ruthe was desperately jealous of her husband and Yvonne; Yvonne was jealous of anything and everyone who interfered with her pleasure.

Almost inevitably there follows in the wake of jealousy the misery of tragedy; but when Mrs. Ruthe was murdered, and although it seemed easy to detect the murderer, it unexpectedly proved a baffling mystery.

In this story, with her customary brilliance of characterization and description, Miss Peterson presents her readers with an intriguing problem. *7s. 6d.*

The Silver Arrow

ANTHONY WYNNE

Author of "Murder of a Lady" (2nd impression), "The Blue Vesuvius", etc.

Mr. Wynne presents our old friend, Dr. Eustace Hailey, with a problem that almost overcame him—almost but not quite. Rollo Bowmark was called a "wizard of finance". More poet than money-maker, all that he touched nevertheless turned to gold. So his disappearance from a house on the Solent convulsed the exchanges. Within a day or two, as the circumstances became known, dismay changed to horror. Here, it seemed, was murder walking by day, yet wholly invisible. Only the silver arrow pointed the way to understanding. . . .   *7s. 6d.*

The Hangman's Guests

STUART MARTIN

Author of "Capital Punishment", "The Trial of Scotland Yard", etc.

In *Capital Punishment* the author showed the penal code as viewed through the eyes of a criminal. In *The Trial of Scotland Yard* he showed the code through the eyes of the official hunters of criminals. In *The Hangman's Guests* he reaches the apex of the triangle. It is a clash between the opposing forces of criminal investigation, the final battle over criminal liability.

The hangman comes to the prison to do his terrible duty. He relates to the chaplain his researches and his objectives. And then he reveals his true personality. Who is the greater criminal, the official who ruthlessly pursues his victim seeking punishment, or the humanitarian who desires to rescue through pity ?   *7s. 6d.*

UNIFORM EDITION OF THE FAMOUS
RAFAEL SABATINI
HISTORICAL ROMANCES

The World is Rafael Sabatini's background and he ranges all history for his plots. France during the revolution, the Italy of the Renaissance, England under the Stuarts, America under the Georges—all come alike to this versatile author. In this uniform edition it is now possible to collect your favourite writer in a style which is at once beautiful and inexpensive.

SCARAMOUCHE
CAPTAIN BLOOD
THE TRAMPLING OF THE LILIES
THE SEA HAWK
ANTHONY WILDING
LOVE-AT-ARMS
THE BANNER OF THE BULL
THE SHAME OF MOTLEY
THE CAROLINIAN
FORTUNE'S FOOL
ST. MARTIN'S SUMMER
BELLARION

THE SNARE
THE TAVERN KNIGHT
HISTORICAL NIGHTS' ENTERTAINMENT. Series I
HISTORICAL NIGHTS' ENTERTAINMENT. Series II
THE GATES OF DOOM
THE LION'S SKIN
THE STROLLING SAINT
BARDELYS THE MAGNIFICENT
THE JUSTICE OF THE DUKE
THE HOUNDS OF GOD

Other titles will be added from time to time.

LEATHER. Brown Lambskin, rounded back, gilt top, gold blocked side and back, special end papers, printed in choice and newly-set clear type on pure paper. 5s. *net*

CLOTH. Blue Art Cambric, rounded back, gold blocked side and back, printed in choice and newly-set clear type on pure paper. 3s. 6d. *net*

UNIFORM EDITION OF NOVELS BY
PHILIP GIBBS

"Sir Philip Gibbs is a typical and topical product of his age; he is the apostle of youth and of idealism; a reasoned and not a reckless optimist, disciplined rather than disillusioned".

THE STREET OF ADVENTURE

THE MIDDLE OF THE ROAD

HEIRS APPARENT

YOUNG ANARCHY

THE CUSTODY OF THE CHILD

HELEN OF LANCASTER GATE

OLIVER'S KIND WOMEN

THE RECKLESS LADY

UNCHANGING QUEST

BACK TO LIFE

A MASTER OF LIFE

LITTLE NOVELS OF NOWADAYS

VENETIAN LOVERS

OUT OF THE RUINS

THE AGE OF REASON

DARKENED ROOMS

INTELLECTUAL MANSIONS, S.W.

Other titles will be added from time to time.

LEATHER. Red Lambskin, rounded back, gilt top, gold blocked side and back, facsimile autograph, special end papers, printed in choice and newly-set clear type on pure paper. F'cap 8vo. 5s. net

CLOTH. Blue Art Cambric, rounded back, gold blocked side and back, facsimile autograph, printed in choice and newly-set clear type on pure paper. F'cap 8vo. 3s. 6d. net

The Works of
The Late Right Honourable
THE EARL OF BIRKENHEAD
P.C., G.C.S.I., D.C.L., LL.D., B.Litt.

FAMOUS TRIALS OF HISTORY

"They are the very stuff of which tragedy is made . . .
richer in plot than the most ingenious novel."—*Daily Mail.*

11th impression, illustrated, 21s. net

MORE FAMOUS TRIALS

"Unlike most sequels, the book is, on the whole, even better
than its predecessor."—*Daily Mail.*

"The book, as a whole, supplies a remarkable series of
psychological studies among every class of society and is
full of living interest."—*The Times.*

3rd impression, illustrated, 21s. net

TURNING POINTS IN HISTORY

Lord Birkenhead, with his vast experience in many spheres
of life, and with a mind made astute through a triumphantly
successful period at the bar, has here selected and discussed
what were and are, in his opinion, the crucial turning points
in history. Ranging from the Conversion of Saint Paul to
the Problem of the Dantzig Corridor and from the Navigations
of Columbus to the Coming of the Bolshevist, this volume
contains material for endless debate and discussion.

4th impression, illustrated, 21s. net

Hutchinson's Sports & Pastimes Library

The authors of the books in this series are all acknowledged authorities on their respective subjects and as such need no introduction.

Each volume fully illustrated. 4s. 6d. net

INSECT ARTIZANS AND THEIR WORK
EDWARD STEP, F.L.S.

(With 54 illustrations on art paper.)

"A volume of sheer delight."—*Daily Graphic.*
"Full of marvels . . . a captivating book."—
Literary World.
"A really good book."—*Manchester Guardian.*

BIRD BEHAVIOUR   *FRANK FINN, F.Z.S.*

(With 44 illustrations on art paper.)

"Mr. Finn's book reveals him as that uncommon creature among animal observers who can use his eyes and his head too. The combination is rare."—*Westminster Gazette.*

MESSMATES. A BOOK OF STRANGE COMPANIONSHIPS
EDWARD STEP, F.L.S.

(With 64 illustrations from photographs.)

"An enthralling picture."—*Evening Standard.*
"Well written and entertaining . . . as amusing as it is instructive . . . the illustrations are many and excellent."

THE COURTSHIP OF ANIMALS
W. P. PYCRAFT, A.L.S., F.Z.S.

(With 40 illustrations on art paper.)

". . . a volume of absorbing interest . . . there is hardly a page in this delightful book which the reader will care to slip."—*Westminster Gazette.*

Hutchinson's Famous Library

WILD FRUITS OF THE COUNTRYSIDE
F. EDWARD HULME

(With 36 coloured plates by the author
and 25 illustrations from photographs.)

"A most agreeable as well as an instructive
handbook."—*Tribune.*

BRITISH FRESH-WATER FISHES
SIR HERBERT MAXWELL, F.R.S.

(With 24 coloured plates.)

"This delightful book with its numerous
coloured plates, is invaluable to every fisher-
man and naturalist."

**TOADSTOOLS AND MUSHROOMS OF THE
COUNTRYSIDE**
EDWARD STEP, F.L.S.

(With 8 coloured plates and 128 other illustrations.)

Ten years were taken in collecting the photographs for this book and the subject is dealt
with lucidly and in non-technical language.

BIRDS OF THE COUNTRYSIDE
FRANK FINN, F.Z.S.

(With 12 coloured plates, 118 other illustrations and many outline drawings.)

"Nature students will find it an invaluable
companion."—*Morning Post.*

EGGS AND NESTS OF BRITISH BIRDS
FRANK FINN, F.Z.S.

(With 154 eggs reproduced direct from Nature in
colours, 74 eggs in black and white, and other
illustrations.)

If you are interested in the latest news of the latest books, fill in this form and despatch it to the publishers who will send you, free of charge, each issue of

THE BOOKLOVER,

a magazine devoted entirely to news of the latest books.

Please send me, free of charge, each issue of

THE BOOKLOVER.

Name..

Address..

....

HUTCHINSON & CO. (PUBLISHERS), LTD.
34-36 PATERNOSTER ROW, LONDON, E.C.4